It was a force
smile. Ben felt i
gut. His flesh lea

This is not *what I need*

But then he thought…*why not?* He'd finished with his latest in a long string of socialites. What was to stop him from exploring this attraction further?

Ben almost laughed. Because this wasn't just attraction he was suddenly feeling. This was lust—an emotion he was not unfamiliar with. But this time it felt stronger. Much stronger.

Impossible to ignore.

Impossible not to pursue.

He could hardly contain the burst of triumph he experienced when she noticed him assessing her, and he heard her sharply indrawn breath, watched her reef her eyes back to the road as if the hounds of hell were after her.

And perhaps they were, he thought darkly. Be damned with his conscience! Be damned with common sense! He had to have her. And soon.

Miranda Lee is Australian, and lives near Sydney. Born and raised in the bush, she was boarding-school-educated, and briefly pursued a career in classical music before moving to Sydney and embracing the world of computers. Happily married, with three daughters, she began writing when family commitments kept her at home. She likes to create stories that are believable, modern, fast-paced and sexy. Her interests include meaty sagas, doing word puzzles, gambling and going to the movies.

Recent titles by the same author:

MASTER OF HER VIRTUE
CONTRACT WITH CONSEQUENCES
THE MAN EVERY WOMAN WANTS
NOT A MARRYING MAN

TAKEN OVER BY THE BILLIONAIRE

BY

MIRANDA LEE

Published in Great Britain 2014
by Mills & Boon, an imprint of Harlequin (UK) Limited,
Eton House, 18-24 Paradise Road, Richmond, Surrey, TW9 1SR

ISBN: 978-0-263-25031-2

Harlequin (UK) Limited's policy is to use papers that are natural, renewable and recyclable products and made from wood grown in sustainable forests. The logging and manufacturing processes conform to the legal environmental regulations of the country of origin.

Printed and bound in Spain
by Blackprint CPI, Barcelona

TAKEN OVER BY THE BILLIONAIRE

CHAPTER ONE

MURPHY'S LAW STATED that if anything could possibly go wrong, then eventually it would.

Jess did not subscribe to this theory, despite the fact that her surname was Murphy. But her father was a firm believer. Whenever anything annoying or frustrating happened, such as a flat tyre when he was driving a bride to her wedding—Joe owned a hire-car business—then he blamed it on Murphy's Law: bad weather at the weekends; down-turns in the stock market. Recently, he'd even blamed the defeat of his favourite football team in the grand final on Murphy's Law.

Admittedly, her dad was somewhat superstitious by nature.

Unlike her father, Jess's view of unfortunate events was way more rational. Things happened, not because a perverse twist of fate was just waiting to spoil things for you without rhyme or reason, but because of something someone had done or not done. Flat tyres and stock-market crashes didn't just happen. There was always a logical reason.

Jess didn't blame Murphy's Law for her boyfriend suddenly having decided last month that he no longer wanted to drive around Australia with her, having opted instead to go backpacking around the whole, stupid world for the next year! With a mate of his, would you believe? Never mind that she'd just gone into hock to buy a brand-new four-wheel drive for their romantic road trip together. Or that she'd started thinking he might be Mr Right. The truth, once she'd calmed down long enough to face it, was that Colin had caught the travel bug and obviously wasn't ready to settle down just yet. He still loved her—he claimed—and had asked her to wait for him.

Naturally, she'd told him what he could do with that idea!

Neither had Jess blamed Murphy's Law for recently having lost her much-loved part-time job at a local fashion boutique. She knew exactly why she'd been let go. Some cash-rich American company had bought up the Fab Fashions chain for a bargain price—Fab Fashions was in financial difficulties—and had then sent over some bigwig who had threatened the managers of all the stores that, if they didn't show a profit by the end of the year, all the retail outlets would be closed down in favour of online shopping. Hence the trimming of staff.

Actually, Helen hadn't wanted to let her go. Jess was an excellent salesgirl. But it was either her or Lily, who was a single mother who really needed her job, whereas Jess didn't. Jess had a full-time job during the week working at Murphy's Hire Car. She'd only taken the weekend job at Fab Fashions because she was mad about fashion and wanted to learn as much as she could about the industry, with a plan one day to open her own boutique or online store. So of course, under the circumstances, she couldn't let Helen fire poor Lily.

But she'd seethed for days over the greed of this American company. Not to mention the stupidity. Why hadn't this idiot they'd sent over found out why Fab Fashions wasn't making a profit? *She* could have told him. But, no, that would have taken some intelligence. And time!

Before she'd been let go last weekend, she'd asked Helen if she knew the name of this idiot, and she'd been told he was a Mr De Silva. Mr Benjamin De Silva. Some searching on the Internet just this morning had revealed a news item outlining the takeover of several Australian companies—including Fab Fashions—by De Silva & Associates, a private equity firm based in New York. When she looked up De Silva & Associates, Jess discovered that the major partner and CEO was Morgan De Silva, who was sixty-five years old and had been on the Forbes rich list for yonks. Which meant he was a billionaire. He was divorced—surprise, surprise!—with one son, Benjamin De Silva: the idiot they'd sent out. A clear case of nepotism at work, given his lack of intelligence and lateral thinking.

The office phone rang and Jess snatched it up.

'Murphy's Hire Car,' she said, trying not to let her irritation show through in her voice.

'Hi, there. I have a problem which I sure hope you can help me with.'

The voice was male, with an American accent.

Jess did her best to put aside any bias she was currently feeling towards American males.

'I'll do my best, sir,' she said as politely as she could manage.

'I need to hire a car and driver for three full days, starting first thing tomorrow morning.'

Jess's eyebrows lifted. They didn't often have people wanting to hire one of their cars and drivers for that length of time. Mostly, Murphy's Hire Car did special events which began and ended on the one day: weddings; graduations; anniversary dates; trips to Sydney airport; that sort of thing. Based on the central coast a couple of hours north of Sydney, they weren't an overly large concern. They only had seven hire cars which included three white limousines for weddings and other flash events, two white Mercedes sedans for less flash events and one black limousine with tinted windows for people with plenty of money who wanted privacy.

Recently her father had bought a vintage blue convertible Cadillac but it wouldn't be ready for hiring till next week, having needed new leather seats. Jess knew without even looking up this weekend's bookings on the computer that she wouldn't be able to help the American. They had several weddings on. Not uncommon given that it was spring. 'I'm sorry, sir, but we're fully booked this weekend. You'll have to try someone else.'

His weary sigh elicited some sympathy in Jess. 'I've already tried every other hire car company on the Central Coast,' he said. 'Look, are you absolutely certain you can't wangle something? I don't need a limo or anything fancy. Any car and driver would do. I have to be in Mudgee for a wedding on Saturday, not to mention the stag party tomorrow night. The groom's my best friend and I'm the best man. But a drunk driver ran into me last night, wrecked my rental and left me unable to drive myself. I've a bunged up right shoulder.'

'That's terrible.' Jess hated drivers who drank. 'I truly wish I could help you, sir.' Which she genuinely did. It would be awful if he couldn't make it to his best friend's wedding.

'I'm prepared to pay over and above your normal rates,' he offered just as she was about to suggest he try one of the larger hire car firms in Sydney. They could surely send a car up to him lickety-split. He might even have success hiring an ordinary taxi.

'How much over and above?' she asked, thinking of the hefty repayments she had to make on her SUV.

'If you get me a car and driver, you can name your own price.'

Wow, Jess thought. This American had to be loaded. He could probably afford to charter a helicopter—not that she was going to suggest such a thing. Jess wasn't about to look a gift horse in the mouth.

'Okay, Mr…er…?'

'De Silva,' he said.

Jess's mouth dropped open.

'Benjamin De Silva,' he elaborated.

Jess's mouth remained agape as she took in this amazing coincidence. With his being American and having such a distinctive name, he *had* to be the same man!

'Are you still there?' he finally asked after twenty seconds of shocked silence.

'Yes, yes, I'm still here. Sorry, I…er…was distracted for a moment. The cat just walked onto my keyboard and I lost a file.' In actual fact, the family moggie was sound asleep on a sun-drenched window sill, a good ten metres away from Jess's desk.

'You have a *cat* in your office?'

He actually sounded appalled. No doubt there were no cats allowed in the pompous Mr De Silva's office.

'This a home-run business, Mr De Silva,' she said somewhat stiffly.

'I see,' he said. 'Sorry. No offence intended. So, can you help me or not?'

Well, of course she could help him. And it was no longer just a question of money. For how could she possibly give up the opportunity to tell the high and mighty Mr Benjamin De Silva what was wrong with Fab Fashions?

Surely there would be plenty of opportunities somehow to bring up her lost job during the course of their very long drive together. Mudgee was a long way away. She'd never actually been there but she'd seen it on the map when she and Colin had been planning their trip. It was a large country town in the central west of New South Wales, a good five- or six-hour drive from here, maybe longer, depending on the state of the roads and the number of times her passenger wanted to stop.

'I can take you myself, if you like,' she offered. 'I am well over twenty-one, a qualified mechanic and an advanced driving instructor.' She only helped out in the office on Mondays and Thursdays. 'I also own a brand-new four-wheel drive which won't have any trouble negotiating the roads out Mudgee way.'

'I'm impressed. And extremely grateful.'

And so you should be, she thought a little tartly.

'So where exactly are you now, Mr De Silva? I'm presuming you're on the Central Coast somewhere.'

'I'm staying in an apartment at Blue Bay.' He gave her the address.

Jess frowned as she tapped it into the computer, wondering why a businessman like him would be staying up here instead of in Sydney. It seemed odd. Maybe he was just doing the tourist thing whilst he was in the country. Combining business with pleasure, as well as going to his best friend's wedding.

'And the address in Mudgee where I'll be taking you?' she asked.

'It's not actually *in* Mudgee,' he replied. 'It's a property called Valleyview Winery, not far from Mudgee. It's not difficult to find. It's on a main road which connects the highway to Mudgee. After you drop me off, you could stay at a motel in Mudgee till I need you to drive me back here again on the Sunday. At my expense, of course.'

'So you won't actually need me to drive you anywhere on the Saturday?'

'No, but I'll pay you for the day just the same.'

'This is going to be ridiculously expensive, Mr De Silva.'

'I'm not worried about that. Name your price and I'll pay it.'

Jess pulled a face. It must be nice never having to worry about money. She was tempted to say some exorbitant amount but of course she didn't. Her father would be appalled at her if she did such a thing. Joe Murphy was as honest as the day was long.

'How about a thousand dollars a day, plus expenses?' Mr De Silva suggested before she could calculate a reasonable fee.

'That's too much,' she protested before she could think better of it.

'I don't agree. It's fair, under the circumstances.'

'Fine,' she said briskly. Who was she to argue with Mr Moneybags? 'Now, I will need some other details.'

'Like what?' he demanded in a rather irritated tone.

'Your mobile phone number,' she said. 'And your passport number.'

'Okay. I'll have to go get my passport. I won't be long.'

Jess smiled whilst he gathered the information he wanted. Three thousand dollars was a very nice sum.

'Here we are,' he said on returning, and read out the number.

'We also need a contact name and number,' she said as she typed in the details. 'In case of an emergency.'

'Good grief. Is all this strictly necessary?'

'Yes, sir,' she said, wanting to make sure he was the right man. 'Company rules.'

'Fine. My father will have to do. Mum's on a cruise. But Dad does live in New York.'

'I did assume he'd be American, Mr De Silva. You have an American accent. His name and number, please?'

'Morgan De Silva,' he said and Jess smiled. She'd *known* it had to be him!

He rattled off a phone number which she quickly typed in.

'Do you want to pay for this via your credit card or cash?' she asked crisply.

'Which would you prefer?'

'Credit card,' she said.

'Fine,' he said, a decided edge creeping into his voice. 'I have it here.'

He read out the number. American Express, of course.

'Okay. That's all done. We'll deduct one thousand dollars in advance and the rest on completion.'

'Fine,' he bit out.

'What time would you like me to pick you up tomorrow morning, Mr De Silva?'

'What time do you suggest? I'd like to be out there by mid-afternoon. But first, could we dispense with the "Mr De Silva" bit? Call me Benjamin. Or Ben, if you'd prefer.'

'If you like,' she said, slightly taken aback by this offer. Australians were quick to be on a first-name basis but she'd found people from other countries weren't quite so easy going. Especially those who were wealthy. Maybe Mr De Silva wasn't as pompous as she'd originally thought.

'As to time,' she went on with a little less starch in her own voice, 'I would suggest that I pick you up at seven-fifteen. That way we'll avoid the worst of the traffic. Any earlier and we'll run into the tradies plus Sydney commuters. Any later and it'll be the people going to work at Westfield's, not to mention the mothers taking their kids to school.' Lord, but she was babbling on a bit. She could almost hear him sighing down the line.

'Seven-fifteen it is, then,' he said abruptly as soon as

she gave him the opportunity to speak. 'I'll be waiting outside so we don't waste time.'

Jess's eyebrows lifted. She'd picked up a few well-heeled tourists in her time and they rarely did things like that. They always made her knock, were often late and never helped her with their luggage—if it was a trip to the airport, that was, and not just a day out somewhere.

'Excellent,' she said. 'I won't be late.'

'Perhaps you should give me *your* mobile phone number, just in case you don't show up for reasons outside your control.'

Jess rolled her eyes. It sounded like he was another subscriber to Murphy's Law. But what the heck? She was used to it.

'Very well.' And she rattled off her number.

'And what should I call *you*, Miss…er…?'

'Murphy. Jessica Murphy.' She was about to say he could call her Jess—everyone else did—but simply couldn't bring herself to be that friendly to him. He was still the enemy, after all.

So she said a businesslike goodbye instead and hung up.

CHAPTER TWO

BEN SIGHED AS he flipped his phone shut and slipped it into his jeans pocket. The last thing he wanted to do was be driven all the way to Mudgee tomorrow by Miss Jessica Murphy, qualified mechanic and advanced driving instructor, he thought grumpily as he headed for the drinks cabinet. She'd declared herself well over twenty-one. More likely well over forty. And plain as a pikestaff to boot!

Still, what choice did he have after that doctor at Gosford hospital had declared him unfit to drive for at least a week? Not because of the excuse he'd given over the phone just now. His right shoulder *was* stiff and bruised but quite usable. It was the concussion he'd suffered which was the problem, the doctor having explained that no insurance company would cover him till he had a signed medical clearance.

Stupid, really. He felt fine. A little tired and frustrated, maybe, but basically fine.

Ben scowled as he sloshed a good two inches of his mother's best bourbon into one of her crystal glasses. He supposed he should be feeling grateful he'd found a hire car at all, not irritated. But Miss Jessica Murphy had got right up his nose. There was a fine line between efficient and officious and she'd certainly been straddling it. He half-regretted making the offer for her to call him Ben, but he'd had to do something to warm the old tartar up, otherwise the drive tomorrow would be worse than tedious.

If only his mother had been here, Ben thought as he headed for the kitchen in search of ice. She could have driven him. But she wasn't. She was off on a South Pacific cruise with her latest lover.

Admittedly, this one was older than her usual. In his mid-fifties, Lionel was only a few years Ava's junior. And he was currently employed—something in movie production—so he was a big improvement on the other fortune-hunting toy-boys who'd graced her bed over the years since his parents' divorce.

Not that his mother's affairs bothered him much these days. Ben had finally grown up enough to know his mother's personal life was none of his business. A pity she didn't return the favour, he thought as he scooped a few cubes of ice from the fridge's automatic ice-dispenser and dropped them in his glass. She was always asking him when he was going to get married and give her grandchildren.

So maybe it was better she wasn't here right now. The last thing he wanted was outside pressure about his relationship with Amber. He was having enough trouble as it was, deciding whether he should give up the romantic notion of marrying for love and settle for what Amber was offering. At least if he married Amber he wouldn't have to worry about her being a fortune hunter, which was always a problem when a man was heir to billions. Amber was the only daughter of a very wealthy property developer, so she didn't need a meal ticket in a husband.

In all honesty, Ben hadn't been under the impression that Amber wanted a husband at all yet. She was only twenty-four and was clearly enjoying her life as a single girl with a glamorous though empty job at an art gallery, a full social calendar and a boyfriend who kept her sexually satisfied. But, just before his trip down under, Amber had suddenly asked Ben if he was ever going to propose. She said she loved him, but she didn't want to waste any more time on him if he didn't love her back and didn't want marriage and children.

Of course he hadn't been able to tell her that he loved her back, because he didn't. He'd said that he liked her a lot but did not love her. Ben had been somewhat surprised when she'd replied that she would be happy enough with his liking her a lot. He'd assumed—wrongly, it seemed—that a woman genuinely in love would be more heartbroken by his own lack of love. Apparently not! She'd given him till Christmas to make up his mind. After that, she would be looking elsewhere for a husband.

Ben lifted the bourbon to his lips as he wandered back into the living room and over to the glass wall which overlooked the beach. But he wasn't really looking at the ocean view. He was recalling how he'd told Amber that he would think about her offer whilst he was in Australia and give her an answer on his return.

And he *had* been thinking. A lot. He did want marriage and children. *One* day. But, hell, he was only thirty-one. On top of that, he wanted to feel more for his future wife than he currently felt for Amber. He wanted to fall deeply in love, and vice versa, the kind of love you had no doubts over. The kind which would last. Divorce was not on his agenda. Ben knew first-hand how damaging divorce was to children, even when the parents were civilised about it, as his own parents had been. His workaholic father had sensibly and generously given Ben's mother full custody of Ben, allowing her to bring him back to Australia, with the proviso that Ben spent some of his school holidays with him in America.

Ben had still been devastated to find out that his parents

no longer loved each other. He'd only been eleven at the time, and totally ignorant of the circumstances which had led to the divorce. It was testament to his parents' mutual love of their son that they'd never criticised each other in front of him, never blamed each other for the break-up of the marriage. They'd both just said that sometimes people fell out of love and it was better that they live apart.

Ben had hated coming to Australia at first, but he eventually grew to love this wonderful laid-back country and his life out here. He'd loved the school he'd been sent to and the many friends he'd made here. He'd especially loved his years at Sydney University, studying law and flat-sharing with Andy, his very best friend. It wasn't till he'd graduated that his father had finally told him the ugly truth: that his mother had trapped him into marriage by getting pregnant. She'd never loved him. She'd just wanted a wealthy husband. Yes, he'd also admitted to having been unfaithful to her, but only after she'd confessed the truth to him one night.

His father had claimed he hated hurting Ben with these revelations but believed it was in his best interests.

'You are going to inherit great wealth, son,' Morgan De Silva had said at the time. 'You need to understand the corrupting power of money. You must always keep your wits about you, especially when it comes to women.'

When a distressed Ben had confronted his mother, she'd been furious with his father, but hadn't denied she'd married the billionaire for his money, though she'd done her best to explain why. Born dirt-poor but beautiful, she'd had a tough childhood but had finally made it as a model in Australia and then overseas, having been taken on by a prestigious New York agency. For several years she'd made very good money but just before she'd turned thirty she'd discovered that her manager hadn't invested her money wisely, as she'd believed, instead having wasted it all on gambling.

Suddenly, she'd been close to broke again and, whilst she'd still been very beautiful, her career hadn't been what it once was. So, when the super-wealthy Morgan De Silva had come on the scene, obviously infatuated with the lovely Australian blonde, she'd allowed herself to be seduced in more ways than one. She'd been attracted to him, she'd insisted, but had admitted to Ben that she didn't love his father, saying she doubted he'd loved her either. It had just been a case of lust.

'The only thing your father loves,' she'd told Ben with some bitterness, 'is money.'

Ben had argued back that this wasn't true. His father loved *him*. Which belief had prompted his move to America shortly after his graduation from university.

Not that he'd cut his mother out of his life altogether. She'd been a wonderful mother to him and he still loved her, despite her faults and flaws. They talked every week or so on the phone, but he didn't visit all that often, mostly because he rarely had the time.

Life since going to the States had been full-on. An economics post-graduate degree at Harvard had been followed by an intense apprenticeship in the investment business. There'd been a few snide remarks when he'd made his way quickly up the ladder at De Silva & Associates, but Ben believed he'd earned his promotion to an executive position in his father's company, along with the seven-figure salary, the sizeable bonuses, the flash car and the equally flash New York apartment. Along the way, he'd also earned the reputation for being a bit of a playboy, perhaps because his girlfriends didn't last all that long. Invariably, after a few weeks he would grow bored with them and move on.

Never once had he fallen in love, making him wonder if he ever would.

It was a surprise to Ben that his relationship with Amber had lasted as long as it had—eight months—possibly because he didn't see all that much of her. He was working very long hours. He'd never thought himself in love with her. She was, however, attractive, amusing and very easy to be with, never fussing when he was late for a date or when he had to opt out at the last minute. Never acting in that clinging, possessive way which he hated.

She'd also never once said she loved him in all those months, so her recent declaration had come out of the blue.

Ben had been startled at first, then flattered, then tempted by her proposal, possibly because of his father's mantras, on marriage.

'Rich men should always marry rich girls,' he'd said more than once, along with, 'Rich men must marry with their heads. Never their hearts.'

Sensible advice. But it was no use. Ben knew, deep down in *his* heart, that marriage to a girl he didn't love would be settling for less than he'd always wanted. A lot less.

So his answer had to be no.

Ben considered ringing Amber and telling her so immediately, but there was something cowardly about breaking up over the phone or, God forbid, by text message. She'd already asked him not to call or text her whilst he was away, perhaps hoping that he would miss her more that way.

Frankly, just the opposite had happened. Without phone calls and text messages, the connection between them had been broken. Now that he'd made his final decision, Ben felt not one ounce of regret. Just relief.

When his phone suddenly vibrated in his pocket, Ben hoped like hell it wasn't Amber. But it wasn't her, the caller

ID revealing it was his father. Ben frowned as he lifted the phone to his ear. It wasn't like his father to call him unless there was a business problem. Morgan De Silva wasn't into social chit-chat.

'Hi, Dad,' Ben said. 'What's up?'

'Sorry to bother you, son, but I was thinking about you tonight and decided to give you a call.'

Ben could not have been more taken aback.

'That's great, Dad, but shouldn't you be asleep? It must be the middle of the night over there.'

'It's not that late. Besides, you know I never sleep much. What time is it where you are?'

'Mid-afternoon.'

'What day?'

'Thursday.'

'Ah. Right. So you'll be off to Andy's wedding in a couple of days.'

'I'm actually driving up to his place tomorrow.' For a split second Ben contemplated telling his father about the accident and his fiasco about finding a hire car, but decided not to. Why worry him unnecessarily?

'Nice boy, Andy.'

His father had met Andy when Ben had brought him to America for a holiday. They'd gone skiing with Morgan and had a great time.

'So, when do you think you'll be back in New York?' his father asked.

'Probably not till the end of next week. Mum's away on a cruise and doesn't get back till next Monday. I'd like to spend a day or two with her before I fly home.'

'Of course. Why don't you stay a little longer? Have a decent holiday? You deserve it. You've been working way too hard.'

Ben stared out at the beach and the ocean beyond. In

truth, it had been a couple of years since he'd had more than a long weekend off, his mother recently having accused him of becoming a workaholic, just like his father.

'I might do that,' he said. 'Thanks, Dad.'

'My pleasure. You're a good boy. Give my regards to your mother,' his father said abruptly, then hung up.

Ben stared down at his phone, wondering what in the hell that had been all about.

CHAPTER THREE

JESS WAS GLAD to get out of the house the following morning before her parents were up and about. Her mother had started going on and on the night before about her taking a risk, driving some stranger all the way out to Mudgee and back.

'He might be a serial killer for all you know,' she'd said at one stage.

She hadn't stopped with the doomsday scenarios till Jess had told her everything she knew about Mr Benjamin De Silva, including his being the son of a super-rich American businessman whose company had taken over several Australian firms, including Fab Fashions.

'He's not a serial killer, Mum,' she'd informed her mother firmly. 'Just a man with more money than sense.'

To Jess's surprise, her sometimes pessimistic father had taken her side in the argument.

'Jess knows how to look after herself, Ruth,' he'd said. 'She'll be fine. Just give us a call when you get there, love, and put your mother's mind at rest. Okay?'

She'd happily agreed to do so, but hadn't trusted her mum not to start up again this morning, so she'd packed an overnight bag the night before, then risen early, giving her time to take some extra care getting ready. Under the circumstances, she didn't want to look like a dag. Or a chauffeur, for that matter—so she'd already dismissed the idea of wearing her usual driving uniform of black trousers with a white shirt which had *Murphy's Hire Car* emblazoned on the breast pocket.

She did wear black trousers. Rather swish, stretchy ones which tapered in at the ankles and made the most of her long legs, combining them with a V-necked white T-shirt topped with a floral jacket which she'd made herself. Jess was an excellent dressmaker, having been taught how to sew by her gran. She dithered a bit over how much make-up to wear, opting in the end to play it conservative, using just a bit of lip gloss and a light brushing of mascara. Her clear olive skin did not really need foundation, anyway. She then scooped her thick, black hair back up into a ponytail, wrapping a red scrunchie around it which matched the red flowers in the jacket. Finally, she pulled on a pair of very comfy black pumps before bolting out of the house by six-thirty, a good twenty minutes before she needed to leave.

The drive from Glenning Valley to Blue Bay would take fifteen minutes at most. Probably less at this time of day. She filled in some time having breakfast at a local burger bar, after which she drove leisurely towards the address she'd been given. Jess knew the area well. Whilst there were still lots of very ordinary weekenders around, any property on the beach front was worth heaps. Most of the older buildings which had once graced the shoreline had been torn down, replaced by million-dollar units and multi-million-dollar homes. Over the last decade, Blue Bay had become one of *the* places to live on the coast.

It wasn't till she turned off the Entrance Road into the long street which led down to Blue Bay that Jess felt the first inkling of nerves. Though normally a confident and rather outspoken girl, she suddenly realised it wasn't going to be easy bringing up the subject of Fab Fashions with the man responsible for taking over the company. If truth be told, he would probably tell her to mind her own business. He also wouldn't be pleased with the fact that she'd looked him up on the Internet.

Maybe she should forget about the probably futile idea of trying to save Fab Fashions and just do what Mr De Silva had hired her to do—drive him out to Mudgee and back. Alternatively, maybe she would wait and see what kind of man he was; if he was the kind to listen or not. He hadn't sounded too bad over the phone. Maybe a little frustrated, which was understandable, considering he'd just had a car accident and all his plans had gone awry. And he *had* asked her to call him Ben, which was rather nice of him. She almost felt guilty now that she hadn't asked him to call her Jess in return.

Jess wondered how old he was. Probably about forty, she guessed. If he looked anything like his father—there'd been a photo of Morgan De Silva on the Net—then he'd be short, with a receding hairline and a flabby body from a sedentary lifestyle and too many long business lunches.

'Oh, dear,' she sighed.

Jess was no longer looking forward to today in any way, shape or form.

After letting out the breath she'd been unconsciously holding, she started scanning the numbers on the post boxes, soon realising that the number she was looking for would be on the left and right down the end of the street. Truly, what else had she expected? The son of a billionaire wouldn't be staying anywhere but the best.

The sun was just rising as she approached a block of apartments which carried the right number and which, yes, of course, overlooked the beach. A man was already standing on the pavement outside the building. Beside him sat a black travel case on wheels, across which was draped a plastic zip-up suit bag.

Jess tried not to stare as she pulled into the kerb beside him. But it was difficult not to.

He wasn't short with a receding hairline and flabby body. Hell, no. He was anything but. He was very tall and slim, with broad shoulders and the kind of well-chiselled face you saw on male models in magazines advertising aftershave or expensive watches. High cheekbones, a strong, straight nose and a square jawline. His hair was a light sandy colour, cut short at the sides and slightly longer on top, brushed straight back from that oh, so handsome face. His skin was lightly tanned, his eyes blue and beautiful. His clothes were more what she'd been expecting. Sort of. Dark-grey trousers and a long-sleeved blue business shirt which was open at the neck and which had a pair of sunglasses tucked into the breast pocket.

Jess dragged her eyes away from him, switched off the engine, then climbed out of the car, her thoughts somewhat scattered. Who would have imagined he would be so good-looking? Or so *young*? He couldn't be more than early thirties. Maybe even younger.

'Mr De Silva, I presume?' she asked as she stepped up onto the pavement less than a metre from him. Up close, he was even more attractive, if that were possible.

'You can't possibly be Miss Murphy,' he returned, the hint of a wry smile teasing one corner of his nicely shaped mouth.

She bristled at his comment. 'I don't see why not.'

He shook his head as he looked her up and down. 'You're not what I was expecting.'

'Oh?' she returned stiffly. 'And what were you expecting?'

'Someone a little older and a little less…er…attractive.'

Jess thanked the Lord she wasn't a blusher. For if she had been she might have gone bright red under the openly admiring gaze of those beautiful blue eyes.

'That's nice of you to say so, Mr De Silva. I think,' she added, wondering if she'd sounded old and ugly on the phone.

'I told you to call me Ben,' he said, and smiled at her, a full hundred-watt smile which showed perfect American teeth and a charm which was just as dazzling.

Oh my, Jess thought, trying not to be too dazzled.

Not without much success, given she just stood there staring at him whilst her heartbeat did the tango and she forgot all about Fab Fashions.

'Perhaps we should get going,' he said at last.

Jess gave herself a mental shake. It wasn't like her to go ga-ga over a man, even one as impressive as this.

'Yes. Yes, of course,' she said, still far too breathlessly for her liking. 'Do you need help with your bags?' she added, recalling what he'd said about having a banged-up right shoulder.

'I can manage,' he returned. 'Just open up the back for me.'

He managed very well. Managed the passenger door without any help either.

By the time she climbed into the driving seat and belted up, Jess had taken control of her wildly dancing heartbeat, having told herself firmly to get a grip and stop acting like some awestruck schoolgirl. She was twenty-five years old, for pity's sake!

Taking a deep breath, she reached for her sunglasses and put them on.

'Would you mind if I called you Jessica instead of Miss Murphy?' he said before she could even start the engine.

Jess winced. She hated being called Jessica. 'I'd rather

you call me Jess,' she replied, and found herself throwing a small smile his way.

'Only if you promise to call me Ben,' he insisted as he snapped his seat belt into place.

Jess suspected that women—no, people in general—rarely said no to Ben De Silva. His combination of looks and charm were both seductive and quite corrupting. Already she wanted to please him. Yet she wasn't, by nature, a people pleaser. Jess had always had a mind of her own and a mouth to match. Suddenly, however, all she wanted to do was smile, nod and agree with everything Ben said. Already he was Ben in her head.

'Okay. Ready, Ben?' she said as she reached for the ignition and glanced over at him again.

Dear heaven but he *was* gorgeous! He smelt gorgeous too. She did like men who wore nice aftershave.

'As soon as I put these on,' he replied, pulling his own sunglasses out of his pocket.

They were very expensive looking. God, now he looked like a movie star, a very sexy movie star, the kind a girl fantasised over in the privacy of her bedroom.

Jess's susceptibility to this man was beginning to annoy her. Next thing she'd know, she'd start flirting with him. Which wasn't like her at all! Gritting her teeth, she checked her rear and side mirrors, executed a perfect three-point turn, then accelerated up the street. Neither of them said anything for a full minute or two, Ben being the first to speak.

'I must thank you again, Jess, for doing this for me.'

'You don't have to thank me. You're paying for the privilege.'

'Still, I can see you probably had to put yourself out to do this. I would imagine a girl as attractive as yourself would have better things to do over the weekend than work.'

'No, not really.'

'You didn't have to break any dates?'

'Not this weekend.'

'That surprises me. I would have thought you'd have a boyfriend.'

'I did,' she bit out. 'Till recently.'

'What happened?'

She shrugged. 'We were going to go on a road trip together around Australia. That's why I bought this four-wheel drive. Anyway, at the last moment he decided he didn't want to do that. Instead, he took off backpacking around the world with a mate.'

Jess felt, rather than saw, Ben's startled look. When driving a client, she rarely took her eyes off the road.

'He didn't ask you to go with him?' he quizzed, his shocked tone soothing Jess's still lingering hurt over Colin's defection.

'No. He did ask me to wait for him, though.'

'I hope you said no.'

She laughed as she recalled her quite volatile reaction. 'I said a little more than just no.'

'Good for you.'

'Perhaps. Colin said I have a sharp tongue.'

'Really? I find that hard to believe.'

Was he mocking her?

A quick glance showed a perfectly straight face. A perfectly straight, very handsome face. Jess decided he was just making conversation, which was better than sitting there saying nothing all the way to Mudgee.

'He also said I was bossy and controlling.'

'No!'

He *was* mocking her. But not unkindly.

She sighed. 'I suppose I am a bit controlling. But I just like things to be organised. And to be done properly.'

'I'm somewhat of a perfectionist myself,' Ben said. 'Ah, there's Westfield's. Not far to the motorway now.'

Jess frowned. 'How come you know Westfield's? I thought this was your first visit to Australia.'

'Not at all,' he said. 'I've spent a lot of time here. Well, in New South Wales, at least. My parents are divorced, you see. You already know my father's American, but my mother's Australian. She owns the apartment in Blue Bay. I actually went to boarding school in Sydney. That's where I met Andy—he's the one who's getting married.'

'Goodness!' she exclaimed. 'I had no idea.'

'Well, why would you?' he said, sounding puzzled.

Jess suppressed a groan. As the saying went, *oh, what a tangled web we weave when first we practise to deceive.*

It actually went against Jess's grain to be less than honest with people. But her intentions had been good. Hopefully, Ben wouldn't be too annoyed with her if she told him the truth. She really didn't want to drive all the way to Mudgee watching what she said and didn't say. And, yes, she supposed she did still hope to discuss the future of Fab Fashions with him. He seemed very approachable and a lot smarter than she'd given him credit for. But that didn't make the act of confessing any easier.

'Oh gosh, this is just so awkward. I suppose I simply *have* to tell you now. I...I just hope you won't be too annoyed.'

CHAPTER FOUR

BEN HAD NO idea what she was talking about. 'Tell me what?' he asked.

'The thing is, Ben...' she started, obviously with great reluctance.

'Yes?' he prompted when she didn't go on.

She pulled a face. 'I just hope you understand.'

'Understand *what*?' he demanded to know.

'Just wait, will you, till we're safely on the motorway?'

Jess turned right onto the ramp which took them down to the highway, heading north.

'I have a confession to make,' she said at last, then hesitated again.

'Go on,' Ben said with more patience than he was feeling.

'The thing is... I knew who you were yesterday on the phone once you said you were Benjamin De Silva.'

Ben tried to assimilate what Jess was actually saying, but failed.

'What exactly do you mean by who I was?'

'I mean, I knew you worked for De Silva & Associates and that you were Morgan De Silva's son.'

Ben could not have been more taken aback.

'And how come you knew that?' he said, sounding more confused than angry. 'I wouldn't have thought my father was all that well known in Australia. He keeps a low public profile. Same with myself.'

Her sigh was heavy. 'You might understand better if I tell you I used to have a part-time job at a Fab Fashions boutique in Westfield's till last weekend, when the manager had to let me go.'

'Ah,' Ben said, light dawning. Though what she was doing working part-time in a fashion boutique at all was a mystery. She'd said she was a mechanic, hadn't she? And an advanced driving instructor.

There was no doubt that Jess was a surprising girl in more ways than one. You could have knocked him over with a feather when she'd turned up, looking nothing like the middle-aged battle-axe he'd been envisaging. Not only was she young—surely no more than mid- to late-twenties—she was also hot looking. Normally he went for blondes, not brunettes. But he found Jess quite delicious with her full lips, flashing dark eyes and seriously great legs. She also had an engaging and rather amusing personality. That boyfriend had been a fool, letting her go.

'Yes, ah…' Jess said somewhat sheepishly. 'I asked Helen…she's the manager…what the problem was and she told me about this American company taking over Fab Fashions and threatening them with closure if they didn't make a profit before the end of the year. I was so mad I found out what your name was and looked you up on the Internet. Not that I found out much about you,' she added hastily. 'Mostly it was about your father and the company he founded. Anyway, when an American chap rang yesterday and told me his name was Benjamin De Silva, I nearly fell off my chair.'

Ben didn't doubt it.

'So why on earth did you agree to drive me anywhere?'

he asked her. 'I would have thought you would have told me to drop dead.'

'Good heavens, no. What would have been the point of that? Look, the truth is that I had this crazy idea that during our long drive out to Mudgee I could somehow bring Fab Fashions into the conversation. I imagined you'd be surprised at the coincidence that I'd once worked for them but that you wouldn't be suspicious. I'd then tell you what I thought could be done to make Fab Fashions more profitable. I know that sounds terribly arrogant of me but I do know fashion. It's a lifelong passion with me. My grandmother was a professional seamstress and she taught me everything she knew. I've also done a design course online and I make a lot of my own clothes.'

'I see,' Ben said slowly. She was serious, he realised, but truly there was probably no saving Fab Fashions. Retail was in a terrible shape worldwide. He'd only given them till the end of the year because he hadn't wanted to play Scrooge. His father had wanted him to shut them down straight away, having bought them only because it came as a package deal along with other companies which had much better prospects and assets.

But Ben wasn't about to tell Jess that. Not yet, anyway.

'So why did you look so surprised when we first met today?' he asked, trying to get the full picture.

Jess frowned.

'You did stare at me, Jess,' he went on when she didn't say anything.

'Yes… Yes, I did, didn't I?' she said, seeming a little flustered. 'The thing is…there was a photo of your father on the Internet and…well…you don't look much like him, do you?'

Ben had to smile. She really didn't have a tactful bone in her body. Or maybe he meant artful. Yes, that was it. Jess was not, by nature, a deceiver. She was open and honest. He suddenly wished that something could be done with Fab Fashions, just to please her.

'No,' he agreed. 'I take after my mother.'

'She must be very beautiful.'

Ben suppressed another smile with difficulty. Lord, but she was quite enchanting. And totally ingenuous in her honesty. She wasn't trying to flatter him, or flirt with him. Which was a change. It was years since Ben had encountered a girl who did neither in his company.

'Mum was very beautiful when my father married her,' he said. 'She still is, despite being over sixty. She was quite a famous model in her time. But that came to an end when she married Dad. After their divorce, she came back to Sydney and started up a modelling agency. Did very well too. Sold it for heaps a couple of years back. But perhaps you already knew all that, did you? From the Internet?'

'Heavens, no. The only personal information was that your father was divorced with one son, Benjamin. The article was all about business. It didn't say a word about your mother.'

Ben imagined that was his father's doing. He was a powerful man and still very bitter about the divorce. He rarely spoke of his ex-wife, which made his parting words on the phone last night extremely surprising.

Give my regards to your mother...

Odd, that.

'Ben, I'm really very sorry for prying into your life like that,' Jess suddenly blurted out, perhaps interpreting his thoughtful silence for annoyance. 'I realised as soon as I met you that I shouldn't have done it. But I didn't mean any harm. Truly.'

'It's all right, Jess,' he said reassuringly. 'I haven't taken offence. I was just thinking about Fab Fashions,' he invented. 'And wondering what we could do about it. Together.'

'Oh,' she said, and fairly beamed over at him, her smile lighting up her face in a way which went beyond beauty.

It was a force of nature, that smile. He felt it deep down in his gut. Very deep down.

His flesh leapt and he thought, *Uh-oh. This is not what I need right now.*

And then he thought...why not? He'd finished with Amber. What was to stop him from exploring this attraction further?

Ben almost laughed. Because this wasn't just attraction he was suddenly feeling down south of the border. This was lust, an emotion he was not unfamiliar with. But this time it felt stronger. Much stronger.

Impossible to ignore.

Impossible not to pursue.

Though not too seriously. He'd be going back to America soon. All he could fit in was a short fling.

His conscience pricked him. Jess didn't come across as the kind of girl who indulged in short flings. Though, maybe he was wrong. Maybe she'd be only too willing to go along with whatever he wanted. After all, he was the son of a billionaire, wasn't he? That made him super-attractive to women. On top of that, she already thought him very beautiful.

'You'd honestly listen to what I have to say about Fab Fashions?' she asked him eagerly.

'I'd be mad not to,' he replied, since this would give him a viable excuse to spend more time with her whilst he was in Australia. 'You're obviously a clever girl, Jess, with lots of smarts.'

'I'm not all that smart,' she said with delightful self-deprecation.

'I don't believe that.'

'Look, there's smart and there's smart. School smart, I wasn't. But I've always been good with my hands.'

Ben wished she hadn't said that, his eyes drifting over to where her hands were wrapped around the steering wheel. Hell, but he wanted those hands wrapped around *him*. Caressing him, stroking him, teasing him, whilst she did delicious things with her mouth. Such thoughts sent hot blood roaring through his veins, giving him an instant and quite painful erection.

Ben gritted his teeth as he tried to will his aroused body back into line. He was not a man who liked tipping out of control, even sexually. *Especially* sexually. Ben liked to be the boss in the bedroom, or wherever it was he chose to have sex. He enjoyed having total control of the action, along with his partner, which meant he had to have total control over himself, something which he'd practised and perfected over the years.

'Is that why you became a mechanic?' he asked, pleased with how normal he sounded despite his wayward flesh continuing to defy him.

Her shrug showed surprising indifference to her choice of career. 'Before Dad started up his hire car business, he owned a garage. Not up here. Down in Sydney. Anyway, all my brothers became mechanics and I just followed suit.'

'So when did you move up to the Central Coast?'

'A good few years back now,' she replied. 'I'd just finished my apprenticeship. I know I had my twenty-first birthday party up here so I must have been nineteen or twenty. I'm not sure of the exact year. Why?'

'Just making conversation, Jess,' he said, searching his mind for more safe topics. He could not believe that he still had an erection. 'You're not using your GPS, I see. So I guess you know the way to Mudgee.'

'It's pretty straightforward. We stay on the motorway till we reach the New England Highway, heading for Brisbane. But we turn off onto the Golden Highway just before Singleton. Then we don't get off that road till the turn-off to Mudgee. Easy peasy.'

'You sound like you've been this way a dozen times before.'

'I've driven to Brisbane via the New England Highway once or twice but I've never been along the Golden Highway before. Or to Mudgee, for that matter. I checked it up last night on the Internet.'

'I've never been this way before either,' he admitted.

Her glance carried curiosity. 'You've never been to your best friend's place before?'

'Yes, of course I have. Several times. But you take a different route when you're driving from Sydney.'

'Oh yes, of course. I didn't think of that. You said you went to boarding school in Sydney, is that right?'

'Yes. Kings College. It's near Parramatta. Do you know it?'

CHAPTER FIVE

A MOMENTARY FLASH of pique had Jess's hands tightening around the steering wheel. Just because she'd said she wasn't school smart didn't mean she was ignorant. Of course she knew of Kings College. It was one of the best private schools in Sydney. Despite it being located in the western suburbs, it was a far cry from the humble high school she'd gone to only a few miles away.

'Yes. I know it,' she said, thinking how way out of her league this man was. 'It's a very good school.'

'That's where I met Andy.'

'Your best friend?'

'Yes. We went on to study law together at Sydney Uni as well.'

Oh, Lord. Now he'd studied law at Sydney University, another prestigious establishment. Jess knew what it took to get into law. Which showed Ben was very school smart. But then, she'd guessed that already.

What next? she wondered. He probably wintered in the ski fields of Austria every year. And took his girlfriend to Paris for romantic weekends.

This last thought gave her a real jolt. Jess hadn't thought of Ben as having a girlfriend, which was very stupid of her. Of course he must have, a man like him. Not a wife, though.

When she'd asked him for a contact name and number yesterday he hadn't mentioned a wife.

A fiancée was still on the cards, however.

'And now your best friend is getting married,' she said, trying to make her voice cool and conversational, not like she was dying of curiosity. 'Are *you* married, Ben?' she asked.

'No,' he said.

'Engaged?'

'No.'

She'd gone too far now to stop. 'You must have a girlfriend back home.'

'Not any more. I did have a girlfriend. But, like yours, that relationship has now gone by the board.'

'She *dumped* you?' Jess said with total disbelief in her voice.

'Not exactly…'

'Sorry. I'm prying again.'

'I don't mind,' he said. 'I enjoy talking to you. Actually, *I'm* the one who decided to call it quits. I just haven't had the opportunity to tell Amber yet. I only decided last night.'

Amber, Jess thought with a curl of her top lip. A typical name for the type of girl he would date. She sounded beautiful. And rich. Jess hated her, till she remembered Ben was breaking up with her. Since that was the case, she could afford to be less bitchy. But she was still curious.

'What went wrong?'

'She wanted marriage and I didn't.'

'I see,' she said. What was it with men these days that they shied away from commitment?

When Jess found herself surrendering to a sinking feeling, she decided a change of subject was called for. She thought of returning to the problems with Fab Fashions but for some strange reason her enthusiasm for that project had lost some of its appeal. It was probably a waste of time, anyway. So she turned to that old favourite to fill awkward moments in a conversation. The weather.

'I'm so glad it's a nice sunny day,' she said with false brightness. 'There's nothing I hate more than driving in the rain. Though the recent rain was greatly appreciated. We had a terribly dry winter. Now everything's lovely and green.'

Ben turned his head to gaze at the countryside. 'It does look good. I can't say the same for this road, though. It's deplorable for a main highway. All cracked and patched up.'

'That's because it's built over the top of coal mines,' Jess explained. 'It suffers from subsidence. Still, that's Australia for you. We're notorious for our dreadful roads.'

'That's because the country is too big for your population. Not enough taxes for proper infrastructure.'

'Not enough taxes!' Jess exclaimed, putting aside her uncharacteristic desire to please and giving vent to her usual outspokenness. 'We're one of the highest taxed countries in the world!'

'Not quite. Australia's only number ten. Most European countries pay higher taxes.'

'Not America, though,' Jess argued. 'People can become rich in America. It's hard to become rich in Australia unless you're a crook or a drug dealer. Though, come to think of it, bankers are doing pretty well at the moment,' she added a touch tartly. 'My dad works his bum off and still only makes a living. Mum and Dad haven't had a decent holiday in years.' She didn't call five days in Bali last year a decent holiday.

'That's a shame. Everyone must have holidays these days or stress will get you in the end.'

'That's what I keep telling them.'

'How old are they?'

'Dad's sixty-three. Mum's fifty-nine.'

'Close to retirement age, then.'

'Dad says he'd rather die than retire.'

'My dad says the same thing,' Ben said. 'He loves working.'

Loves making money, you mean, Jess thought but didn't say.

'You mentioned brothers earlier,' Ben said. 'How many do you have?'

'What? Oh…er…three.'

'I always wanted a brother. So, Jess, tell me a bit about these brothers of yours.'

Jess shrugged. There seemed no point not telling him about her family. They had to talk about something, she supposed.

'Connor's the oldest,' she said. 'He's thirty-six. Married with two boys. Then there's Troy. He's thirty-four and married too, with twin girls. They're eight,' she added, smiling as she thought of Amy and Emily, who were the sweetest girls. 'Then there's Peter, who's closest to me at twenty-seven. He's not long married and his wife is expecting a bub early next year.'

'No sisters?'

'No, no sisters.'

'So you're the baby of the family.'

'Not a spoilt one, I can assure you,' she said, though this was a lie. Her brothers had indulged her shamelessly. And had been very protective of her when the boys had started hanging around. They were the reason she hadn't had a boyfriend till she'd left school. Because they kept frightening them off. Peter, especially. Jess had been a virgin till she was close to twenty.

'I suppose you want kids as well. I saw you smiling when you talked about the twin girls.'

'I'd love at least two children,' Jess admitted. 'But getting married and having children is not high on my list of wants right now. I'm only twenty-five. First, I'd like to travel all around Australia. That's why I bought this little darling,' she added, tapping the steering wheel. 'Because it can cope with whatever terrible roads Australia can throw at me.

'Oh look, there's the turn-off to the Hunter Valley vineyards,' she pointed out. 'If you're staying up on the Central Coast for a while after you get back from your friend's wedding, then that's one of the places you should visit. It's lovely at this time of the year. Lots of great places to stay and terrific wine to taste. You can even go up in a balloon. Colin and I did that not long ago and it was fantastic.'

'Had you been going out with this Colin fellow for long?'

'Just over a year.'

'And you were serious about him?'

'Serious enough,' she admitted. 'To be honest, I thought I was in love with him. But I can see now that I wasn't.' How could she have been? Colin had been gone from her life less than a month and she already had the hots for another man.

'For what it's worth, Jess,' that other man said, 'I think this Colin was a total idiot, leaving a girl like you behind.'

Jess could not help glancing over at Ben. His head turned her way and their eyes would have met if they hadn't both been wearing sunglasses. Even so, something zapped between them like a charge of electricity, taking Jess's breath away. And suddenly she knew, as surely as she knew that she should get her eyes back on the road ahead quick smart, that Ben fancied her as much as she fancied him. And, whilst the realisation of his sexual interest was exciting and flattering, it also terrified the life out of her.

CHAPTER SIX

BEN COULD HARDLY contain the burst of triumph he experienced when he heard her sharply indrawn breath, then watched her reef her eyes back on the road like the hounds of hell were after her.

Perhaps they were, he thought darkly. Be damned with his conscience. Be damned with common sense! He had to have this girl. And soon.

Jess was annoyed with herself for feeling flattered by Ben's interest. Why shouldn't he fancy her? she reasoned with more of her usual self-confidence. She was an attractive girl, with a nice face and figure. And, yes, super legs. Okay, so she probably wasn't a patch on this Amber female, but *she* was over in New York and Jess was right here. On top of that, he didn't want Amber. *No, no, be honest here, Jess, it wasn't Amber he didn't want, just marriage.* No doubt he would have continued their sexual relationship if she hadn't put the hard word on him. The truth was he was out here in Australia, probably feeling a bit lonely, and suddenly there she was, with no boyfriend and availability written all over her stupid face!

Jess was dragged out of her frustrating train of thought by the sudden end of the motorway. She hadn't even seen the signs to slow down. Rolling her eyes at herself, she made a careful left at the roundabout onto the New England Highway and set sail for the Golden Highway. Thankfully, Ben had fallen silent. No doubt he was working out when to make a pass whilst she was working out how she was going to act when that happened.

As Jess drove on silently, she wondered why she couldn't be like other girls—the ones who could sleep with guys on a first date, or even on meeting them for the first time at a pub, or club, or disco or whatever. She could never do that. She found the idea repulsive. And dangerous. She had to get to know the guy first. And like him. Had to see that he liked her too. Liked her enough to wait for her. Till she felt ready to go all the way.

She'd made Colin wait for weeks. Jess suspected Ben wouldn't wait weeks for her.

Not that she wanted him to. Lord, what was happening to her here? This wasn't like her at all! But Ben wasn't like any man she'd ever met before. It wasn't just a question of his movie-star looks, although they were hard to ignore. There was something else. A cloak of confidence which he wore without effort and which she found incredibly attractive. And very sexy. He would be a fantastic lover, she was sure. Very experienced. Very...knowledgeable. He would know exactly what to do and how to do it to make sure she always came.

A shiver rippled down her spine at this last thought. She didn't always come during sex. But she would like to.

'When are we going to make our first stop?' Ben suddenly piped up. 'I'll need to have a coffee fairly soon.'

Jess suppressed a groan as she realised that she'd once again become distracted from her driving. It took an extreme effort of will to drag her overheated mind away from those corrupting thoughts and put it to the task of estimating exactly where they were, quickly realising that they couldn't be far from the turn-off onto the Golden Highway.

'Denman is about half an hour from here,' she said, having studied the route and memorised all the towns and services on the way. 'I checked it up on the Internet. It's a small historic town down in a valley with a nice pub and a couple of cafés. If that's too far off for you, we could drive into Singleton, but then we'd have to double back.'

'No. No doubling back. Denman sounds fine. You wouldn't happen to have any pain killers with you, would you? I should have taken a couple this morning but forgot.'

Jess only then remembered his bad shoulder. 'There's some in the glove box,' she said. 'And a bottle of water in your door, if you want to take the tablets straight away.'

'Thanks.'

'How bad is your shoulder?' she asked, happy to have something safe to talk about.

'It's a bit stiff and sore this morning, but honestly it's fine. I could have driven, but the doctor at the hospital said no. Not because of the shoulder—I had a mild concussion as well.'

'Best you didn't drive, then.'

'I'm glad I couldn't—I wouldn't have met you.'

Jess could not stop her heart swelling with pleasure. Yet she knew what he was about. She'd seen how her brothers had acted with girls whose pants they wanted to get into. She'd watched them lay the compliments on thick and fast. And she'd watched those silly girls lap them up, then give her brothers what they wanted in no time at all.

Maybe that was why *she'd* acted differently with boys who came onto her. Or she had, till this handsome devil had come along.

He'd thrown a spanner in her works all right. Jess

could not believe she was thinking of having a one-night stand with him. Or that just the thought of it made her heart race faster than a Formula One car on the starting blocks.

CHAPTER SEVEN

'WHAT A LOVELY little town this is,' Ben said.

They had stopped and were sitting at a table on the veranda of an old farmhouse which had been converted into a café, sipping their just-delivered coffee and looking out onto a quite lovely garden full of flowering shrubs. Ben knew nothing about gardening and plants but he knew what he liked. It was the same way with art. He never bought art on the so-called reputation of the artist. He only bought what he liked.

He glanced over the table at Jess and thought how much he liked her too. Maybe that was why his desire for her was so strong. During the last half-hour of the drive, he'd been thinking how he could be alone with her this weekend in a place suitable for seduction. And he'd finally come up with a plan which would work, provided she went along with the idea.

'So, Jess,' he said. 'I think it's about time you started telling me what's wrong with Fab Fashions. I didn't want to talk business during the drive; I just wanted to drink in the wonderful scenery. But now that we've stopped...'

She put down her cup, then looked up at him with those big brown eyes of hers, the kind of eyes a man could drown in. He almost wished she'd put her sunglasses back on. But she'd left them hooked over the sun visor in the four-wheel drive. Lord, but they were expressive eyes. He could only hope that his own didn't give away his innermost thoughts, since he'd removed his sunglasses a couple of minutes earlier and popped them back into his shirt pocket.

'You honestly want to hear my ideas?' she said, sounding somewhat sceptical.

Not really, he conceded privately. They were a waste of time. But it was part of his plan.

'But of course,' he said.

Her face lit up and, yes, so did her eyes. Guilt threatened, but he pushed it firmly aside. Guilt, Ben conceded, was no match for lust.

'Okay. Well, for starters there's its name. "Fab Fashions" implies it caters for the young where in fact most of the stock in Fab Fashions is targeted towards the more mature woman. Either change the name or change the stock. I would suggest change the name; there are enough clothes around for teenagers.

'Then you should change your buyers. Get people in who aren't just buying to price. Someone who knows what's in fashion and what is comfortable to wear. The more mature lady wants comfort as well as style. Also, it might be a good idea to stock more of the most common sizes instead of just buying across the board. Most women over forty are not size eight! And of course you *should* have an online store too. To fall behind the times is stupid.'

Ben was surprised and impressed. All her suggestions made sense. They might even work. 'You really know your stuff, don't you?'

'I told you…fashion is a genuine passion with me. On top of that, I hate to think of all those people losing their jobs. If every owner shut their stores during a down-turn in the economy, the country would go to the wall. Surely it's not always about profit, is it, Ben? I mean…everyone has to take the bad times with the good, especially big companies like yours.'

'It's not always quite as simple as that, Jess.'

She bristled. 'I knew you'd say that.'

'I didn't say I wasn't prepared to do what you suggested. What say we have a think over the weekend and see if we can find a fab new name which would lend itself to a successful marketing campaign?'

Jess's frown was instant. 'But we don't have any spare time this weekend. You have to go to a stag party tonight and the wedding's tomorrow. I suppose we could talk on the drive home.'

'We could,' he said. 'But when I'm excited about something, I like to get straight to it,' he added with considerable irony and another tweak to his conscience. 'How about I give Andy a ring and organise for you to stay at the winery over the weekend instead of some motel in Mudgee? They have a small cottage on the property away from the main house which is very comfy. We could stay there together.'

'Together!'

'There's two bedrooms, Jess. Of course, there won't be much time for talking tonight, since I'll be at Andy's bachelor party. But the wedding's not till four the next afternoon. That should give us plenty of time to talk. And, speaking of the wedding, I'm sure I could wangle you an invitation.' If she didn't have a suitable dress, he would take her into Mudgee and buy her one.

Wariness warred with temptation in her eyes. 'Won't Andy think it odd, you asking him to invite a virtual stranger to his wedding?'

'But you're not a stranger, Jess. I already know more about you than most of my past girlfriends. On top of that, we're now business colleagues. I'll tell Andy you're a marketing consultant I've hired to help me with Fab Fashions and who kindly offered to drive me up here after I had that unfortunate car accident. There's no need to mention anything about you working for a hire car company, is there?'

Jess shook her head. Did he honestly think she didn't know what he was doing? She wasn't a fool. But there was simply no saying no to him.

'You do like to take over, Ben, don't you?'

His smile was both charming and sexy at the same time. 'What can I say? People tell me I'm bossy and controlling.'

Jess laughed. He was a clever devil. But totally irresistible.

'I'm sure Andy's folks will still think it odd, you asking for us to stay together in that cottage.'

'In that case, I'll say we're dating.'

'But we're not!'

'We will be, come Sunday. I have every intention of asking you out once we get back to the coast.'

'I might say no.'

'Will you?'

'No.'

He grinned at her. 'Great. No problems, then. I'll tell Andy you're my new girlfriend.'

Jess sighed. 'You are incorrigible.'

'I'm smitten, that's what I am.'

She just stared at him. *She* was the one who was smitten. *He* just wanted to get into her pants.

'I think you should know in advance, Ben, that I don't sleep with a guy on a first date.' Or she hadn't, till he'd come along.

There was that hint of a smile again. 'Who said anything about sleeping?'

'Very funny. You know what I mean.'

'Yes, of course I do. Let me assure you, Jess, that I would always be respectful of your wishes.'

Mmm…meaning he was very confident that he could seduce her in no time flat. Which he could, of course. But she had to make some kind of stand. Her pride demanded it.

'Fine,' she said. 'Just so you understand my feelings in advance. I don't want to have to fight you off at the end of the night.'

'I appreciate you being straight with me, Jess. I admire honesty.'

Oh, dear. She hoped she didn't look too guilty. Because of course she was probably going to sleep with him. How could she possibly say no? He was the sexiest man she'd ever met.

'Soon as I finish this coffee, I'll ring Andy,' Ben said, looking very pleased with himself.

He made the call out of earshot, walking around the garden as he talked. Jess wondered what he was telling his friend. She hated to think it was one of those 'nudge-nudge, wink-wink, say no more' conversations where Ben and his best friend were becoming co-conspirators in her supposed seduction. She would hate that. Still, Andy had already to know that Ben hadn't been out here in Australia for long. So how could she possibly be a proper girlfriend? She was just someone he'd met and fancied, but who would be quickly forgotten once he flew back to America.

Now that she was thinking straight, Jess also doubted Ben would really do anything about Fab Fashions. His interest in her ideas was just a ploy to keep her sweet. It also crossed Jess's mind as she watched Ben chatting away to his friend that she wouldn't be the first girl he'd installed in that cottage for the weekend. He was the sort of guy who would always have a willing girl on his arm. And in his bed. Jess would just be one in a long line of conquests.

She didn't like that thought, or the other thoughts she'd been having since he'd left her at the table.

Feeling decidedly disgruntled, Jess stood up, thanked the lady who ran the café and marched back to her four-wheel drive.

CHAPTER EIGHT

AFTER BEN FINISHED his call to Andy, he went back to the table on the veranda, only to find it empty. He glanced around and saw that she was out by the SUV, standing with her arms crossed and her face not at all happy. Ben wondered what had gone wrong during the last ten minutes. And there he'd been, thinking all his plans for the weekend were on track. Andy had accepted his entire story about Jess and agreed to put them both in the cottage. He'd also said there would be no problem with her coming to the wedding tomorrow.

Her body language worsened as he walked towards her, her manicured but unvarnished fingertips digging into the sleeves of her floral jacket.

'What's wrong?' he asked straight away.

Her mouth tightened. 'I don't like lies, that's what's wrong! I'm not your girlfriend, Ben. Not really. Not yet, anyway. Why, you haven't even kissed me yet!'

Jess could not believe she'd just said that. It sounded dreadful, like she was *asking* him to kiss her.

'Well, that can be easily fixed,' he returned, his eyes dropping to her mouth as he reached out and took firm possession of her shoulders.

Oh, Lord, she thought as panic set in.

He didn't rush anything; her arms dropped to her sides

long before he actually kissed her. He gathered her against him very slowly, his eyes holding hers captive as easily as he was holding her body. The descent of his head was just as slow, Jess's heart pounding against her ribs by the time his lips made contact with hers. Even then, he didn't kiss her properly, just brushed his mouth over hers. Once. Twice. Three times. Finally, her tingling lips gasped apart, desperate for more.

But he denied her desire. And, in doing so, deepened it. She moaned when his head lifted, her eyes glazed as they stared up at him.

'Will that do for now to raise your status to girlfriend?' he said, shocking her with his cool manner. She was on fire inside. Yet he seemed totally unmoved.

'Like I said, lovely Jess,' he went on, 'I'm smitten with you. Seriously smitten. I'm already planning on extending my stay here in Australia to spend more time with you. And, since you don't like lies, let me say right here and now that I doubt very much if I can fix Fab Fashions, even with your very excellent ideas.'

He was a wicked devil, she decided shakily, using honesty now to seduce her.

'But I'm willing to give it a try,' he added, 'if it makes you happy.'

What to say to that? She could hardly admit that Fab Fashions wasn't high on her personal agenda right at this moment. All she could think about was being with this man.

At the same time, she didn't want Ben thinking he could play her for a fool.

Pulling herself together, Jess did her best to imitate his controlled demeanour.

'It would be nice to try to turn things around,' she said. 'So, yes, it would make me very happy.'

'Good. And, whilst I'm in the mood for confession,' he

went on, 'my reason for organising for us to stay together at the cottage was something far more...intimate.'

Ben was watching her eyes closely and decided she wasn't upset by his admission. Just the opposite, in fact. There was a glittering of dark excitement in their gorgeous depths. She was trying to act cool with him but her eyes gave her away. Besides, he'd felt her tremble in his arms just now. And that frustrated moan of hers had been very telling. She wanted him as much as he wanted her. He hadn't dared deepen that kiss for fear of losing it himself. Jess really did have a powerful effect on him. Much more than Amber ever had.

'Not tonight, unfortunately,' he said with true regret, 'Since I'll be otherwise occupied. But I thought by tomorrow night, after the wedding, I'd be in with a chance.'

'Did you now?' Jess threw at him, desperate to find some composure, not to mention her pride.

His beautiful blue eyes glittered with amusement, not to mention supreme confidence. 'Let's just say I was hopeful.'

'You'll need to improve your kissing technique.'

'Really? And there I was, thinking you'd enjoyed being teased.'

Jess shook her head in defeat. He was just too clever for her. And way too knowing. 'You are incorrigible.'

'And you're irresistible.'

Jess said nothing to that, but her mind kept ticking over. Oh yes, he was a wicked devil all right, with all the right words and all the right moves. She wondered how many women he'd had in his life.

Lots, she supposed.

And she would be just one more.

Not the happiest of thoughts.

'I think we should get going now,' she said abruptly. It

was almost ten; it had taken them longer to get to Denman than she'd estimated.

'Good idea,' he said.

They climbed in and belted up, both of them reaching for their sunglasses at the same time, Jess careful not to look over at him lest she give away even more of her vulnerability to this man. She hated Ben thinking he was onto a sure thing tomorrow night. Though, of course he was. No point in denying it to herself. But that didn't mean she had to act like some gushing nincompoop who was overwhelmed by his attentions.

'I thought we'd stop at Cassilis for lunch,' she said matter-of-factly as she started the engine. 'Sandy Hollow is the next town but it's too close. After that, it's straight to your friend's place.'

'Sounds like a good plan.'

'We should easily arrive by mid-afternoon, depending on how long you want to stop for lunch.'

'I guess that would depend on how quickly we get served.'

Very quickly, as it turned out. They settled on a pub lunch, eaten out in the very pleasant beer garden. Jess ordered just the one glass of white wine with her steak and salad, since she was driving, whilst Ben decided on a schooner of beer with his. But they ate slowly and talked a lot. And, whilst the conversation was very superficial, all the while Jess was aware of a dangerous excitement growing deep inside her. Every time she looked at Ben a sexual image jumped into her head. When he forked some food into his mouth, she found herself staring at that mouth and thinking of how it would feel kissing, not her mouth so much, but other more intimate parts of her body. His hands brought similar sexy images. They were rather elegant hands. Well-manicured with long fingers and rounded tips. Jess imagined them doing darkly delicious things to her.

Her bottom tightened with shock at her thoughts, for Jess was not that sort of girl. Or so she'd imagined up till now. Her boyfriends so far had been rather lacking in imagination when it came to foreplay, which was perhaps why she hadn't come every time. Not that she hadn't enjoyed herself. She liked male bodies, especially well-built ones. Sex with Colin had been somewhat better, perhaps because he liked her being on top. Which she liked too. Perhaps because of that controlling nature of hers, or because she always came that way.

Jess glanced over at Ben and wondered again how many women he'd had in his life. Which sent Amber into her mind.

Jess wished Ben had already broken up with her. She wanted to tell him to ring her and do it, right now! But she didn't have the courage—or the gall—to say so. It would be a waste of time, anyway. For what would it matter in the end? The cold, hard truth was that eventually he would leave her and go back to America anyway. He didn't want marriage. She was just a girl he'd met out here whom he fancied and whom he meant to have.

A part of Jess was flattered by his determined passion for her. But she didn't deceive herself into thinking this would ever be a serious romance. They were just ships passing in the night. She decided—perhaps in protection of her fluttering female heart—that she would think of him as an experience. An adventure. Possibly even an education. For Jess knew, as surely as she knew the house wine she was drinking was rubbish, that sex with Ben would be unlike anything she'd ever experienced before.

Falling for a man like Ben, however, would be a stupid thing to do. *Very* stupid.

'You've gone quiet on me,' Ben said.

Jess perked up immediately. She didn't want Ben to think she was worried about anything. Which she was, somewhat. But forewarned was forearmed. Now that she'd decided to go down this road, she was determined to do so in a positive state of mind. There were worse things that could happen to a girl than an affair with the handsome son of a billionaire. Not that Ben's having money mattered to her. Jess had never been overly impressed by wealthy people. They never seemed all that happy, for one thing. But Ben's privileged background had given him a confidence and polish which was very attractive.

'I was thinking I should ring Mum soon,' she said with a quick smile. 'And reassure her that I'm still alive.'

'What? Surely she wasn't worried about you driving? You're an excellent driver.'

'No. Mum has every faith in my driving abilities. She was worried that you might be a serial killer.'

The shock on his face was classic.

'I assured her that you weren't. You were just a rich businessman with not an ounce of intelligence to save your soul.'

He pretended to look offended. 'You *do* have a sharp tongue, don't you?'

His eyes narrowed as men did when they were challenged. 'I'm actually quite intelligent.'

'I've yet to see evidence of that fact.' Lord, but she was actually loving this. She'd never sparred verbally with Colin, or any of her other boyfriends. She'd never flirted like this either. But it was such fun.

'I'll have you know that I was dux of my school.'

'Yes, but that's just school smart, Ben, which is a lot different from street smart. How can you possibly be street smart when you were born with a silver spoon in your mouth?' It was a lovely mouth, though. The more she studied it, the more she liked it. His bottom lip was full and sensual, whilst his top lip was thinner and harder. She suspected Ben could be stubborn as well as arrogant. Maybe even a little ruthless. But there was something decidedly sexy about a man being ruthless. You wouldn't want to marry a ruthless man, but having an affair with him was a different matter entirely.

'Keep that up and your mother might have something to worry about,' he quipped, his beautiful blue eyes sparkling with good humour. 'Women have been strangled for less.'

She smiled, and was still smiling when they left the hotel and set off again. It wasn't till they were well down the road to Mudgee that she realised she *hadn't* rung her mother.

'Is this the road Andy lives on?' she asked.

'Yes, I'm sure it is.'

'Are we nearly there yet?'

'I think so. It's been a while since I've been up here but I'll recognise the place once I see it.'

'In that case I'd like to stop for a sec and make that phone call to Mum,' she said, pulling off the road and parking under the shade of a tree.

Her mother answered on the second ring.

'Jess?'

'Yes, Mum.'

'Are you okay? Are you there yet?'

'Yes, Mum, I'm almost there and I'm fine. Mr De Silva wasn't a serial killer after all,' she added, at which Ben shook his head at her. 'He's really quite nice,' she added, and pulled a face at him.

He smiled a crooked smile.

'That's a relief. A girl can't be too careful, you know.'

'Mr De Silva's friend lives at a winery along this road.

After I drop him off, I'll head into Mudgee and book into a motel. Look, I'd better go. I'll give you another call later tonight. Bye for now. Love you.'

'Why didn't you tell her you were staying at the winery?' Ben asked as she gunned the engine and pulled out onto the road. 'I thought you didn't like lies.'

'Don't be silly, Ben. She's my mother. All girls lie to their mothers. We do it to protect them from worry.'

He laughed. 'That's a good one. But I suppose it would be a bit hard to explain.'

'Very. Now, how far along this road is Valleyview Winery?'

'Not too far now. I recognise that place over there. I'm sure it's just along here on the left. Yes, there it is now.' And he pointed high up to the left.

Her eyes followed the direction of his finger, landing on an impressive federation-style homestead built on the crest of a hill so that its wraparound verandas could take advantage of the valley views.

'The driveway is not far now,' Ben added. 'Yes, there it is.'

Jess slowed, then turned into the driveway, passing through widely set stone gateposts, one of which doubled as a post box, the other having the name 'Valleyview Winery' carved into the stone and painted black so that it stood out. The driveway was relatively straight and nicely tarred, bisecting gently sloping paddocks which held rows and rows of grapevines.

'So, does this place belong to Andy or his parents?' she asked, Jess only then realising they hadn't really talked about Andy, or the upcoming wedding, at all. They'd been totally taken up with each other.

'His parents. And the house is actually not as old as it looks. His folks built it while we were at boarding school together. His dad was a stock broker in Sydney but made enough money to retire early, so he decided to indulge his hobby and start up a winery.'

Jess suppressed a sigh. She should have known Ben's best friend would be rich.

'And what does Andy do?'

'He's now the official wine-maker here. He did law like me when he first left school, but decided after we graduated that it wasn't for him, so he went to France and studied wine-making with the masters. Then he came back and took over. Till then his dad hired a professional wine-maker. Apparently, it's not an art you can learn from a how-to book.'

'I dare say.'

As they drew near to the house, three people emerged onto the front veranda. Two men and a woman. Jess presumed it was Andy and his parents. The younger of the two men separated himself from the others and hurried down some side steps which led to a large tarred area at the side of the house where she was about to park.

'This do?' she asked Ben as she pulled to halt.

'Perfect,' he said, already unclicking his seat belt. In no time he was out and hugging his best friend with a big bear-hug.

Andy wasn't as tall as Ben, she noted as she climbed out from behind the wheel, but he was nice looking, with dark hair, brown eyes and even features.

'Long time no see, bro,' Andy said, finally disengaging from the hug.

Ben shrugged. 'Been busy in the Big Apple.'

'You know what they say, mate, about all work and no play. Still, you're in Australia now, the land down under where the weather is hot and so are the girls. Speaking of hot girls, I presume this is Jess,' he added, giving her the once-over with appreciative eyes.

'How intuitive of you,' Ben mocked. 'Jess, this smart Alec is Andy.'

'Hi, there, Jess,' he said, and came forward to give her a peck on the cheek. 'Lovely to meet you.'

'Are you sure it's all right for me to stay here?' she said in reply. 'I wouldn't like to put your mother to any extra trouble.'

'No, no, she's fine with it. The cottage is always ready for guests and Mum's very easy going. Come inside and have some afternoon tea. And some of Mum's blueberry muffins—the ones you like, Ben. You know, Jess, I'm not sure what it is about Ben here, but women fuss over him like mad.'

'Search me,' she returned with a straight face. 'It's not as though he's handsome or charming or anything like that.'

Andy stared at her for a second, then laughed a big belly laugh. 'Oh, that's priceless. You can keep this one, Ben, if you like.'

'I do like,' Ben whispered in her ear as he slipped a possessive arm around her waist and steered her towards the house.

But, even as she quivered inside with delicious pleasure at his touch, Jess knew Ben had no intention of keeping her. They would be together whilst he was here. And then he would go back to America and it would all be over.

CHAPTER NINE

ANDY'S PARENTS WERE as lovely as their home. Jess had been half-expecting that they would be snobbish, since they were wealthy and owned a winery. But they were anything but. Whilst obviously well-educated and well-spoken, both of them were very down to earth and welcoming, insisting immediately upon introduction that she call them Glen and Heather.

Afternoon tea had been set up in the main living room which had French doors leading out onto the veranda. Heather explained that it was a little too breezy today to have it out there, a wind having sprung up seemingly out of nowhere.

Jess had just finished her cup of tea and was popping a second delicious mini muffin into her mouth when a nearby phone rang. Not the ring tone of a mobile. The unmistakable sound of a landline.

'Do excuse me,' Heather said, moving over to a long sofa table which rested against the wall and on which sat a phone, along with some very nice pieces of pottery.

Jess tried not to listen but it was impossible once she heard Heather make a sound which was halfway between a gasp and a groan.

'Oh, my dear, that's most unfortunate,' she said to whoever she was talking to. 'So what are you going to do? Yes, yes, I'll get Andy for you right away.'

Andy's attention must already have been grabbed because he jumped up immediately and rushed to take the phone from his mother. It didn't take Einstein to realise he was talking to his fiancée and that something had gone wrong. Heather, thank God, quickly enlightened the rest of them.

'Catherine's matron of honour has been rushed to hospital with a threatened miscarriage. Anyway, she's okay, but she has to stay in bed for at least a week and can't be at the wedding tomorrow. She's naturally very upset. Catherine is too. I suppose she'll just have to move the other bridesmaid up to be opposite you, Ben. It means it will be a very small bridal party, but what else can she do?'

Murphy's Law had struck, was Jess's immediate thought. And cruelly. She felt terribly sorry for them all, but especially the bride.

'She could always put Jess in her place,' Ben suddenly suggested.

Jess threw him a horrified look. 'Don't be ridiculous, Ben. Andy's fiancée doesn't even *know* me.'

'In that case, we'll take you over to her place and she can meet you,' he said in his usual taking over fashion. 'She only lives next door. It's not an ideal solution, Heather,' he said, turning his attention to Andy's mother, 'but it *is* a solution.'

'Well, yes, I…I suppose so,' Heather said before Jess could object again. 'It would also make Krissie feel better. She thinks she's spoiled her best friend's wedding. Not to mention the wedding photos. Catherine was only having the two bridesmaids and now she's down to one.'

'It's a perfectly sensible solution,' Glen said with typical male pragmatism. 'Andy!' he called out. 'Ben here said Jess would be willing to take Krissie's place, if it's all right with Catherine.'

Jess held her breath whilst Andy explained Ben's suggestion to his bride.

'She's Ben's new girlfriend,' Andy went on when he was obviously asked for further explanation. 'Her name is Jess. They only met recently. Over some business deal in Sydney. Anyway, Ben got his rental car totalled by some drunk and Jess offered to drive him out here… She'll look great in the wedding photos.'

Jess cringed, not sure now if she wanted the bride to say yay or nay. Still, it wasn't as though she wouldn't have been at the wedding anyway. And if it made everyone a bit happier… After all, weddings were supposed to be happy occasions.

Andy turned to face Jess. 'She says thanks heaps for the offer. Says you've really saved the day, but she would still have to see you asap. Something about whether the dress would fit you or not. It might need altering. Krissie was pregnant, after all.'

'Fine,' Ben said, standing up. 'Tell Catherine we'll be over straight away.'

After Andy relayed Ben's message, he shot his friend a droll look. 'She says *I'm* not allowed to come. Something about my not being allowed to see any of the dresses before the big day.' He rolled his eyes and placed his hand over the phone. 'Women! *Truly.*'

'No sweat, Andy. Tell Catherine we're on our way.' Taking Jess's hand, Ben pulled her to her feet, made his excuses to an understanding Glen and Heather, then steered Jess from the room.

'Make sure you're back for tonight, Ben,' Andy threw after them.

'Will do,' Ben threw back.

Jess resisted resorting to belated objections on the way out. What was done was done.

'Don't be angry with me,' Ben said as they climbed into their respective seats in the SUV.

'I'm not,' Jess said with a somewhat resigned sigh, then started the engine. 'But it might be an idea if you didn't always presume I would do whatever you wanted. A girl likes to be consulted first.'

He seemed startled by her stand. Clearly, he was used to women kow-towing to him all the time.

'Sorry,' he said. 'I was just trying to fix things for Andy.'

'Yes, I know that. That's why I'm not angry.'

'Good. But I will try to be more thoughtful in future. Right, you just turn left when we hit the main road and it's the next driveway along. Catherine's parents own a horse stud. Racehorses.'

'So they're rich too?'

'Not as rich as Andy's folks. But, yes, they're well off.'

'Do you have any poor friends?'

Ben hesitated before answering.

'Not many,' he said.

'I thought not,' she said drily. Rich people mixed with rich people. She was the odd one out here.

'There's the driveway,' he said, pointing.

This one was more impressive than Andy's driveway, with a huge, black iron archway connecting the tall brick gateposts with the name 'Winning Post Stud' outlined in red. The road itself—which was concreted rather than tarred—was lined with white-painted wooden fences behind which grazed the most beautiful horses Jess had ever seen, some of them with foals at foot. She wasn't a horse person herself but her father liked a flutter on the races and she always had a bet on the Melbourne Cup every year. Often won too, which piqued her dad considerably, since she knew next to nothing about form. Mostly she just picked names that she liked.

The house itself was similar in style to Heather and Glen's but genuinely old, made of stone rather than wood. It was also two-storeyed with iron lacework on the verandas and lots of chimneys.

Jess parked outside the large shed behind the house.

'Before we go in, exactly what did you tell Andy about me?'

'I said you were a marketing consultant I'd met connected with Fab Fashions. But I did let him think we'd met a week or so back, not this morning.'

His reminding her that they'd just met today startled Jess. It underlined just how far they'd come in a few short hours. She should have been more shocked, she supposed. But she was beyond shock. When she shook her head in a type of confusion, he leant over and brushed his lips over hers.

'Don't stress the small stuff, Jess,' he murmured against her quivering mouth. 'Just go with the flow.'

When his head lifted she blinked up at him. He wasn't a flow, she realised. He was a raging current which threatened to carry her out to sea and leave her there, like so much flotsam.

'Ah, here's Catherine, and presumably the other bridesmaid, come to meet us,' Ben said and reached for the door handle.

With an effort, Jess pulled herself together.

Catherine turned out to be a right sweetie. Late twenties, Jess guessed. Above-average height, with an athletic figure and blonde hair. Possibly not a natural blonde, but it suited her. She was very attractive with blue eyes and a warm, friendly manner. Nothing bitchy or snobby about her at all. Jess didn't like her bridesmaid nearly as much, perhaps because she made eyes at Ben from the moment she made an appearance. Her name was Leanne and she and Catherine had gone to boarding school together at some college in Bathurst, along with Krissie, who was the only one of the three friends who'd married so far.

'The teachers at school called us "the unholy trinity",' Catherine said, smiling.

'We *were* a bit naughty,' Leanne trilled.

'I can't believe that,' Ben said, annoying Jess with his flirtatious tone. If he was trying to make her jealous, then he was being successful!

After a little more idle chit-chat, Jess and Ben were led inside the house, where they refused offers of another afternoon tea from Catherine's harried-looking mother. Her name was Joan, a handsome woman, but way too thin, with anxious eyes.

'We just had afternoon tea at Andy's place,' Ben explained.

'I see,' she muttered, then gave Jess a frowning once-over. 'You're a lovely looking girl, dear, but I don't think you're going to fit into Krissie's dress.'

'I don't think so either,' Catherine agreed. 'Luckily, she's about the same height as Krissie, but I'd say she's a good size smaller. Krissie's put on some weight since getting pregnant. But no worries, Mum. At least she's not too big. There's nothing Doris could do to make the dress bigger, but making it smaller is not so much of a problem.

'Doris is a lady in Mudgee who does alterations for Mum and me,' she explained to Ben and Jess. 'I'll give her a call once I know what needs to be done. Meanwhile, we should go upstairs and try the dress on post haste. Then I'll ring her. No, no, you stay down here, Ben,' Catherine added when he went to follow them. 'You're not allowed to see the dresses either. You might tell Andy about them and that's bad luck. Mum, take Ben into the living room and put the TV on.'

It rather amused Jess to see the look on Ben's face. Clearly, he wasn't used to being told what to do, especially by women. Most of them probably said yes to him all the time. Jess realised it would do Ben good if she rejected him tomorrow night. But she couldn't see that happening. She would kick herself if she let him go back to America without spending at least one night with him.

Not knowing what it would have been like would haunt her for ever!

'Don't worry,' Catherine said in a conspiratorial whisper as she led Jess up a large, curving staircase, a reluctant Leanne in their wake. 'He won't go anywhere whilst we're gone.'

Jess laughed. 'Well, he can't, can he? He can't drive.'

'Gosh, that must be hard for him. I know Andy would die if he couldn't drive. Is Ben badly hurt?'

'Only his ego,' Jess replied.

'He's very sweet,' Leanne defended from behind them. 'And very rich.'

'Is he?' Jess said casually.

'You said his dad was a billionaire, didn't you, Catherine?'

'That's what Andy told me,' Catherine confirmed.

Jess shrugged. 'Well, that's his dad, not him.'

'But he's an only child,' Leanne persisted as Catherine led Jess into her bedroom, which was huge.

'I'm not interested in Ben for his money,' she said a bit sharply.

'Are you serious about each other?' Catherine asked.

'We've only just met, but we like each other a lot I think…' Jess replied. She didn't want anyone thinking she was that easy. *She* didn't like thinking she was going to be that easy.

Catherine smiled over her shoulder. 'Well, let's get this dress on and see what has to be done.'

The dress was pale-pink chiffon lined with satin, strapless in style with a seam straight under the bust from which the skirt fell in feminine folds to the floor. It was a sweet dress—not Jess's usual style, but surprisingly it looked good on her, the pale pink suiting her strong colouring. It was not a colour she ever chose for herself, thinking she needed bolder colours.

The dress was too large in the bust line, however. The bodice was just too wide. It needed to be taken in at the side seams which would be a time-consuming job; both the chiffon and the lining would have to be carefully unpicked before being resewn. Thankfully, it was the right length, Krissie obviously being of a similar height to Jess. And, whilst the matching shoes were half a size too large, it was better than them being too small.

Catherine tipped her head to one side as she looked Jess over. 'It actually looks better on you than it did on Krissie. But I won't be telling her that,' she added with a quick smile. 'She feels bad enough as it is. Anyway, I'll just give Doris a call. She altered my wedding dress for me a couple of weeks ago when I lost weight. I'm sure she won't mind, since it's an emergency.'

But as it turned out Doris was in Melbourne visiting her sister.

Murphy's Law at work again, Jess thought silently as she took off the dress and put her own clothes back on again. But at least she could do something about the dismay which had already entered the bride-to-be's face.

'It'll be all right, Catherine,' she said soothingly. 'I can fix the dress. I know exactly what to do. And, before you ask, I have my trusty sewing machine sitting in the back of my four-wheel drive.'

Both Catherine and Leanne gaped at her.

'But...but...' Catherine stammered, not looking too certain about Jess's offer.

Jess smiled reassuringly. 'You don't have to worry. I'm a very experienced dressmaker. It was my profession before I went into marketing,' she added, backing up Ben's little white lie. 'I made this jacket myself, you know, and I think it's a pretty good design.'

'You can say that again!' Catherine exclaimed. 'I've been envying it ever since you arrived.'

'Me too,' Leanne gushed. 'Floral jackets are very *in* this spring.'

'But tell me something, Jess,' Catherine said, looking puzzled. 'Do you *always* travel around with your sewing machine?'

Jess realised immediately she could hardly say that, until fate had stepped in and changed everything, she'd been going to do some sewing whilst she was stuck in a motel room for most of the weekend.

'Lord, no,' she said, laughing. 'I simply forgot to take it out of the car after I did some sewing at a girlfriend's place last weekend. How lucky is that?' As little white lies went, it wasn't too bad, except that it made Jess realise she didn't have girlfriends the way Catherine did. When she'd left Sydney to come live on the Central Coast she'd drifted away from all the female friends she'd made at school. She did see a couple of them occasionally but they weren't in her life on a regular basis. In truth, she didn't actually have any female friends now that Colin had debunked, her recent social life having been more his mates and *their* girlfriends.

Jess had never thought of herself as being lonely before. She did have a large family, but suddenly she envied Catherine her girlfriends.

Still, she didn't entertain her negative feelings for long, vowing instead to do something about her lack of girlfriends once she got back home. Maybe she would join a gym. Or a sports club of some kind. She'd been good at basketball at school, her above-average height giving her an advantage. Yes, she'd join a basketball club. For females only. Jess suspected that after Ben went back to America she would want a spell away from male company for a while.

Her heart lurched at this last thought but she steadfastly ignored it.

'How about I drive Ben back to Andy's place?' she suggested. 'Then come back and get stuck into the dress? It could take a couple of hours. I don't want to rush things. I want to get it right.'

Catherine beamed at her. 'Jess, you are a life saver! You must stay here for dinner,' Catherine added. 'Then afterwards we can have a little hen party of our own. I mean, there's no point in your returning to Andy's place. He and Ben are going out on the town in Mudgee tonight. A few of their mates from uni are staying at a motel there, so they're having a big get-together. I did tell Andy not to stay out too late or do anything seriously stupid, but you know Aussie men when they get a few beers into them. Ben might sound like an American these days, but he's an Aussie boy through and through.'

Jess didn't agree with Catherine on that score. Ben was nothing like any Aussie boy she'd ever met.

'At least the wedding's not till four-thirty,' Catherine added. 'So they have time to recover.'

'Where is the wedding, Catherine?' Jess asked.

'We're having it outside in Mum's rose garden, with a

celebrant officiating. And the reception will be in a marquee set up on the back lawn. It's due to go up first thing in the morning. Once that's done, the wedding planner and her lot will swoop in and set everything else up.'

'You booked a wedding planner?' Jess said, surprised. She would want to plan her own wedding right down to the last detail.

'Gosh, yes. I knew it would be a nightmare if I did it. Mum would want to help, but the poor love gets in a flap over the least little thing. The lady I hired has been fantastic. She's arranged everything, right down to the cars and the flowers. She even took me down to Sydney and helped me choose the dresses. Not that it's a large wedding. Only about a hundred guests. This business with Krissie and her dress is the first hiccup there's been.'

'Is the weather forecast good for tomorrow?' Jess asked, worried that Murphy's Law might raise its ugly head again at the last minute. She was beginning to be a serious believer.

'Perfect. Warm, with no rain in sight. Okay, let's get ourselves downstairs and I'll reassure Mum whilst you drop Ben back at Andy's. But don't be away too long,' she added, flashing Jess a knowing smile. 'No hanky panky, now. Keep that till after the wedding.'

CHAPTER TEN

'ARE YOU SURE you can do this, Jess?' Ben said as Jess sped down the driveway. 'I mean, altering a dress can't be the same as making one from scratch.'

'It won't be any trouble. Gran did a lot of alterations and I used to help her. I earned my first pocket money that way.'

'You are full of surprises, aren't you?' he said, smiling over at her. 'A good person to have around, I would imagine. I dare say you can cook as well.'

Jess shrugged. 'I'm not bad. Mum's better, though. Can you cook? Or is that a silly question?'

'Not at all. I think all men should be able to cook a bit, especially ones who live alone. I can make a mean omelette, and my mushroom risotto has received several compliments.'

Jess laughed. 'I dare say it has.' She could imagine Amber gushing over every single thing he did. She could hear her now: *Oh, Ben, darling, you are so clever. And talented. And handsome. And rich.*

No, no, Amber wouldn't actually say that last bit. She would not be as obvious as Leanne. Or as envious. Because Amber would have money of her own. Jess was sure of it.

His sideways glance was sharp. 'Do I detect some sarcasm in that remark?'

Her returning glance was brilliantly po-faced. Or so she thought.

'Not at all.'

He chuckled. 'You little liar, you. You enjoy taking the Mickey out of me.'

'That's a very Aussie saying. Maybe you're not as American as you sound.'

'What's wrong with being American?'

'Absolutely nothing.' It was his being a *filthy rich* American that was the problem.

'You're not going to sleep the night at Catherine's place, are you?' he asked abruptly.

Jess frowned at this question. 'I wasn't planning to, but what difference would it make if I did? You're going out and from what I gather you'll be home very late.'

'I just want you to be there in the morning. I want to have breakfast with you and talk to you some more.'

'Okay,' she agreed. 'But do try to be quiet when you get in. I'm going to be tired after doing that dress. I don't want to be woken by drunken revellers.'

'I have no intention of getting drunk tonight,' he surprised her by saying. 'I don't want to be hung-over tomorrow, thank you very much. I have plans for tomorrow night which require me to be fit and well.'

'Oh,' she said, and for the first time in her life Jess blushed. But it wasn't the blush of embarrassment, it was the blush of heat. Sexual heat.

'Don't miss Andy's place,' he said.

'What? Oh, God, I forgot where I was for a moment.' She glanced in the rear-view mirror as she braked sharply before turning into Andy's driveway.

'Thinking of tomorrow night?' he asked in a low, oh, so sexy voice.

Jess refused to act rattled by him, even though she was.

'But of course,' she said, her cool tone a total contrast to the inferno raging inside her.

Ben should not have been surprised by her bald honesty. Jess didn't play games. But Ben had games very much in mind for tomorrow night. He didn't want sex with her to be over quickly. He wanted to savour it. To savour her. He also wanted the love-making to last and last and last.

'How many lovers have you had, Jess?'

'Not as many as you've had, I'll bet,' she countered, thinking he had a hide to ask her that. 'Now, could we stop talking about sex?' She reefed the car to a ragged halt. 'You sit here whilst I go get Andy, and I'll explain things, then find out where this guest cottage is. And, before you object, you're not fooling me by pretending you can get in and out of your seat without some pain in your shoulder because I know differently. So just be a good boy and sit still for a while.'

She didn't give him a chance to come back with some witty riposte because she was off in a flash, running up the side steps of the house, leaving Ben to ponder just how good a boy he was going to be tonight. And he wasn't talking about at the stag party.

The temptation to come home early was acute. He could easily make some excuse pertaining to his car accident—claim a crippling headache from the concussion, or an appallingly painful shoulder. It *was* sore, but nothing to write home about.

No, he decided in the end. He would wait. Waiting often made the sex better. And Jess would be even more inclined to be thoroughly seduced.

Tomorrow night would be a first for him in more ways than one. His first wedding. His first brunette. The first girl in a decade who didn't seem overly impressed with his being Morgan De Silva's son and heir.

Now, that really would be a first!

CHAPTER ELEVEN

THE GUEST COTTAGE was cute and quite a long way from the main house, set on a smaller hill and surrounded by trees. Made of weatherboard, it had a pitched iron roof, covered porches front and back and a hallway which cut the cottage in two. On the left on entering was a lounge followed by a dining room and then the kitchen. On the right were two bedrooms separated by a bathroom, followed by a utility room and walk-in pantry. All the rooms were delightfully furnished in comfy, country-style furniture which was probably newer than it looked. Apparently, it had once been a miner's cottage, and had been on the property when Andy's parents had bought the place.

Andy had shown them the way to the cottage personally, which was a relief to Jess. Nothing like a third person being present to prevent Ben doing something which she didn't want him to do. Not yet, anyway. If truth be told, she was terrified of that moment when he would stop the talk and walk the walk, so to speak. She'd always thought herself quite good at sex but, on a scale of one to ten, she doubted she came much above a five. She would hate it if he found her a disappointment.

She quickly put her overnight bag in the smaller of the two bedrooms, insisting that Ben have the front room with the queen-sized bed, since he was too big for a single bed.

He didn't argue, just sat down on the side of the bed and bounced up and down, as though testing it for comfort. Andy carried Ben's things into the room whilst Jess hovered in the doorway.

'I'll come back with some more provisions shortly,' Andy told them. 'Some stuff for breakfast. There's already white wine in the fridge, and red wine in the cupboards, along with coffee, tea and biscuits, etc. But I'll bring down some fresh bread, eggs and bacon.'

'Well, I won't be here,' Jess returned before he could escape. 'I have to get back to Catherine's. I won't be back till late tonight.'

'Oh, right. I forgot. I also forgot to thank you for what you're doing, Jess. Catherine rang me and told me about the dress. You are one clever girl, isn't she, Ben? Fancy being able to sew like that.'

'She's amazing,' Ben said.

Jess just smiled, awake to his many compliments.

The moment they were alone Ben gave her a narrow-eyed look. 'You won't be staying in that bedroom tomorrow night.'

She glowered at him, never being at her best when men started ordering her around. 'Maybe I will,' she bit out. 'If you start acting like some jerk.'

That sent him back in his heels. 'What do you mean?'

'I run my own race, Ben. I don't like men telling me what to do and when to do it.'

'Is that so?'

Ben stood up and strode over to her, taking her firmly by the shoulders and pulling her hard against him. She didn't struggle, or protest. Just stared up at him with wide, dilated eyes. Ben could actually feel her galloping heartbeat. She thought she didn't like to be ordered around, but he knew that a lot of strong-minded women liked their lovers to take charge.

It came to him that she'd probably never had a dominant lover before. What an exciting thought!

He could hardly wait for tomorrow night to come.

'When the time is right, Jess,' he said quietly, his eyes intense on hers, 'you *will* like me telling you what to do. Trust me on this. But, for now, perhaps you should get going. Because if you stay I won't be responsible for what might happen.'

Jess left the cottage in a fluster, her body cruelly turned on and her thoughts totally scattered.

Trust him, he'd said. To do what? Turn her into some kind of mindless sex slave?

At this moment she didn't doubt he could do it. If she let him.

Did she want that to happen?

The answer to that question lay in her thudding heart and rock-hard nipples.

Suddenly, Jess was overwhelmed by a wave of desire so strong that she almost ran off the road. Giving herself a savage mental shake, she slowed down to a crawl, then turned shakily into Catherine's driveway, proceeding very carefully up the cement road, grateful now that she had a job to do which would take her most of the evening; *very* grateful that she had no reason to go back to that seductive cottage till well after Ben had left with Andy for their night on the town. Thank heavens he wouldn't get home till the small hours of the morning. By which time she would be sound asleep.

Jess had to laugh over that one. There would be no sleeping for her tonight.

But at least she could pretend she was asleep.

Things didn't turn out quite like that, however. Jess finished the dress around nine-thirty, after which she refused all offers of wine, saying she was tired, then drove back to the cottage. In actual fact she'd only just remembered that she'd promised to give her mother a ring. This she did whilst she opened a bottle of the white wine resting in the door of the fridge. She poured herself a large glass, sipping it as she sat at the kitchen table, and gave her mother an edited version of what had happened, telling her the truth about the dramas over the wedding and how she'd fixed the dress tonight, plus the plan for her to be a substitute matron of honour the next day. Naturally, she didn't mention anything about her being thought of as Ben's girlfriend or that she was staying with him, alone, in this cottage. She admitted staying as a guest at the winery but that was all.

'It sounds like it's been a rather surprising trip so far,' her mother said.

'It certainly has,' Jess agreed with considerable irony as she poured herself a second glass of wine.

'You'll have to ring me tomorrow night and tell me all about the wedding.'

Jess winced. She could hardly tell her mother why that wasn't going to happen.

'Mum, the wedding's not till late in the afternoon. By the time the reception is over and I get to bed, it's going to be very late and I'm going to be exhausted. I'll call you on Sunday morning. But not too early, mind. I might sleep in.' Jess was grateful that her mother couldn't see inside her head at this moment, as the images in there were not fit for a caring mother's consumption.

'Oh, all right,' her mother said. 'But don't forget to take some photos. I'd love to see what you looked like. What you *all* looked like, actually. Which reminds me. What does this Ben fellow look like? You said he was nice but I have a feeling he's good-looking, am I right?'

'Yes, he's very good-looking,' she admitted, struggling to keep her voice calm in the face of a looming panic attack over her sexual inadequacies. 'And very tall.'

'Tall, dark and handsome, eh?'

'No, he's actually fair-haired, with blue eyes.'

'And how old, did you say?'

'I don't know. Early thirties, perhaps.'

'And rich?'

'Filthy rich, Mum. His father's a billionaire.'

'Goodness. And did you tell him that you lost your job at Fab Fashions because of him?'

'I did mention it. And he promised to see what he could do.'

'Well, that was nice of him. But did he mean it?'

The jury was still out on that score. 'Maybe. I guess we'll have to wait and see, Mum. Now, I really must go. I'm tired.' That was a lie. She had so much adrenaline flowing through her body at the moment that she had no hope of sleeping. That was why she was downing all this wine; sometimes wine made her sleepy. Unfortunately, it didn't seem to be working.

'Driving can be very tiring,' her mother said. 'Goodnight, darling. Sleep tight. Love you.'

Jess suddenly came over all emotional.

'Love you too, Mum,' she choked out, then hung up.

Jess decided after her third glass of wine that it definitely wasn't working. So she put the half-drunk bottle back in the fridge and headed for the bathroom. A long, hot bath filled in another hour but didn't relax her one iota. She'd just emerged from the bathroom, dressed in a nightie, when she heard a car screech to a stop in front of the cottage. Running to the front living room, Jess peered through the curtains in time to see Ben climb out of the back of a taxi.

Flustered—what on earth was he doing home this early?—she whirled to make a dash for the bedroom, in her haste catching her left foot under the curled up corner of a rug. She cried out as she fell, her hands bracing themselves to protect her face whilst her knees hit the wooden floorboards with a painful thud.

Ben heard Jess cry out as he made his way up onto the front veranda. He dashed inside, switching on the hall light and calling her name at the same time.

He found her sitting back on her haunches in the semi-dark on the living-room floor, dressed in a red satin nightie with spaghetti straps which showed off her gorgeous figure. Her lovely hair was down, spread over her shoulders in dishevelled disarray, adding to the criminally sexy picture she presented.

'What happened?' he asked, and held out his left hand to help her up.

'I fell over,' she said, but made no move to take his hand, her eyes on her ground. 'My foot got caught under the rug.'

'I see,' he said, not seeing at all. What was she doing in this room, anyway? The lights weren't on. Neither was the television. 'Well, do you want to take my hand or are you going to stay there all night?' he said, his tone betraying his inner frustration.

She glanced up at him.

Jess only just managed not to groan out loud. God, but he looked utterly gorgeous dressed in grey stone-washed jeans, an open-necked white shirt and a fabulous looking charcoal-grey jacket.

Finally, she placed her hand in his, his fingers closing tightly around hers as he pulled her to her feet.

'What on earth are you doing home *this* early?' she asked whilst she tried to ignore the direction of his gaze. Right where her erect nipples were poking against the red satin. Maybe he would think she was cold. Though she wasn't, having turned off the air-conditioning when she'd got home. The temperature had dropped considerably once the sun had gone down but it was a nice twenty-three degrees inside the cottage.

'Do you want the truth?'

'Of course.'

'I told Andy I had a vicious headache and that if he wanted me on deck tomorrow, then I should go home.'

'And do you? Have a vicious headache?'

'No. I simply couldn't stop thinking about you.'

Jess tried not to let his flattering words seduce her but it was way too late for such a futile struggle.

'I've been thinking about you too,' she admitted somewhat shakily.

'So do I still have to wait till tomorrow night?'

She shook her head.

She half-expected him to kiss her then but he didn't. Instead, he just smiled.

'I need a shower,' he said. 'I smell of beer. Can I tempt you to join me?'

The desire to lick her suddenly dry lips was intense but somehow she resisted. Jess swallowed instead, putting some moisture into her mouth. 'I…I've just had a bath,' she said, her voice thick and throaty.

'Then you can come and watch.'

Jess blinked at him, her mouth falling open briefly before snapping shut again.

'All right,' she said, wondering if this was what he'd meant earlier about her liking him telling her what to do.

She did. Which was weird. If Colin or any of her other boyfriends had suggested the same thing to her, she would have told them to get lost. Bathrooms were private places, in her opinion. They weren't places where you *watched*. Yet she wanted to watch Ben shower, didn't she? She wanted to see him naked. Wanted to do all sorts of things she'd never done before.

Her head spun at the thought.

When she didn't move, he frowned at her. 'You've changed your mind already?'

Changed her mind? Was he insane? How could she possibly change her mind when she'd already lost it?

She shook her head.

'Good,' he said, and held out his hand to her again.

CHAPTER TWELVE

BEN LIKED THE way Jess let him lead her meekly into the bathroom. He could tell she was turned on, the same way he was. Even the slightest touch turned him on with her. It was quite incredible, the effect she had on him. But nothing he couldn't control, now that she was being deliciously cooperative.

He settled her, somewhat stunned-looking, on the side of the claw-footed bath, then started undressing.

Jess could not believe she was doing this, sitting there watching whilst Ben took all his clothes off in front of her. But, dear heaven, it was exciting!

After he kicked off his shoes, he removed his jacket and then his shirt, revealing an upper half which didn't look like it spent all day seated behind a desk. He must work hard in a gym, she decided, or go swimming a lot. His light tan suggested this might be the case. He had broad shoulders, one of which carried a nasty bruise. But it didn't seem to stop his arm working. His chest muscles were wide and well-toned, his stomach a surprising six-pack. Very little body hair, she noted, and liked.

Jess held her breath when he whipped the belt out of his jeans, but he just dropped it on the floor, then ran the zipper down. When his hands hooked under the waist band

and pushed down, she finally let go of the air trapped in her lungs.

He was wearing black underpants, made out of a silky material which hid nothing.

She wondered if he was as big as he looked. Jess had always believed that size *did* matter. To a degree. She liked a man to be well built in that area.

He was. Bigger than her previous boyfriends. And magnificently erect. Circumcised, with only a smattering of fair hair at the base. She knew he would feel—and taste—fantastic.

He stood facing her, a golden Adonis in every way.

'Now you, Jess,' he commanded. 'Stand up and take that nightie off. I want to see all of you.'

She stood up onto shaky legs, utterly compelled to obey him. Her belly tightened as she slowly slipped the straps off her shoulders, first on, then the other. She wasn't wearing any undies. She never wore undies to bed. The nightie slid down her body with a whoosh, pooling around her feet on the tiled floor.

His gaze dropped down to those feet first, then gradually travelled upwards, lingering on the neatly waxed V of curls between her thighs, before lifting to her breasts.

'Beautiful,' he said.

Jess knew she was attractive, but she'd never considered herself beautiful. She had physical flaws, like most people. Couldn't Ben see that her nose was too big for her face? So was her mouth. The back of her thighs had some dimples of cellulite which no amount of massage or cream could remove, though he wouldn't see that unless he ordered her to turn around.

Jess suspected Ben wasn't about to do that. He was enjoying looking at her breasts too much. Admittedly, they were the best feature of her figure. Full and high, with perky pink nipples that grew astonishingly in size when they were played with. Or when she was excited. Which she was right now. God, yes. Her whole breasts seemed to be swelling under his hot, hungry eyes, though perhaps it was just Jess's ragged breathing.

'No more arguments or excuses, Jess,' he said thickly. 'You're coming into that shower with me and then we're going to bed. Together.'

Once again, she obeyed him, blindly and without protest, letting him pull her with him into the shower cubicle. And it was there, as the hot jets of waters did dreadful things to her hair, that he cupped her face and finally kissed her properly.

Jess had been kissed many times in her life. And by men who were quite good kissers. But Ben kissing her was a once-in-a-lifetime experience. She felt its effect through her whole body right down to her toes. It overwhelmed her. Then obsessed her. She could not get enough of it. And of him. When at last his head lifted, she sank against him in total surrender, her arms wrapping tightly around his waist.

'Are you on the pill, Jess?'

She pulled back enough to glance up at him. 'What?'

'Are you on the pill?'

Her mind cleared a little. 'Well…yes…but…'

'You still want me to use protection.'

'Please,' she said, despite being tempted to say no. *Just do it to me. Right here and now.*

'In that case, I think we should cut this shower short this time.'

Again, no protest from her. She just stood there whilst he switched off the taps, then reached for one of the towels hanging on the rack, rubbing rather roughly at her dripping hair before giving himself a brisk rub down. Then he scooped her up in his arms and carried her back to his bedroom.

Jess shivered as he laid her gently down on top of the bed, goose bumps springing up over her body.

'Are you cold?' he asked as he lay down next to her, propping himself up on his left side.

'A little,' she lied.

'Do you want to get under the covers?'

She shook her head.

'I've been wanting to do this all day,' he said, and bent his lips to hers once more, his right hand sliding up into her still damp hair.

His return to gentle kisses surprised her at first, then entranced her. She sighed under their soft sweetness. Gradually, however, the pressure of his mouth grew stronger. When his teeth nipped at her lower lip, she gasped, and his tongue slipped inside once more, Jess moaning softly as it explored the sensitive skin of her palate. She gasped again when a hand covered her right breast, playing with her nipple in ways she'd definitely never experienced before: soft rubbing with his palm interspersed with quite painful pinching till it was on fire.

And all the while he kept on kissing her, his tongue alternately snaking deep, then withdrawing before plunging in again. When his hand moved across to her other nipple, she felt momentarily bereft for the abandoned one. If he could have played with both at the same time, she would have been in heaven. Or hell. Jess could not work out if she was in agony or ecstasy. Not that she cared, as long as he didn't stop.

He stopped, both the kissing and the nipple pinching, leaving her moaning in dismay till she realised why he'd stopped. Already he was down there with that knowing mouth and tongue of his, making her groan and squirm as he licked and sucked and showed her that all her other lovers had been seriously ignorant of a woman's body. Ben knew exactly what to do to bring her to the brink of coming, not once but several times. How he knew when to back off, she wasn't sure. Maybe it had something to do with his fingers being deep inside her all the while. Maybe he could feel the way her muscles tightened when she came close to coming.

His head lifted at last. 'Enough, I think,' he muttered, then collapsed on his back beside her, breathing very heavily.

She levered herself up onto her elbow and stared over at him. 'You're not stopping, are you?'

'Just for a few seconds. I need a breather, and then I have to get a condom on. I put two in that top drawer this afternoon,' he said, nodding towards the bedside chest next to her. 'Get one for me, would you, Jess?'

Jess wondered if Ben always used protection, even when his girlfriends were on the pill. She had a feeling that he did. Maybe he was worried that one of them might try to trap him into marriage. Seriously rich men would have to worry about such things, she imagined. If this Amber wanted to marry him enough, it wouldn't be beyond her to do such thing.

'Put it on for me,' he said after she extracted one from the drawer.

Oh, Lord, Jess thought as she opened the foil packet and turned back to him. She *had* put a condom on before. Just not whilst she was in such an excited state. She found it extremely difficult with her hands shaking so much. When Ben groaned, she shot him a worried look.

'Am I hurting you?'

His smile was both tortured and wry. 'Oh, honey, you're killing me. But not in the way you think. Would you mind being on top?'

'You want me on top?' she echoed. Whilst it was her favourite position, she hadn't imagined it would be Ben's. Earlier on, he'd seemed keen to be the one in control. And whilst it had turned her on, being ordered around, she was happy to have their roles reversed for a while. Though the position had been *his* idea, come to think of it.

'I would have thought you'd like being on top,' he said.

'I do quite like it,' she confessed.

'Then what are you waiting for?'

What, indeed?

Ben's stomach tightened when she moved to straddle him, his heart thundering in his chest when she took hold of him and presented the bursting tip against the entrance to her body. He could feel the heat and the wetness of her, but he couldn't see it. She wasn't one of those girls who totally denuded herself of body hair, her sex protected by a smattering of soft dark curls. Ben rather liked that. It was different. She was different. In every way. There was no pretence about her. She was sweet and very natural, and he wanted her as he'd never wanted any woman before. His excitement was so great that he had no patience with playing games tonight. He wanted her now!

A groan escaped his lips as she pushed him inside, her flesh slowly swallowing his with a silky snugness which was incredibly pleasurable. He braced himself mentally against what it would feel like when she moved. He didn't want to come too soon. Hell, no. That would never do!

Jess had been right. It felt incredible with him deep inside her, filling her totally. He obviously liked it too, judging by the look on his face. Though was it rapture she was seeing, or torture? A mixture of both, she imagined. Men could be very impatient at this stage. So she kept her movements slow and gentle at first, lifting her hips only slightly before lowering herself down again. But it wasn't long before her own desire for satisfaction took over, urging her to lift her hips higher, then to plunge down harder. She tried not to think about anything but her sexual pleasure, valiantly ignoring the emotional responses which hovered at the edges of her brain. This wasn't love, she told herself firmly. This was just sex. Great sex, yes, with an utterly gorgeous man. But still just sex. *Enjoy it, girl. Because you could go the rest of your life without finding a lover like Ben.*

Their coming together distracted her totally from any thought of love, her own orgasm so intense that all she could think about were the physical sensations. The electric pleasure of each spasm, plus the wonderful relief from the tension which had gripped her all evening. Finally, when it was over, every pore in her body succumbed to a huge wave of languor. She collapsed across him, totally spent, sighing a long, sated sigh when he wrapped his arms around her, his lips in her hair.

'That was fantastic,' he whispered. '*You're* fantastic.

'No, don't move,' he said when she tried to lift her head. 'I want to fall asleep like this, with me still inside you. My only regret is that we can't do it again. I'm just too damned tired all of a sudden. But I'll make it up to you tomorrow. I promise. Just stay where you are, you delicious thing. Stay,' he repeated, his voice slurring a little.

Within thirty seconds, he'd fallen asleep.

Less than a minute later, she followed him.

CHAPTER THIRTEEN

BEN WOKE TO the smell of bacon cooking, plus no Jess in bed with him. Hell, he'd really passed out last night. And slept for a good ten hours, he realised with amazement as he glanced at his watch. And whilst he regretted not waking—he hadn't intended sex with Jess to be so short and swift—the long sleep had done him a lot of good. His shoulder was one hundred percent better and he felt marvellous.

Ben fairly leapt out of bed, calling a hurried, 'Good morning,' out to Jess before bolting for the bathroom. After a very quick shower, he wrapped a towel around his waist, then made his way to the kitchen, anxious to see Jess again. She glanced over her shoulder as he walked in, her lovely eyes lighting up at the sight of him.

'You look good in a towel,' she said, smiling.

'And you look good in anything,' he returned, his gaze raking over her from top to toe. She was wearing the same fitted black trousers again, but her top was different, a simple scoop-necked sweater in a bright-green colour which suited her dark hair and olive skin. She wasn't wearing any make-up and her hair was up, secured on top of her head in a rather haphazard fashion. On closer inspection, he could see she'd wrapped it around itself in a knot, a few bits and pieces already escaping. Her lack of artifice continued to enchant him. Amber was always fully made up and her hair groomed to perfection before showing herself in the morning.

Jess made Amber look terribly shallow. And impossibly vain.

'Flatterer,' she said, laughing, then turned back to the stove.

'That smells good,' he said, coming up behind her to slide his arms around her waist.

Jess tried not to stiffen at his touch, having determined to act naturally with him. It had been difficult not to ogle his beautiful body when he'd come into the kitchen just now, but she'd managed, telling herself all the while that a sophisticated New York woman wouldn't ogle. She would sail through the morning after the night before with style and panache. She wouldn't ask for reassurances that he wanted more from her than sex. She would be pleasant and easy going. Slightly flirtatious, yes, but nothing heavy.

So, when Ben placed a hand under her chin and turned her face towards his, she hid her momentary panic and let him kiss her. Fortunately, it wasn't too deep, too long a kiss. But, oh…how her heart raced, her head instantly filling with images of him scattering everything off the kitchen table with one sweep of his arm and taking her on it then and there.

His eyes were glittering when his head lifted. 'If that bacon wasn't already cooked,' he said, 'I'd have *you* for breakfast.'

'Really,' she replied with superb nonchalance. 'I might have something to say about that.'

His eyes carried the knowledge she was bluffing. 'Come now, Jess, let's not play games this morning. You and I both know that what we shared last night was something special. And highly addictive. But you're right. We should eat first.'

'Your bruise looks much better,' she said, turning her attention back to the breakfast. 'When bruises start going all the colours of the rainbow, it usually means they're on the mend. Now, sit down, for Pete's sake, and let me get on with this.'

'You sound like you're familiar with bruises,' he said, pulling out a chair at the kitchen table and sitting down.

'I have three brothers,' she reminded him. 'There wasn't a day that they didn't come home from school with bruises.'

'Habitual fighters, were they?'

'No. Just physical.'

'Like you. You're very physical. And very sexy.'

Jess felt some dismay—and irritation—that Ben's focus seemed to be all about sex. She was more than that… wasn't she?

Somehow, she managed to serve up toast, bacon and eggs without burning anything. Ben ate his with relish, Jess just picking at hers. She'd always been a girl who lacked appetite when she was upset about something. She tried telling herself she was foolish to expect anything more than sex from Ben, but it was a losing cause.

'You didn't eat much,' Ben remarked after he finished his breakfast.

'I'm not very hungry. I had some coffee before you got up.'

'You're not one of those girls who lives on coffee, are you?'

'Not usually.'

'You don't need to lose weight, Jess. Your body is absolutely gorgeous just the way it is.'

Jess struggled not to show her feelings on her face. But did he *have* to concentrate on her body?

'I'm glad you think so. By the way, you said yesterday we could have a talk about Fab Fashions this morning.'

He seemed genuinely taken aback. 'Yes, I know I did. But that was before last night.'

Jess glared at him across the table. 'You mean you don't have to pander to me any more because we've already had sex.'

Ben hid his guilt well. Because she was right, wasn't she? But, damn it all, he wasn't about to waste time talking about business when he could be having sex with her again.

'No,' he said carefully. 'That's not true. Though what we shared last night does change things, Jess. It was so very special. We can talk about Fab Fashions during the drive home tomorrow. And every day next week. Meanwhile, we probably only have a couple of hours to ourselves before we both have to get ready for the wedding this afternoon. What time do you have to be over at Catherine's?'

She seemed mollified by his explanation. 'I said I'd be there at three. But I have to do my hair first. Catherine and Leanne are having their hair done at a hairdresser's in Mudgee this morning, but I prefer to do my own hair. I'm better at it than the hairdresser.'

He smiled. 'I have no doubt you are. Okay, Andy said he's going to collect me around two-thirty. We're all getting ready together up at the house before heading over to Catherine's around four. Apparently, it doesn't do for the groom's party to be late arriving.'

'You haven't been in a bridal party before?'

'Actually, no, I haven't. Have you?'

'I was a bridesmaid at all of my three brothers' weddings.'

'Maybe next time you'll be the bride.'

'I doubt it,' she said, her voice sharp.

'Don't you want to get married?'

'Well, yes, I do. Eventually. That's what we do in our

family. But I'm prepared to wait till the right man comes along. After Colin, I'm not in any hurry.'

Ben wasn't in any hurry either. But it did cross his mind that Jess would make some man a wonderful wife.

'And what would make him the right man?' he asked.

Jess shrugged. 'That's a difficult question. For starters, he'd have to be reasonably successful in whatever he's chosen to do in life. I like men who are confident.'

'Would he have to be rich?'

'Not rich like you, Ben De Silva. I would never marry a man as rich as you.'

Ben felt perversely offended. 'Really? A lot of women would.'

'Yeah. Silly, greedy ones like Leanne. And already rich ones like your Amber.'

Ben frowned. 'Why makes you think Amber's rich?'

Jess stood up and started clearing the breakfast things away. 'Am I wrong?' she threw at him.

'No. She *is* rich. Or, her father is.'

'I thought as much.'

Ben laughed. 'You're not jealous, are you, Jess? You have no reason to be. Amber's history.'

His accusing her of jealousy was very telling. Because she was. Horribly so. Jess turned her back on him and walked over to the sink. She'd be history too one day soon. It was just a matter of time. And geography.

His suddenly taking firm possession of her shoulders startled her. She hadn't even heard him get up.

'Don't be angry with me, Jess. Come back to bed. We can talk about Fab Fashions there, if you like. We can multi-task.'

She couldn't help it. She laughed. 'Men can't multitask.'

'Don't you believe it,' he said as he pulled her back hard

against him. 'I can talk and get an erection at the same time. See?' he said and rubbed himself against her bottom. 'There's proof.'

She laughed some more.

'I love it when you laugh,' he murmured as he nuzzled her neck. 'But I love it more when you come. The sounds you make, the way your insides squeeze me like a vice... You drove me crazy last night. Drive me crazy again, lovely Jess. With your mouth this time. And those hands you're so damned good with.'

She was the one who was being driven crazy. No man had ever said things like that to her. He made her want to do *everything* with him. Oh, God...

She didn't say a word, just whirled in his arms and kissed him. And he kissed her back, a long, wet wildly passionate kiss which scattered her brainwaves and turned her body to liquid.

'Come on. Back to bed,' he said when he finally came up for air.

'Bed?' she echoed, dazed.

His smile was wry. 'Yeah. You know. The furniture thingy with sheets and pillows where you go to sleep at night. But we're not going to sleep in it today, beautiful,' he added. 'Not even for a single second.'

CHAPTER FOURTEEN

'Do you think I'm doing the right thing?'

Jess almost shook her head at the bride in exasperation. After all, why ask *her*? She knew next to nothing of Catherine's relationship with Andy. It was also rather late to have second thoughts with the bridal party about to make its way over to the rose garden where the groom would be impatiently waiting. They were already twenty minutes behind schedule. At the same time, Jess did feel some sympathy for the girl. Her mother was not the most reassuring of mothers—the woman had spent the last two hours in tears—and marriage *was* a big step, especially in this day and age when divorce was rife and the 'for ever' kind of love seemed like a pipe dream. But, as they said in the classics, better to have loved and lost than never to have loved at all!

'Do you love Andy, Catherine?' Jess asked quickly.

'Yes, of course.'

'There is no *of course* about it. Lots of girls marry for reasons other than love.'

'Not me.'

'Nor me. And does Andy love you?'

'Yes, I'm sure he does.'

A sudden thought crossed Jess's mind. 'You're not pregnant, are you?'

'Lord, no. No. But we do plan on having children.'

'Sounds like you don't have any reason for last-minute doubts, Catherine. Now, come on, girl, we're already running late. Though, before you go, let me say you look absolutely gorgeous!' Which was true. Her dress was a bit OTT in Jess's opinion, but it suited Catherine's feminine blonde beauty.

'Oh.' The bride fairly beamed. 'You look gorgeous as well. And you too, Leanne.'

Leanne preened whilst Jess just smiled. Yes, they did all look very nice.

'Aren't you girls ready yet?' Catherine's father snarled at them.

Jess had disliked the man within seconds of having met him. He was one of those larger than life men who was absolutely full of himself. Jess decided with sudden insight that his bombast could explain why Catherine's mother was a nervous wreck and why perhaps Catherine was afraid of marriage. If Andy had been anything like her father in character—which fortunately he didn't seem to be—then she would have every right to be hesitant.

Jess decided to put him on the spot. 'Don't you think your daughter looks absolutely divine?'

'What? Oh, yes, yes. Very nice. Now, let's go.'

Jess and Leanne exchanged rolling eyes which told it all. Jess decided if her father ever said she just looked *nice* on her wedding day she would throttle him.

Thinking of her own future wedding day thoroughly distracted Jess as they made their way from the house over to the rose garden, making her only dimly aware of her surrounds. She'd done her best to put a halt to her escalating feelings for Ben during the hours she'd spent with him earlier on, focusing on the physical and not the emotional. But her heart had been as impossible to control as her body. It had soared every time she'd touched him. But it had been performing oral sex on him which had been the killer. She had loved the way he'd lost control under her mouth and hands. He hadn't wanted to, she was sure. But he'd seemed as powerless to stop himself as she'd been. Not that that meant anything. She wasn't that naïve.

They'd used the only remaining condom in no time, with a still turned-on Jess eventually offering to go and get the condom she kept in her bag which was in the other bedroom. Ben had followed her there, pulling her down onto the rug by the bed where he'd taken her on all fours, squeezing her nipples as she came. It was the first time in her life that she'd had sex that way and she'd loved it, giving rise to the hope that she wasn't falling in love, just suffering from an intense case of lust.

Ben had been wrong about their not actually sleeping. When he'd carried her back to bed after that rather rough mating on the floor, she'd passed out, not waking till Ben had started shaking her shoulder.

'Oh, Lord!' she'd exclaimed, sitting bolt upright and pushing her tangled hair out of her eyes. 'What time is it?' Ben was dressed, she'd immediately noted. Not in what he would be wearing at the wedding. Just jeans and a top.

'Shortly before two-thirty. Andy will be here any moment. You said you had to do your hair.'

Jess had grimaced. 'I'll have to shampoo it again. It's a mess.'

Just then there'd been a knock on the front door, Andy calling out as he'd opened it and walked into the hallway. Panicked, Jess had grabbed a sheet to cover herself, Ben unable to get to the open doorway in time before Andy had been standing in it.

'Oh, sorry,' Andy had said hurriedly on seeing an obviously naked Jess in the bed. 'I'll…er…wait for you outside, Ben.'

'No sweat.' He'd turned to throw Jess an apologetic glance. 'Sorry about that, my darling. See you at the wedding.'

Jess recalled that her heart had turned over at his calling her his darling. It turned over again when she caught sight of him standing with Andy at the end of the strip of red carpet which had been rolled out between the rows of decorated seats. No doubt the groom and the other groomsman looked almost as good as Ben in their black dinner suits. But Jess didn't see anyone or anything else but him, smiling at her. Talk about tunnel vision!

Some taped wedding music started up and she floated down the makeshift aisle, unaware of the admiring whispers from the guests, aware of nothing but Ben's eyes upon her.

Bloody hell, Ben thought as Jess walked slowly towards them. *She is just so damned desirable!*

'You are one lucky guy, mate,' Andy murmured out of the side of his mouth. 'That is one hot babe.'

'You ought to talk,' Ben managed to whisper back when the bride finally came into view. But he hardly noticed Catherine or heard the ceremony. He just went through the motions, producing the rings on cue, thankful that it was a relatively short service. He could not wait to be alone with Jess again.

His first opportunity to speak to her was at the signing of the register which they did to one side after Catherine and Andy had been declared man and wife.

'You look very pretty in pink,' he whispered as he passed her the pen. 'But I prefer you in nothing.'

He noticed her hand trembling as she signed her name. It excited him, the way he could turn her on like that. She wasn't like other girls he'd slept with. She seemed less experienced and more capable of being surprised. That, in itself, was very arousing. The temptation to push her sexual boundaries was acute, especially since she was obviously a highly sexed girl. She'd loved going down on him. He'd loved it too. It worried Ben, though, the tendency he had to lose control with her on occasion.

Next time, he would not let that happen. Ben had a penchant for erotic fun and games, first sparked when he'd had an affair with an older woman during his university days. She'd been a mature student who liked being dominated in bed, teaching Ben all there was to know about such role playing. Ben had enjoyed playing lord and master to the hilt. He still did. Ben already had an idea in mind for tonight, an idea which he hoped Jess would go along with. He felt pretty sure that she would.

Damn, but it was going to an excruciatingly long evening!

Jess could not believe how long the evening proved to be. The photos had been tedious, as had the serving and eating of the three-course meal. It wasn't till coffee and cheeses were served that Ben finally stood up to make the best man speech.

He didn't look at all nervous. Which irritated her. Perhaps because it underlined how confident a person he was. Which was perverse. Hadn't she told him she liked confident men?

She actually didn't mind *liking* Ben. She would never have had sex with him if she hadn't liked him. She just didn't want to fall in love with him.

'Ladies and gentlemen,' Ben began. 'Firstly, let me thank you all for coming here today to celebrate Andy's marriage to Catherine who, might I say, is the most beautiful bride I have ever seen.'

Not just confident, Jess thought ruefully, but a silver-tongued charmer.

'For those who don't know me personally, you might be wondering what a chap with an American accent is doing as Andy's best man. Trust me when I say I might sound like a Yank, but if you scratch the surface you will find an Aussie through and through.'

Cheering from the guests.

'Andy and I go way back. He was my best friend all through boarding school and then through law school. He was always there for me. Always. And I love him. Sorry, Andy, I know you don't like mushy. Now, I know it is traditional to embarrass the groom by telling stories of things he got up to in his pre-wed life, but I have struggled to think of anything which Andy ever did which was stupid or reckless. Of course, I have been living in the US of A for the past ten years, so perhaps a few potential slip-ups have eluded me. I did hear a rumour that when he was in France he burnt the candle at both ends, so to speak.'

Laughter from the guests.

Ben smiled. 'But I do not believe a word of it. From what I saw last night at Andy's stag party, his candle is still in full working order.'

More laughter from the guests. And a horrified glance from the bride.

'Just kidding, Catherine. Andy's was the best behaved stag party I have ever attended. On a serious note, folks, believe me when I say that Andy is the most sensible, smartest man I have ever known. It's testimony to his brain power that he has chosen such a lovely girl as Catherine as his life partner. They are a well-matched couple who love each other dearly. Such love is a precious gift, one which should be treasured. And protected. And toasted. So, will you please all be upstanding and charge your glasses…'

Everyone obeyed, especially Jess, who had been moved by the last part of Ben's speech. Love was indeed precious, especially true love. Colin hadn't truly loved her. As for Ben… No point in going there!

'To Andy and Catherine,' Ben said loudly as he held up his own glass.

All the guests repeated his words as they clinked glasses and drank.

Jess did likewise, then sat back down, feeling suddenly drained. More speeches followed and, finally, Andy stood up to speak. He did not have Ben's gift of the gab, or the same smooth delivery, but what he said was sweet and touching. It actually brought tears to Jess's eyes, which she had to blink back swiftly when he proposed a toast to the bridesmaids, explaining how Jess had had to step in at the last moment and how grateful they were to her.

Jess sat there, her right hand fingering the lovely silver and diamond pendant Andy had given the bridesmaids earlier. Catherine had received a magnificent pair of diamond-drop earrings. When Jess had insisted to Catherine that they give her pendant to Krissie afterwards, Catherine had said no, she and Andy would buy Krissie something special for the baby when it came.

They really were a very nice couple. And, yes, very much in love. Jess couldn't help envying them their happiness. She was no longer pleased that Ben planned to stay in Australia a little longer. She knew the score. He wanted hot sex with her after which he would wing his way back to New York and forget she ever existed. And by then, she could very well be left behind with a broken heart.

Common sense demanded she have no more to do with Ben after this weekend was over. But common sense was no match for the sexual heat which had been charging through her veins ever since they'd signed the marriage certificate together. A few hot words whispered in her ear and she had almost combusted on the spot. Her still-erect nipples burned as they pressed against the satin lining of her dress, her belly tight with sexual tension. She couldn't wait for this reception to be over so she could be with Ben again. She could not wait!

But she *had* to wait, she accepted wretchedly. Dear God, but she was in over her head here with this man.

At last they moved along to the cake-cutting part. Soon would come the bridal waltz, after which the serious partying would begin. Though tempted, Jess decided not to drink too much, so there wouldn't be a problem with driving back to the cottage as soon as they could leave.

Which wouldn't be any time soon, Jess realised with some dismay. No way could the best man leave till the bride and groom had gone—only a couple of hours to go, but it seemed like an eternity.

'Care for a dance, ma'am?' asked a voice with a thick, southern accent.

Jess's head jerked around to find Ben standing behind her chair with a goofy smile on his face.

'They say a fella's best chance to get lucky at a wedding is with one of the bridesmaids,' he added, acting like some redneck out of the hills.

Jess had to smile. *He* obviously hadn't been sitting there, all churned up. This was all just fun and games to him!

'Well, I sure wouldn't want to disappoint a fella as handsome as you,' she returned saucily. There was no point in being a wet blanket. Though dancing with him was going to be sheer torture.

'Aw, shucks, ma'am,' Ben returned, twisting his hands

together in fake embarrassment. 'You shouldn't say things like that to a shy boy from Alabama.'

Jess laughed as she stood up. 'Now you sound like a character from one of those Doris Day, Rock Hudson movies.'

'Yeah, I know,' he said, dropping the fake southern accent as he steered her onto the dance floor. 'Those old movies have a way of drawing you in. I gather you like them too,' he added, and pulled her into his arms.

Jess melted into him and closed her eyes, savouring the feel of his body against hers whilst trying to contain her ever-increasing excitement.

'Mum does,' she said. 'I sometimes watch one with her. She likes happy endings.'

'And you? What kind of movies do you like?'

Oh, Lord, now he wanted to chat! She tried not to sigh. 'I guess something which is both entertainment and escape. I don't go to the movies to watch things that are too real. I can't stand stories about drug dealers or war or people who are mean and cruel.'

'You like reading?'

'I'm not as avid a reader as Mum. I spend a lot of my spare time sewing. But I do like a good thriller.'

'Romances?'

'One or two. I did read a certain erotic romance which swept the world by storm.'

'And did it give you a few delicious ideas?' he murmured against her ear.

She shivered as his lips made contact, his tongue tip dipping inside. But only for a split second.

She groaned softly when his head lifted, suppressing another groan when the other groomsman, Jay, tapped Ben on the shoulder and suggested they change partners.

Ben no more wanted to dance with Leanne than fly a

kite, but what could he do? He'd been brought up to be polite, to have proper manners. So he smiled and handed Jess over to Jay whilst he did his duty and danced with the very silly Leanne.

'So, how long have you known Jess?' was the first thing Leanne said, her voice as curious as her eyes.

'Not that long,' he replied, his own eyes drifting over to where Jay was holding Jess too darned close, in his opinion.

'She's very attractive, isn't she?' Leanne went on.

Ben agreed.

'Girls like that can get any man they want,' she said with an envious sounding sigh.

Ben thought of Colin doing a flit but didn't mention him.

Leanne fluttered her eyes up at him. 'It must be difficult for a really rich man like you to know if a girl likes him for himself or his money.'

Ben was astonished at the sly bitchiness behind Leanne's remark. 'I'm not that rich, Leanne.'

Leanne smiled a knowing smile. 'Maybe not now but you will be one day. I mean, your daddy's a billionaire, according to Catherine. Not that I think Jess is a gold-digger. She's a very sweet girl.'

'You're certainly right there,' Ben stated, thinking to himself that Leanne was a nasty piece of work. Of all the girls he'd ever been with, Jess was the *least* likely to be with him for his money. If anything, his wealth was a mark against him. Hadn't she said she would never marry a man as rich as he was?

It was a relief when Andy tapped him on the shoulder and handed him over to Catherine. Let *him* put up with Leanne's malicious prattle. He'd had enough of her for one night. Ben had to smile, however, when within less than a minute Andy whirled Leanne over to Jay and gave her back to him, happily dancing with Jess instead.

Which made Ben happy as well. He didn't mind Jess dancing with Andy. He certainly hadn't liked her dancing with Jay. Hadn't liked another man holding her that close and possibly trying to crack onto her.

Ben frowned as he realised just how possessive he was beginning to feel about Jess. It wasn't like him to be jealous. He'd always despised that kind of self-destructive emotion. But with Jess he just didn't have the control over his emotions that he usually had. He didn't have as much control over his body either.

It had been a battle to stop himself from having an erection all evening, finally losing the war when he'd taken her in his arms just now. Not that anything showed. His dinner jacket covered the evidence of his almost obsessive desire. But he could *feel* it, damn it. Not just in his flesh, but in his mind. Never had he wanted a woman as much as he wanted Jess. He could not wait to strip that infernal dress off her and do all the things he wanted to do to her.

CHAPTER FIFTEEN

'THANK GOD THEY'RE GONE,' Ben muttered under his breath as Andy and Catherine drove off in their much-decorated car. The happy couple were spending their wedding night in a nearby, very swanky guest house, which was fortunate, given Andy had imbibed quite a lot of champagne. Ben hadn't touched a drop; he needed a clear head and an un-intoxicated body for the games he had in mind for Jess tonight. It possibly would be the last opportunity to indulge himself with her in such a fashion. He did have full access to his mother's apartment at Blue Bay tomorrow night—she didn't get back till Monday—but Jess might not be willing to stay the night with him there. It was obvious that she still lived at home and still had to answer to her parents. Her mother, anyway.

Meanwhile…

Jess spotted Ben standing at the edge of the throng of guests who'd gone outside to watch the bride and groom depart. He'd been in a distracted mood the last hour or so. Not talking much. Not drinking either. She'd kept her consumption to a minimum, but then she had to drive. He didn't.

When she came up to him, he was frowning.

'Why are you frowning like that?' she asked him. 'Is your shoulder aching?' She wouldn't put it past him to have lied to her about his arm. Men hated to admit to any weakness, especially physical ones.

'No,' he said, giving her an odd look. 'It's fine. And more than capable of giving you a good spanking when the time comes.'

Jess sucked in sharply. 'Spanking?' she repeated in shocked tones even as the picture of her being bent naked over his thighs zoomed into her mind.

She stared up at him, her whole head whirling as she tried to work out if the idea excited or repulsed her.

'I think you might enjoy the experience. But only if you want me to, Jess,' he continued in that soft, seductive voice he often adopted. 'I would never force you to do anything you didn't want to do.'

But that was the problem, wasn't it? Once he started on her, she wanted to do whatever he wanted to. Already she was wondering what it would feel like to be spanked.

Jess struggled to act cool when she was anything but. 'I…I'll think about it,' she said. And of course that was another problem. Thinking about doing sexual things with him invariably turned her on. She was already turned on. Had been all evening. Now, her body temperature and her desire metre were zooming off the charts.

'Come on,' he said brusquely. 'Let's get out of here.'

Jess hesitated. 'But shouldn't we say goodbye to people first?'

'Who do you have in mind? We'll see Glen and Heather in the morning before we leave. We can say goodbye to them then.'

'But we won't see the bride's parents in the morning. We should say goodbye to them. It's only polite.'

Ben grimaced. 'You can, if you like. I can't stand either of them. I'll wait here for you. Don't be long.'

She whirled away from him and raced back into the

marquee, taking less than five minutes to say the appropriate goodbyes and collect her bouquet. He was still looking impatient when she returned to his side.

'What took you so long?' he growled as he steered her in the direction of the main house and her parked SUV.

She could not contain a surge of exasperation, shrugging off his bruising hold and grinding to a halt. 'For pity's sake, Ben, what's got into you all of a sudden? You're acting like a jerk.'

He sighed. 'Sorry. Just impatient to be alone with you, that's all.'

'Oh.' Trust him to say the one thing guaranteed to defuse her anger.

'Do you have your keys with you?' he asked when they approached her vehicle.

'Yes, of course.'

'Good. Now, get in and drive.'

She got in, tossed her bouquet in the back, then drove, all conversation between them ceasing during the five minutes it took to negotiate the short trip back to the cottage. By the time she pulled up in front of the small porch, her stomach was churning and her heart was pounding behind her ribs.

Was she really going to let him spank her?

Oh, Lord, she thought, and let out a panicky rush of air.

Ben heard her ragged sigh and recognised the reason behind it.

'Don't be nervous,' he said gently.

'I am a bit. I've never been spanked before.'

'I gathered that. Have you ever been tied up before?'

Her eyes went like saucers. 'No. I...I thought they only did things like that in books and in brothels.'

'Lots of real people like to play erotic games. Which is all I'm suggesting. Nothing serious. I'm not into humiliation or pain. I just want to give you pleasure, Jess. You can say no at any stage to anything you don't like.'

'But...but I might not know that I don't like it till you've done it.'

'I see.' God, but she was delightful. And delicious. And he wanted her like crazy. 'I promise to take things slowly, then. Give you time to say no before things go too far.'

'Oh. All right.'

'Let's go.'

He took her into the bathroom first where he undressed her—slowly, as he'd promised. The sight of her fiercely erect nipples revealed that she was genuinely enjoying herself. So far. She gasped when he tweaked one of the pink peaks, then groaned when he did the same to the other one.

'Still a little tender?' he enquired as he quickly disposed of his own clothes.

'A little,' she confessed shakily.

'But not too tender,' he said, and she shook her head.

'Good. Here, I think I should take off that diamond pendant as well. We wouldn't want it to get broken, would we?'

Her head whirled whilst he undid the clasp, then placed the pendant on the vanity along with his expensive looking wrist-watch. He hadn't taken his watch off last night, she recalled. But then he hadn't spanked her last night.

Oh, God.

Her heartbeat went up another notch.

'We'll have a shower together first,' he said. 'But no touching from you, beautiful. You are *way* too good with your hands.'

Ben turned her back to him whilst he washed her, making her moan when he rubbed the soapy sponge back and forth between her legs, her peach-like buttocks clenching tightly together when he moved his attention to them. By the time he switched off the water and turned her to face him, he knew she was ready for him to do whatever he wanted. Her eyes were glazed over and her lips had fallen apart as she panted for breath.

Ben thought she had never looked more beautiful or more desirable. He almost decided to bypass the foreplay in favour of straightforward sex but he suspected Jess was by now looking forward to the experience. Ben could only hope that he would be able to control himself during what was usually a lengthy game.

He stepped out of the cubicle and reached for the two white towelling robes which were hanging on the back of the door. After putting one on, he handed the other robe to Jess.

'Put that on,' he ordered.

When she did so without question, he wanted her all the more.

'No, don't do it up,' he said, and reached for the sash, sliding it through the side loops before wrapping it around his left wrist.

He had to take her hand and lead her back to the bedroom. By the time they got to the side of the bed, she was trembling. But he felt certain it was no longer from nerves.

'You should be dry by now. So you won't be needing that robe.'

'But you've still got yours on,' she protested.

'That's the idea.'

When she hesitated, he bent and whispered in her ear. 'Yours is not to reason why, Jess. Yours is just to lie back on that bed and let me give you pleasure.'

His breathing quickened as she obediently took off the robe and lay down on the bed, her head on the pillows.

'No, not that way,' he said and she just stared at him, sucking in sharply when he turned her over onto her stomach.

'Just say no if you want me to stop,' he said.

She didn't say no, but she did bury her face in the pillow.

Gently, he took both her hands and placed them in the small of her back, then looped her wrists together with the sash from the robe. Not tightly, but enough so that she would feel bound and helpless. Which was the point, of course. That was what would excite her to fever pitch. Finally, he removed the pillow from under her face and slid it under her hips, raising her buttocks in the most erotic and inviting fashion.

When Ben stepped back to examine his handiwork, the sight of her like that took his breath away. Dear God, she was just so sexy looking. And totally at his mercy! It was a heady combination. And, whilst he was fiercely erect, all of a sudden Ben wasn't so concerned about his own satisfaction but how Jess was feeling. He hated to think she might be afraid to say no at this stage.

'Are you all right, Jess?' he asked softly. 'Do you want me to continue?'

CHAPTER SIXTEEN

WAS HE INSANE? She would die if he didn't continue. She'd never been so excited in her whole life!

'I'm fine,' she said, her voice high-pitched and raspy. 'Please don't stop.'

He laughed a short, sexy laugh. 'Your wish is my command.'

Now *that* was a laugh, Jess thought. *He* was the one doing the commanding. But didn't she just love it!

No touching from you, beautiful... Put that on... You won't be needing that robe.... Just lie back on that bed and let me give you pleasure...

'It's just a game, Jess,' he said. 'You can stop me at any time. Okay?'

'Okay,' she mumbled.

The first crack of his hand on her right buttock brought a gasp of shock, rather than pain. Though it did sting. Jess buried her face into the quilt, determined not to cry out again. Another slap followed. Then another, his hand moving from left to right in a slow, relentless rhythm till both her buttocks were burning. And red, no doubt. Yet despite her discomfort—oh, yes, her whole bottom was stinging like mad—she didn't want to tell him to stop. There was something exquisitely pleasurable in the whole experience. She held her breath between slaps in anticipation of his large palm making contact with her soft skin, biting her bottom lip each time it happened. The slaps began coming at a slower interval now, her time of waiting extended till she almost pleaded for more. When he finally stopped altogether, she groaned in frustration.

'That's enough,' she heard him say.

But he didn't untie her. Instead, the bed dipped as he lay down beside her. She saw he was naked now when she twisted her head to look at him.

'So what did you think?' he asked her.

'I think,' she choked out, 'that if you don't have sex with me in the next ten seconds, then you're a dead man.'

He smiled. 'You're not really in a position to give orders right now, are you, darling Jess?'

'Ben,' she said pleadingly. 'Please.'

'If you insist.'

She couldn't believe it when he didn't untie her first, just spread her legs wide and moved around between them. She moaned when he rubbed his tip against her, her teeth digging into her lower lip to stop herself from screaming.

'So wet,' he muttered.

Ben was close to losing it. Time to get a condom on, he realised, before things got out of hand.

Thank God Andy had given him a good supply so he had one at the ready.

She cried out when he entered her, her bottom moving frantically against him with an urgency which betrayed a cruel level of frustration. He wasn't much better, grabbing her hips with bruising fingers and setting up a savage rhythm, forgetting everything but what his flesh was feeling at that moment. The heat. The urgent need. The madness of it all. Her stunningly violent climax only preceeded his by a second or two, Ben thrilling to the way she cried out as she came.

Jess lay there afterwards, stunned yet totally sated. A draining languor started seeping into her limbs, her eyelids growing heavier and heavier. Ben was lying across her back, his own breathing now slow and heavy. She desperately wanted to stay awake. But sleep would not be denied. It came quickly, with Jess's wrists still bound.

Ben fell asleep too, still slumped across her back.

He woke first, momentarily confused by where he was. And then he remembered. Everything.

He groaned as guilt consumed him. How could he possibly have left her that way? She didn't wake as he carefully withdrew, then even more carefully untied her. She stirred slightly when he slid the pillow out from under her hips, but she didn't wake, thank God, though she did curl herself up into a semi-foetal position. After throwing a sheet over her far too delicious derrière, he headed for the bathroom.

A quick shower later and he was back in the bedroom, standing at the side of the bed and staring down at her still body. Ben supposed he really had nothing to be guilty about; Jess had obviously enjoyed herself. Ben was never absolutely sure if his girlfriends went along with his demands because they were genuinely on the same sexual wavelength or because he was Morgan De Silva's son and heir. He definitely had no such doubts with Jess. Damn it, but he wished she lived in America.

Maybe he would ask her to go back with him. He could get her a job and lease her a nice little apartment. Or she could even move in with him.

Ben frowned at this last thought. His father had warned him never to do that: have a woman move in with him. Not unless they were married. As much as Jess claimed she would never marry a rich man, she hadn't seen his New York lifestyle. His thirty-square apartment overlooking Central Park had a lap pool on the roof plus a fully equipped gym and spa room. He had a wardrobe full of designer suits and hand-made shoes, a Ferrari in the underground car park and an expense account which allowed him to dine at all of New York's finest restaurants. He also had access to the company's private jet which flew him to Acapulco for weekends in the summer and Aspen in the winter.

That kind of lifestyle could corrupt even the nicest girl, especially if she'd never experienced such luxury. Which Jess obviously hadn't.

No, best not ask her to go back to America with him. Best he do what he'd originally intended: have a holiday fling with Jess, then leave it at that. It wasn't as though he was in love with her. He just liked and admired her a lot. And wanted her like mad. Already he had another erection, tempting him to climb back into bed and wake her. He didn't think she'd mind.

Ben sensibly armed himself with protection first, then climbed in under the sheet and curved his body around hers, spoon fashion. She stirred immediately, stiffening against him when he began to caress her breasts. Obviously they were still sensitive from all the attention he'd been giving them, so he moved lower, stroking her stomach, then her thighs.

'Yes please,' she choked out when he pressed himself against her still-wet sex.

A wave of tenderness engulfed Ben as he slid into her. God, but he'd never felt anything like this for a girl before. She was just so sweet, yet so sexy at the same time. A girl in a million.

He took his time, setting up a gentle rhythm, loving the sounds she made, loving the way she wriggled against him as her excitement grew. And, when he knew he was close to coming himself, he touched her in a way that would guarantee her release as well.

They came together, Ben startled as another wave of emotion hit him. Not just tenderness this time, but something deeper. Much deeper. He held her tightly in his arms afterwards and wondered if he was finally on the verge of falling in love.

CHAPTER SEVENTEEN

JESS WAS WOKEN by Ben shaking her shoulder again, plus the sound of her phone ringing.

'I was in the kitchen making coffee when it rang,' he explained as he handed it to her.

Jess tried to take the phone, sit up and cover her bare breasts at the same time, but failed.

What the heck? she thought despairingly. It wasn't anything he hadn't seen before. Yet, strangely, she felt shy in front of Ben all of a sudden. Jess supposed it wasn't every day that one woke to such memories. In a way, it didn't seem real. Had she really let him tie her up and spank her? Obviously she had, if her still-tender bottom was anything to go by.

'It's my mother,' she said, trying to look and sound cool. 'Would you mind?' She waved him away.

He smiled, turned and left the room. Thank God. The infernal man was stark naked. Obviously, he never suffered from shyness.

'Hello, Mum,' she said into the phone. 'It's a little early, isn't it? I've only just woken up. Can I tell you all about the wedding when I get home?'

'I guess so. But, before you go, I was also ringing to remind you that today is family barbecue day. I thought you might have forgotten.'

She had, actually. It was a once a month tradition where the family got together at her parents' place.

'I was thinking that you could ask Ben to come along. Your father and I would love to meet him.'

Meaning *she'd* like to see what he looked like. Her mother was a very intuitive woman and had probably picked up something from Jess's voice.

'I'll ask him, Mum,' she said. 'But I won't guarantee that he'll say yes. He might just want to get home after such a long drive.'

'I see. Well, how about you call me when you stop and tell me if Ben's coming or not?'

'Will do. Now, I must go, Mum.'

'Before you go, did the wedding go off all right yesterday? No other Murphy's Law disasters?'

'Everything was perfect, Mum,' she said. 'I'll ring you later. Bye.'

Rising, Jess dashed for the bathroom, where the sight of her pink bridesmaid dress draped over the bath reminded her of the submissive scenario Ben had insisted upon in there. That was where her loss of will-power had all started, of course. In that shower. By the time he'd turned off the water, she'd been so excited that he could have done anything to her and she would not have objected.

The speed with which he'd turned her into a submissive sex slave was quite shocking. So why wasn't she more shocked this morning? Maybe it was because underneath all that S&M role-playing Ben was a nice man. A decent man. She felt confident that he would never hurt her for real. Look at the way he'd made love to her later in the night, so gently and rather sweetly. She'd enjoyed that time even more than all the other times so far. And there'd been quite a few already, Jess thought ruefully. Ben couldn't seem to keep his hands off her. In more ways than one!

After a rather quick shower, Jess rubbed some of the body lotion she found in the vanity into her buttocks. They were still a little on the tender side, but nothing major. Once her teeth were cleaned and her hair up in a pony-tail, she hurried into the other bedroom where she took out some fresh clothes: a pair of three-quarter length white trousers and a navy-and-white striped top. Slipping white sandals onto her feet, she headed for the kitchen where Ben was thankfully now wearing the white bathrobe which had been on the bedroom floor earlier. He was sitting at the kitchen table with some toast and coffee in front of him.

'I think your mother's checking up on you,' he said.

'Possibly. It's hard to put anything past my mum.'

'Not for the want of your trying, though,' he said, smiling at her.

Lord, but he was devilishly attractive when he smiled like that, even with slightly bleary eyes and a stubbly chin.

'She wanted to know how the wedding went. And to invite you to our family barbecue tonight.'

His eyebrows lifted, then fell. 'Do *you* want me to go, Jess?'

She shrugged. 'I doubt you'll enjoy it much. Mum will give you the once-over, then Dad'll probably give you the third degree, if he thinks you're interested in me.'

'Which I am.'

It annoyed Jess, his saying that. Because he wasn't really interested in her in that way. He just wanted to have more sex with her whilst he was here in Australia. Okay, so Ben was basically a good man, but he was also spoiled and selfish. It wasn't all his fault, of course. He'd been born beautiful and into great wealth: both very corrupting factors. He'd probably developed his liking for kinky sex because he'd had so much sex in his life he'd got bored with straightforward love-making. Which was a pity. Because he did straightforward love-making very well indeed.

Jess sighed. 'I honestly don't think you should go.'

'Why not?'

'For the reasons I just told you.'

'But I want to meet your parents.'

Jess rolled her eyes. 'For pity's sake, *why*?'

'Because I want to ask them to give you this week off so we can go to Sydney and work together on Fab Fashions. I thought we might stay down there instead of driving up and down the motorway every day. Mum has a flat in Bondi we could use.'

Jess didn't know what to say. She wanted to go, of course. Wanted the opportunity to do something about Fab Fashions. And, yes, she wanted to spend more time alone with Ben, especially some more of his very exciting brand of sex. She'd be lying if she didn't admit that, especially to herself. But at the back of her mind, in that place reserved for difficult decisions, she knew if she did this, then she was sure to become even more emotionally involved with him.

'I...I don't know, Ben,' she said hesitantly, turning away to make herself some coffee. 'Like you said, there's probably no fixing Fab Fashions. We'd just be wasting our time.'

'I don't agree. We'll have that chat on the drive home and come up with a new name, one which will lend itself to a successful marketing strategy. Because you're right, Jess. Companies like ours shouldn't just bail out when things get tough. We can afford to ride some losses for a while, especially when the alternative means that people will lose their jobs.'

Jess wanted to believe he meant it. But she didn't. Companies like De Silva & Associates were all about making profits. They didn't give a damn about the little people. Which was what she was. One of the little people.

Jess finished making her coffee, then carried it over to the table. 'I'm sorry, Ben,' she said, pulling out a chair and sitting down, 'but I'd rather not. I'm a mechanic, not some marketing expert.'

'So you're giving up on Fab Fashions?'

'I've told you what's wrong with the business. You're an intelligent man. I'll put my thinking cap on during the drive back and come up with a name which might suit. Then it's up to you to do something with it.'

He looked at her long and hard, then shrugged. 'Okay. If that's the way you want it.'

What she wanted at that moment was never to have met Ben De Silva.

'I still wouldn't mind coming to that barbecue, Jess.'

'No, Ben. I'd rather you didn't.'

He frowned at her. 'Why is that?'

'I don't want my parents knowing what we've been up to this weekend. And they will. Mum will take one look at us together and she'll know.'

'We're consenting adults, Jess. Our having sex isn't a crime.'

'No, but it's very unlike me, Ben, to hop into bed so quickly. Mum's sure to jump to the wrong conclusion.'

'Which is?

'That I've fallen madly in love.'

Again, she was on the end of another long, thoughtful look.

'I take it that hasn't happened?'

'You know it hasn't. We've been having a dirty weekend, Ben. That's all.' It went against her grain to describe their weekend in such a crude fashion, but it was the truth after all.

'I don't see it that way, Jess. I like you. A lot. And I want to see more of you.'

'You mean you want to have more kinky sex with me whilst you're in Australia.'

He pursed his lips in obvious annoyance. 'You make it all sound so tacky. Yes, of course I want to have more sex with you, but not just kinky sex. I enjoy making love to you in more traditional ways as well. I also want to spend time with you out of bed.'

Jess's laugh was a little bitter. 'Yes, I noticed you like having sex out of bed too.'

His blue eyes flashed with frustration. 'Very funny. Just remember, you're the one who knocked back my offer of our working together on Fab Fashions.'

'I can live with that. I can't live with you taking me for a fool.'

He sat bolt upright in his chair, his face furious. 'I would never do that. I think you're one of the smartest girls I've ever met. And the most stubborn. I suppose if I asked you to go back to New York with me, you'd say no to that as well!'

Jess could not have been more taken aback. Or more speechless.

'Well?' he snapped when she said nothing. 'What *would* you say to such an offer?'

Jess gathered in a deep breath, then let it out slowly. 'I would say thank you very much, Ben, but no thank you. My life is here, in Australia. I wouldn't be happy in New York.'

'How do you know?'

'I just know.'

His eyes carried exasperation. 'Most girls would jump at the chance. For Pete's sake, Jess, you wouldn't have to pay for a thing. You could stay in my apartment and have the holiday of a lifetime.'

The word 'holiday' reaffirmed what Jess already knew. He wasn't seriously interested in her. Not the way she would have liked. But then, that was never going to happen. He'd already said he didn't want to get married. She was just a passing amusement, one which he hadn't grown bored with yet.

'Couldn't we just leave things the way they are, Ben? I'm happy to go out with you whilst you're staying up on the coast. I like you a lot, but I don't want to go to America with you.'

Ben should have been relieved, he supposed, that she hadn't jumped at his somewhat impulsive offer. But he wasn't. He was bitterly disappointed. He'd wanted to show her New York, wanted to give her the time of her life.

'Fine,' he bit out.

'Please don't think me ungrateful, Ben,' she went on, her eyes softening on him. 'It was a very generous offer. But it's best I stay here in Australia.'

He sighed, then smiled at her. 'So we're still on for dinner tomorrow night?'

Jess smiled back at him. 'Of course. Where are you going to take me?'

'I have no idea. I'll ask Mum when she gets back tomorrow. She knows all the best local restaurants. But you'll have to pick me up. I'm not allowed to drive till I get that stupid medical clearance. Hopefully by Tuesday that'll be done and I can drive Mum's car.'

'So your mother will be there when I pick you up?' she said, sounding a bit panicky.

'Yes, but you don't have to worry. Mum's really quite nice, despite everything.'

'What do you mean by that?'

'I'll explain on the drive back,' he said, thinking he shouldn't have made such a leading comment. But it was too late now. Besides, it would give them something to talk about. Telling Jess all about his mother's exploits over the years would take some time. 'I'll go shower and shave whilst you have breakfast. Then we should get going.'

CHAPTER EIGHTEEN

BY THE TIME they stopped at Sandy Hollow for lunch, Jess had a much better understanding of why Ben wasn't interested in marriage. To find out that your mother had married your father for his money must have come as a bitter blow. Still, it had been good of his father not to say anything till Ben had turned twenty-one. That way, Ben had been able to grow up loving his mother who, though materialistic, had obviously been a good mother to him.

Despite that, Jess could just imagine how Ben had felt when his mother had admitted she'd trapped his father into marriage with a pregnancy and had never loved him. His money was what she'd loved. Yes, there were reasons for her materialism, but the bottom line was still not very nice. Her actions certainly wouldn't have engendered faith in her son's own relationships with the opposite sex. Given he would one day be as rich as his father, Ben would always be on the lookout for signs that his girlfriends were gold-diggers. Which was an awful way to have to live.

But it did also explain why Ben concentrated on sex when he was with a girl he liked. Sex was safe, especially the kind of sex he indulged in. Such goings-on kept his girlfriends at a distance, both physically and emotionally. Jess realised that the only time he'd had sex face to face with her had been when she'd been on top. But even then he'd adopted the role of voyeur rather than that of a loving partner.

'Neither of your parents have married again,' she remarked once they sat down to another pub lunch. Different pub but similar food. A steak sandwich and salad. 'Why is that, do you think?'

Ben shrugged. 'Mum always said she would marry again if she ever fell in love. But that's unlikely to happen, given the type of man she usually dates—all young, handsome studs without much between their ears. Mum does like intelligence when she's out of bed.'

Jess tried not to look shocked at his talking about his mother's sex life in that fashion.

'But who knows? This fellow she's gone on the cruise with seems a different kettle of fish. Not so young and he actually works. I'll find out more when she gets home tomorrow. As far as Dad is concerned… This might sound silly but I think Mum was the only woman Dad ever truly loved. Though don't get me wrong. He was unfaithful to her during their marriage. Had several mistresses going at once, apparently. He still has women running after him, despite being sixty-five and not the best-looking man in the world. Money is a powerful aphrodisiac,' he added drily.

Jess sighed. 'I can understand now why you don't want to get married.'

'What?' Ben said, almost knocking his drink over. 'I never said I didn't want to get married.'

Jess frowned. 'But you did. When I asked you why you broke up with Amber you said she wanted marriage and you didn't.'

'Not with *her* I don't. I don't love her. That doesn't mean I wouldn't consider it with anyone else at some stage.'

'Oh,' Jess said, startled by this turn of events. Not that

it changed anything. Ben might want marriage at some stage, but it wouldn't be to an ordinary girl like her.

Ben stared across the table at Jess and wondered if that was why she'd refused to come to New York with him. Because she wanted marriage and she thought he didn't. Not that he was about to propose. He did, however, feel more strongly about Jess than any girl he'd ever met.

He decided then and there that he would ask her to come to New York with him again later in the week. Meanwhile, he'd show her the time of her life every night. And, yes, behind the scenes he'd even do something about that damned Fab Fashions.

'Are you absolutely sure you don't want me to come to your family barbecue?' he asked coolly before picking up his steak sandwich and taking a big bite.

She was tempted. He could see she was tempted.

'I promise to be on my best behaviour,' he added once his mouth was temporarily empty.

She laughed. 'It's not you I'm worried about. It's my mother.'

Ben didn't give a damn if her mother realised they were sleeping together. Mothers had never been a problem to him. They usually liked him a lot. 'I can handle your mother,' he said.

Lord, but he was an arrogant devil. But she did so like him. And she wanted him like mad. Already she was regretting not going to New York with him, even if it *was* only for a holiday. Still, she suspected Ben hadn't totally given up on that idea. Jess wondered what she would say if he asked her again.

Hopefully, she would have the courage—and the common sense—still to say no. But, dear Lord, she did have a lot of trouble saying no to him.

'I'm coming to that barbecue,' he announced firmly,

'And that's final. Now, about that new name for Fab Fashions; I've given it some thought. What do you think of Real Women? It would lend itself to a good advertising campaign. Clothes for real women, et cetera, et cetera.'

The take-over man in action again, Jess thought. Telling her he was coming, then changing the subject.

She had to smile. He was clever all right.

'I think it's a great name,' she said. 'I love it.'

He beamed across the table at her. '*Finally* she agrees with something I've suggested!'

'I can be agreeable,' she said. 'When it's a sensible suggestion.'

'Coming to New York with me is just as sensible.'

'Ben,' she said with a warning look. 'Just leave it, will you?'

'Okay. I will. For now. But I make no promise to do so indefinitely.'

They both fell to eating their meals, Jess doing her best to stop thinking about her potentially dangerous feelings for Ben. Once again she wished she could be like other girls. Most would jump at the chance of going to New York with him, even if it didn't lead to anything permanent.

But maybe it would; she started hoping as she ate. How would she know unless she agreed? She'd gone to bed with Ben initially because she knew she'd regret it if she didn't. Maybe she'd regret not going to New York with him and not giving their relationship a chance.

But it *wasn't* a relationship, her more pragmatic side argued. It was just a fling, or an affair, for want of a better word. Ben had never said he loved her. Not that he would. It was way too early for a man of his natural wariness to make such a declaration. She certainly wasn't about to tell him she was close to falling for him either. That would only give him power over her. He had enough of that already.

No, she wouldn't be foolish enough to admit that. But she would think about going to New York with him and, when he asked her again, she probably would say yes.

'That steak was quite good,' Ben said, wiping his mouth with a paper serviette.

'My dad cooks much better steak on the barbecue,' Jess told him. 'And Mum's salads are way better.'

'In that case, I'm in for a treat later today.'

'Just don't let my brothers give you too much beer.'

'Why? You're worried I might not be able to perform when you take me home?'

'What? No, of course not! Ben De Silva, haven't you had enough sex for one weekend?'

'There's no such thing as too much sex.'

'There is if it involves getting your bottom spanked,' she whispered so that the people at the next table couldn't hear.

He frowned. 'Sorry. I did get a little carried away last night. In that case, you can have today off.'

She tried to be annoyed with him but she simply couldn't. Instead, she smiled. A slightly wry smile, but still a smile. 'One day, some woman is going to tell you where to go, Ben De Silva.'

He nodded. 'You could be right there. And I have a feeling she's sitting across the table from me.'

I wish, Jess thought. But she just laughed, then finished off her coffee. Ten minutes later, they were back on the road and heading for home, turning off the motorway just after three-thirty.

CHAPTER NINETEEN

JESS'S HOME WAS bigger than Ben had expected, a two-storeyed, family-sized house in blond brick, with the biggest shed that Ben had ever seen sitting in a nearby paddock. A workshop, obviously, plus garaging for the hire cars. Two of the three massive roller doors were open and Ben could glimpse several cars within. The land around the house was bigger than he'd expected too, at least five acres. It was a lovely looking property with well-tended gardens, rolling lawns and enough trees to give privacy and shade.

Jess drove her SUV off the driveway onto a large square of gravel by the side of the house, the clock on her dash showing five to four as Ben climbed out. Jess had explained on the way that the barbecue wouldn't start till five-ish, so they had some time before her brothers and their families descended upon them.

'What a lovely place,' he said straight away.

Jess smiled. 'We like it. Mum will be in the kitchen, preparing the salads. You can meet her first. This way...'

'I presume that's the office,' he said as he walked past a converted double garage which had sliding glass doors at the front with 'Murphy's Hire Car' in big, black letters engraved on it.

'Yes,' she said. 'That's mostly Mum's domain. I help out when Mum's shopping or plays bowls or just needs a break. Mum, we're here,' Jess called out as she opened the front door.

A woman appeared at the end of the hallway, light behind her forming the silhouette of someone much shorter than Jess, and somewhat plumper.

'Goodness, but you made good time. I didn't expect you till four-thirty at least.'

When she came forward, Ben saw her more clearly. She looked nothing like Jess, being short, with ash-blonde hair and blue eyes. Attractive for her age, though.

'Hello, there,' she said, smiling as she looked him up and down. 'You must be Ben.'

'And you must be Mrs Murphy,' he replied, stepping forward to give her a kiss on the cheek. 'Lovely to meet you.'

Jess could not believe the look on her mother's face. It was the kind of look you saw on the face of a female fan of a rock star. Truly!

'Oh, don't call me that.' Her mother fairly simpered at him. 'Call me Ruth.'

Jess gained some satisfaction in the thought that he wouldn't charm her father so easily. Joe Murphy was a tough nut to crack. He wasn't going to be impressed by a New Yorker who'd never had dirt under his fingernails in his life.

'In that case, Ruth,' Ben said, flashing those brilliant white teeth of his, 'would you kindly point me to the nearest bathroom?'

Her mother didn't point. She escorted Ben herself to the small powder room next to the family room, leaving Jess standing there in the hallway like some shag on a rock.

Jess sighed, then trudged upstairs to use the toilet in the main bathroom. By the time she made it downstairs, Ben was ensconced on one of the kitchen stools, chatting away happily to her mother whilst she worked on the various salads.

'That's a terrific new name Ben's come up with for Fab Fashions, isn't it?' she directed at Jess as she joined them.

'Fantastic,' Jess agreed, at which Ben slanted her a narrow-eyed glance. Had he heard the slight sarcasm in her voice?

'You might get your job back there soon,' Ruth rattled on.

'You never know, Mum. I presume Dad's in the shed working on that blue Cadillac?'

'Yes, the seats finally came yesterday. He's been working on them all day.'

'I think I should take Ben out to meet Dad before the others get here, don't you?'

'Oh, but I just put the kettle on for a cup of tea. Ben says he likes tea more than coffee. Same as me.'

'We won't be long, Mum,' she said, then gave Ben a look which brooked no protest.

He slid off the stool and followed her back down the hallway and out of the front door.

'You *are* bossy and controlling,' he said as she marched in the direction of the shed with him in her wake.

'And you're a serial charmer,' she snapped.

He laughed. 'Better than being a serial killer.'

'I suggest you curtail that silver tongue of yours with my sisters-in-law. The Murphy men are known to be extremely jealous.'

'What about the Murphy women?' he threw at her.

'Them too. So watch yourself.'

'I like your being jealous.'

'Of course you do. It suits your male ego, which is insufferably large.'

'So will something else be if you keep that up. I get turned on by feisty women.'

She gave up at that point, throwing her hands up in the air in defeat.

She was glad that her father chose that moment to walk out of the shed, wiping his hands on a towel as he did so.

'I thought I heard someone,' he said, coming forward. 'You must be Ben,' he said, and held out his hand.

Ben shook it, thinking that this was where Jess got her striking looks. Joe Murphy was one handsome fellow, with thick black hair sprinkled liberally with grey and the deepest, darkest brown eyes, which at that moment were surveying him with considerable thoughtfulness.

'So, how did your weekend go?' he asked Ben, not Jess. 'The wedding go off okay in the end?'

'It was close to perfect,' Ben said. 'Jess here was marvellous, the way she stepped in. You heard about what happened, did you?'

'Oh yes, Ruth told me all about it. Look, I just have to finish a job here and I'll be over to clean up and get the barbecue ready. You ever cook on a barbecue, Ben?'

'Lots of times,' he said. 'I was brought up here in Australia.'

'No kidding; I didn't know that. So that's how your best friend turned out to be Australian.'

'Yep,' Ben said, sounding more Ocker by the minute. 'We went to school together in Sydney.'

'Fancy that.'

'So, what's this job you're doing, Mr Murphy? Can I help?'

'I doubt it. I'm just putting some new seats into an old Cadillac convertible I bought. The kids like to hire cars like that for their graduation night.'

'My dad collected vintage cars at one stage. Which model Cadillac is it?'

Jess could not believe it when they went off together, talking cars. Spluttering, she whirled and stormed back to the house, only just managing to have her exasperation under control by the time she reached the kitchen.

'Where's Ben?' her mother asked straight away.

'Helping Dad with the Cadillac, would you believe? I'll have tea, though, if you're making it.'

'Can you get it yourself, dear? I really need to go spruce myself up a bit. I can't wear this old thing when we have a guest like Ben.'

'He's just a man, Mum, not some movie star.'

'Well, he looks like a movie star. I know you said he was handsome, Jess, but he's beyond handsome, with that smile and those eyes. I've never met a man quite like him. I dare say you haven't either. He makes Colin look very ordinary. And I thought *he* was good-looking.'

When Jess sighed, her mother gave her a sharp look.

'Did something happen with Ben over the weekend that I should know about?'

Jess kept a straight face with difficulty. 'Like what?'

'You know what, girlie.'

'I think, Mum, that my sex life is my private business, don't you?'

Her mother looked at her for a long moment before smiling an understanding smile. 'Of course it is. You're a grown woman. But let me just say that I don't blame you, love. If I were thirty years younger I would have done exactly the same thing.'

Jess stared after her mother as she walked off. She'd been expecting the third degree, or disapproval, or something! She certainly hadn't expected her mother's reaction to Ben to be so blindly approving. Couldn't she see that her daughter's leaping into bed with such a man was fraught with danger to her happiness? She should have been warning her off him, not saying she would have done exactly the same thing!

Jess sighed. The man was a devil all right. With way too much sex appeal. And way too much charm. Even her father liked him. No doubt her whole family would fall under his spell in no time flat.

Still, if they did, she would at least be able to relax a bit and enjoy the barbecue instead of being on tenterhooks all the time. This last weekend might have been exciting but it hadn't exactly been relaxing!

CHAPTER TWENTY

BEN WAS HELPING Joe with the barbecue when Jess joined them, a huge black-and-white cat in her arms.

'You haven't been plying Ben with too much beer, have you, Dad?' Jess said in a teasing but loving voice which Ben could never imagine using with his own father. Or his mother, for that matter. He'd thought he had a good relationship with both his parents but seeing Jess interacting with her parents was a real eye-opener.

So was her interaction with the rest of her family. She was so warm with them, caring and considerate, asking after their well-being when they arrived with real interest, not just giving lip-service. He could see how much they loved her back as well. The children had flocked around her, vying for her attention. Even the damned cat loved her, yet he'd been warned by Joe not to touch Lazarus, as he was known to scratch. When he'd commented on the cat's name, he'd been told that Lazarus had been stillborn but Jess had resurrected him with the kiss of life.

Ben didn't doubt it. She was a girl of many talents, and a wealth of stubbornness. He still could not believe she'd refused to come to New York with him. But he had no intention of giving up on that score.

'The boys want Ben to go play cricket with them and the kids,' Jess said. 'I'll take over for him here,' she offered before dropping the cat gently onto the paved pergola which stretched across the back of the Murphy house.

'Can you play cricket?' Joe asked as Jess took the fork Ben had been using to turn the steak and sausages. 'I gather it's not a popular sport in America.'

Ben grinned. Could he play cricket or what? He'd been captain of his school's A-grade cricket team. But best not mention that. That would be bragging.

'Don't forget, Joe,' he replied, still smiling. 'I went to an *Australian* school. A *boy's* boarding school, where sport was compulsory. We played footie in winter and cricket in summer.'

'Right. Off you go, then. Just don't go hitting the ball into that thick bush over there. Can't count the number we've lost in there over the years.'

Ben resolved to peg back his batting ability a bit. No need to be a smart Alec.

Jess watched Ben stride off, a wry smile on her face. If she knew Ben, he would be anything but an ordinary cricket player. He wasn't ordinary at anything he did. He was an exceptional man, with exceptional abilities and exceptional social skills.

She was still amazed at how he instinctively knew what to talk about with every member of her family. He talked cars with her father, sport with her brothers and the advances in technology with her very smart sisters-in-law. He didn't mention his wealth when he was introduced, or sit back and play the role of honoured guest. He was happy to help with the food and very happy to drink beer. She imagined that over in New York his social life was very different. He'd go to fancy restaurants and fancy parties where they'd eat caviar and drink the most expensive champagne.

Jess frowned at this last thought. She would be uncomfortable with that kind of life. It was shallow, in her opinion. And snobbish. And way out of her league. She was a simple girl at heart with simple wants, like love, marriage and a family. She wasn't cut out for the high life.

Such thoughts renewed her resolve not to go to New York with him, if and when he asked her again. Jess suspected she would not enjoy the experience. The sex part, yes. And possibly some of the sightseeing. New York was a fabulous city, she was sure. But she shrank from the idea of meeting any of Ben's American friends or ex-girlfriends; shrank from being looked down upon by the type of people he mixed with.

The barbecue finished early, as the younger children got tired and the older ones had to go to school the next day. Ben seemed reluctant to leave, however, staying to help clear up and to have a final beer with her father. It was after ten before Jess could drag him away.

'You have a wonderful family, Jess,' was the first thing he said on the way back to Blue Bay. 'You're very lucky.'

'Yes, I am,' she agreed. 'By the way, my mother knows about us.'

His head jerked her way. 'You *told* her?'

'No, she guessed. Like I said, she's very intuitive.'

'How much does she know?'

'No details. Just that we've had sex.'

'That's good, then. She won't worry if you get home late.'

'She'll still worry. That's a mother's job. Frankly, I was surprised at how calm she was over my sleeping with you.'

'That's because she knows I'm one of the good guys.'

'Hmm. I doubt that's the reason. Now, I'm not coming

inside with you tonight, Ben,' she went on firmly, determined not to weaken and be seduced by him. Again. 'I'm dropping you off and going straight home.'

'Fair enough.'

She blinked her surprise at his easy acceptance of her stance. Maybe he was tired. Yes, that was probably it. He'd had a very tiring weekend.

In no time she was pulling into the kerb. She did get out to open the boot and, yes, she let him give her a kiss goodnight after he'd placed all his things on the pavement. Not too long a kiss, as it turned out, both their heads lifting when his phone rang. Frowning, Ben rifled the phone out of his pocket and stared at the ID.

'Damn,' he said. 'It's Amber.'

'Aren't you going to answer it?' Jess asked, trying not to sound as sick as she was suddenly feeling.

'I might as well,' Ben said. 'She has to know sooner or later that it's over between us.'

He put the phone to his ear. 'Hello, Amber. I thought you said we weren't to contact each other till I got back.'

Jess just stood there, listening to a one-sided conversation, her stomach tight with tension.

'What?' he suddenly snapped. 'Say that again?'

Jess watched as Ben suddenly lost all his normal glow, his face going a ghastly ashen colour. Whatever Amber was telling him had to be dreadful.

'No, no,' he choked out. 'I'll come home straight away. Tell the funeral home to delay things till I can be there to make the arrangements.'

Jess's heart sank. She could think of only one person's funeral which would make Ben look this way. His father must have died. Oh, dear God, poor Ben…

'No, I don't want you to help,' he was saying, his voice under control again. 'No, Amber, I don't want to marry you either. I'm sorry but I've met someone else… Yes, an Australian girl… Yes, yes, I do,' he said and looked a startled Jess straight in the eye. 'I'll be bringing her back with me.'

Jess's mouth fell open. It was still open when Ben put his phone back in his pocket.

'Please don't say no, Jess. My father died of a massive coronary last night. I can't bury him alone,' he said brokenly.

Jess's heart turned over at the raw grief in his face. Even if she had decided not to go to New York with him if he asked again, she would say yes to this. How could she turn her back on the man she loved when he was at his most vulnerable? Because, of course she loved him. She couldn't deny it any longer. Not to herself, anyway.

'Yes, of course I'll come with you,' she said gently.

'Thank you. I don't know what I would have done if you'd said no. I need someone I care about by my side, Jess. If you're there, I'll make it through.'

Jess's breath caught at his words. 'You really care about me, Ben?'

'Yes, of course I do. You care about me too, don't you? I refuse to believe you're just with me for the sex.'

'Of course I'm not!' she blurted out, shocked that he would think such a thing.

He sighed a deep sigh. 'That's a relief. Let's go inside and start making plans.'

His mother's apartment was as she'd imagined it to be. Very spacious and modern with large windows, polished wooden floors and Italian leather furniture.

'I'll get onto the airline,' Ben said, 'whilst you ring your parents. You do have a current passport, don't you?' he added sharply.

'Yes,' she answered.

'Good. I'll make my calls from the kitchen. You stay here.'

Her mother answered on the second ring, her voice anxious.

'What is it, Jess? Have you had an accident?'

'No, Mum,' she said, then launched into an explanation of events.

'And you're going to go back to New York with him?' her mother said, sounding shocked.

'Yes, Mum.'

'When?'

'As soon as possible. Ben's on to the airline now.'

'But you hardly know the man, Jess.'

'I know him better than I ever knew Colin.'

'You love him, don't you?'

'Yes, Mum. I do.'

'Does he love you back?'

'I'm not sure.'

'You do realise that with his father dying he'll be a very rich man.'

'Yes, Mum. I'm not stupid.'

'But…'

'We'll talk more when I get home, Mum,' she said as Ben walked back into the room. 'Gotta go.'

'Well?' she asked Ben straight away.

'Our flight leaves first thing in the morning. We'll have to leave here around four to be there on time. But we can sleep on the plane. We're flying first class.'

First class, Jess thought with less enthusiasm than most girls would have had. She'd never flown first class before. But that was what Ben probably did every time.

'What clothes will I need?' she asked, trying to be practical in the face of her mounting concern.

'Something black for the funeral, I guess. It's cool in New York so make sure you have a jacket. Other than that, just trousers and tops and a dress for going out at night. I can buy you anything else you might need.'

Jess conceded that he could certainly afford to buy her anything she needed, now that he was a billionaire. But she didn't want him to do that. She didn't like him thinking he could buy her as well if he wanted to.

Just what was she supposed to be by his side? Girlfriend or mistress?

She doubted he had fiancée in mind. But who knew? Love did make one hope.

'How long will you want me to stay?' she asked, doing her best to sound nonchalant.

For ever, Ben thought. But he knew it was too soon to say that. Too soon to tell her that he loved her. He wished now he hadn't said as much to Amber. She was sure to be at the wake and she might say something.

Well, too bad if she did. It was the truth.

'As long as you like,' he answered. 'It's up to you.'

CHAPTER TWENTY-ONE

THEY BOTH MANAGED to sleep on the very long flight to New York, which was just as well, because as soon as they landed and were allowed to use their mobile phones again it was all systems go. Ben didn't stop making phone calls during the rather long, slow drive from the airport to wherever his apartment was located. Jess did send her mother a text saying they had arrived safely but her attention was more on her surrounds. She had never seen so many tall buildings, so many people or such thick traffic. Sydney was small compared to New York. She stopped herself just in time from gushing when she spotted the Empire State Building. She wasn't there as a goggle-eyed tourist but as Ben's support system during this very difficult time for him.

Jess remained discreetly silent in the taxi. Though, they weren't called taxis here, were they? They were called cabs. When they finally pulled up outside a swish looking apartment building, she did her best not to do or say anything gauche which would embarrass Ben. But she was seriously impressed, both by the uniformed porter who took care of their luggage, and the doorman who said hello to Ben in a very deferential manner. Inside, the lobby was just as impressive, with marble floors and a huge, fresh flower arrangement sitting on a circular table underneath a massive chandelier. The security guard behind the desk in the corner nodded to Ben as he steered Jess over to the bank of lifts against a side wall.

'Everything's arranged,' Ben said briskly once the lifts doors closed and they were alone. 'The funeral will be at two tomorrow afternoon with the wake afterwards at Dad's apartment. My apartment's not large enough to cater for so many people.'

Not large enough? Jess thought in amazement when she walked into his apartment. The main living room was ginormous with ten-foot ceilings and tall French doors which opened out onto a very large balcony. All the walls were white, which only added to the feeling of space. On them hung some of the loveliest paintings Jess had ever seen. She hardly knew which one to look at first. Or where to look at all. The furniture was obviously very expensive, an eclectic mix of modern and antique.

'Goodness, Ben,' she said. 'How many people are you expecting at the wake if this place isn't big enough to house them?'

'Two hundred, at least,' he replied. 'Dad had a lot of business colleagues.'

'What about friends and relatives?'

'Not too many of those. Dad was an only child and his parents are long gone. So are his aunts and uncles. He possibly has a few cousins somewhere but he never kept in touch with them.' Ben gave a crooked smile. 'There might be the odd mistress or two attending, wondering if he's left them anything. But I fear they'll be disappointed. Dad told me not long ago that he left everything to me.'

Ben watched Jess's eyes when he said this, wondering if his being a billionaire would make any difference to her. Quite frankly, he didn't care if it did. He loved her and he had every intention of marrying her. He understood now how his father had felt when he'd proposed to his mother. Love did have a blinding effect on one.

But Jess was nothing like his mother. Ben felt sure of that.

'Amber might be there,' he said, feeling that he should warn Jess in advance. 'Her father was a close business associate.'

'That's okay,' she said. Though it wasn't. Not really. Jess supposed there was a small part of her which was curious to meet this Amber. But she could have managed well without the experience.

The doorbell rang. It was the porter delivering their luggage.

'Leave it just inside,' Ben directed, getting out his wallet and handing the man a note.

'I'd forgotten you have to tip everyone here,' Jess said after the porter had left. What a different country America was from Australia.

'You'd better believe it,' Ben said. 'No tip, no service.'

She didn't much like that, but didn't say anything.

'Will you be staying with me in the master bedroom?' he asked her. 'Or do you want one of the guest rooms?'

'Where do you want me to stay?' she returned, suddenly feeling nervous. Realising that she loved him seemed temporarily to have banished any desire for the exciting love-making they'd shared. Now, she just wanted him to hold her in his arms and make love to her like they were normal people.

'With me, of course.'

'Okay. As long as you don't...you know...'

His eyes clouded over. 'You needn't worry. I'm not in the mood for fun and games at the moment, Jess.'

'No, no, of course not. I just...' She stopped, then let out a long sigh. 'I'm sorry. That was insensitive of me. Of course you don't want to do things like that at the moment. I know exactly how you must be feeling. When my grandmother died last year, it felt like someone had taken a huge jagged spoon and scraped a great big hole out of my heart. I'm sure that's how you're feeling at this moment. Maybe even worse. He was your father.'

He looked at her with such sad eyes. 'I think he knew something was wrong with him. They say sometimes people have a premonition of their death from a heart attack, even when there are no actual symptoms.'

'Yes, I've heard that's true,' Jess said.

'He rang me, you know. On the night before we drove out to Mudgee. It wasn't like him to ring unless it was to discuss business. But he just chatted away. And then, right before he hung up, he said, "give my regards to your mother". I thought that was a bit odd at the time. Now I think it was because he knew he was going to die and he wanted to put all that old bitterness behind him.'

Ben gave an unhappy sigh. 'I did send Mum a text in the taxi about Dad dying and she answered me; said how sad it was for me but not to expect her to fly over for the funeral. I knew she wouldn't come, that's why I went ahead with the arrangements for tomorrow. She believed Dad hated her. But she's wrong about that. I think he actually loved her.'

'Yes. Of course he did,' was all Jess could think of to say.

Just when Ben looked as though he was going to burst into tears, he dragged in another deep breath, then straightened his spine.

'Dad would expect me to be strong,' he said.

Jess wanted to tell him that tears didn't make a man weak but she knew it would have been a waste of time.

Her father had never cried in front of her, neither had her brothers. It was just the way lots of men were.

'I'll put these in the bedroom,' he said as he picked up their bags and headed down a hallway.

Jess followed him with a heavy heart.

The master bedroom was magnificent, of course. Lavishly furnished with a king-sized bed and everything anyone could possibly want, including a huge flat-screen TV built into the wall opposite the bed. Ben opened the door of a walk-in dressing room which proved bigger than her bedroom back home. She tried not to gape as she hung up her outfit for the funeral, but the extent of Ben's wardrobe was mind-boggling. How could one man wear so many suits?

She unpacked the rest of her things silently, thankful that she'd thought to bring her newest and best nightie. To wear something cheap in this place wouldn't seem right. It was made of white satin, adorned with white lace. The colour would even match the room, which was mainly white and grey, not a single piece of dark wood in sight.

'I dare say you'd like to freshen up after that very long flight,' Ben said. 'And no, I won't be joining you in the shower, so you don't have to worry. I also don't want to go out to dinner tonight. I'll order something in for us. Will Chinese do, or would you prefer something else?'

'No, no. I love Chinese food,' she said.

'Good. Take your time in the bathroom. Have a bath, if you'd prefer.'

Jess hated how sad he looked. She instinctively walked over and put her arms around him, hugging him tightly. 'It's going to be all right, Ben,' she said as one did when one didn't know what else to say.

He hugged her back for a long moment before extricating himself from her arms and giving the weariest sigh.

'Dear, sweet Jess,' he said and laid a gentle hand against her cheek. 'Maybe it will be all right. In time. Meanwhile, tomorrow is going to be hell.'

CHAPTER TWENTY-TWO

IT WAS WORSE than hell, Jess decided by five the following afternoon. Firstly, it had rained overnight and she'd frozen to death, both in the church and at the cemetery. She did have a jacket, one which matched her black crepe skirt, having chosen to wear the black Chanel-style suit she'd made to attend her grandmother's funeral. But even though it was lined it wasn't a warm outfit. Everyone else, she saw, was wearing overcoats. Some were wearing hats. She didn't even own a hat!

She'd warmed up a little during the drive from the lawn cemetery back into the city, though Ben hadn't said a word. Obviously, he'd been in a pretty bad place in his head after having to deliver the main eulogy, then watch his father's coffin being lowered into the ground. He'd held her hand so tightly whilst that had happened, she'd thought her fingers would break. She hadn't known what to say to make him feel any better so she'd said nothing.

But none of that compared to the hell the wake proved to be. Jess had felt intimidated from the moment she'd set foot in that mausoleum of an apartment Ben's father had owned. Maybe if she'd been able to stay by Ben's side she would have been able to cope better. But people kept taking him away from her, smarmy men in black suits with sucking-up manners and ingratiating voices. Everyone seemed to want his ear now that he was no longer the heir but the man himself. It was all quite sickening. And depressing.

Time ticked away very slowly spent with people she didn't know, making conversation with her about things she knew nothing about. When one particularly snobbish woman asked her what she did for a living, Jess rather enjoyed telling her that she was a mechanic. The expression on her snooty face was horrified. Anyone would have thought she'd said she was a garbage collector.

Finally, just after the grandfather clock in the main hallway struck five, an exasperated Jess scooped up a glass of white wine from a passing waiter and slipped out onto one of the many balconies, hopeful of finding some solitude and peace.

But she wasn't about to be so lucky. A svelte blonde who'd been at the funeral, and who'd stared daggers at Jess across the graveside, followed her out onto the balcony.

'Well, hello there,' the blonde said. 'You must be Ben's new girlfriend, the one he told me about over the phone.'

It didn't take a genius to conclude who the blonde was.

Amber wasn't beautiful, Jess decided. But she was attractive, and she shouted money with her super-sleek hairdo, her shiny complexion and her expensive-looking black sheath dress. No doubt they were real diamonds twinkling in her ears, Jess wished that she was wearing the diamond pendant Andy had given her at the wedding. But she'd left it at home in her jewellery case.

Despite knowing that her own outfit didn't look home-made it suddenly felt home-made. And dated. Which was silly.

'Hi,' Jess returned, refusing to feel intimidated any more today. 'I presume you're Amber. Ben told me all about you too.'

Amber's smile was not at all nice. 'Did he, now? I'll bet he didn't tell you what he and I used to get up to.'

Jess hated to think of Ben doing with this creature what he'd done with her. But there was no use pretending that some of it wouldn't have happened. Ben obviously had a penchant for erotic fun and games.

'I wouldn't dream of questioning Ben over what he did with his previous girlfriends,' she said coolly. 'What's past is past.'

The blonde laughed. 'In that case, you might be in for a few surprises, sweetie. But let me warn you…if you've set your cap at marrying the dear boy, then it might be wise to play a more conservative role. I tried to accommodate his kinky little demands and it didn't get me anywhere in the end. Not that I enjoyed any of it, but a girl will do just about anything, won't they, when there are billions at stake.'

'So it seems.'

Jess and Amber whirled at the sound of Ben's voice.

Amber went a guilty shade of pink whilst Jess just stared at him.

'Amazing what you learn after a relationship is over,' he said, still glaring at Amber. 'If I'd known your father was on the verge of bankruptcy, then I'd have better understood your sudden declaration of love. Not to mention your timely proposal.'

'Ben, I…I…'

'Save it, Amber,' he snapped.

'*She* doesn't love you,' Amber retaliated spitefully. 'She just wants your money, the way your mother wanted your father's money. For God's sake, just look at her. She's a nothing from down under. A nobody!'

Jess stepped forward and slapped Amber's face before she could think better of it. 'I do so love him,' she spat at the stunned blonde. 'And I am *not* a nobody!'

All of Amber's face went bright red, not just the palm print on her cheek. 'I'll sue you for assault, you bitch. And you too, you bastard—for breach of promise. I'll make you pay for wasting all that time on you.'

Ben's look in return was chillingly cold. 'Give it your best shot, sweetheart. I have billions at my disposal and you've got what? A dead-broke father and a dead-end job, working for peanuts in an art gallery.'

Amber opened her mouth to say something, then just whirled and stormed off.

Ben stared at Jess who was feeling somewhat shattered by the nasty incident.

'Did you mean it?' he asked her. 'Do you really love me?'

Tears pricked at her eyes. 'Of course I do. Why do you think I'm here?'

'Amber just said it's for the money.'

'Amber's a fool. And so are you, if you think that.'

'I don't think that. That's why I love *you*.'

Jess gaped at him then burst into tears. He gathered her close and pressed his lips into her hair. 'I love you,' he murmured. 'And I want to marry you.'

Jess wept all the harder. Because how could she marry this man and live this life with him? She would hate it. And soon she would hate him.

Finally, when the crying had stopped and she could gather enough courage, she pulled back from him and lifted still, wet eyes to his. 'I do love you, Ben,' she said shakily. 'Very much. But I can't marry you. I'm sorry. I just can't.'

CHAPTER TWENTY-THREE

'I DON'T UNDERSTAND why you won't marry me,' Ben raged when he finally got Jess back to his apartment. 'If you love me the way you say you do, then what's the problem? Hell on earth, Jess, I can give you anything you want.'

'That's the problem, Ben. I don't want what you can give me. I don't want to live this kind of life,' she said, sweeping her right arm around at his apartment. 'It's too much. We wouldn't have any real friends. Neither would our children.'

'That's ridiculous. I have real friends.'

'No, you don't. There wasn't a single person there tonight who was a real friend. The only real friend you have is Andy in Australia, and that's because you met him when you weren't so rich. Being a billionaire means you can't live an ordinary life, Ben. As your wife, I won't be able to live an ordinary life either. You'll want me to go to toffee-nosed dos and dinner parties all the time with people that I despise. You'll want me to stop making my own clothes. You'll insist I have a stylist and a designer wardrobe. Our children will have nannies and bodyguards and be sent to snobby boarding schools whilst we stay at home and *entertain*. I'm sorry, Ben, but that's not what I want for my children. That's not what I want for *me*.'

He stopped pacing around the living room and sent her a disbelieving look. 'You really mean this, don't you?'

'I do,' she said, even though her heart was breaking.

He swore, then strode over and yanked her hard against him. 'I could make you change your mind,' he ground out darkly.

'No, Ben,' she said firmly. 'You couldn't.'

'Even if I promise you the world?'

'Especially if you promise me the world.'

'Then you don't really love me,' he growled and threw her from him.

When she almost fell over he grabbed her again, but not so roughly this time, his expression both apologetic and desperate. 'I'm sorry. God, I'm sorry. I would *never* hurt you, Jess. But please, don't do this. I beg of you. Stay with me. I need you. I love you. I won't let you go!'

Jess was not at her best when cornered. 'You can't stop me, Ben.'

'Then go, damn you.' And, before she could say another word, *he* was gone, slamming the front door behind him.

She waited for hours but he didn't come back. She tried his phone but it was turned off. Clearly, he didn't want her contacting him. She couldn't rest, just paced the apartment, her mind awhirl with regrets and recriminations.

It had been cruel of her to reject Ben's proposal like that on the same day that he'd buried his father. It was no wonder he'd lost his temper with her. She'd hurt him. Terribly. At the same time, Jess could not deny that what she'd said had been true. She knew she wouldn't be happy living this kind of life. And he wouldn't be happy with her as his wife. They lived in different worlds. She had always led a simple life whereas Ben lived like *this*, she thought, her gaze once again taking in the sheer luxury of her surrounds.

In the end, Jess made an agonising decision. She packed,

then went downstairs and got the doorman to summon a cab for her.

'JFK airport,' she told the driver in a broken voice.

She cried all the way to the airport where she had to wait some time before she could get a flight out. Just before she boarded, she sent Ben an explanatory and deeply apologetic text message. She didn't want him to worry about where she was, but she also didn't want him to follow her. The plane she caught set down in San Francisco, where she changed planes for the long flight back to Sydney. When she checked her messages, there wasn't one from Ben.

Jess didn't sleep much on the plane—she was travelling economy—so by the time she reached Mascot she was very tired and seriously depressed. She caught the bus over to the long-distance car park where she'd left her four-wheel drive, then literally had to force herself to drive home. Fortunately, it wasn't peak hour in Sydney, so it only took her a couple of hours. Even so, by the time she pulled into the driveway at home, she was totally wrecked.

Her mother must have heard a vehicle pull up outside; the front door was flung open just as Jess staggered up to it.

'Jess!' she exclaimed. 'Good heavens. I didn't expect it to be you. I was just having morning tea when I heard a car. What are you doing back so soon?'

'Mum, I can't talk now. I have to go to bed.'

'Can you just give me a clue as to what's happened?' Ruth asked as she followed her weary daughter up the stairs.

Jess stopped at the top step. 'If you must know, Ben told me he loved me and wanted to marry me.'

'He did?'

'I turned him down.'

'You turned him down?' Ruth repeated, somewhat stunned.

'Mum, he's too rich. I would have been miserable.'

'It wouldn't have been an easy life,' her mother said, feeling terribly sorry for her obviously heartbroken daughter. But she was proud of her too. Jess had a very sensible head on her shoulders. There weren't many girls who could turn down a man like Ben.

'Mum, I have to go to bed,' Jess said, tears threatening once more.

'You do that, darling. I'll go tell your father that you're home.'

'What?' was Joe's first reaction. 'She turned him down, did you say?'

'Yes,' Ruth said with a sigh.

'Ben won't take that lying down,' Joe said. 'He'll come after her.'

'Do you think so, Joe?'

'You mark my words. That man's crazy about our Jess. He'll be on our doorstep in less than a week.'

But he wasn't.

A week went by. Then two weeks. Then three.

Still no contact from Ben, either by phone, email or in person.

Joe couldn't believe it. Ruth wasn't quite so surprised. Maybe it was a case of out of sight, out of mind. Men, she believed, fell out of love more quickly than women.

On the following Sunday, Ruth did suggest Jess ring *him*, but this was vehemently rejected.

'No, Mum, there's no point. He's not going to give up his lifestyle for me and I'm not going to give up mine for him. That's the bottom line. So he's being sensible, not contacting me. It would only delay the inevitable. And make it even harder for me to move on.'

'But you're not moving on,' Ruth pointed out, frustrated. 'You're not even sewing any more!'

'Give me time, Mum. It's not even been a month.'

It had been, in fact, three weeks, four days and five hours since she'd last seen Ben, Jess thought bleakly. And even longer since she'd slept in his arms. Which she had the night before the funeral. It had been quite wonderful to have Ben make love to her, face to face, then to fall asleep with her head on his chest and her arms around him. She would remember the way that had felt for ever.

That Sunday night, Jess dreamt a futile dream where she and Ben got married somewhere overlooking a beach. An Australian beach. Shelley Beach, she recognised after she woke. It was an upsetting dream because that was only what it would ever be. A stupid dream! God, was she ever going to get over that man? Maybe she should have said yes and been miserable in New York, for this was just as bad, living life without him. Maybe worse!

She had to work in the office that day. Unfortunately, it turned out not to be a busy day for Murphy's Hire Car with hardly any phone calls or bookings coming in. She had way too much time to twiddle her thumbs, drink endless cups of coffee and think depressing thoughts. By the time twelve o'clock came, Jess had had enough. She stood up from her desk, deciding that she needed distraction or she'd go stark, raving mad. She would go to the movies, find herself a silly comedy. Or an action flick. Putting on the answering machine, she made her way from the office over to the house where she found her mother in the kitchen, packing away the food shopping.

'Mum, I think I'll go to the movies this afternoon. Do you mind?'

'Not at all. I'll look after the office.'

'Thanks, Mum.'

Ruth Murphy watched her daughter walk off slowly, thinking to herself that it would take Jess a long time to get over Ben. A small, selfish part of Ruth was glad that nothing had come of their relationship. She could not bear to think of her only daughter going off and living in America. At the same time, she could not bear to see her so unhappy.

Sighing, she finished putting away the shopping, made herself a sandwich and coffee, then toddled over to the office. After checking the answering machine—there'd been no calls—she ate her lunch, then picked up the book she kept there for reading when the office was slow. But she'd only finished a few pages when the phone rang.

'Murphy's Hire Car,' she said brightly.

'Hello, Ruth.'

Ruth sat up straight once she detected the American accent.

'Is Jess there?'

'No,' she said, feeling both anxious and defensive at the same time. 'Jess isn't here at the moment. Are you calling from New York?'

'No, Ruth. I'm parked just down the road from your place.'

Oh, dear Lord, he *had* come after her, like Joe had said.

'I tried Jess's phone several times but it's turned off.'

'She's at the movies.'

'At the movies?' He sounded puzzled, as though he couldn't imagine why she would be at the movies at this time of day.

'She needed to get out of the house, Ben. She's been very down since she came back from New York.'

'Did she tell you what happened?'

'Yes, she did. We're a very close family. There are no secrets between us.'

'I love your daughter, Ruth. And I mean to marry her.'

Ruth was taken aback by the fierce determination behind his words.

'In that case, what took you so long to come after her?' she couldn't help throwing at him.

'I needed time to change my life so that she would accept my proposal.'

'What do you mean? How have you changed your life?'

'I would rather discuss that with Jess, if you don't mind. Though, there is something I'd like to ask her father first, if he's here.'

'Well, yes, he is. He's working on one of the cars.'

'I'll be there shortly.'

When Ben hung up, Ruth just sat there in a total panic. Clearly, Ben meant to ask Joe for Jess's hand in marriage. What else could it be? She should have warned Ben that he might not get so civil a reception from Joe. He was mad as a hatter with Ben. Alternatively, she could race down to the shed and warn Joe that Ben had come to win Jess over.

But she'd dithered too long, Ruth realised when she saw a white sedan speed past the office on its way to the shed.

Joe heard a car pull up outside, but he was underneath one of the limousines when the driver walked in, so all he saw was a clean pair of trainers and some bare legs under cream shorts.

'Are you there, Joe?' Ben called out.

Joe's temper had already flared by the time he slid out from under the limo and stood up to face his visitor. 'You took your bloody time, didn't you?' he snarled. 'My girl's been in a right state over you.'

'I'm sorry about that, Joe. To be honest, I was in a right state myself when she turned me down. Took me a day or two to see sense after she left, but then I got to thinking more rationally and I realised she was right. We wouldn't have been happy living in New York. But it took some time to fix things so that we would be happy.'

'What kind of things?'

'I would prefer to discuss that with Jess first. Let me just say that I think she'll accept my proposal after I tell her what I've done. But I guess there's no harm in you knowing that I've come home to Australia to live. Permanently.'

Joe was both stunned and relieved. 'That's good news, Ben. Really good news. Ruth will be especially thrilled. So you're going to ask my girl to marry you again, is that it?'

'That's the plan. But I want to do it right, Joe, so I'm asking you first for your daughter's hand in marriage. I know that your approval would mean a lot to her.'

Joe could not have been more pleased. Or more proud.

'You have my full approval, Ben. But I sure hope you haven't bought the ring yet.'

Ben's heart plummeted at this statement. 'You think she might still say no?'

'Hell, no. But she'll want to pick the thing herself, if I know my Jess. That's one strong-minded girl.'

'Tell me about it.' Ben laughed. 'Now, I'd better get going.'

'Good luck,' Joe shouted as Ben made his way back to the car. 'You're going to need it!' he chuckled to himself.

CHAPTER TWENTY-FOUR

NAUSEA SWIRLED IN Ben's stomach as he headed for Westfield's and the movie theatre. A lack of confidence was not something he was familiar with. Admittedly, his ego had been brutally crushed by Jess's refusal to marry him back in New York. He had, in fact, lost a day or two indulging his sorry self in a serious drinking binge, which was most unlike him. But once he'd sobered up, and realised a future without Jess was unthinkable, he'd attacked all the changes necessary to his lifestyle in a very positive state of mind. Not once had he entertained the thought that he would not succeed in winning Jess over.

But now, suddenly, he wasn't so sure.

Maybe, during these last few weeks of silence, Jess had decided that she didn't love him after all. Maybe it was a case of out of sight, out of mind, rather than absence making the heart grow fonder. Her being 'in a right state', as her father had described, could have been her realising that it wasn't love she'd been suffering from but lust. Maybe she even regretted letting him do the things he'd done to her. Though, damn it, he was sure she'd enjoyed everything at the time. She wasn't like Amber, just doing what he wanted in the bedroom with an eye on his money. Hell, Jess was nothing like Amber at all. He really had to stop thinking all these negative thoughts. Negativity never achieved anything!

By the time Ben pulled into the large car park, he'd regained some of his confidence and composure. Once parked, he quickly checked Jess's mobile; it was still turned off. Climbing out from behind the steering wheel, he locked the car, then hurried into the shopping centre, heading through the food court and stopping at a spot where Jess would have to pass by as she exited the cinema complex.

Jess stood up as soon as the credits started coming up. The movie had been quite funny in parts. She'd managed to laugh once or twice. But the moment she exited the cinema her depression returned. What on earth was she going to do? Sit and have a coffee, she supposed wearily. No way was she going home yet. It was only just three.

She wandered slowly along the carpeted hallway which separated the numerous theatres, her blank eyes not registering the few people who passed her. Monday afternoon—especially on a warm spring day—was not rush hour at the movies. She did not bother to look at the advertisement posters on the walls like she usually did, not caring what blockbuster movies were about to hit the screens. Her mind was filled with nothing but one subject. She'd almost reached the food court just outside the cinema when someone called her name.

Her eyes cleared and there he was, standing right in front of her.

'Oh, my God,' was all she could say. 'Ben.'

When he smiled at her, she almost burst into tears. But she caught herself in time.

'What are you doing here?' she said, her sharp tone a cover for her confusion. She wanted to believe that he'd come for her, but it seemed too good to be true. And yet here he was, looking as handsome as ever.

'Your mother said you were at the movies. So I came and waited for you to come out.'

'You rang my *mother*?'

'I tried your mobile first, but it was turned off, so I rang Murphy's Hire Car and your mum answered.'

'Oh…'

'Is that all you've got to say?'

'Yes. No. What do you expect me to say? I'm in shock. I mean, you haven't rung or texted me at all. I thought you were finished with me.'

'It was you who finished with me, Jess.'

Her grimace carried true pain. 'I did what I thought was right. For both of us. So why *have* you come, Ben? Please don't ask me to go back to New York with you and marry you. That would just be cruel. I gave you my reasons for saying no and they haven't changed.'

'But you're wrong there, Jess. Lots of things have changed.'

'Not really. You're probably richer than ever now.' Hadn't she read somewhere that billionaires earned thousands of dollars a day from their many and varied investments? Or was it thousands every minute?

'What say we go have a coffee somewhere a little more private and I'll explain further?'

'There is nowhere here more private,' Jess said, waving at the open-plan and rather busy food court. People might not be flocking to the movies on a Monday but, since October had tipped into November, Christmas shopping had begun.

'I seem to recall there was a small coffee shop down that way on the right,' Ben said. 'Come on, let's go there.'

Jess didn't say a word as he led her away. She was still trying to work out what could possibly have changed.

The café he was referring to was half-empty with tables and booths to choose from. Ben steered her to the furthest booth where a sign on the back wall said you had to order at the counter.

'Would you like something to eat with your coffee?' he asked.

'No thanks.'

'Fine. What would you like? Flat white? Latte? A cappuccino?'

'A flat white,' she answered. 'No sugar.'

'Right.'

Jess tried not to ogle him as he got their coffee, but he looked utterly gorgeous in cream cargo shorts and a black polo shirt. His hair had grown a bit, she noted. It suited him longer. But then, he'd look good no matter what he wore or how long he grew his hair. Fate was very cruel to have her fall in love with a man with so many temptations.

As Jess waited for him to come back with the coffee, she tried to get her head around him suddenly showing up like this. Obviously he thought he *could* get her to change her mind. And maybe he was right. She'd been so miserable. And she'd missed him so much. Missed his love-making as well. Seeing him again reminded her of what an exciting lover he was. Exciting and dangerous and downright irresistible!

In the end, she looked down at where her hands were twisting nervously in her lap, not glancing up till he put her coffee in front of her, then sat down with his.

'Thank you,' she said politely, not really wanting coffee at all. Her stomach was in a mess. But she picked it up and had a small sip before putting it back down again. 'Now, would you mind telling me what's going on?'

He looked deep into her eyes. 'What's going on is that I still love you, Jess. And, yes, I still want to marry you.'

Oh, God, he *was* cruel.

'I don't doubt that, Ben, since you're here,' she replied. 'But sometimes love isn't enough.'

He reached over and touched her on the hand. 'You might change your mind on that when you hear what my love for you has achieved.'

It was hard for Jess to think straight when he was touching her. 'What are you talking about?'

'Well, first of all, I've come home to Australia to live.'

Her heart leapt. 'You *have*?'

'Yep. I knew you would never live with me in New York so I quit my job, then sold my majority interest in Dad's company to his partners.'

Jess just stared at him.

'After that, I used the money from the sale to set up a charity trust fund that gives financial assistance to people affected by natural disasters. We do seem to have a lot of them nowadays. Dad always gave lots of money to whatever disaster relief effort was going on, but he often worried if the money actually made it to where it was meant to go. I took this on board, so I'm the CEO of the fund. *I* decide when and where the money goes. The capital is safely invested so it should last for yonks. I don't take a salary or expenses myself, but I had to employ a couple of professional charity workers to oversee the day-to-day transactions and they do get paid. Other than that, all the money earned by the trust will go where it should go.'

Jess could only shake her head at him. 'You gave *all* your money away to charity?'

'Not all of it. Just what I inherited from the sale of Dad's company. Which, admittedly, was the majority of his estate. I still have his cash account—which was considerable—plus the money from the sale of his real-estate assets. When they're finally sold, that is. This includes his furnished apartment in New York and another one in Paris. They should bring in about twenty to thirty million each. If you include all the artwork he invested in over the years, you can add several more million. Though, I might donate them to various museums around the world. Yeah, I think I'll do that. The upshot is I'm still a multi-millionaire, Jess. Just not a billionaire. I knew you wouldn't marry a billionaire, but there's nothing attractive about poverty either.'

Jess's shock was beginning to change to wonder. 'You did all that for me?'

'The strange thing is, Jess, even though I initially gave away most of my money to win you back, after I actually did it, it felt good. Very good. They say there's more pleasure in giving than receiving and they're darned right. Anyway, as you can imagine, all that organising takes some considerable time, even when you're doing your own legal work. Which is why it took me this long to get here. I still might have to fly back occasionally, to attend to fund business, but Australia will be my permanent home from now on. It has to be, since I'm going to have an Australian wife. One whom I can't bear to live without.'

'Oh, Ben,' she said, the tears coming now. 'I can hardly believe it.'

Ben was struggling now to retain his own composure. 'Then your answer is yes this time?'

'Yes,' she choked out as she dashed away her tears. 'Of course it's yes.'

'Thank God,' he said, slumping back against the seat. 'I was worried you might still say no. And so was my mother.'

Jess blinked in surprise. 'You told your mother about us?'

'But of course. She's been at me to get married and have children for years. She'll be over the moon when I tell her.'

'You want children as well?' Jess said, still in a state of shock.

'Hell, yes. As many as you want. And if I know you, Jess, that will be more than one or two.'

'Yes, I'd like a big family,' she confessed. 'So when did you tell your mother about us?'

'Last night. I stayed at her apartment in Bondi. I flew in late, you see, too late to come up here. Though in the end, I stayed up even later, telling Mum everything. Then, would you believe it, I slept in. Didn't make it up to the coast till after lunch. Like I already told you, when you didn't answer your phone I rang Murphy's Hire Car and your mum answered.'

Jess was still a bit dumbstruck by everything Ben had done for her. 'I hope Mum was nice to you.'

'Very nice. So was your dad, after I asked him for your hand in marriage.'

'You actually asked Dad for my hand in marriage?'

'I wanted to do everything right, Jess. I didn't want anything to go wrong this time.'

'Oh, Ben, you make me feel awful.'

He frowned. 'Why awful?'

'Because you've done everything for me and I've done nothing for you.'

Done nothing? Ben looked at this wonderful girl whom he loved and he thought of all the things she'd done. Firstly and most importantly, she'd loved him back, not for his money but for himself—Ben the man, not the heir to billions. She'd also made him see what was important in life. Not fame and fortune but family and community. Not a high-flying social life but a simpler life, full of fun and friends and children. Oh yes, he couldn't *wait* to have children with Jess. What a lucky man he'd been the day he'd rung Murphy's Hire Car and met her.

But Ben knew if he said all that she'd be embarrassed. So he just smiled and said, 'Happiness is not nothing, Jess. You make me happy, my darling.'

'Oh,' she said, and looked like she was going to cry again.

'No more tears, Jess. You can cry on our wedding day, if you like, but not today. Today is for rejoicing. Now, drink up your coffee and we'll go buy you an engagement ring. There must be a decent jewellery store here somewhere.'

Half an hour later, the third finger of Jess's left hand was sporting a diamond solitaire engagement ring set in white gold, not as large and expensive as one Ben would have chosen.

'It's not how much it costs, Ben,' she'd told him firmly when she'd made her choice. 'But the sentiment behind it. Besides, I wouldn't like to make my very nice sisters-in law envious. They don't have engagement rings with diamonds the size of Ayer's Rock.'

Ben lifted his eyes to the ceiling. 'Fine. But don't go thinking I intend to buy a house with any constraints on it. I aim to have everything you and I want in it.'

'Fair enough,' Jess said, thinking to herself that that was fine by her. She wasn't a jewellery person but she'd always wanted a truly great house.

'Okay,' Ben said. 'Now that the ring business is all sorted out, take me along to that Fab Fashions store you used to work in.'

'But why?' she asked, puzzled. 'You don't own it any more.'

'Ah, but you're wrong there. When I sold Dad's company, that's the one asset I arranged to keep—the Fab Fashions chain. Dad's partners were only too happy to let me have it for nothing. They all consider it a right lemon, but I reckon that with your advice we could make a go of it. So what do you think, Jess? Can you help me out here?'

Jess's heart swelled with happiness. What an incredibly thoughtful man Ben was! And very clever. He knew exactly the way to her heart. And she told him so.

He grinned. 'Andy always said that no one should get between me and the goal post.'

She smiled. It wasn't every day that a girl liked being called a goal post.

'Does Andy know about your dad dying?' she asked on a more serious note.

'Not yet. They're still on their honeymoon. But they get back next week. Perhaps we could drive up and visit them one weekend soon, now that we're engaged. Stay in that nice little cottage for a night or two before they knock it down. Andy's planning on building a family home on that site in the New Year. Till then, they're living in the main house.'

Jess's heartbeat had quickened at the mention of the cottage, which immediately evoked the most wickedly exciting memories.

'That would be nice,' she said rather blandly. Wow, what an understatement! She could hardly wait.

He gave her a narrow-eyed look. Then he laughed. 'You don't fool me, Jess Murphy. You liked those fun and games as much as I did.'

'Yes,' she admitted. 'But I think they should be kept for special occasions, not an every-day event. I like the way you made love to me that night in New York, Ben. I thought you liked it too.'

'I did. Very much so. Okay, we'll keep the fun and games for special occasions, and weekends in nicely private cottages. Now, take me to Fab Fashions.'

* * *

Helen was surprised when Jess walked in on the arm of the most handsome man she'd ever seen. He reminded her of a young Brad Pitt.

'Hello, Helen,' Jess said, looking oddly sheepish. 'This is Benjamin De Silva, the American businessman who took over Fab Fashions.'

'Please call me Ben,' the American said and extended his hand. 'Jess has been telling me about the difficulties you've encountered since my order came through for you to make a profit before Christmas or be closed.'

Helen shook his hand whilst wondering what on earth was going on here.

'I just wanted to personally deliver a new order to you. There will be no closing down, and come the New Year there will be huge changes to Fab Fashions. A new name and brand-new stock, plus an extensive advertising campaign to go with it. Till then, I'd like you to put all of your current stock on sale at fifty-percent off. Get rid of it all. Oh, and one more thing—Jess has just agreed to become my wife.'

Jess was still smiling when Ben steered her out of the shopping centre ten minutes later.

'Did you see the look on Helen's face when you said we were engaged?' she said.

'She did seem a little shocked.'

'Shocked? She couldn't speak for a full minute and that's not like Helen at all.'

'Well, she soon made up for it. What do you think of her idea of stocking more accessories for the clothes?'

'It's a good one. Ladies love accessories. We already had a few bits of jewellery, but that could be increased, and I think some scarves, handbags and even shoes could do well.'

'We'll have to invite her to the wedding,' Ben said. 'She's nice.'

'She is. And so is her husband.'

'Then we'll invite them both.'

Jess's heart swelled with pride at the man by her side. He'd changed in so many ways. Still a 'take charge' kind of man, but she liked that about him. Still charming too. But there was more sincerity behind his charm. More depth of feeling.

'So, where have you parked your car?' she asked once they were out on the pavement. 'You do have a car this time, don't you?'

'Yes, I rented one till I knew whether I was going to actually buy a car or a plot in Wamberal Cemetery in anticipation of my throwing myself off a cliff after you turned me down again.'

Jess sucked in sharply. 'You wouldn't have done that, would you, Ben?'

'Nah. I would have gone back to New York, become a movie producer and made millions.'

'You're not going to become a movie producer here, are you?' Jess said, horrified at the thought.

'Are you kidding me? I'm going to buy myself a place on the beach, have half a dozen kids and take up golf.'

'You're not going to work?'

'Well, I do have Fab Fashions to sort out. I also might go into business with your dad, doing up vintage cars. I was very impressed with what he's done with that Cadillac. I could be the money man and he could do the actual work.'

'Sounds good to me, provided you've got enough money left to support me and all those children.'

'I have more than enough. Now, whilst we're making serious plans here, when can we actually get married? I'd like to do it asap.'

'Ben De Silva, I'm going to have a proper wedding. And I aim to plan it all myself. That takes time.'

'How much time? It only takes a month to get a licence.'

'It'll be Christmas in just over a month, which is a big celebration in our family. No way can our wedding be organised before then.'

'What about January? Or February?'

'I don't like January or February for weddings either. It's way too hot. How about March?'

'I can live with March,' Ben said. 'Just.'

'March it is, then,' Jess said happily. 'Now, let's go and tell Mum and Dad the good news.'

EPILOGUE

March, four months later...

THE LIGHTNING AND thunder started around ten in the morning. Jess and her parents rushed out onto the back veranda and stared up at the suddenly leaden sky, which had a rather ominous green colour.

'Murphy's Law,' Joe grumbled. 'You'd think it would leave me alone on my only daughter's wedding day.'

'It's not Murphy's Law, Dad,' Jess said, despite feeling disappointed. They'd been going to have the wedding ceremony at a picturesque open-air spot overlooking Toowoon Bay. 'It's just a storm.'

'No, it's bloody Murphy's Law!' he growled.

'I'm not going to let a little bit of rain spoil my big day, Dad. We have Plan B, don't we, Mum? We decided when we booked the Shelley Beach golf club for the reception that if it rained we could always have the ceremony there. They have some lovely balconies with nice views of the ocean and the golf course. If needs be, I'll give the club a call later. Everything will work out, Dad.'

It was at that point that it started to hail, denting even Jess's positive spirit.

'The wedding's not till three,' Ruth pointed out. 'It will probably have passed over by then.'

The hail was gone quite quickly but heavy rain continued all morning, resulting in several panicky phone calls from Jess's bridesmaids, who were all at the hairdresser's. None of them had stayed at Jess's place overnight, but were due out there as soon as they'd had their hair and make-up done. Jess reassured them that they had a Plan B, and told them to stop worrying, after which she went upstairs to do her own hair and make-up.

Just after midday, the rain finally stopped. The girls arrived around one, looking gorgeous, the sun making its appearance shortly before the bride and her four bridesmaids were due to leave.

Jess beamed her happiness at Catherine, whom she'd asked to be her matron of honour. They'd become good friends over the last few months. Andy, of course, was Ben's best man. Catherine was pregnant, but only two months gone, so hopefully there would be no last-minute dramas. Jess's three sisters-in-law were her other bridesmaids, thankfully none of them pregnant at the moment. Pete's wife, Michelle, had given birth to a baby girl two months earlier but had got her figure back very quickly. Jess had made the dresses for the wedding party, all of them strapless and full-length. Jess's bridal gown was in ivory silk and the bridesmaids' in a pale-yellow shantung.

The bride's bouquet, made from yellow and white roses, reached from her waist to just above the hem of her dress. The other bouquets were smaller with just white roses. Jess had chosen a white rose for Ben's lapel and yellow ones for the other men.

Ruth hadn't let Jess make *her* dress, however, choosing a lovely blue mother-of-the bride outfit from Real Women, which now had an excellent range of elegant clothes for the more mature lady. After an Australia-wide marketing campaign during January, the chain of stores was beginning to do quite well. No great profit as yet, but it was early days.

'See, Joe?' Ruth said a little smugly. 'I knew the sun would shine on our daughter's wedding. She's a lucky girl. Now, I must get going. See you all soon at Toowoon Bay.'

Jess watched her mother drive off in the family sedan whilst her father escorted her over to the first of the gleaming white wedding cars.

'Your mother's right,' he said to Jess once they were settled in the roomy back seat. 'You *are* a lucky girl to snare yourself a man like Ben. But then, he's a lucky guy to have a girl as special as you for his wife. Not to mention so exquisitely beautiful.'

'Please don't say things like that to me, Dad,' Jess said, her eyes pooling with moisture. 'I don't want to cry and ruin my make-up.'

'You won't cry, darling daughter. You're too sensible for that.'

But he was wrong. Jess almost cried as soon as she saw Ben standing there waiting for her with a look of such wonder and love in his eyes. She came even closer to weeping when he promised to love her till his dying days. She definitely would have cried when the celebrant announced that they were husband and wife, but Ben saved the day by kissing her with such passion that she forgot all about tears.

After that she didn't think about crying, being swept along with all the things which had to be done—first the photos at Toowoon Bay, then more at the golf club, followed by the greeting of the guests, pre-dinner champagne on the balconies and then the official part of the reception.

She smiled her way through all the speeches. Andy was suitably funny and Ben wonderfully complimentary about his beautiful bride. She smiled during the cake-cutting and the bridal waltz. She smiled and laughed with

Catherine whilst she changed into her going-away outfit, a chic white linen dress with red accessories. She and Ben planned to spend their wedding night at the Crown Plaza at Terrigal and the following day they were setting off on that long-awaited road trip around Australia; Jess's trusty four-wheel drive was already parked at the hotel. Not only was it parked but packed with every provision they could possibly need.

It wasn't till Jess was saying her goodbyes to her parents that tears suddenly flooded her eyes.

'Come now, Jess,' Joe said in a choked up voice as he hugged her. 'You don't want to spoil your make-up, do you?'

Jess laughed, then wiped away her tears. 'Absolutely not,' she said. 'But they aren't unhappy tears. I was just thinking what wonderful parents you and Mum are.'

'Oh, go on with you,' Joe said, though he seemed pleased. Ruth, however, started to look a bit weepy.

'Jess is right,' Ben said, stepping forward from where he'd been saying goodbye to his own mother. 'You are both wonderful. So we got our heads together and decided to give you both a little personal something. Here…' And he handed Joe a rather large envelope which had a well-known travel agency's logo on the outside.

'What on earth have you done?' Joe said as he opened the envelope and pulled out the printed itinerary of a very extensive trip around Europe.

'Now, we don't want to hear any objections,' Ben went on as a very wide-eyed Ruth looked over her husband's shoulder and read where they would be going. Knowing that they weren't seasoned travellers, Ben and his mother had booked guided tours as well as a long cruise down the Rhine. It would take them a good four months to do it all, the various tours taking in almost every country in Europe, finishing in Italy.

'Your departure date is not till late April. It's not a good idea to holiday in Europe in the dead of winter if you don't have to,' he added. 'As for Murphy's Hire Car...Jess's brothers will look after that till you get back. They assured me it's not a busy time of the year, anyway.'

'But it says we'll be travelling first class,' Ruth said, amazed.

Ben's mother, who'd been standing nearby, suddenly came forward, her arm linked with Lionel's. 'Please don't worry about the cost,' Ava said. 'I have more money than I need. Besides,' she added, smiling coyly at her partner, 'Lionel has decided to make an honest woman out of me and he has buckets of money himself, haven't you, darling?'

Darling Lionel just smiled.

'Now,' Ava raced on, 'I've been to all those places in Europe and it would be a real shame for you not to go whilst you're young enough to enjoy it. Oh, and Ruth, you and I are going clothes shopping in Sydney before you leave. I know exactly what you'll need.'

Ruth beamed at her. 'I'd love that, Ava.'

'And Lionel can take Joe clothes shopping at the same time,' Ben suggested.

'I'd be only too happy to,' Lionel agreed. 'If Joe wants me to, that is.'

Joe grinned. 'Sounds good to me. Can't have Mother showing me up, can I?'

'That's all settled, then,' Ben said, looking pleased with himself. 'Then, when we both get back from our holidays, Joe, we'll get right to work on that vintage car idea I told you about.'

'Too right,' Joe said, clapping Ben on the back.

'Hey!' Jess exclaimed, pretending to be piqued. 'Where does that leave me?'

'You can stay at home and clean that big house I bought you,' Ben said.

'But I didn't want such a big house. That was your idea.'

'You didn't say no.'

The three parents rolled their eyes at each other.

'Are these two having their first marital spat?' Andy said on joining them.

'I hope not,' Joe said.

Jess and Ben looked at each other, then laughed. 'We're just kidding. We both love our house.' It wasn't on a beach; Ben had decided he needed more room if and when he had sons. Their new purchase sat on a five-acre lot at Matcham, a rather exclusive rural enclave not far from the coast. The house was huge with six bedrooms, three bathrooms, a four-car garage, a tennis court and, of course, a solar-heated pool. They had already planned to have Christmas there the following year, Jess aiming to make it a very special occasion.

Thinking this last thought sent another thought into Jess's mind.

'Is a wedding night a special occasion?' she whispered to Ben once they'd said their final goodbyes and climbed into the back of the waiting limousine.

His eyes widened in mock horror. 'Are you suggesting what I think you're suggesting?'

'Not quite. I don't want to have to drive all that way tomorrow with an iffy bottom.'

'Hush up, wife. The driver might hear.'

'You're no fun any more,' she said sulkily.

Ben had actually refused to make love to her all week, saying she had to learn to wait.

'No fun!' Ben exclaimed. 'Might I remind you what we got up to just last month in Andy's cottage?'

'Hush up, husband. The driver might hear.'

Ten minutes later, they were safely alone in the bridal suite, which was beautifully furnished and quite seductive, with its big bed and mounds of pillows.

'If you must know,' Ben said as he busied himself with the waiting champagne bottle, 'I packed a little box of surprises which might come in handy during our rather elongated honeymoon.'

Jess's heart leapt. 'What kind of surprises?'

'Just a few naughty little items which I found on a website. You'll find out if and when required. But we certainly don't need anything like that tonight. Tonight is meant for more romantic sex. Though even romantic sex requires that clothes be removed. Why don't you get naked, my lovely wife, whilst I pour us some of this splendid champagne?'

'Aren't you going to get naked too?' a fiercely turned-on Jess asked after she'd complied.

He walked over to her slowly and handed her a glass. 'All in good time, my darling,' he murmured with wicked lights dancing in his beautiful blue eyes. 'All in good time.'

* * * * *

'You planned this,' she accused in a hushed tone, because her throat was working to swallow down her rising anger.

'I plan everything, Inez,' he replied simply.

She looked into his face. The indomitable determination stamped on Theo's harsh features sent a wave of anxiety through her. She started to speak, to say the words that seemed unreal to her, and her mouth trembled. His gaze dropped to the telling reaction and she immediately clamped her lips together. Showing weakness would only get her eaten alive.

Not that she wouldn't be anyway.

A bubble of hysteria threatened. She swallowed and held his gaze.

'You want me to be your *mistress*?'

He laughed long and deeply. 'Is that what you would call yourself?'

She flushed. 'How else would you describe what you've just demanded of me? This *keeping* me? What you're suggesting is archaic enough to be described as such. Or does *plaything* more suit your pseudo-modernistic outlook?'

'No, Inez. I don't like the term *plaything* either. I have no intention of playing with you. What I foresee for us is much more grown-up than that.'

The sexual intent behind the statement was unmistakable.

Rather than being offended or shocked, Inez found herself growing breathless. Excited.

No!

'Yes,' he murmured, as if he'd read her mind.

THE UNTAMEABLE GREEKS

Rich, powerful and impossible to resist

Sakis, Arion and Theo Pantelides—three formidable brothers who have risen up from the darkness of their pasts to conquer the world. Powerful, gorgeous and fabulously wealthy, these deliciously arrogant Greeks can have any woman they want—but none will ever tame them.

Until now?

WHAT THE GREEK'S MONEY CAN'T BUY
April 2014

Sakis is hungry to give in to the forbidden temptation of his buttoned-up PA—but will the cynical Greek pay the price for breaking his golden rule?

WHAT THE GREEK CAN'T RESIST
June 2014

Perla Lowell is the last woman Arion should want yet he can't deny himself one night with this irresistible temptress—but what will happen when the dark-hearted Greek discovers the consequences of succumbing to his desire?

WHAT THE GREEK WANTS MOST
December 2014

Business tycoon Theo Pantelides is in Brazil for one reason only—revenge. Bedding his enemy's beautiful socialite daughter Inez da Costa is an unexpected bonus—but will Theo's desire cost him more than he ever imagined?

WHAT THE GREEK WANTS MOST

BY

MAYA BLAKE

Published in Great Britain 2014
by Mills & Boon, an imprint of Harlequin (UK) Limited,
Eton House, 18-24 Paradise Road, Richmond, Surrey, TW9 1SR

ISBN: 978-0-263-25031-2

Harlequin (UK) Limited's policy is to use papers that are natural, renewable and recyclable products and made from wood grown in sustainable forests. The logging and manufacturing processes conform to the legal environmental regulations of the country of origin.

Printed and bound in Spain
by Blackprint CPI, Barcelona

Maya Blake fell in love with the world of the alpha male and the strong, aspirational heroine when she borrowed her sister's Mills & Boon® at age thirteen. Shortly thereafter the dream to plot a happy ending for her own characters was born. Writing for Harlequin Mills & Boon® is a dream come true. Maya lives in South East England with her husband and two kids. Reading is an absolute passion, but when she isn't lost in a book she likes to swim, cycle, travel and Tweet!

You can get in touch with her
via e-mail at mayablake@ymail.com,
or on Twitter: www.twitter.com/mayablake

Recent titles by the same author:

THE ULTIMATE PLAYBOY
(The 21st Century Gentleman's Club)
WHAT THE GREEK CAN'T RESIST
(The Untamable Greeks)
WHAT THE GREEK'S MONEY CAN'T BUY
(The Untamable Greeks)
HIS ULTIMATE PRIZE

To my editor, Suzanne Clarke,
for your unfailingly brilliant insight and support!

CHAPTER ONE

THEO PANTELIDES ACCELERATED his black Aston Martin up the slight incline and screeched to a halt underneath the portico of the Grand Rio Hotel.

He was fifteen minutes late for the black tie fund-raiser, thanks to another probing phone call from his brother, Ari.

He stepped out into the sultry Rio de Janeiro evening and tossed the keys to an eager valet who jumped behind the wheel of the sports car with all the enthusiasm Theo had once felt for driving. For life.

The smile that had teased his lips was slowly extinguished as he entered the plush interior of the five-star hotel. Highly polished marble gleamed beneath his feet. Artistically positioned lighting illuminated the well-heeled and threw the award-winning hotel's design into stunning relief.

The hotel was by far the best of the best, and Theo knew the venue had been chosen simply because his hosts had wanted to show off, to project a false image to fool him. He'd decided to play along for now.

The right time to end this game would present itself. Soon.

A sleek designer-clad blonde dripping in diamonds clocked him and glided forward on sky-high stilettos, her strawberry-tinted mouth widening in a smile that spelled out a very feminine welcome. And more.

'Good evening, Mr Pantelides. We are so very honoured you could make it.'

The well-practised smile he'd learnt to flash on and off since he was eighteen slid into place. It had got him out of trouble more times than he could count and also helped him hide what he did not want the world to see.

'Of course. As the guest of honour, it would've been crass not to show up, no?'

She gave a little laugh. 'No, er, I mean yes. Most of the guests are already here and taking pre-dinner drinks in the ballroom. If there's anything you need, anything at all, my name is Carolina.' She sent him a look from beneath heavily mascaraed eyelashes that hinted that she would be willing to go above and beyond her hostess duties to accommodate him.

He flashed another smile. '*Obrigado*,' he replied in perfect Portuguese. He'd spent a lot of time studying the nuances of the language.

Just as he'd spent a lot of time setting up the events set to culminate in the very near future. For what he planned, there could be no room for misunderstanding. Or failure.

About to head towards the double doors that led to the ballroom, he paused. 'You said most of the guests are here. Benedicto da Costa and his family. Are they here?' he asked sharply.

The blonde's smile slipped a little. Theo didn't need to guess why. The da Costa family had a certain reputation. Benedicto especially had one that struck fear into the hearts of common men.

It was a good thing Theo wasn't a common man.

The blonde nodded. 'Yes, the whole family arrived half an hour ago.'

He smiled at her, effectively hiding the emotions bubbling beneath his skin. 'You've been very helpful.'

Her seductive smile slid back into place. Before she could grow bolder and attempt to ingratiate herself further, he turned and walked away.

Anticipation thrummed through his veins, as it had ever

since he'd received concrete evidence that Benedicto da Costa was the man he sought. The road to discovery had been long and hard, fraught with pitfalls and the danger of letting his emotions override his clear thinking.

But Theo was nothing if not meticulous in his planning. It was the reason he was chief troubleshooter and risk-assessor for his family's global conglomerate, Pantelides Inc.

He didn't believe in fate but even he couldn't dismiss the soul-deep certainty that his chosen profession had led him to Rio, and to the man who'd shattered what had remained of his tattered childhood twelve years ago.

Every instinct in his body yearned to take this to the ultimate level. To rip away the veneer of sophistication and urbanity he'd been forced to operate behind.

To claim his revenge. Here. Now.

Soon...

He grimaced as he thought of his phone call with his brother.

Ari was beginning to suspect Theo's motives for remaining in Rio.

But, despite the pressure from his family, neither Ari nor Sakis, his older brothers, would dare to stop him. He was very much his own man, in complete control of his destiny.

But that didn't mean Ari wouldn't try to dissuade him from his objective if he'd known what was going on. His oldest brother took his role as the family patriarch extremely seriously. After all, he'd had to step up after the secure family unit he'd known for his formative years had suddenly and viciously detonated from the inside out. After his father had betrayed them in the worst possible way.

Theo only thanked God that Ari's radar had been momentarily dulled by his newfound happiness with his fiancé, Perla, and the anticipated arrival of their first child.

No, he wouldn't be able to stop him. But Ari...was Ari.

Theo shrugged off thoughts of his family as he neared

the ballroom doors. He deliberately relaxed his tense shoulders and breathed out.

She was the first thing he saw when he walked in. His lips started to curl at his clichéd thought but then he realised she'd done it deliberately.

The dress code for this event had been strictly black and white.

She wore red. And not just any red. Her gown was blood-red, provocatively cut, and it lovingly melded to her figure in a way that made red-blooded males stop and stare.

Inez da Costa.

Youngest child of Benedicto. Twenty-four, socialite… seductress.

Against his will, Theo's breath caught as his gaze followed the supple curve of a breast, a trim waist and the flare of her hips.

He knew each and every last detail of the da Costas. For his plan to succeed, he'd had to do what he did best. Dig deep and extract every last ounce of information until he could recite every line in the six-inch dossier in his sleep.

Inez da Costa was no better than her father and brother. But where they used brute force, blackmail and thuggery, she used her body.

He wasn't surprised lesser men fell for her Marilyn Monroe figure. A true hourglass shape was rare to find these days. But Inez da Costa owned her voluptuousness and confidently wielded it to her advantage. Theo's gaze lingered on her hips until she moved again, dropping into conversation with the consummate ease of a practised socialite. She had guests eating out of her hands, leaning in close to catch her words, following her avidly when she moved away.

As he advanced further into the room, she turned to speak to another male guest. The curve of her bottom swung into Theo's eye line, and he cursed under his breath as heat raced up through his groin.

Hell, no.

His fists curled, willing his body's unwanted reaction away. It had been a while since he'd indulged in a mindless, no-holds-barred liaison. But this was most definitely not the time for a physical reminder, and the instigator of that reminder was most definitely not the woman he would choose to end his short dry spell with.

He exhaled in a slow, even stream, letting the roiling in his gut abate and his equilibrium return.

As he made his way down the stairs to join the guests, the deep-seated certainty that he was meant to be here—in the right place at the right time—flared high.

If Pietro da Costa's love of excess hadn't led him down the path of biting off more than he could chew, this time in the form of commissioning a top-of-the-line Pantelides super-yacht he could ill afford, Theo wouldn't have flown down to Rio to look into the da Costas' finances three years ago.

He wouldn't have become privy to the carefully hidden financial paper trail that had led right back to Athens and to his own father's shady dealings almost a decade and a half ago.

He wouldn't have dug deeper and discovered the consequences of those dealings for his family. And for him personally.

Memory stirred the unwanted threads of anxiety until it threatened to push its way under his control like Japanese knotweed. Gritting his jaw, he smashed down on the poisonous emotion that had taken too much from him already. He was no longer that frightened boy unable to stem his fears or chase away the screaming nightmares that plagued him.

He'd learned to accept them as part of his life, had woven them into the fabric of his existence and in doing so had triumphed over them. Which wasn't to say he wasn't determined to make those who'd temporarily taken power from him pay dearly for that error. No, that mission he was very much looking forward to.

Focusing his gaze across the room to where Benedicto and his son held court among Rio's movers and shakers, he strategised how best to approach his quarry.

Despite the suave exterior he tried to portray with his tailor-made suit and carefully cropped hair, Benedicto could never mask his lizard-like character for very long. His sharp, angular face and reptilian eyes held a cruelty that was instinctively felt by those around him. And Theo knew that he honed that characteristic to superb effect when needed. He bullied when charm failed, resulting in the fact that half of the people in this room had attended the fund-raiser tonight just to stay on Benedicto's good side.

Five years ago, Benedicto had made his political aspirations very clear, and since then he'd been paving the way for his rise to power through mostly unsavoury means.

The same unsavoury means Theo's own father had used to bring shame and devastation to his family.

Grabbing a glass of champagne, Theo sipped it as he slowly worked his way deeper into the room, exchanging pleasantries with ministers and dignitaries who were eager to find favour with the Pantelides name.

He noticed the moment Benedicto and Pietro zeroed in on his presence. Bow ties were surreptitiously straightened. Smiles grew wider and spines straighter.

He suppressed a smile, deliberately turned his back on the father and son and made a beeline for where the daughter was smiling up at Alfonso Delgado, the Brazilian millionaire philanthropist, who was her latest prey.

'If you want me to host a gala for you, Alfonso, all you have to do is say the word. My mother used to be able to throw events like these together in her sleep and I've been told that I've inherited her talent. Or do you doubt my talents?' Her head tilted in a coquettish move that most definitely would've made Theo snort, had his eyes not been drawn to the sleek line of her smooth neck.

Alfonso smiled, his expression beginning to closely resemble adoration.

Forcing himself not to openly grimace, Theo took another sip of champagne and brushed off an acquaintance who tried to catch his eye.

'No one in their right mind would doubt your talent. Perhaps we can discuss it over dinner one night this week?'

The smile that started to curve her full, glossy lips forced another punch of heat through him. 'Of course, I would love to. We can also discuss that pledge you made to support my father's campaign…?'

Theo moved closer, deliberately encroaching on the space between the two people in the centre of the room.

Alfonso's attention jerked towards him and his smile changed from playboy-charming to friendly welcome.

'*Amigo*, I wasn't aware that you had returned to my beloved country. It seems we cannot keep you away.'

'For what I need to achieve in Rio, wild horses couldn't keep me away,' he replied, deliberately keeping himself from glancing at the woman who stood next to Alfonso. He breathed in and caught her scent—expensive but subtle, a seductive whisper of flowers and warm sunshine.

His friend's eyes gleamed. 'Speaking of horses—'

Theo shook his head. 'No, Alfonso, your racehorses don't interest me. Speedboat racing, on the other hand… Just say the word and I'll kick your ass from one end of the Copacabana to the other.'

Alfonso laughed. 'No can do, my friend. Everyone knows underneath that tuxedo you're part shark. I prefer to take my chances on land.'

A delicate clearing of a throat made Alfonso turn, a smile of apology appearing on his face as he slipped back into playboy mode. For the ten years that Theo had known him, Alfonso had had a weakness for curvy brunettes.

Inez da Costa had curves that required their own danger

signs. His friend risked being easy prey for whatever the da Costas had in mind for him.

'Apologies, *querida*. Please allow me to introduce you to—'

Theo stopped him with a firm hand on his shoulder. 'I'm perfectly capable of making my own introductions. Right now, I think you're needed elsewhere.'

Alfonso's eyes widened in confusion. 'Elsewhere?'

Theo leaned and whispered in his friend's ear. Shock and anger registered on Alfonso's face before his jaw clenched and he reined his emotions back in. His gaze slid to the woman next to him and returned to Theo's.

Taking in a deep breath, he held out his hand. 'I guess I owe you one, my friend.'

Theo took the proffered hand. 'You owe me several, but who's counting?'

'And I shall repay you. *Até a próxima*.'

'Until next time,' Theo repeated. He heard the disbelieving gasp from Inez da Costa as Alfonso walked away without another glance in her direction.

A thread of satisfaction oozed through him as he tracked his friend to the ballroom doors. Scanning the room, he saw Pietro da Costa's thunderous look in his sister's direction.

Theo lifted his glass to his lips and took a lazy sip then turned his attention to Inez da Costa.

Her large brown eyes were filled with anger as she glared at him.

'Who the devil are you and what did you say to Alfonso?'

CHAPTER TWO

THEO DIDN'T LIKE the idea that he'd been less than one hundred per cent thorough in covering every angle in his investigations.

His surveillance of Inez da Costa had been from afar simply because until recently he'd deemed her involvement in his investigation peripheral at best.

The extent of her role in her father's organisation had only come to light a few days ago. But even then he should've recognised her power.

Now, at the first proper sight of what was turning out to be the jewel in Benedicto da Costa's crown, the essential cog in the sinister wheel that his enemy was intent on using to his full advantage, he experienced a pulse of heat so strong, so powerful, he sucked in a quick breath.

Up close, Inez da Costa's heart-shaped face was flawless…breathtaking, her skin a silky, vibrant complexion even the best cosmetics couldn't hope to produce.

Not that she hadn't attempted to enhance her beauty even further. Her make-up was impeccable, her lids smoky in a way that drew attention to her wide, doe-like stare.

Long-lashed eyes that bored into him with unwavering demand and a healthy dose of suspicion. Her nose flared with pure Latin ire and her full lips parted as she released another agitated breath.

The pictures in his dossier did her no justice at all. Flesh and blood wrapped in red silk from cleavage to toe, she made his senses ignite in a way he hadn't felt in a long time. The earlier pull deep in his groin returned. Harder.

'I asked you a question.' Her voice held a hint of dark sultriness that reminded him of a warm Santorini evening spent drinking ouzo on a deserted beach. And the mouth that framed her words, painted a deep matt red, reminded him of what happened on the beach after the ouzo had been consumed and inhibitions were at their loosest.

She glanced over his shoulder and Theo's jaw clenched at the thought that she was more concerned with the departing Alfonso than she was with him.

'Why is one of my guests walking out the door right this moment?'

'I told him that if he didn't want a noose slipped around his neck before he was ready to be hog-tied, he needed to stay away from you.'

Her parted mouth gaped wider, showing a row of perfect white teeth. *'Excuse me—?'*

'You're excused.'

Eyes the colour of dark caramel flashed. 'How dare you refer to me as such—?'

'Careful, *anjo*, you're causing a scene. *Pai* would not be happy to see his event ruined by a tantrum now, would he?'

Her eyes didn't stray from his, her stare direct and cutting in a way that made it difficult for him to look away. Or maybe it was because, despite the boldly challenging stare, he spied a quickly hidden vulnerability that tweaked his radar?

'I don't know who you think you are but perhaps you need to be educated in the etiquette of social gatherings. You don't deliberately set out to insult your host or—'

'My intention was quite simple. I wanted to get rid of the competition.'

'The *competition?*'

The doors to the larger ballroom where the dinner fund-raiser was to be held were thrown open. Theo turned to her. 'Yes. And now Alfonso's gone, I have you all to myself. And, as to who I am, I'm Theo Pantelides, your VIP guest of honour. Maybe you should add another bullet point to your rules of etiquette. That the hostess should know who her most important guests are?'

Her mouth started to drop open but she caught her reaction and pursed her lips.

'You're Theo Pantelides?' she muttered.

'Yes, so I suggest you make nice with me to stop me from leaving. One high net worth guest departing before dinner may be excusable. Barely. Two will certainly not go down well with your crowd. Now, smile and take my arm.'

Inez reeled under the steely punch packed behind the suave, sophisticated exterior and charming smile.

Theo Pantelides.

This was the man her father and Pietro had talked about. The one who would be taking over majority shares in Da Costa Holdings until after the elections. The one her brother Pietro had referred to as an arrogant bastard.

Well, he certainly was arrogant all right. The swiftness with which he'd dispatched Alfonso and assumed he could control her confirmed that assertion. As to whether he was a true bastard...well, that was something to be determined. But so far all signs pointed in that direction.

What she hadn't been aware of was that the man spoken of with such scorn would be so...visually breathtaking.

'I thought you would be older.' The words tripped from her tongue before she could stop herself.

'As opposed to young, virile and unbelievably handsome?' he drawled.

Shock jolted though her at his unapologetic, irritatingly justified confidence. Because he undeniably was. A full head of vibrant jet-black hair was common enough among her countrymen. Even his hazel eyes, sculpted cheekbones and square jaw were conventional in the polo-loving jet set crowd her father and brother encouraged her to associate with.

On this man, though, the whole combination had been elevated several hundred notches to an entirely different level of magnetism that demanded attention and got it. There was a quality about the way he carried himself, his broad shoulders unyielding, that spelled a tough inner core anyone would be foolish to mess with.

And yet that danger Inez could feel rising off him was… compelling. Alluring.

She found her gaze drifting over his face, past the tiny dimple in his chin to the dark bronze throat as he lazily swallowed a mouthful of champagne.

She inhaled a sharp dart of air as she watched his Adam's apple move. Then jerked back when her fingers flexed suddenly with the urge to touch him there.

Santa Maria!

She fought to remember her anger at this stranger. As much as she detested her role in tonight's events—the blatant begging for campaign funds disguised as a charity event—she couldn't let opportunities slip through her fingers.

It was the deal she'd made with her father.

An education in return for serving her time. In six short weeks she would be free to pursue her dreams. Free of her father's influence, of the sleazy, horrifying rumours that had been part of her childhood and what had driven her mother to quiet despair when she thought she wasn't being observed.

She needed to focus, not moon over how coarse this arrogant stranger's faintly stubbled jaw would feel against her skin.

'*Make nice?* After you rudely interrupted my conversation and sent my guest for the evening running without so much as a goodbye?'

'Think about that for a minute. Do you really want a man who would abandon you so easily on the strength of a few whispered words?'

Genuine anger replaced the momentary sensory aberration. 'That you needed to whisper those words instead of state them in my hearing makes me wonder just how confident you are of your manhood.'

Inez was used to being the butt of male jokes. Pietro and her father had mocked and dismissed her career ambitions until the day she'd picked up her suitcase and threatened to leave home for good.

But she was still shocked when the man in front of her threw back his head and laughed. Even more so when the sight of his strong white teeth and the genuine twinkling merriment in his eyes sent her pulse racing. An alien tingling started in her belly and spread outward like fractured lightning.

'Did I say something funny?'

Light hazel eyes speared hers. 'I've been challenged on a lot of things, *querida*, but never over my manhood.'

The political career her father so desperately craved produced men who could fake confidence with the best of them. She'd seen political candidates on a clear losing streak fake bravado until they were on the verge of looking totally ridiculous.

This man oozed confidence and power so very effortlessly it was like a second skin. Couple those two elements with the dangerous magnetism she could feel and Theo Pantelides was positively lethal.

Over her thundering heartbeat, she heard the master of ceremonies announce that the fund-raiser she'd so carefully orchestrated—the platform that would see her achieve her freedom—was about to begin.

Beyond one broad shoulder of the man who seemed to have sucked the air from the large ballroom, she saw her father and Pietro heading towards her.

Her father would want to know what had happened to Alfonso. The Brazilian businessman had promised to host a polo match on his large ranch where he bred the finest thoroughbreds. Securing a time and a date and a campaign donation had been her job tonight.

A much needed win this man had cost her.

Frustrated anger flared anew.

'This can be resolved very easily, Inez,' Theo Pantelides murmured in her ear. His voice was deep. Alluring. To hear him use her given name, the version her half-American mother had so lovingly bestowed on her, made her momentarily lose her bearings. A state that worsened when his hot breath washed over her neck.

Barely managing to suppress a shiver, she snapped herself back into focus. 'Don't say my name. In fact, don't speak to me. Just...just go away!'

Inez knew she was on the verge of displaying childish behaviour but she needed to regroup quickly, find a solution to a situation that had been so cut and dried fifteen minutes ago.

She watched her father and brother approach and the dart of pain that resided beneath her breastbone twisted. For a long time she'd yearned for a connection with them, especially after *Mãe* had been so cruelly ripped from their lives following a fall from a racehorse a week before Inez's eighteenth birthday. But she'd soon realised that she was alone in the pain and loneliness brought on by the loss of the mother who'd been her everything. Pietro had been given no time to grieve before their father had stepped up his grooming campaign. As for Benedicto himself, he'd barely finished burying his wife before resuming his relentless pursuit of political power.

The only other male she'd foolishly thought was honourable had turned out to be just as ruthlessly power-hungry as the men in her family.

Constantine Blanco—one lesson well and truly learned.

'I see the rumours were false after all,' the man who loomed, large and imposing, in front of her drawled in that deep voice of his, capturing her attention so effortlessly.

She pushed down the bitterness that swirled through her at the thought of what she'd allowed to happen with Constantine. How low she'd sunk in her need for love and a desire for a connection.

'What rumours?' She infused a carelessness in her voice she was far from feeling.

'The ones that said you exhibit grace and charm with each bat of your eyelids. At the moment all I can see is a hellcat intent on scoring grooves into my skin.'

'Then I suggest you stay away from me. I wouldn't want to ruin your *unbelievably handsome* face now, would I?'

She hurried away from his magnetic presence towards where the tables had been set out with highly polished sterling silver cutlery and exquisitely cut crystal. At twenty thousand dollars a plate, the event was ostensibly to raise money for the children trapped within Rio's *favelas*, a cause dear to her heart.

Shame it had to be tainted with power-hungry sharks, mild threats to secure votes and…devastatingly handsome rogues with piercing hazel eyes who made her breath catch in a frighteningly exciting way…

The direction of her thoughts made her stumble lightly. Catching herself, she smiled at a guest who slid her a concerned glance.

Each table was set for eight. Her father had insisted their table was placed in the centre, where all eyes would be on them.

With Alfonso's unexpected departure, the empty seat would stick out like the proverbial sore thumb once the Secretary of State and his wife and the other power couple had taken their places.

She had no choice but to bump someone to the high table. All she needed to figure out was who—

'Staring at the empty seat will not make your departed guest suddenly reappear, *senhorita*,' the deep voice uttered from behind her.

That hot shiver swept up her spine again.

Before she could summon an appropriately scathing retort, her chair and the one bearing Alfonso's name were pulled back.

'What are you doing?' she demanded heatedly under her breath. She continued to stare down at the place setting, unwilling to look up into those hazel eyes. Something in their light depths made her hyperaware of her body, of her increased heartbeat. As if she was prey and he was the merciless predator.

It was preposterous. She didn't like it. But it was undeniable.

'Saving your skin. Now, smile and play along.'

'I'm not a puppet. I don't smile on command.'

'Try. Unless you want to spend the rest of the evening sitting next to the equivalent of an elephant in the ballroom?'

Something in his voice made her forget her vow not to look into his eyes. Something...peculiar. Her head snapped up before she could stop herself.

Their eyes clashed. And she found herself in that hyperaware state again. She forced herself to breathe through it. 'You created the very situation you now seem intent on fixing. Why don't you save us both time and state what your agenda is?'

A look passed over his face. Too quickly for her to decipher but whatever it was made her breath catch in a totally different way from before. Warning spiked the hairs on her nape.

'I merely want to redress the situation a little. And, as talented as you seem to think you are at hiding it, I can see my actions caused you distress. Let me help make it better.'

'So you cause me grief then swoop in to save me like a knight in shining armour?'

'I'm no one's knight, *senhorita*. And I prefer Armani to armour.'

He pointedly held out her seat.

Casting a swift glance around, Inez saw that they were attracting attention. Short of causing a scene, there was nothing she could do. Willing her facial muscles to relax into a cordial smile, she slowly sat down and watched as Theo Pantelides folded himself into the seat next to her.

He reached for his champagne at the same time as she reached for her water glass. The brush of his knuckle against her wrist made her jump.

'Relax, *anjo*. I've got this,' came the smooth, deep reassurance.

A hysterical laugh bubbled up her throat, curbed at the last minute by a cough. 'Pardon me if that assurance brings me very little comfort.'

He lifted the glass she'd abandoned and held it out to her. 'Tell me, what's the worst that could happen?'

She took the glass and stared into the sparkling water. The need to moisten her dry throat had receded. 'Believe me, the worst already has happened.'

For a long time she'd hidden from the truth—that her father had his heir, and she was a useless spare part.

Pain writhed through her and her breath grew shaky as her throat clogged with anger and bitterness.

'Get yourself together. Now isn't the time to fall apart. Trust me, Delgado may be a good friend but he has a wandering eye.' The hard bite to his tone cut a path through her emotions.

Setting the glass down, she faced him. 'I have been toyed with enough to last me a century, and I know your business here tonight has nothing to do with me, so do me a favour, *senhor*, and tell me straight—what do you want?' she whispered fiercely. She noted vaguely that her heartbeat was once again on rapid acceleration to sky-high. Her fingers shook and her belly churned with emotions she couldn't have named to save her life.

'First of all, cut out the *senhor* bit. If you want to address me in any way, call me Theo.'

'I will address you how I see fit, Mr Pantelides. And I see that once again you have failed to give me a straight answer.'

'No, I've failed to jump when you say. You need to be taught a little patience, *anjo*.'

She lifted a deliberately mocking brow. 'And you propose to be the one to teach me?'

That wide, breathtaking smile appeared again. Just like that, her pulse leapt then galloped with a speed even the finest racehorse would've strained to match.

What was going on here?

'Only if you ask nicely.'

She was searching for an appropriately cutting response when her father reached the table with the rest of the guests.

He cast her a narrow-eyed glance before his gaze slid to Theo Pantelides.

'Mr Pantelides, I had hoped for a few minutes of your time before the evening started properly,' her father said as he took his seat across the table.

Inez wasn't sure whether she imagined the slight stiffening in the posture of the man beside her. Her senses were too highly strung for her to trust their accuracy. Searching his profile as he stared at her father, nothing in his face gave any indication as to his true feelings.

'I'm all for mixing business with pleasure. However, I draw the line at mixing business with the plight of the poor. Let the *favela* kids have their cause heard. *Then* we will attend to business.'

The firm put-down sent an arctic chill around the table. The Secretary's wife gave a visible gasp and her skin blanched beneath her overdone make-up. Pietro, who'd just approached the table as Theo replied, gripped the back of his chair, anger embedded in his face.

Silence reigned for several fraught seconds. Her father flicked a glance at Pietro, who yanked back his seat and sat down. The hands her brother placed on the table were curled into fists and for a moment Inez wondered if his famous temper was about to be let loose on their guests.

Benedicto smiled at Theo. 'Of course. This cause is extremely dear to my heart. My own mother was brought up in the *favelas*.'

'As indeed you were, no?' Theo queried silkily.

Again, the Secretary's wife gasped. She reached for her wine glass and took a quick gulp. When she went to take another, her husband surreptitiously stayed her hand and sent her a stern disapproving look.

Her father nodded to the waiter, who stood poised with a bottle of the finest red wine. He took his time to savour his first sip before he answered.

'You are quite mistaken, Mr Pantelides. My mother managed to escape the fate most of her lot failed to and bettered her life long before she bore me. But I inherited her fighting spirit and her determination to do what I can for the bleak place she once called home.'

Theo's eyebrow quirked. 'Right. I may have been misinformed, then,' he said, although his dry tone suggested otherwise.

'I assure you misinformation is rife when it comes to the ploys of political opponents. And I have been told more than once that only a foolish man believes everything he reads in the papers.'

Theo slashed a smile that had a definite edge to it across the table. 'Trust me, I know a thing or two about what lengths newspapers will go to achieve a headline.'

'We seem to have lost Alfonso. Would you care to explain his absence, Inez?' Pietro's voice slid through the conversation.

Anger still rippled off him and Inez was acutely aware that he hadn't directly addressed Theo Pantelides.

Before she could speak, the man in question turned to her brother. 'He was called away suddenly. Emergency business elsewhere. Couldn't be helped. Since I was there when he took his leave, your sister offered me his seat and I graciously accepted, didn't you, *anjo*?'

She saw Pietro's eyes visibly widen at the blatant endearment. Just as swiftly, they narrowed and she could almost see the wheels spinning in a different direction as his gaze swung between her and Theo Pantelides.

No! Never! Her fingers curled into fists and she glared at him until he looked away.

'Well, perhaps Delgado's loss is our gain, *sim*?' her father prompted.

Again Theo smiled. Again her heart thudded hard at the sheer magnetism of his smile, even though it sorely lacked any humour.

The man was an enigma. He'd inveigled his way onto the top table, then proceeded to insult his host, just as he'd insulted her.

Inez had little doubt her father would unleash his anger at the slight later.

But right now she was more puzzled by the man next to her. What was his game plan? If he was in a position to acquire a controlling share of their company then clearly he was a man of considerable means. But he wasn't Brazilian. That much she knew. So why was he interested in her father's political ambitions?

She realised she was staring when that proud head turned and gold-flecked hazel eyes captured hers, one eyebrow quirked in amusement.

Hastily averting her gaze, she picked up her glass and took another sip.

Thankfully, the master of ceremonies chose that moment to climb onto the podium to announce the first course and the first speaker.

Inez barely tasted the salmon mousse and the wine that

accompanied it. Nor did she absorb the speech given by the health minister about what was being done to help the poor.

Her hyperawareness of the man beside her interfered with her ability to think straight. The last time she'd felt anything remotely like this, she'd wandered down a path she'd hated herself for ever since. She'd almost given herself to a man who had no use for her besides using her as a pawn.

Never again!

Six more weeks. She needed to focus on that. Once her father was on his campaign trail, she could start her new life.

She'd heard the rumours about her father's ruthless beginnings when she was growing up; a couple of her school friends had whispered about unsavoury dealings her father had been involved in. Inez had never found concrete proof. The one time she'd asked her mother, she'd been quickly admonished not to believe lies about her family.

At the time, she'd assured herself that they weren't true. But the passage of time had whittled away that assurance. Now, with each day that passed, she suspected differently.

'You look as if the world is coming to an end, *anjo*,' the man she was desperately trying to ignore murmured. Again the endearment rolled off his tongue in a deep, seductive murmur that sent shivery awareness cascading over her skin.

'I hope you're not going to ask me to smile again, because—' She gasped as he took her hand and lifted it to his mouth.

Firm, warm lips brushed her skin and Inez's stomach dipped in sensual free fall that took her breath away. Desperately, she tried to snatch her hand back.

'What the hell do you think you're doing?' she snapped.

'Helping you. Relax. If you continue to look at me like you want to claw my eyes out, this won't work.'

'What exactly *is* this? And why on earth should I play along?'

'Your brother and father are still wondering why Delgado

left so abruptly. Do you want to suffer the third degree later or will you let me help you make it all go away?'

She eyed him suspiciously. The notion that there was something going on behind that smooth, charismatic façade didn't dissipate. In fact, it escalated as he stared down at her, his features enigmatic save for that smile that lingered on his wide, sexy mouth.

'Why do you want to help me?' Again she tried to take back her hand but he held on, one thumb smoothing over her inner wrist. Blood surged through her veins at his touch, her pulse racing at the spot that he so expertly explored.

'Because I'm hoping it would persuade you to have lunch with me tomorrow,' he replied.

His gaze flicked across the table. Although his expression didn't change, she again sensed the tension that hovered on the edge of his civility. This man didn't like her family. Which begged the question: what was he doing here investing in their company?

He swung that intense stare back to her and she lost her train of thought. Grabbing it back, she shook her head.

'I'll have to refuse the lunch offer, I'm afraid. I have other plans.'

'Dinner, then?'

'I have plans then, too. Besides, don't you have business with my father tomorrow?'

'Our business won't take longer than me signing on a dotted line.'

'A dotted line that gives you a permanent controlling share in my family's company?'

His eyes gleamed. 'Not permanent. Only until I have what I want.'

CHAPTER THREE

'And what is it you want?'

'For now? Lunch. Tomorrow. With you.' Another pass of his thumb over her pulse.

Another roll of sensation deep in her belly. The temptation to say yes suddenly overcame her, despite the warning bells shrieking at the back of her mind.

She forced herself to heed those warning bells. Her painfully short foray into a relationship had taught her that good looks and charm often hid an agenda that would most likely not benefit her or her heart. And Theo Pantelides had metaphorical skull and crossbones stamped all over him.

'The answer is still no,' she replied, a lot sharper than she'd intended.

His lips compressed but he shrugged. As if her answer hadn't fazed him.

And it probably hadn't. He was one of those men who drew women like bees to pollen. He could probably secure a lunch date with half of the women in this room and tempt the other married half into sin should he choose to.

With his dark, exquisite looks and deep sexy voice, he could have any woman he chose to display even the mildest interest in.

The thought that he would do just such a thing punched so fierce a reaction in her belly that she suppressed a shocked gasp.

What on earth is wrong with me? She needed to get herself back under control before she did something foolish—like discard her plans for tomorrow in favour of spending more time with this infuriatingly self-assured, visually stunning man.

Giving herself a fierce pep talk, she pulled her hand from his grasp.

She folded her hand in her lap and wrapped her other hand over her wrist. But suddenly her own touch felt…inadequate.

She was saved from exploring the peculiar feeling when the lights dimmed and the projector started reeling pictures of miles and miles of rusted shingle roofs that formed the world famous Rio *favelas.*

Her father climbed onto the podium to begin his speech.

The tale of despair-driven prostitution, violence, gang warfare and kidnapping of innocents, and the need to do whatever was needed to help was one she'd heard at many fund-raisers and charity dinners.

She clenched her fist. Knowing that half the people in here, dripping in diamonds and tuxedos worth several thousand dollars, would've forgotten the plight of the *favela* residents by the time dessert was served made her silently scream in frustration.

The need to get up, to walk out almost overwhelmed her but she stayed put.

There would be no running. No walking away from the work she'd committed herself to, nor walking away from the formative minds that were depending on her.

Fierce pride tightened her chest at the part she was playing in the young lives under her charge. And the fact that she'd managed to change that part of her own life without her father or brother's interference.

She refocused as her father finished his speech to rousing applause. The projector was shut off and the lights grew brighter.

She reached forward for her glass of wine and noticed that she was once again the focus of Theo's gaze.

'Should I be offended that I'm being so comprehensively ignored?' he asked.

'It's not a state you're used to, I expect?' With her surroundings once more in focus, she noticed the looks he was getting from women on other tables. She didn't delude herself that any of them were interested in his views on politics or world peace. No, each and every one of them would vie for much more personal, much more physical contact with the lean, broad-shouldered man next to her, whose hands casually caressed his wine glass stem in a way that made her think indecent thoughts.

She noticed the young famous actress on the next table where Theo should have been sitting gazing over at him, and again felt the sharp edge of an unknown emotion pierce her insides.

His smile grew hard. 'You'd be surprised.'

Curiosity brought her gaze back to his. 'Would I? How?'

'That question makes me think you've formed an opinion of me.'

'And that answer convinces me that you're very good at deflecting. You may fool others, but you do not fool me.'

He stared at her for a moment before one corner of his mouth lifted. Abruptly, he stood and held out his hand. 'Dance with me, *anjo*, and enlighten me further as to what you think you know about me.'

The demand was silky and yet implacable. In full view of the other guests, her refusal would be extremely discourteous.

Her heart hammered as she slowly slid her hand into his and let him draw her to her feet.

Emotions she was trying and failing to suppress flared up at the warmth and firmness of his grip. Fervently, she prayed for time to speed up, for the evening to end so she could be free of this man. Her reaction to him was puzzling in the extreme and the notion that she was being toyed with unsettled her more with each passing second.

As they skirted the table to head for the dance floor, her gaze met her father's. Expecting approval for accommodating the man whose business he was so obviously keen to garner, she was taken aback when she saw his icy disapproval.

Through the elite Rio grapevine she knew Alfonso Delgado's net worth and knew he couldn't afford to acquire a controlling share of Da Costa Holdings. So why did her father disapprove of a man who was clearly superior in monetary worth to Alfonso?

'You really have to do better with your social skills than this. Or I'll have to do something drastic to retain your attention.' The hard bite to Theo's voice slashed through her thoughts. 'Or were you really that into Delgado?'

'No, I wasn't.'

Her immediate denial seemed to pacify him. 'Then tell me what's on your mind.'

Inez found herself speaking before she could snap at him not to issue orders. 'Have you ever found yourself in a position where everything you do turns out wrong, no matter how hard you try?'

'There have been a few instances.' He pulled her close and slid an arm around her back. Heat transmitted to her skin via the soft material of her dress and flooded through her body. This close, his scent washed over her. Strong but not overpowering, masculine and heady in a way that made her want to draw even closer, touch her mouth to the bronze skin just above his collar.

Deus!

'You think this is one of those occasions for you?'

'I don't think; I know.'

'Why?'

Her laugh grated its way up her throat. 'Because I have a perfectly functioning brain.'

'You're worried because your father and brother are displeased with you?'

'Everything else this evening has gone according to plan except…'

'Delgado. You're worried that your father offered you up on a silver platter because he seems to think you're a prize worth winning and now he'll demand to know what you did wrong.'

Her eyes snapped to his, the insult surprisingly painful. 'What do you mean by *seems to think*? What do you know about my father? Or about me, for that matter?'

Theo forced himself not to tense at the question. Or let the fact that her body seemed to fit so perfectly in his arms impact on his thinking abilities. 'Enough.'

'Do you always go around making unfounded remarks about someone you've just met?'

He let a small smile play over his mouth. 'Enlighten me, then. Are you a prize worth winning?'

'There's no point enlightening you because it will serve no useful purpose. After tonight you and I will never meet again.'

She took a firm step back. Attempted to prise herself out of his arms. He held her easily, willing back the thrum of anger and bitterness that rose like bile in his throat.

'Never say never, *anjo*.'

Her fiery brown eyes glared at him. 'Don't.'

He feigned innocence. 'Don't what?'

'Don't keep calling me that.'

'You don't like it?'

'You have no right to slap a pet name on someone you just met.'

The hand holding hers tightened. 'Calm down—'

'No, I won't calm down. I'm not an angel. I'm certainly not *your* angel.'

'Inez.' A warning, subtle but effective.

Inez's pulse stalled, then thundered wildly through her veins.

'Don't,' she whispered again. Only this time she wasn't sure what she pleaded for.

He leaned closer until his mouth was an inch from her ear. When he breathed out, warmth teased her earlobe. 'Don't use your given name? It's either that or *anjo*. All the other words are only appropriate for the bedroom.'

Heat flamed through her belly as indecent thoughts of rumpled sheets, sweaty bodies and incandescent pleasure reeled through her mind.

She shook her head to dispel the images and heard his low laugh.

When she stared up at him, his eyes blazed down at her with a hunger that smashed through her body. Her nipples slowly hardened and the fire raged higher as his lips parted on another heart-stopping smile. Unable to help herself, her eyes dropped to the sensual curve of his mouth.

'I think it's my turn to say *don't*. Not if you don't want to be thrown over my shoulder and raced to the nearest cave.'

She forced a laugh despite the sensations rushing through her. 'This is the twenty-first century, *senhor*.'

'But what I'm feeling right now isn't. It's very basic. Primeval, in fact.'

He swerved her out of the path of another couple and used the move to draw her even closer. At the fierce evidence of his arousal against her stomach, Inez swallowed hard.

Her confusion escalated.

Constantine had been charismatic and breathtaking in his own right. But he'd never made her feel like *this*, not even in the beginning…before everything had gone disastrously wrong.

Thinking of the man who'd broken her heart and betrayed her so cruelly threw much needed ice over her heated senses. She'd made a fool of herself over one man. Foolishly believed he was the answer to her prayers. She was wise enough now to know Theo Pantelides wasn't the answer to any prayer, unless it was the crash and burn type.

'I believe I've fulfilled my obligatory dance duty to you. Perhaps you'd like to find a more unwitting female to club over the head and drag to your cave?' She injected as much indifference into her voice as possible.

'That won't be necessary. I've already found what I'm looking for.'

Theo watched several emotions chase over her features before Inez da Costa regained her impeccable hostess persona.

Although he silently cursed himself for his physical reaction, he was thankful she realised her effect on him.

Let her think she held the power. Allow her to believe that he could be manipulated to her advantage. Or, rather, her father's advantage.

Her reaction to Delgado's departure had shown him that fulfilling her role as her father's Venus flytrap was most important to Inez da Costa. Or was it something else? Did she hope to bag *herself* a millionaire while serving her father's purpose? She came from a family ruthless in its pursuit of wealth and power. Was that her underlying agenda?

That knowledge demanded that he rethink his strategy. The conclusion he'd arrived at was surprising but easily adaptable.

He had an opportunity to kill a few more birds with one stone. With any luck, he would conclude his business in Rio in a far shorter time than he'd already anticipated if he played his cards right.

Inez tried to wrench herself from his grasp once more. The primitive feelings he'd mentioned so casually a moment ago resurfaced. When she tugged harder, he forced himself to release her. Her soft hand slid from his, leaving a trail of sensation that made his groin pound and his blood heat.

The plan he'd hatched solidified as he gazed down into

her heart-shaped face, saw her fighting to stop her clear agitation from messing with her breathing.

Theo hid a smile.

Either she was offended at his primitive declaration or she was turned on by it. Since she wasn't slapping his face, he concluded that it was the latter.

His gaze dropped lower, and the sight of her tightly beaded nipples against her gown made his own breathing stall in his chest. Lower still, her tiny waist gave way to those tempting hips that his palms ached to explore.

Even as he talked himself into believing his reaction would ultimately serve his purpose, a part of Theo was forced to acknowledge that he hadn't reacted this strongly to a woman in a very long time. Everything about her brought his senses to roaring life in a way only the thought of revenge had for the past decade.

Revenge...retribution over the person who had created such chaos in his life.

He gritted his teeth as the sound of tinkling laughter and animated conversation refocused his mind to his task and purpose.

'Good evening, Mr Pantelides. I hope you enjoy the rest of your evening,' Inez said stiltedly.

She turned and walked off the dance floor before he could reply. Not that he felt like replying. Although he'd mostly kept on track throughout the evening, a large part of him had become far too consumed by her seductive presence.

Inez da Costa was only one part of the game. To keep on track he needed to keep his head in the *whole* game.

He headed for the bar and sensed the moment Benedicto and his son halted their conversation and moved pincer-like towards him.

Dreaded anxiety washed over his senses but he forced himself to breathe through it.

I am no longer in that dark, cold place. I am in light. I am free...

He tersely repeated the short statement under his breath as he tossed back the shot of vodka and set it down with cold, precise care.

He was no longer weak. No longer helpless.

And he most certainly would never be put in a position to beg for his life. Ever again.

By the time they reached him, he'd regained control of his body.

'Senhor Pantelides—'

'We're about to become business partners—' his gaze slid over Pietro's head to where Inez was holding court in a group of guests; the sleek line of her neck and the curve of her body sent another punch of heat straight to his groin '—and hopefully a little bit more than that. Call me Theo.'

The younger man looked a little taken aback, but he rallied quickly, nodded and held out his hand. 'Theo...we wanted to hammer down a time to discuss finalising our agreement.'

He took Pietro's hand in a firm grip. Benedicto started to offer his hand. Theo deliberately turned away. Catching the bartender's eye, he held up his fingers for three more drinks. By the time he faced them again, Benedicto had lowered his hand.

Theo breathed through the deep anger that churned through his belly and smiled.

'Tomorrow. Ten o'clock. My office. I'll have the documents ready for us to sign.'

This time it was Benedicto who looked taken aback. 'I was under the impression that you wanted to iron out a few more details.'

Theo's gaze flicked back to Inez. 'I had a few concerns but they no longer matter. Your campaign funds will be ready in the next twenty-four hours.'

Father and son exchanged triumphant looks. 'We are pleased to hear it,' Benedicto said.

'Good, then I hope the three of you will join me for dinner tomorrow evening to celebrate our new deal.'

Benedicto frowned. 'The three of us?'

'Of course. I expect that, since this is a family company, your daughter would wish to be included in the celebrations? After all, the company was her mother's family's business before it became yours, Senhor da Costa, was it not?' he queried silkily.

The older man's eyes narrowed and something unpleasant slid across his face. 'I bought my father-in-law out over a decade ago but yes, it's a family business.'

Bought out using money he'd obtained by inflicting pain and merciless torment.

The bartender slid their shots across the polished counter.

Theo picked up the nearest shot glass and raised it. 'In that case, I look forward to welcoming you all as my guests tomorrow evening. *Saúde.*'

'*Saúde*,' Benedicto and his son responded.

Theo threw back the drink and this time didn't hold back from slamming it down.

Again he saw father and son exchange looks. He didn't care.

All he cared about was making it out of the ballroom in one piece before he buried his fist in Benedicto da Costa's bony face. The urge to tear apart the man who'd caused his family, caused *him*, so much anguish reared through him.

The sound of his phone vibrating in his jacket pocket brought a welcome distraction from his murderous thoughts.

'Excuse me, gentlemen.' He walked away without a backward glance, gaining the double doors leading out to the wide terrace before activating his phone.

'Heads up, you're about to get into serious trouble with Ari if you don't fess up as to why you're really in Rio,' Sakis, his brother, said in greeting.

'Too late. I've already had the hairdryer treatment earlier this evening.'

'Yeah, but do you know he's thinking of flying down there for a face-to-face?'

Theo cursed. 'Doesn't he have enough on his hands being all loved up and taking care of his pregnant fiancé?' He wasn't concerned about a confrontation with Ari. But he was concerned that Ari's presence might alert Benedicto to Theo's true intentions.

So far, Benedicto da Costa was oblivious as to the connections Theo had made to what had happened twelve years ago. The older man had been very careful to erase every connection with the incident and sever ties with anyone who could bear witness to the crime he'd committed. He hadn't been careful enough. But he didn't know that.

Having another Pantelides in Rio could set off alarm bells.

'You need to stall him.'

'He's concerned,' Sakis murmured. Theo heard the same concern reflected in his brother's voice. 'So am I.'

'It needs to be done,' he replied simply.

'I get that. But you don't need to do it alone. He's dangerous. The moment he guesses what your true intentions are—'

'He won't; I've made sure of it.'

'How can you be absolutely certain? Theo, don't be stubborn. I can help—'

'No. I need to see this through myself.'

Sakis sighed. 'Are you sure?'

Theo turned slowly and surveyed the ballroom. Rio's finest drank and laughed without a care in the world. In the centre of that crowd stood Benedicto da Costa, the reason why Theo couldn't sleep through a single night without waking to hellish nightmares; the reason anxiety hovered just underneath his skin, ready to infest his control should he loosen his grip for one careless second.

Inexorably, his eyes were drawn to the female member of the diabolical family. Inez was dancing with a man whose blatant interest and barely disguised lust made Theo's fist curl over the cold stone bannister.

His stomach churned and adrenaline poured through his system the same way a boxer experienced a heady rush in the seconds before a fight. This fight had been long coming. He would see it through. He had to. Otherwise he feared his demons would never be exorcised.

He'd lived with them for far too long, and they needed to be silenced. He needed to regain complete, unshakeable hold of his life once more.

His other hand tightened around his mobile phone, his heart thundering enough to drown out the music. He spoke succinctly so his brother would be in no doubt that he meant every word.

'Am I sure that I need to bring down the man who kidnapped and tortured me for over two weeks until Ari negotiated a two million ransom for my release? *Hell, yes.* I'm going to make him feel ten million times worse than what he did to me and to our family and I don't intend to rest until I bring all of them down.'

CHAPTER FOUR

'A DOUBLE-SHOT AMERICANO, *por favor.*' Inez smiled absently at the barista while she tried to juggle her sketchpad and fish out enough change from her purse to pay for the coffee.

It was barely nine o'clock and yet the heat was already oppressive, even more than usual for a Thursday morning in February. Normally, she would've opted for a cool caffeine drink but her energy levels needed an extra boost this morning.

She'd slept badly after the fund-raiser last night. And what little sleep she'd managed had been interspersed with images of a man she had no business thinking, never mind dreaming, about.

And yet Theo Pantelides's face had haunted her slumber...still haunted her, if truth be told.

The last time she'd seen him he'd been leaning against the terrace bannister outside the ballroom, his eyes fixed firmly on her. Inez wasn't sure why her attention had been drawn outside. All she knew was that something had compelled her to look that way as she danced with a guest.

Even from that distance the tension whipping through his frame had been unmistakable, as had the blatant dark promise in his eyes as his gaze raked her from head to toe.

More than anything she'd wished she could lip-read when she'd watched his lips move to answer whoever was at the other end of his phone conversation.

That last look plagued her. It'd held hunger, anger and another emotion that she couldn't quite decipher. Brushing it off, she smiled, accepted her coffee and headed outside. She was a little early for her class with the inner city kids but she hadn't wanted to spend another moment at the tension-fraught breakfast table with her father and brother this morning.

In contrast to Pietro's third degree as to what exactly had happened with Alfonso Delgado, her father had been cold and strangely preoccupied. The moment he'd stood abruptly and left the table, she'd made her excuses and walked away.

Even Pietro's reminder that they had a dinner engagement she couldn't recall making hadn't been worth stopping to query. All she'd wanted was to get out of the mansion that felt more and more as if it was closing in on her.

'*Bom dia, anjo.*' The deep murmured greeting brought her thoughts and footsteps to a crashing halt.

Theo leaned casually against a gleaming black sports car, a pair of dark sunglasses hiding his eyes from her. But her full body tingle announced that she was the full, unwavering focus of his gaze. Her breath stalled, her heart accelerating wildly as her pulse went into overdrive.

'What the hell are you doing here?' she blurted before she could stop her strong reaction.

Aside from the devastation his tall, lean suited frame caused to her insides, the thought that he could discover where she was headed or what she did with her Tuesday and Thursday mornings made her palms grow clammy. By lunchtime today, if Pietro were to be believed, Theo would be firmly entrenched as a business partner in her family's company. Which meant constant contact with her family. Which meant he could disclose parts of her life she wasn't yet ready to disclose to her family.

'Are you following me?' she accused hotly as she approached him, her senses jumping with the possibilities and consequences of her discovery.

'Not today. My trench coat and fedora are at the laundry.'

'Keep them there. In this heat, you'd boil to death.'

A smile broke across his face. 'Do I detect a little un-ladylike relish in your voice, *anjo*?'

'What you detect is high scepticism that you're here by accident and not following me,' she snapped.

'You give me too much credit, *agape mou*. I asked for the best coffee shop in the city and I was directed here. That you're here too merely confirms that assertion. Unless you go out of your way to sample bad coffee?'

Before she could respond, he straightened and reached for the hand wrapped around her coffee. Curling his hand over hers, he brought his lips to the small opening on her coffee lid and tilted the cup towards him.

He savoured the drink in his mouth for a few seconds before he swallowed.

Inez fought to breathe as she watched his strong throat move. The slow swirl of his tongue over his lower lip caused darts of sharp need to arrow straight between her legs.

'Delicious. And surprising. I would've pegged you for a latte girl.'

'Which goes to show you know next to nothing about me,' she retorted.

He slowly raised his sunglasses and speared her with his mesmerising eyes. Although a smile hovered over his sensual lips, some unnameable tension hovered in the air between them. A charged friction that warned her all was not as it seemed.

Hell, she knew that. Theo Pantelides spelled danger. Whether smiling or serious, dallying with him was akin to playing with electricity. Depending on his mood, you could either receive a mild static frizzle or a full-blown electro-cution. And she had no intention of testing him for either.

'*Sim*, I don't know enough about you. But I intend to remedy that situation in the near future.'

She shrugged. 'It is your time to waste.'

He merely smiled and turned towards his car.

'I thought you came to get coffee?' she probed, then bit her lip for prolonging a meeting she wanted over and done with. Last night she'd told herself to be thankful that she would never see this man again. And yet, here she was, feeling mildly bereft at the notion that he was leaving.

He paused and his gaze slid over her. Immediately, she became supremely conscious of the white shorts and blue tank top she'd hurriedly thrown on this morning. Her hair was caught up in a ponytail because it helped keep it out of the way during her class. Her face was devoid of make-up except for the light sunscreen and the gloss she'd passed over her lips. All in all, she projected a much different image this morning than the sophisticated hostess she'd been last night.

Catching herself wondering whether he found her wanting now, she mentally slammed the thought down. She didn't care what Theo thought of her.

'I have the kick I need to keep me going. See you tonight.'

'Tonight? Why would you be seeing me tonight?' she demanded.

His smile slowly disappeared as his gaze slid over her again. This time, his hot gaze held an element of possessiveness that made her fight to keep from fidgeting under his keen scrutiny.

Stepping back, he activated a button on his car key and the door slid smoothly upward. She watched, completely captivated, as he lowered his tall masculine frame inside the small space. A touch of a slim finger on a button and the engine roared to life.

'Because I want to see you. And I always get what I want, Inez,' he said cryptically, his tone suddenly hard and biting. 'Remember that.'

I always get what I want.

Another shiver of apprehension coursed down her spine.

All through the two art and graphic design classes she

taught from ten till midday, the infernal words throbbed through her head as if someone had set them on repeat.

She managed to keep her focus, barely, as she demonstrated the differences between charcoal and pencil strokes to a group of ten-year-olds. Once or twice she had to repeat herself because she lost her train of thought, much to the amusement of her pupils, but the satisfying feeling of imparting knowledge to children who would otherwise have been left wandering the streets momentarily swamped the roiling emotions that Theo had stirred with his unexpected appearance this morning.

The suspicion that he had been following her didn't go away all through her hurriedly taken lunch and the meeting she'd scheduled with the volunteer coordinator at the centre.

Her decision to forge her own path by seeking a permanent position at the centre had solidified as she'd tossed and turned through the night.

Seeking her independence meant finding a paying job. To do that she needed more experience, which she hoped her longer hours spent volunteering would give her.

Thanks to her father's interference, all she had was one semester at university. It wasn't great but, until such time as she could further her education, it was better than nothing. That plus her volunteering was a starting point.

A starting point that was greatly enhanced when the coordinator agreed to increase her hours to three full days.

She was smiling as she activated her phone on the way to her car after leaving the centre.

The first text was from Pietro, reminding her that they were dining out that evening. With Theo Pantelides.

The unladylike curse she uttered won her a severe look of disapproval from an elderly lady walking past. The urge to text back a refusal was immediate and visceral.

After last night and this morning, exposing herself to the raw emotions Theo provoked was the last thing she needed.

And even more than her suspicions this morning, she

had a feeling he'd engineered this dinner. Hell, he'd as much as taunted her with it with his last words to her this morning.

As much as she tried to think positive and hope that the dinner would be quick and painless, a premonition gripped her insides as she slid behind the wheel and headed home.

'*Filho da puta.*' Her brother's habitual crude cursing wasn't a surprise to her. That it had seemingly come out of nowhere was.

'What's wrong?' She eyed him as they stepped out of the car at the marina of the exclusive Rio Yacht Club just before seven p.m.

She pulled down her box-pleated hem and wished she'd worn something a little longer than the form-fitting mid-thigh-length royal-blue sleeveless dress. The traffic had been horrendous and she'd arrived home much later than planned. The dress had been the nearest thing to hand. Now she stared down at the four-inch black platform heels she'd teamed with it and grimaced at the amount of thigh and legs on show.

The light breeze lifted a few strands of her loose hair as she turned to her brother and saw him jerk his chin towards the largest yacht moored at the far end of the pier. 'Trust Pantelides to rub my nose in it,' he said acerbically.

She looked from the sleek black, gold-trimmed vessel back to her brother. 'Rub your nose…what are you talking about?'

With a sullen look, he strode off down the jetty. 'That's my boat.'

'*Yours*? When did you buy a boat?'

'I didn't. I couldn't. Not after the mess up with *Pai*'s last campaign. That boat was supposed to be mine!' Dark anger clouded his face.

Her heart jumped into her throat. 'Pietro, a boat like that costs millions of dollars. Besides that very unsubtle hint that

I in any way stood in the way of your acquiring it—which is preposterous, by the way—there's no way you could ever have afforded a boat like that, so—'

'Forget it. Let's go and get this over with. It's bad enough *Pai* pulled out of coming tonight. Now I have to schmooze for both of us. You have to play your part, too. It's clear Pantelides's got a thing for you.'

Disgust and anger rose in her and she snatched her hand away from Pietro when he tried to lead her down the gang-plank.

'I won't participate in another of your soulless schemes. So you may as well forget it right now.'

'Inez—'

'No!' Feelings she'd bottled up for much longer than she cared to think about rose to the surface. 'You keep asking me to throw myself at prospective investors so you can fund *Pai*'s campaign. You're his campaign manager and yet you can't seem to function without my help. Why is that?'

Pietro's eyes darkened. 'Watch your mouth, sister.'

'Show me some respect and I'll consider it,' she challenged.

'What the hell has got into you?'

'Nothing that hasn't always been there, Pietro. But you need me to point it out to you so I will. I'm done. If you want me to accompany you as your *sister* to Theo Pantelides's dinner, then I will. If you have another scheme up your sleeve, then you might as well forget it because I am not interested.'

Her brother's lips pursed but she saw a hint of shame in his eyes before his gaze slid away. 'I don't have time to argue with you right now. All I ask, if it's not too much, of course, is that you help me secure this deal with Pantelides, because if we lose his backing then we might as well pack up and head back up to the ranch in the mountains.' He set off down the jetty.

She hurried to keep up, picking her way carefully over

wooden slats. 'But I thought everything was done and dusted this morning?' she asked when she caught up with him.

Anxiety slid over Pietro's face. 'Pantelides cancelled the meeting. Something came up, he said. Except I know it was a lie. I have it on good authority he was parked outside a coffee shop chatting up some girl when he was supposed to be meeting us to finalise the agreement.'

Inez stumbled, barely catching herself from toppling headlong into the water a few feet away.

'*You're having him watched?*' How she managed to keep her voice even, she didn't know.

Petulance joined anxiety. 'Of course I am. And I'd bet my Rolex that he's doing the same to us.'

The thought of being the subject of anyone's surveillance made her skin crawl, even though a part of her had reluctantly accepted the truth: that her father's business dealings weren't always legitimate. But hearing her brother admit it made her stomach turn.

And if that was the way Theo Pantelides conducted his business as well…

She pressed her lips together and looked up as Pietro strode past the potted palm lined entrance to the Yacht Club.

'Aren't we dining in there?'

He shook his head. 'No. We're dining on my…on *his* boat,' he tossed out bitterly.

Inez glanced at the yacht they were approaching.

This close, the vessel was even more magnificent. Its sleek lines and exquisite craftsmanship made her fingers itch for her sketching pad. She was so busy admiring the boat and yearning to capture its beauty on paper that she didn't see its owner until she was right in front of him.

Then everything else ceased to register.

He wore a black shirt with black trousers, his dark hair raked back from his face. Under the soft golden lights spilling from the second deck his sculpted cheekbones and strong jaw jutted out in heart-stopping relief.

At the back of her mind, Inez experienced a bout of irritation at the fact that he captured attention so exclusively. So effortlessly.

Even as he shook hands with Pietro and welcomed him on board the *Pantelides 9*, his eyes remained on her. And God help her, but she couldn't look away.

On unsteady feet, which she firmly blamed on the swaying vessel, she climbed the steps to where he waited. When his eyes released hers to travel over her body, she grappled with controlling her breath. She reached him and reluctantly held out her hand in greeting.

'Thank you for the dinner invitation, Mr Pantelides.'

With a mocking smile, he took her hand and used the grip to pull her close. Despite her heels, he was almost a foot taller than her, easily six foot four. Which meant he had to lean down quite a bit to whisper in her ear, 'So formal, *anjo*. I look forward to loosening your inhibitions enough to dissolve that starchy demeanour.'

Her pulse, which had begun racing when his palm slid against hers, thundered even harder at his words. 'I can see how not having a woman fall at your feet the moment you crook your finger can present a challenge, *senhor*. But you really should learn the difference between playing hard to get and being plainly uninterested.'

His eyebrow quirked. 'You fall into the latter category, of course?' he mocked.

'*Sim*, that is exactly so.'

He looked towards where Pietro had accepted a glass of champagne from a waiter and was admiring the luxuriously decorated deck, at the end of which a multi-coloured lit jet pool swirled and shimmered.

When his gaze re-fixed on hers, there was a steely determination in his eyes that sent a shiver down her spine. All the earlier alarm bells where Theo was concerned clanged loudly in her brain.

'Then I will have to get a little more inventive,' he murmured silkily before dropping her hand.

Inez clenched her fist and fought the urge to rub the tingling in her palm. She didn't want him getting inventive where she was concerned because she had a nasty feeling she wouldn't emerge unscathed from the encounter.

But she kept her mouth shut and followed him onto the deck. The cream and gold décor was the last word in luxury and opulence. Plump gold seats offered comfort and a superior view onto the well-lit marina and the open sea to their right. To their left, the lights of Rio gleamed, with the backdrop of the huge mountain, on top of which resided the world-famous Cristo Redentor.

A sultry breeze wafted through the deck as a waiter served more flutes of champagne. She took a glass as Pietro rejoined them. His glass was already half empty and she watched him take another greedy gulp before he pointed a finger at Theo.

'I wish you'd given me the chance to make you another offer for this boat before you pulled the plug on our sale agreement, Pantelides.'

Theo's jaw tightened before he answered. 'You had several opportunities to make good but you failed to close the deal. So I cut my losses.' He shrugged. 'Business is business.'

Pietro bristled. 'And cancelling our meeting today? Was that for business too, or pleasure?'

Theo's eyes caught and held hers. Inez held her breath, wondering if he was about to give her up. His eyes gleamed with a mixture of danger and amusement. Somehow he'd sensed that he held her in his power. And he relished that power. Her hand trembled slightly as she waited for the axe to fall.

'I'm not in the habit of discussing my other business interests, or my pleasurable ones, for that matter. But, suffice it to say, what kept me away from our meeting was very much worth my time.' His gaze swept down, lingering over her breasts and hips in a blatant appraisal that made her breathing grow shallow. When his eyes returned to hers, Inez was sure all the oxygen had been sucked out of the atmosphere.

'Our business together should be equally worth your time,' Pietro countered.

Theo finally set her free from his captivating gaze. Narrow-eyed, he glanced at Pietro.

'Which is why I rescheduled for this evening. Of course, your father chose not to grace us with his presence. So the song and dance continues, I guess.' The hard edge was definitely in his tone again, prompting those alarm bells to ring louder.

Pietro muttered something under his breath that she was sure wasn't complimentary. He snapped his fingers at the waiter and swapped his empty glass for a full one.

'Well, we'll be there at the appointed time tomorrow. We can only hope that you will not be delayed…elsewhere.'

The upward movement of Theo's mouth could in no way be termed a smile. His eyes flicked back to her. 'Don't worry, da Costa, I intend to hammer out the final points of our agreement tonight. When I turn up to sign tomorrow, it will be with the knowledge that all my stipulations have been satisfied.'

The firm belief that his statement was connected to her wouldn't dissipate all through dinner. As a host, Theo was effortlessly entertaining. He even managed to draw a chuckle from Pietro once or twice.

But Inez couldn't shake the feeling that they were being toyed with. And once or twice she caught the faintest hint of fury and repulsion on his face, especially when her father's name came up.

She shook herself out of her unsettling thoughts when the most mouth-watering dessert was set down before her.

Whatever Theo was up to, it was nothing to do with her. Her father had managed their family business with enough savvy not to be drawn into a scam.

With that comforting thought in mind, she picked up her spoon and scooped up a mouthful of chocolate truffle-topped cheesecake.

Her tiny groan of delight drew intense eyes back to hers. Suddenly, the thought of dishing out a little of the mockery he'd doled out to her tingled through her. Keeping her gaze on his, she slowly drew the spoon out from between her lips, then licked the remnants of chocolate with a slow flick of her tongue.

His nostrils flared immediately, hunger darkening his eyes to a leaf-green that was mesmerising to witness. With another swirl of her tongue, she lowered the spoon and scooped up another mouthful.

His large fist tightened around the after-dinner espresso he'd opted for and she momentarily expected the bone china to shatter beneath his grip. But slowly he released it and sat back in his chair, his eyes never leaving her face.

'Enjoying your dessert, *anjo*?' he asked in that low, rough tone of his.

She hated to admit that the endearment was beginning to have an effect on her. The way he mouthed it made heat bloom in her belly, made her aware of her every heartbeat… made her wonder how it would sound whispered to her at the height of passion. *No!*

'Yes. Very much.' She fake smiled to project an air of nonchalance.

He smiled at her mocking formality. 'Good. I'll make a note of it for the next time we dine together.'

Before she could tell him she intended to move heaven and earth to make sure there wouldn't be a next time, Pietro lurched to his feet. 'I never got the chance to inspect my…this boat before the opportunity to buy it was regrettably taken away. You won't mind if I take a look around, would you?' he slurred.

Theo motioned the hovering waiter over. He murmured to him and the waiter went to the deck bar and picked up a handset. 'Not at all. My skipper will give you the tour.'

A middle-aged man with greying hair climbed onto the deck a few minutes later and escorted a swaying Pietro towards the stairs.

Inez watched him go with a mixture of anxiety and sympathy.

'He's drunk.' Her appetite gone for good, she set her spoon down and pushed the plate away.

'You say that as if it's my fault,' he replied lazily.

'Did you really have to do that?' She glared at him.

He raised a brow. 'Do what, exactly?'

'This was supposed to be Pietro's boat.' No matter how unrealistic that notion had been, her brother didn't deserve to be humiliated like this.

'*Supposed* being the operative word. We had a *gentleman's* agreement.' That hard bite was back again, sending trepidation dancing along her nerve ends. 'He didn't hold out his end of the deal.'

'Regardless of that, do you have to rub his nose in it like this?' she countered.

'As I said before, I'm a businessman, *anjo*. And I currently have a yacht worth tens of millions of dollars that needs an owner. The Boat Show starts next week. I relocated aboard in order to get it in shape for prospective buyers, otherwise our dinner would have taken place at my residence in Leblon and your brother's delicate feelings would've been spared.'

She frowned. 'You're selling the boat?' The thought of the beautiful vessel going to some unknown, probably pompous new owner made her nose wrinkle in distaste. The design was exquisite, unique…sort of like its owner.

As hard as she tried to imagine it, she couldn't see anyone else owning the boat besides Theo. Not even Pietro. Its black and gold contrasts depicted darkness and light in a complementary synergy—two fascinating characteristics she'd glimpsed more than once in Theo.

'Needs must.'

She looked around the beautiful deck, imagined its graceful lines awash with sunlight, and sighed.

Theo's eyes narrowed as he stared across at her. 'You like the boat.'

'Yes, it's…beautiful.'

He watched her for a few minutes then he nodded. 'Let's make a date for Sunday afternoon. We'll take her out for a quick spin.'

She laughed. 'Unless I'm mistaken, this is a four hundred foot vessel. You don't just take her out for a *quick* spin.'

'A long spin, then. I need to make sure it runs perfectly. If you still like it when we return to shore, I'll keep it.'

Her heart lurched then sped up like a runaway freight train. 'You would do that…for me?'

'*Sim*,' he replied simply.

Genuine puzzlement, along with a heavy dose of excitement she didn't want to admit to, made her blurt, 'Why?'

He strolled lazily to where she stood. This close, she had to tilt her head to catch his gaze. *Darkness and light.* He might have been smiling but Inez could almost reach out and touch the undercurrent of emotions swirling beneath his civility. She jumped slightly when he brushed a forefinger down her cheek.

'Because I intend to keep you, *anjo*. And while you will not have a lot of choice in the matter, I'm willing to make a few adjustments to ensure your contentment.'

CHAPTER FIVE

THEO WATCHED HER grapple with what he'd just said. Unlike her brother, she wasn't inebriated—she'd barely touched her glass of the rich Barolo 2009 he'd specially chosen for their dinner.

She shook her head in confusion. 'You intend to *keep* me?'

Her skin, satin-smooth beneath his touch, begged to be caressed. He gave in to the urge and traced her from cheek to jaw. When she withdrew from him, he followed. He stroked the pulse beating in her neck and pushed back the need to step closer, touch his mouth to the spot.

He'd learnt two things last night.

The first was that Benedicto da Costa, for all his cunning and veneer of sophistication, was still a greedy, vicious snake who thought he could con millions of dollars out of an unsuspecting fool like him.

The second was that Inez da Costa could be a key player in the slow and painful revenge he intended to exact for the wrong done to him. It didn't hurt that the chemistry between them burned the very air they breathed.

In the past Theo had made several opportune decisions by switching tactics at the last minute and making the most of whatever situation he found himself him.

With the newfound information at his fingertips, he'd found a way not only to end the da Costas once and for all, but also to make a tidy profit to boot.

He barely stopped himself from smiling as he looked down into Inez's face. She really was stunningly beautiful. With a mouth that begged to be explored.

'Mr Pantelides?'

'Theo,' he murmured, anticipating her refusal to use his first name.

She blew out an exasperated breath. 'Theo. Explain yourself.'

The unexpected sound of his name on her lips sent a pulse of heat through his body. Followed swiftly by a feeling he recognised as pleasure.

With a silent curse he dropped his hand. Pleasure featured nowhere on his mission to Rio. Nor was standing around, gazing into the face that reminded him of the painting of an angel that used to hang in his father's house.

Pain. Reparation. Merciless humiliation. Those were his objectives.

'There's no hidden message in there, *anjo*. For the duration of my stay in Rio I expect you to make yourself available to me, day and night.'

Her genuine laughter echoed around the open deck. When he didn't join in, she quickly sobered. 'Oh, I'm sorry. But I believe you have me confused with a certain type of woman you must encounter on your travels.'

Theo let the insult slide. He'd told his skipper to take his time with the tour, but even his trusted employee couldn't keep Pietro away for ever. And it looked as if he needed to step up this part of his strategy in order to forward his overall objective.

'I was supposed to sign documents that guaranteed your father's campaign funds this morning but I didn't turn up. Aren't you even a little bit curious as to why?'

A touch of confusion clouded her brown eyes but she shrugged one silky-smooth shoulder that shimmered softly under the deck lights. 'Your business with my father is not my concern.'

A little of that control he kept under a tight leash threatened to slip free. 'You don't care where the money comes from as long as you're kept in the style to which you've grown accustomed, is that it?'

Her eyes widened at the acid leaching from his tone. 'You may think you know me but, I assure you, you've got things wrong—'

'Have I? From where I'm standing it's very evident you're the bait he uses to trap weak, pathetic fools into opening their wallets.'

Her ragged gasp accompanied a look of outrage so near authentic Theo would've believed her reaction had he not seen her in action with Delgado last night.

'If it is your intention to be offensive to show your *machismo*, then *bravo*, you've succeeded,' she threw at him and whirled away.

He caught her wrist before she could take a step.

'Let me go.'

'I've yet to outline my plans, *anjo*.'

'I think you've *outlined* enough. I won't stand here listening to your unfounded insults. I'm going to find Pietro. And then we're leaving.' She tried to free herself. He tightened his grip until he could feel her pulse under his fingers. Furious. Passionate.

His groin stirred and he forced himself to ignore the throb of arousal determined to make itself known. 'You're not leaving here until we have this discussion.'

'What we're having is not a discussion, *senhor*. What you're doing is holding me captive, torturing me with—'

She broke off, no doubt in reaction to his hiss of fury and the flash of icy memory that made his whole body go rigid for one long second.

Theo released her, turned away sharply and shoved his hand through his hair. He noted his fingers' faint trembling and willed himself to stop shaking.

'Th...Theo?' Her voice came from far away, filled with confusion and a touch of concern.

He willed away the effect of the trigger words and forced himself to breathe. But they pounded through his brain nonetheless—*captive, prisoner, torture, darkness...*

Fingers closed over his shoulder and he jerked around. *'Don't!'*

She jumped back, snatching back her hand. It took several more seconds for him to recall where he was. He wasn't in some deep, dark hole in a remote farm in Spain. He was in Rio. With the daughter of the man who continued to cause his recurring nightmares.

'What's...what's wrong with you?' she asked with a wary frown.

He drew in a steady breath and gritted his teeth. 'Nothing. I'll get to the point. The agreement was that I'd take control of Da Costa Holdings and keep a fifty per cent share of the profits in exchange for liquidated funds to finance your father's political campaign. However, the papers your father had drawn up contain a major loophole that I can easily exploit.'

Slowly, his panic receded and he noticed she was absently rubbing her wrist. He quickly replayed his reaction to her touch and breathed a sigh of relief when he confirmed to himself that he hadn't grabbed her in his panic.

She continued to rub her skin and slowly another earthy emotion replaced his roiling feelings. He welcomed the pulse of arousal despite the fact that he had no intention of falling prey to the easy wiles of Inez da Costa. No matter how mouth-watering her body or how angelic her face.

'Shouldn't you be telling my father this, give him a chance to fix the loophole before you sign?'

He smiled at her naiveté. 'Why should I? I stand to gain by signing the agreement as it's drawn up.'

Her brow creased. 'Then why tell me about it? What's

to keep me from telling my father about it the moment I leave here?'

'You won't.'

One expertly plucked eyebrow lifted. 'Again, I think you underestimate me.'

He strode to the extensively stocked bar and poured himself a shot of vodka. 'You won't because if you do I won't sign the agreement in any form. And the offer of financial backing vanishes.'

All trace of colour left her face. 'So this is a blackmail attempt. To what purpose?'

'The purpose needn't concern you. All I want you to know is that there is a loophole which I can choose to exploit or leave alone, depending on your cooperation.'

'But what is to stop you from going ahead with whatever you have planned after I've cooperated with…what exactly is it you want from me?'

'That's the simple part, *anjo*. I want to keep you. Until such time as I tire of you. Then you will be set free.'

When the full meaning of his words finally became clear, ice cascaded down Inez's spine. Despite the warm temperature, she shivered.

Oh, how easily he said the words. As if her answer meant nothing to him. But of course it did. He'd been planning this for a while. The meeting this morning outside the coffee shop—which she was now certain hadn't been coincidental—the dinner invitation that he'd probably known her father wouldn't be able to attend due to his long-standing monthly dinner with the oil minister, the invitation to the yacht, which was sure to cause a reaction in her brother, letting Pietro drink far more than he should've so he'd get her alone…

'You planned this,' she accused in a hushed tone because her throat was working to swallow down her rising anger.

'I plan everything, Inez,' he replied simply.

She looked into his face. The indomitable determination stamped on his harsh features sent a wave of anxiety through her.

She started to speak, to say the words that seemed unreal to her and her mouth trembled. His gaze dropped to the telling reaction and she immediately clamped her lips together. Showing weakness would only get her eaten alive.

Not that she wouldn't be anyway. A bubble of hysteria threatened. She swallowed and held his gaze.

'You want me to be your *mistress*?'

He laughed long and deeply. 'Is that what you would call yourself?'

She flushed. 'How else would you describe what you've just demanded of me? This *keeping* me? What you're suggesting is archaic enough to be described as such. Or does *plaything* more suit your pseudo-modernistic outlook?'

'No, Inez. I don't like the term plaything either. I have no intention of playing with you. No, what I foresee for us is much more grown up than that.' The sexual intent behind the statement was unmistakable.

Rather than being offended or shocked, Inez found herself growing breathless. Excited.

No!

'Yes,' he murmured as if he'd read her mind.

'Whatever term you slap on your intentions, I refuse to be a part of it. I'm going to find my brother—'

He slowly sank onto the plush seat, curved his hand along the back of the chair and levelled one ankle over his knee. 'And tell him that you've dashed his hopes of a possible high profile position in your father's administration because you couldn't take one for the team? I don't think you're in a position to refuse any demands I make, *anjo*.'

'Stop calling me that! And I won't be a pawn in whatever game you're playing with my father and brother. Pietro is well aware of that.'

'Really? Since when? Wasn't serving on your father's

campaign the reason you dropped out of university? Clearly, you play a part in your father's political ambitions or you wouldn't have been trying to fleece poor Alfonso. Why stop now when you're so close to achieving your goals? And why claim innocence when it's something you've done before?'

The hurt that scythed through her was deep and jagged. She wasn't aware she'd moved until she stood over him, glaring down at the arrogant face that wore that oh, so self-assured smile.

'I've never wanted to be this…this person you think I am. I was merely trying to help my family. I misjudged the situation and—'

'You mean you fell in love with your mark.'

She swallowed. 'I don't know what you're getting at.' But deep down she suspected.

'I mean you were set a target and you fell in love with your target. Isn't that what happened with Blanco?'

Light-headedness assailed her as he confirmed her suspicion. 'You know about Constantine?'

'I know everything I need to know about your family, *anjo*. But by all means enlighten me as to why you've been so misjudged.'

His cynicism raked her nerves raw. 'I made a mistake, one that I freely admit to.'

'What mistake do you mean, *querida*? I want to hear it.'

'I misjudged a man I thought I could trust.'

'You mean you meant to use him but found out he intended to use you too?' he mocked. 'Some would call that poetic justice.'

Recalling Constantine's public humiliation of her, the names he'd called her in the press, her stomach turned over. 'You're despicable.' She raised her chin. 'And assuming you're even close to being right, won't I be a fool to repeat that mistake again?'

'No.'

'No?'

His eyes fixed on hers. Serious and intense. 'Because this time you know exactly what you're getting. There will be no delusions of love on either of our parts. No pretence. Just a task, executed with smooth efficiency.'

'But you intend to parade me about as your…lover? What will everyone think?'

He shrugged. 'I don't care what everyone thinks. And I don't much think that bothers you either.'

She shivered. 'Of course it bothers me. What makes you think it won't?'

'You're the ultimate young Rio socialite. You have a dedicated following and young impressionable girls can't wait to grow up and be you.' His mockery was unmistakable.

Heat crept up her cheeks. 'That's just the media spinning itself out of control.'

'Carefully fuelled by you to help your father's status. You're always seen with the right offspring of the right ministers and CEOs. You're the attraction to draw the young voters, are you not?'

She couldn't deny the allegation because it was true. Nor did she want to waste time straying away from the more serious subject of the demand he was making of her.

The demand she wouldn't—*couldn't*—consent to.

But there was something about him…a reassurance… and expectation of acquiescence that made the hairs on her nape stand on end.

'What happens if I refuse this…this sleazy proposal?'

'I sign the agreement then use the company as I wish. I could dismantle it piece by piece and sell it off for a neat profit. Or I could just drive down the share price and watch the company implode from the inside out. But that's all boring business. What do you care?'

Her fists clenched. 'I care because my grandfather built that company from nothing.'

'And now your father's willing to hand it over to a complete stranger just so he can further his political career.'

She pursed her lips and fought not to react. She'd been deeply concerned when she'd first heard how her father planned to raise funds for his campaign. Concerns that had been airily brushed away with reassurances of airtight clauses.

Clauses which Theo had apparently easily loopholed.

Maybe it wasn't too late. She could tell him to go to hell and warn her father and brother about the danger their proposed business partner presented and advise them to walk away. Surely that would be better than admitting the lion into their midst and letting him wreak havoc at whim?

Light hazel eyes watched her with a predatory gleam. 'If you're thinking of warning your family, I'd think twice. Remember how easily I dispatched Delgado?'

She stiffened, recalling how a few whispered words had caused one investor in her father's campaign to walk away. 'You don't mean that,' she tried.

He slowly rose from the chair and towered over her. Every protective instinct screamed at her to step back but she stood her ground. Any show of weakness would be mercilessly pounced on.

'Do you want to test me, *anjo*?' The blade of steel that hovered over the endearment sent a shiver down her spine.

She slowly uncurled her fists and forced herself to breathe. 'What do you expect me to do?'

His smile was equally as predatory as the look in his eyes. 'You will inform your father and brother tomorrow that you and I are an item—our meeting last night sparked a chemistry so hot we couldn't *not* be together.'

A tiny sliver of relief eased her constricted chest. 'If that's all you want, I'm sure I can convince them—'

His mocking smile stopped her words.

'After you tell them that, you'll pack your bags and move in with me.'

Shock slammed her sideways. 'Are you serious?'

He gripped her chin and held her pinned under his gaze. 'I've never been more serious in my life.'

'But…why?'

'My reasons are my own. You just need to do as you're told.'

Do as you're told. Constantine had tried to blackmail her with those very words. When she'd refused he'd spread rumours about her in the newspapers.

Anger grew in her belly. But it was a helpless anger born of the knowledge that there was nothing she could do. Once again she was trapped in a hell that came from trying to do what was right for her family.

Only this time she was to truly pay with her body. In a stranger's bed. Her heart tripped before going into fierce overdrive.

She gazed at Theo's face, then his body. A body she would in the very near future become scorchingly intimate with. The horror she'd expected to feel oddly did not materialise.

'How long exactly will I be expected to *do as I'm told*?' she snapped.

'Until after the elections.'

A horrified gasp escaped her throat and she forcibly wrenched herself from his grip. 'But…that's…the elections are *three months* away!'

'*Sim*,' he replied simply.

'*Sim*? You expect me to put my life on hold for the next three months, just like that?' She clicked her fingers.

He raised an eyebrow. 'Do you want me to repeat the part about you not having a choice?'

She searched his face, trying to find meaning behind his intentions. 'What did my father do? Did he best you at a deal? Bad-mouth you to investors? Because I can't see what would make you want to go down this path of trying to get your own back.'

She watched his eyes darken, and his nostrils flare. All

traces of mockery were wiped from his face as he stared down at her. Only she was sure he wasn't really seeing her.

His usual intense focus dulled for several seconds and his jaw clenched so tight she feared it could crack. Whatever memory he was reliving caused volcanic fury to bubble beneath the harsh, ragged breath he expelled and this time she did take that step back, purely for self-preservation.

Voices sounded on the deck below. In a few minutes Pietro and the skipper would return from their tour. Inez wasn't sure whether to be grateful for the disruption or frustrated that her opportunity to find out Theo's reasons for demanding her presence in his bed had been thwarted.

His gaze sharpened, flicked towards the steps and back to her.

'It's time for your answer. Do you agree to my terms?'

She shook her head. 'Not until you tell me— *what are you doing*?' she blurted as he snapped out an arm and tugged her close.

One large bold hand gripped her waist and the other speared through her hair. Completely captured, she couldn't move as he angled her face to his. The unsettling fury was still evident in his darkened eyes and taut mouth. Despite the heat transmitted from his grip, she shivered.

'You seem to think you can talk or question your way out of this, *anjo*. You can't. But perhaps it was a mistake to expect a verbal agreement. Perhaps a physical demonstration is what's best?'

Despite his rhetorical question, she tried to answer. 'No…'

'Yes!' he muttered fiercely. Then his mouth smashed down on hers.

She'd been kissed before. By casual boyfriends in her late teens who she'd felt safe enough with.

By Constantine, in the beginning, before he'd revealed his true ruthless colours.

Nothing of what had gone before prepared her for the power and expertise behind Theo's kiss. Her world tilted beneath her feet as his tongue ruthlessly breached the seam of her lips. Hot, erotically charged and savagely determined, he invaded her mouth with searing passion. Bold and brazen, he flicked his tongue against hers, tasting her once and coming back for more.

The shocked little noise she made was a cross between surprise and her body's stunned reaction to the invasion.

The hand at her waist pressed her closer to his body. Whipcord strength, sleek muscles and his own unique scent brought different sensations that attacked her flailing senses.

Fire lashed through her belly as liquid heat pooled between her thighs. Her breasts, crushed against his chest, swelled and ached, her nipples peaking into demanding points with a swiftness that made her dizzy.

Deus!

Feeling her world careen even faster out of control, she threw up her hands. Hard muscle rippled beneath her fingers. The need to explore slammed into her. Before she could question her actions, she slid her hands over his warm cotton-covered shoulders to his nape, her fingers tingling as they encountered his bare skin.

He jerked beneath her touch, pulled back with a tug on her hair. Breathing harshly, he stared into her eyes for several seconds. Hunger blazed in his, turning them a dark, mesmerising molten gold that stole what little breath she had from her lungs. Then his eyes dropped lower to her parted mouth.

A rough sound rumbled from his throat. Then he was kissing her again. Harder, more demanding, more possessively than before.

Inez pushed her fingers through his hair as arousal like she'd never experienced before bit deep. This time, when his tongue slid into her mouth, she met it with hers. Boldly, she tried to give as much as she got, although she knew she was hopelessly inadequate when it came to experience.

The hand around her waist tightened and she was lifted off her feet. Seconds later, she found herself on the bar stool, her legs splayed and Theo firmly between thighs exposed by her stance. He came at her again, the force of his sensual attack tilting the stool backwards.

She threw out her hands onto the counter to keep from toppling over. Theo growled beneath his breath, his hands moving upward from her waist to cup her breasts. He moulded her willing, aching flesh so expertly she whimpered and arched into his hold. Beneath her clothes, her tight nipples unfurled in eager anticipation when his thumbs grazed over them. The deep pleasurable shudder made him repeat the action, eliciting a soft cry of pleasure from deep inside her.

'Inez!'

The rapier-sharp call of her name doused her with ice-cold water. She wrenched herself from Theo's hold…or at least she tried to.

The hands that had dropped from her breasts to her waist at the sound of Pietro's return stayed her desperate flight.

'What the *hell* do you think you're doing?' Pietro growled, no longer looking as drunk as he'd been half an hour ago.

'If you need it explained to you, da Costa, then I'm wondering who the hell I'm getting into business with.'

Her brother flushed in anger. 'I wasn't talking to you, Pantelides. But maybe I should ask you what you're doing, pawing my sister like some mad animal.'

Inez desperately tried to pull her dress down. But Theo stood firmly between her thighs, making the task impossible. Her sound of distress drew his attention from Pietro. He stared down at her for a second before he adjusted his stance. But although he allowed her to close her legs and pull her dress down, his hands didn't drop from her waist.

If anything, they tightened, their hold so possessive she fought to breathe.

'Inez was going to tell you tomorrow. But I guess tonight's as good a time as any.'

Pietro's gaze shifted from Theo's face to hers. 'Tell me what?'

'Do you want to do the honours, *anjo*? Or shall I?' he queried softly.

Her heartbeat accelerated but not with the arousal pounding through her bloodstream. She heard the clear warning in Theo's tone. Anything short of what he'd demanded of her would see her family ruined completely.

She opened her mouth. Closed it again and swallowed hard.

A trace of fear washed over Pietro's face. Despite their strained relationship, there'd been times in the past when they'd been close. She knew how much a political career of his own some day meant to him. How much he was pinning his hopes on what her father's campaign would mean to him personally.

She tried again to speak the words Theo demanded she speak. But her vocal cords wouldn't work.

'Would someone hurry up and tell me what's going on?'

Fierce hazel eyes drifted over her face in a look that spelled possession so potent her breath caught.

Theo curled his arm over her shoulders and pulled her into the heat of his body. He drifted his mouth over her temple in an adoring move so utterly convincing she reeled at his skilful deception.

She was grappling with that, and with just how much of the kiss they'd shared had been an exercise in pure ruthless seduction on his part, when he spoke.

'Your sister and I have become…enamoured with each other. We only met last night but already I cannot bear to be without her.' His voice held none of the mockery from before, sparking another stunned realisation of his skill. He stared down at her and she caught the implacable determination in his eyes.

When his gaze reconnected with Pietro's she stared, mesmerised, at his profile then shivered at the iron-hard set to his jaw.

'Tomorrow she will be moving out of your home. And into mine.'

CHAPTER SIX

'*LIKE HELL YOU are*,' Pietro repeated for the hundredth time as their chauffeur-driven car stopped outside the opulent Ipanema mansion she'd grown up in.

She quickly threw open the door and hurried up the steps leading to the double oak front doors although she knew escape wouldn't be easy. Pietro was hard on her heels.

'Did you hear what I said?' he demanded.

'I heard you loud and clear. But you fail to realise I'm no longer a child. I'm twenty-four years old—well over the age when I can do whatever the heck I want.'

He slid a hand through his hair. 'Look, I know I may have pushed you into playing a greater part in *Pai*'s fund-raising campaign. But…I don't think getting involved with Pantelides is a good idea,' he said abruptly.

Inez's heart lurched at his concern but she couldn't reassure him because she herself didn't know what the future held. 'Thank you for your concern but like I said, I'm a grown up.'

He swivelled on his heel in the vast entrance hall of the villa. 'Are you really that into him? I know what I saw on his deck tells its own story but you only met him last night!'

'I hadn't met Alfonso Delgado before last night either and yet you expected me to charm him.'

'*Charm* him, not move in with him!'

'There's no point arguing with me. My mind is made up.'

Pietro's face darkened. 'Is this some sort of rebellion?'

Inez sighed. 'Of course not. But I'd planned to move out anyway, once you and *Pai* started on the campaign trail.'

'Move out and go where? This is your home, Inez,' he replied.

She shook her head. 'My world doesn't begin and end in this house, Pietro. I intend to rent an apartment, get a job.'

'Then don't start by ruining yourself with Pantelides.'

Her throat clogged. 'My reputation is already in shreds after Constantine. I really have nothing left to lose.'

She turned to head up the grand staircase that led to the twin wings of their villa. Behind her, she could still hear Pietro pacing the hallway.

'This doesn't make any sense, Inez. Perhaps a good night's sleep will bring you to your senses.'

She didn't answer. Because she didn't want to waste her time telling him the decision had already been made for her.

For Theo to have gone to the effort of staging that kiss and paving the way for the lies she had to perpetuate, she knew without a shadow of a doubt that his demands were real.

He'd gone to a lot of trouble to set up tonight's meeting. She would be a fool to bait him to see if he would carry out his threat.

Her heart hammered as she undressed and stepped beneath the shower. Slowly soaping her body, she found her mind drifting back to their kiss. The incandescent delirium of it was unlike anything she'd felt before.

Her fingers touched her lips, and they tingled in remembrance.

Tomorrow she was inviting herself into the lion's den to be devoured whole for the sake of her family.

A hysterical laugh became lost in the sound of the running water.

Pietro was finally showing signs of being the brother she remembered before their mother died. Shame that she'd had to sacrifice herself on the altar of their family's prosperity before he'd come round. As for her father…sadness engulfed her at the thought that even if he knew of her sacrifice, he probably wouldn't lift a finger to shield her from it.

Theo's gaze strayed to his phone for the umpteenth time in under twenty minutes and he cursed under his breath.

He'd called Inez this morning and they'd agreed a time of eleven o'clock, two hours before he was due to sign the documents at her father's office.

It was now eleven twenty-five and there was no sign of her. No big deal. She was probably stuck in traffic. Or she hadn't left her home on time, especially if she was packing for a three-month stay.

Besides, women are always late.

Even as a child he'd known this. His mother had never been on time for a single event in her life.

His mother…

Memory rained down vicious blows that had him catching his breath. His mother, the woman who'd been nowhere in sight, either before or after he was kidnapped and held for ransom by Benedicto da Costa's vicious thugs.

For weeks after he'd been rescued and returned home, broken and devastated by his ordeal, he'd asked for his mother. Ari had made several excuses for her absence. But Theo had been unable to reconcile the fact that the mother who'd once treated him as if he'd been the centre of her world suddenly couldn't even be bothered to pick up the phone and enquire about her mentally and physically traumatised child.

No. She'd been too preoccupied with wallowing in her misery following her husband's betrayal to bother with her own children.

Ari had been the one to hold them together after their family was shattered by the press uncovering their father's many shady dealings and philandering ways.

For a very long time he'd laboured under the misconception that out of the three brothers he was the most special in their father's eyes. That just because he was the miracle baby his parents had never thought they'd have, he was their favourite. His kidnapping and what he'd uncovered since had mercilessly ripped that indulgent blindfold away.

Finding out that his father had known about Benedicto da Costa's escalating threats and that he'd done nothing to warn or protect him had forced the cruellest reality on him.

And his mother's response to all that had been to abandon him, together with her other two children, and go into hiding.

Hearing of his father's eventual death had made him even angrier at being robbed of the chance to look his father in the eye and see the monster for himself.

Because, even now, a pathetic part of him clung to the hope that maybe his father hadn't known the full extent of the kidnapping threat; hadn't known that Benedicto da Costa's reaction to being thwarted out of a business deal would be to kidnap a seventeen-year-old boy, and have his torture photographed and sent to his family to pressure them into finding the millions of dollars owed to him.

His phone rang, wrenching him out of the bitter recollections. Glancing down at the number, a bolt of white-hot anger lanced through him. He forced himself to wait for a couple more rings before he answered it. 'Pantelides.'

'*Bom dia*. I've just had a very interesting conversation with my daughter.' Theo detected the throb of anger in Benedicto da Costa's voice and a grim smile curved his own lips. 'She seems determined to pursue this rather *sudden* course of action where you're concerned.'

'Your daughter strikes me as a very determined woman who knows exactly what she wants,' he replied smoothly.

'She is. All the same, I can't help think that this decision is rather precipitate.' There was clear suspicion in Benedicto's voice now.

'Trust me, it's been very well thought through on my part. Tell me, Benedicto, has she left yet?'

'*Sim*, against my wishes, she has left home,' he replied, his voice taut with displeasure.

A wave of satisfaction swept through Theo. 'Good. I'll await her arrival.'

'I hope this will not delay our meeting,' the older man enquired.

'Don't worry. The moment I welcome your daughter into my home, I'll head to your offices.'

An edgy silence greeted his answer and Theo could sense him weighing his words to perceive a possible threat. Finally, Benedicto answered, 'We should celebrate our partnership once the documents are signed.'

Theo's mouth twisted. Benedicto had already moved on from the subject of his daughter. And he noticed there had been no admonition to treat her well, *or else…*

But the knowledge that Benedicto had intensely disapproved of Inez's intentions and had called him to air that disapproval was good enough for him.

'Great idea. Unfortunately, I'll be busy for the next few nights. Perhaps some time next week Inez and I will have you and Pietro over for dinner.'

The fiery exhalation that greeted his indelicate words made Theo's grin widen.

'Of course. I'll look forward to it. *Até a próxima,*' Benedicto said tightly.

Theo ended the call without responding. He absorbed the pulse of triumph rushing through his bloodstream for a pleasurable second before he exhaled.

His plan was far from being executed. But this was a brilliant start.

He looked out of the floor to ceiling window at the sparkling pool and the beach beyond and tried to push away the images that had visited him again last night and the single hoarse scream that had woken him.

A full body shudder raked his frame and he shoved a hand through his hair. Although he'd long ago accepted the nightmares as part of his existence, he loathed their presence and the helplessness he felt in those endless moments when he was caught in their grip.

The single therapy session he'd let Ari talk him into attending had mentioned triggers and the importance of anxiety-detectors.

He laughed under his breath. Putting himself within touching distance of the man responsible for those nightmares would be termed as foolhardy by most definitions.

Theo chose to believe that exacting excruciating revenge would heal him. *An eye for an eye.*

And if he had to suffer a few side-effects during the process, then so be it.

He tensed as his security intercom buzzed. Crossing the vast sun-dappled room, he picked up the handset.

'*Senhor*, there's a Senhorita da Costa here to see you.'

A throb of a different nature invaded his bloodstream. 'Let her in,' he instructed.

Replacing the handset, he found himself striding to the front door and out onto his driveway before he realised what he was doing.

Hands on his hips, he watched her tiny green sports car appear on his long driveway. The top was down and the wind was blowing through her loose thick hair. Stylish sunglasses shielded her eyes from him but he knew she was watching him just as he was studying her.

She brought the car to a smooth stop a few feet from him and turned off the ignition. For several seconds the only sound that impinged on the late morning air was the water cascading from the stone nymph's urn into the fountain bowl. Then the sound of her seat belt retracting joined the tinkling.

'You're late,' he breathed.

She pulled out her keys and opened her door. 'It took

a while to uproot myself from the only home I've ever known,' she said waspishly.

A touch from a well-manicured finger and the boot popped open. He strolled forward, viewed its contents and his eyes narrowed.

'And yet you only packed two suitcases for a three-month stay?' he remarked darkly. 'I hope you don't think you can run back to *Pai*'s house each time you need a new toothbrush?'

She got out of the car.

From across the width of the open top, she glared at him. 'I can afford to buy my own toothbrush, thanks,' she retorted.

Theo nodded. 'Good to hear it.' Unable to stop himself, his gaze travelled down her body.

Faded jeans moulded her hips and her cream scooped-neck silk top left her arms bare. Its short-in-the-front, longer-at-the-back design exposed a delicious inch of golden, smooth midriff when she turned to shut her door and the air lifted the light material.

Heat invaded his groin, once again reminding him of their kiss last night.

The kiss that had blown him clean away and rendered him almost incoherent by the time her brother had rudely interrupted them.

Hell, she'd been so responsive, so intoxicatingly passionate, she'd gone to his head within seconds. What had set out as a hammering-a-point-home exercise to convince her he meant business had swiftly morphed into something else. Something he'd still been struggling to decipher when she'd been hustled off his boat by her suddenly protective brother.

One thing he'd been certain of was that had Pietro been a few more minutes returning to the top deck, Theo was sure he would've had his hands on her bare skin, exploring her in a more earthy way, propriety be damned.

Luckily, he'd come to his senses. And, from here on in, he intended to focus on his plan and his plan alone.

She went to the boot and bent over to lift the first case. The sight of her rounded bottom made a vein throb in his temple.

He stepped forward, grabbed the cases from her and handed them to his hovering butler. 'I'm running late for my meeting. We should have done this last night like I suggested.'

He'd tried. But she'd stood her ground and he had quickly decided that there was nothing to be gained from getting into a slanging match with Pietro da Costa. That he'd also realised that his change of timing was to do with that kiss and nothing to do with his carefully laid plans had had him sharply reassessing his priorities.

'I'm here now. Don't let me stop you from leaving if you wish to.'

He smiled at the undisguised hope in her voice. 'Now what kind of host would I be if I desert you the moment you turn up?'

'The same as the one who blackmailed me into this situation in the first place?' she replied caustically.

There was a thread of unhappiness in her voice that grated at him.

'This will go a lot easier if you accept the status quo.'

'You mean just shut up and *do as I'm told*?' she snapped bitterly as she slammed the boot shut and walked towards him.

Unease weaved through him. With restless shoulders, he shrugged it away. 'No. You can protest all you want. I just want you to be aware of the futility of it.'

She snorted under her breath, a sound that made his smile widen. She had spirit, and wasn't afraid to bare her claws when cornered. Which made him wonder why she withstood the unreasonable control from her father. Were material benefits so important to her?

The heavy glass front door slid shut behind them and he watched her reaction to his house. It was an architectural masterpiece, and had featured in several top magazines before he'd bought it a year ago and ceased all publicity of the award-winning design.

'Wow,' she breathed. 'This place must have cost you a bomb.'

Theo had his answer. Disappointment scythed through him as he watched her move to the bronze sculpture he'd acquired several weeks back.

'I saw the exhibition on this two months ago. This piece is worth a cool half million,' she gasped in wonder. 'And that one—' she pointed to another smaller sculpture he'd commissioned by his favourite New York artist '—is an exclusive piece, worth over two million dollars.'

His lips twisted. 'Should I be worried that you know the monetary value of every piece of art in my house?'

She whirled to face him. 'Excuse me?'

'I hope we can engage in more meaningful dialogue than how much everything is worth. I find the subject of avarice…distasteful.'

Her gasp sounded genuinely hurt-filled. 'I wasn't…I'm just…that's a horrible thing to say, Mr Pantelides.'

His eyebrow lifted. 'I thought I kissed all the formality out of you last night?'

She flushed a delicate pink that made her skin glow. Her expressive brown eyes slid from his and she turned back to examine the room.

It was then that he noticed the faint bruises on her left arm. He was striding to her and lifting her arm to examine the marks before his brain had connected with his body.

'Who did this to you?' he demanded.

Her surprised gaze snapped from his to her arm. Her flush deepened as she swiftly shook her head. 'I…it doesn't matter; it's nothing—'

He swallowed hard. 'Like hell it is.' The idea that his demands on her might have caused this to happen to her made a thread of revulsion rise in his belly. He forced it down and concentrated on her face. 'Tell me who it was.'

She swallowed. 'My father.'

Pure fury blurred his vision for several seconds. 'Your *father* did this to you?'

She gave a jerky nod.

Why the hell was he surprised? 'Has he done anything like this before?' he bit out.

She pressed her lips together in a vain attempt not to answer. A firm grip of her chin, tilting it to his gaze, convinced her otherwise. 'Once. Maybe twice.'

His vicious curse made her shiver. Theo examined the marks, which would grow yellowish by nightfall, and pushed down the mounting fury. 'That son of a bitch will never touch you again.'

Shock made her gasp. 'That *son of a bitch* is my *father*. And I've given you what you wanted, so I expect you to hold up your end of the bargain.'

He frowned with genuine puzzlement. 'Why do you tolerate this, Inez?' He glanced from the bruises to her face. 'You're more than old enough to live on your own. Hell, if money and a rich lifestyle are what you crave, you're sufficiently resourceful to find some wealthy guy who would—'

She snatched her arm from his grasp. It was then that he realised he'd been caressing her soft skin with his thumb. He missed the connection almost immediately.

'I certainly hope you're not about to suggest what I think you are?'

Keen frustration rocked him into movement. 'I'm curious, that's all.'

'I'm not here to satisfy your curiosity. And perhaps you've been lucky enough to be granted a perfect family but not everyone has been afforded the same luxury. We made do with what we… Did I say something funny?' she snapped.

He cut off the mirthless laughter that had bubbled up at

her words. 'Yes. *You're damned hilarious.* You obviously don't know what you're talking about.'

She stared at him with confusion and a little trepidation. 'No. But how can I? We only met two nights ago. And now I'm here, your possession for the foreseeable future.'

The simple statement twisted like live electricity between them. The look in her eyes said she was daring him to react to it. But the off-kilter emotions swirling through his chest made him back away from it. He shouldn't have dealt with her so soon after speaking to Benedicto. He should've left Teresa, his housekeeper, to see to her needs.

He turned and headed for the door. 'I'll show you upstairs. And then I need to go.'

Striding into the hallway, he started up the grand central stairs that led to the upper two floors of his house. After a few steps, he noticed she wasn't behind him.

Turning, he found her paused on the second step, her gaze once again wide and wondrous as she stared around her.

'What?'

'There are no concrete walls.' She looked up at the all-encompassing glass around her. 'Or ceilings.'

He resumed climbing the stairs. 'I don't like walls. And I don't like ceilings,' he threw over his shoulder.

She hurried after him and caught up with him as they neared the first suite of rooms. She regarded him for a few seconds then bit her lip.

He paused with a hand on the doorknob. 'What?' he asked again, trying and not succeeding in prising his gaze from her plump lips.

'I'm not sure whether to take that as a metaphor or not.'

'*Anjo*, there's no hidden meaning behind my words. I literally do not like concrete walls or ceilings.'

She frowned in puzzlement. 'I don't understand.'

'It's very simple. I don't like being closed in.'

'You're...*claustrophobic*?' She whispered the word as if she wasn't sure how to apply it to him.

He shrugged and hurriedly threw open the door, a part of him reeling at what he'd just admitted. 'We all have our flaws,' he retorted.

'Were you born with it?'

His jaw clenched once. 'No. It was a condition thrust upon me quite against my will.'

'But…you seem…'

'Invincible?' he mocked.

Her lips pursed. 'I was going to say self-assured.'

'Appearances can be deceptive, *querida*. After you.' He indicated the door he'd just opened.

She stopped dead in the middle of the room. From where he stood, Theo could see what she was seeing. With the glass walls and white carpet and furnishings and nothing but the view of the blue sky and sea beyond, the vista was breathtaking.

'*Deus*, I feel as if I'm floating on a cloud,' she murmured with an awe-filled voice.

'That is the primary aim of the property. Light, air, no constrictions.'

He'd learned to his cost that constrictions triggered his anxiety and fuelled his nightmares. Which was why every single property he owned was filled with light.

'It's beautiful.'

The strong pulse of pleasure that washed through him had him stepping back. Things were getting out of hand. He needed to walk away, go to his meeting with Benedicto and remind himself why he was in Rio. This need to bask in Inez's presence, touch her skin, indulge in the urge to taste her sensual lips once more needed to killed. He had to stick to his game plan.

'Make yourself at home. I'll be back later. We're going out this evening. Dinner at Cabana de Ouro, then probably clubbing. Wear something short and sexy.'

Her eyes widened at his curt tone but he was already turning away. He didn't stop until he reached the landing.

On a completely unstoppable urge, he looked over his shoulder. Through the glass walls, he saw her frozen in the middle of her suite, her eyes fixed on him.

She looked lost. And confused. And a little relieved.

With grim determination he turned and headed down the stairs. And he hated himself for needing the reminder that Benedicto da Costa had damaged not just him, but his whole family.

The payback should be equal to the crime committed.

The black satin boy shorts she chose to wear were plenty stylish and sexy. They also moulded her behind much more than she was strictly comfortable with but everything else she'd hastily packed was too formal for dinner at Cabana de Ouro, the trendy restaurant and bar in Ipanema. Coupled with the dark gold silk top, with her hair piled on top of her head and gold hoops in her ears and bangles on her wrist, she looked good enough for whatever club Theo intended to take her to after dinner.

Clubbing wasn't strictly her entertainment of choice. But since, for the next twelve weeks, Theo expected her to obey his every command, the least she could do was learn to pick her battles. And she'd already endured one battle this morning in the form of confrontation with Theo. And found out he was claustrophobic.

He'd been right; she'd secretly imagined him to be invincible. The way he carried himself, the innate authority and self-assurance that seemed part of his genetic make up, she'd had no trouble seeing him best each situation he found himself him.

Hearing him admit to a deep flaw that most grown men would be ashamed of had floored her. Coupled with his concern when he'd seen the marks her father had inflicted when she'd announced she was moving in with Theo, she'd been seriously floundering in a sea of uncertainty by the time he'd left her bedroom.

She examined the marks on her arm now and released a shaky breath to see that they were fading. She was shrugging on the shoulder-padded waist-length leather jacket that went with the outfit when she heard Theo's Aston Martin roar into the driveway.

Her fingers trembled as she fastened the long-chained gold medallion necklace at her nape.

He'd left her so abruptly this morning she hadn't had the time to question him about sleeping arrangements. A closer examination of her suite after he'd left had revealed no presence of another occupant, and after talking to Teresa, his housekeeper, she'd found out that the *senhor's* suite was directly above hers, taking up the whole glass-roofed top floor of the house.

The fact that she wouldn't be expected to share his bed immediately should've pleased her. Instead she was more on edge than ever. Or maybe that was what he wanted? That she should be kept guessing, kept on a knife-edge of uncertainty like some sort of game?

Deus!

She'd barely spent one day under his glass roof and already she was being driven mad. His response to her admiring his sculptures had been too infuriating for her to explain how she'd come to acquire such knowledge of sculptures—her late mother's talent. If he wanted to believe Inez appreciated beautiful art purely with dollar signs in her eyes, that was his problem.

Her breath caught as she heard distinct footsteps in the hallway. Teresa had shown her how to shroud the bedroom glass for privacy and she'd activated it before she'd gone in to take a shower. It was still shrouded now although she could make out a faint outline of the towering man who knocked a few seconds later.

'Come in.' She cringed at the husky breathlessness of her voice.

The heavy glass swung back and Theo stood framed in the doorway.

Light hazel eyes locked on her with the force of a laser beam for several seconds before they travelled slowly down her body.

Before meeting him, Inez would've found it hard to believe she could physically react so strongly to a look from a man. Constantine, with all his misleading smiles and false charm, had never affected her like this, not even when she'd believed herself in love with him.

With Theo the evidence was irrefutable—in the accelerated beat of her heart, the tightening and heaviness of her breasts and the stinging heat that spread outward from her belly like a flash fire.

She watched his mouth drop open as his gaze reached her shorts and her own mouth dried at the look that settled on his face.

'What the hell are you wearing?'

'What? I'm wearing clothes, Mr Pantelides,' she snapped, once she was able to get her brain working again.

He stepped into the room and the door slid shut behind him. All at once, she became aware of the sheer size of him, of the restriction in her breathing and the fact that her eyes were devouring his magnificent form.

'Let's get one thing straight. From now on you'll address me as Theo. No more *senhor* and no more Mr Pantelides, understand?'

'Is that an order?' She tilted her chin to see his face as he stopped before her.

'It's a friendly warning that there will be consequences if you don't comply.'

'What consequences?' she huffed.

'How about every time you call me *senhor* I kiss that sassy mouth of yours?'

CHAPTER SEVEN

'EXCUSE ME?' HER voice was a little more breathless. With excitement. *Deus*, what was wrong with her? This man was threatening her family, was effectively turning her life upside down for the sake of some unknown grudge. And all she could think of was him kissing her again.

'No, you're not excused. Use my first name or I'll kiss it into you. Your choice. Now tell me what the hell you're wearing.' His gaze dropped back to her shorts, his eyes glazing with hunger so acute, her heart hammered.

'These are shorts. You said "short and sexy".'

His mouth worked for a few seconds before he nodded. 'I said short, but I don't think I meant that short, *anjo*.'

Heat raced up her neck and she barely managed to stop her hand from connecting with his face. 'They are not that bad.'

His rasping laugh made her face flame. 'Trust me, from where I'm standing, they're lethal.'

'I have nothing else to change into. Everything else is too formal for a club.'

Dark eyes rose, almost reluctantly, to clash with hers. 'I find that very hard to believe.'

'It's true. I didn't have enough time to pack properly. Besides, I didn't take you for…'

His eyes narrowed. 'Didn't take me for what?'

She shrugged. 'You don't strike me as the clubbing type.'

One corner of his mouth lifted. 'Have you been forming impressions about me, *anjo*?'

She kicked herself for that revelatory remark. 'Not really.'

He looked down at her shorts one more time and he turned abruptly for the door. 'I'll be ready to go in fifteen minutes. You can tell me what other impressions you've formed about me at dinner.'

Inez exhaled and realised she hadn't taken a full breath since he'd walked into her presence. Her whole body quivered as she shoved her feet into three-inch platforms and made sure her cell phone and lipstick were in the black and gold clutch.

She caught sight of herself in the hallway mirror as she made her way down and cringed at the feverish look in her eyes.

Reassuring herself firmly that it was anger at Theo for his overbearing treatment of her, she made her way to the living room.

Floodlights illuminated the pool and gardens in a stunning display of shimmering light and shrubbery. Like every single aspect of the building, the sight was so breathtaking her fingers itched with the need to draw.

Setting her clutch down, she went to the large duffel bag she'd brought down this afternoon and took out her sketchpad and pencil.

She was so lost in capturing the vista before her, she didn't sense Theo enter the room until his unique scent wrapped itself around her.

She jerked around to see him standing close behind her, his eyes on her picture.

'You draw?' he asked in surprise.

Unable to answer for the loud hammering of her heart, she nodded.

He reached forward and plucked the pad from her nerveless fingers. Slowly, he thumbed through the pages. 'You're very talented,' he finally said.

Expecting a derogatory remark to follow, like his comment on his art this morning, her eyes widened when she realised he meant it. 'You really think so?' she asked.

He closed the pad and handed it back to her, his eyes speculative as they rested on her face. 'I wouldn't say it otherwise, *anjo*.'

Pleasure fizzed through her. 'Thank you.' She smiled as she stood. Crossing over to her duffel bag, she bent to place the pad back into it.

'*Thee mou!*'

She dropped the pad and hastily straightened. 'What?'

'You bend over like that while we're out and I will not be responsible for my actions, understood?' he growled.

Her mouth dropped open at the dark promise in his voice. A shudder ran through her body as hunger further darkened his eyes. She licked her lip nervously as the atmosphere thickened with sensual charges that crackled and snapped along her nerves.

'We…we don't have to go out if what I'm wearing offends you…Theo,' she ventured hesitantly, sensing that he held himself on the very edge of control.

He inhaled deeply, his chest expanding underneath the dark green shirt and black leather jacket he wore with black trousers. 'That's where you're wrong. What you're offering doesn't offend me in the least. But I'm a red-blooded, possessive male who is finding it difficult not to roar out his primitive reaction to the idea of other men looking at you.' He said it so matter-of-factly she couldn't form a decent response. 'But I'll try to be a *gentleman*. Come.' He held out his arm.

With seriously indecent thoughts of Theo fighting to the death for her flitting through her mind, she crossed the room to his side.

He led them out and held the passenger door of his car open. The first few minutes of the ride to Ipanema was conducted in silence. Every now and then, he raked a hand through his hair and slid a glance at her naked thighs. Each time, he exhaled noisily.

A wild part of her wanted to flaunt herself for him, revel in his very physical reaction to her attire. Another part of her wanted to run and hide from the volatile emotions swirling through the enclosed space of the luxurious sports car.

By the time they drew up in the car park of the exclusive restaurant her pulse was jumping with anxiety. She forced the feeling down and followed him into the restaurant. Finding out they were dining in the even more exclusive upper floor led to all sorts of renewed anxiety as she preceded him up the steps.

The moment they were seated, he leaned forward. 'The moment we return home, I'm burning those shorts.'

She glared at him. 'No, you are not, *senhor!* They're my favourite pair.'

'Then frame them and mount them on a wall. But you most definitely will not be wearing them out again.'

That wild streak widened. 'I thought you would be man enough to handle a little…challenge. Are you saying you're not?'

His eyes narrowed. 'Don't bait a hungry lion, *querida*, unless you're prepared to be devoured,' he grated out.

'Did you tell your last girlfriend how she should dress too?' she challenged.

His mouth compressed. 'My last girlfriend was under the misconception that the more frequently she walked around naked the more interested I would be in her. She lasted ten days.'

Inez's curiosity spiked, along with an emotion she was very loath to name. 'How long did your longest relationship last?'

'Three weeks.'

Her breath caught. 'So why three *months* with me?' she asked.

He looked startled for a moment then he shrugged. 'Because you're not my girlfriend. You're so very much more.'

Inez was struck dumb by his reply. A small foolish part of her even felt giddy, until she reminded herself that she was intended to be nothing but his *mistress*. Again unfathomable emotions wrapped themselves around her heart. She cleared her throat and fought to keep her voice even. 'Why *misconception*?'

'Very few women manage to catch and keep my interest for very long, *anjo*.'

'Because you get bored easily?' she dared.

His lashes swept down for a few seconds before they rose again to capture hers. 'Because my demons always win when pitted against the rigours of normal relationships.'

'*Demons?*'

'*Sim*, *anjo*. Demons. I have a lot of them. And they're very possessive.' A wave of anguish rolled over his face, then it was gone the next instant. He nodded to the hovering *sommelier* and ordered their wine. Another pulse of surprise went through her when she noticed it was the same wine she'd served at the fund-raiser and her favourite.

'The burning is now off the table. Hell, you can even keep the damn shorts. But, for the sake of my sanity, can we agree that you don't wear them outside?' he asked with one quirked eyebrow.

She pretended to consider it. 'What is your sanity worth to me?'

'You think you're in a position to bargain with me, Inez?' he asked, his voice deceptively soft.

'I never pass up an opportunity to bargain.'

He regarded her silently for several minutes. Then he shrugged. 'As long as I achieve my goals in the end, I see no reason why the road to success shouldn't be littered with minor obstacles. Tell me what you desire.'

'Is that what I am, a minor obstacle?'

'Don't miss your opportunity with meaningless questions.'

The need for clarity finally forced her to speak. 'I wish to know exactly what you want of me.'

'Sorry, I cannot answer that.'

She frowned. 'Why not?'

'Because my needs are…fluid.' The peculiar smile accompanying his answer sent a tingle of alarm down her spine.

'So I am to live in uncertainty for the next three months?'

'The unknown can be challenging. It can also be exciting.'

'Is that why you came to Rio? To seek challenge and excitement?'

For several seconds he stared at her. Then he slowly shook his head. 'No, my reason for being in Rio is specific and a well-planned event.'

Inez shivered at the succinct response. 'I can't help but be frightened by your answer.'

Her candid admission seemed to surprise him. 'Why is that?'

'Because I have a feeling it has something to do with my family. Pietro has his flaws but he's never done anything without my father's express approval. Besides, you're much older than him, which makes it unlikely that he's the one you came here for. You're here because of my father, aren't you?'

It took an astonishing amount of control not to react to her simple but accurate summation of the single subject that had consumed him for over a decade.

Thinking back, he realised he'd given her several clues to enable her to reach this conclusion. Somehow, in the mere forty-eight hours that he'd known her, Inez had managed to slip under his guard and was threatening to uncover his true purpose for being in Rio.

He also realised that he'd given her much more leeway than he'd ever intended to when he'd formulated his plan. Inviting her to compromise? Inviting her to state her desires with the knowledge that he was seriously considering granting them?

After his hasty departure this morning he'd realised that he'd let those marks on her arms sway him into going easy on her. *Because he hadn't wanted her to think he was a monster like her father?*

The man who hadn't so much as asked after his daughter when Theo had attended his office to sign the agreement papers?

The man whose eyes had shone with greed and triumph even before the ink had dried on the documents?

No, he was nothing like Benedicto da Costa. He wasn't about to lose any already precious sleep wondering about that little statement.

What he had to be careful of was that his enemy's daughter didn't guess his intentions. He was so very close to having Benedicto right where he wanted him. He couldn't afford to be swayed by a heart-shaped face or the most sinfully sexy pair of shorts he'd ever seen in his life, no matter how acute the ache in his groin.

'Will you please tell me why you're after my father?' she implored softly. The concern on her face appeared genuine and he suddenly realised that, despite Benedicto's treatment of her, Inez cared for her father.

His nostrils flared as bitterness rocked through him. He'd once been in that same position, foolishly believing that the father he'd idolised and loved beyond reason cared just as deeply for him. That he wasn't the fraudster and philanderer the press were making him out to be.

Now, he wanted to rip the blindfold from her eyes, make her see the true monster in the man she called *Pai*. Make her see that her love was nothing but a manipulative tool that would be used against her eventually.

Except he had a strong feeling she already knew, and chose to overlook it. Which made his blood boil even more.

'Why, do you plan to sacrifice yourself to save him?' he taunted.

She gasped, dropping the sterling silver fork she'd been nervously toying with. 'So, it *is* my father!'

He cursed under his breath. 'If you so much as breathe a word in his direction about your suspicions, I'll make sure you regret it for the rest of your life.'

She paled. 'You really expect me to sit back and watch you destroy him?'

'I expect you to hold up your end of the bargain we struck. Live under my roof in exchange for me leaving the loophole in the contract alone. Are you prepared to do that or do I need to plot another plan of action?' he asked, not bothering to hide the threat in his voice.

She stared back at him apprehensively. Her chin rose and her brown eyes burned holes in him but she nodded. 'I'll stick to our agreement.'

When their wine was served, he watched her take a big gulp and curbed the desire to follow suit. He was driving and needed to restrict his drinking. Nevertheless, a sip of the Chilean red went a way to restoring a little order to his floundering thoughts.

Thee mou, he hadn't even fired the first salvo and things were getting out of hand. Why on earth had he shared the presence of his demons with her? And that comment about her being so much more than a girlfriend? He silently shook his head and sucked in a control-affirming breath.

Their dinner progressed in near silence. Theo reminded himself that his main reason for bringing her out hadn't been for conversation. When she refused dessert, he settled the bill quickly and rose to help her out of her seat.

Fire shot through his groin, hard and fierce, as he was once again confronted with the risqué shorts. While they'd been seated, he'd managed to tamp down the effect of those shorts on his raging libido.

Now, as she walked in front of him, he was treated to a mouth-watering sight of her deliciously rounded bottom and stunning legs. With each sway of her hips, he grew harder until he wondered if he had any blood left in his upper extremities that hadn't migrated south.

He was reconsidering his decision not to burn the shorts at the earliest opportunity when he caught a male diner staring in blatant appreciation at her legs.

His growl was low but unmistakable. The man hastily averted his gaze but Theo was still simmering in primitive emotions when they reached the car park.

He followed her to the passenger side but, instead of opening the door for her, he braced his hand on either side of her and leaned in close. With her front pressed against the door, her bottom was moulded into his groin in such a way that she couldn't fail to notice his state of arousal.

Her breathing quickened, but she stayed put. 'What are you doing?'

'Delivering the punishment I promised.'

'Sorry?'

'You called me *senhor* when we were in the restaurant.'

She tried to turn around but he pressed her more firmly against the car. 'I…don't remember.'

'Of course you do. You also thought I wouldn't act on my promise in full view of other diners, didn't you?'

'No, I wasn't—'

'Maybe you were right. Or maybe we both knew I'd want to do more than just kiss you.'

'You're wrong…'

'Am I?'

'Yes…'

'So you'd prefer I let this one slide?' He rocked his hips against her bottom and her breath hitched. 'You won't think me weak?'

Her shocked laugh heated the air around them. 'Only someone foolish would think you weak.'

'I'm not sure whether there's a compliment in there. Is there?'

Her head fell forward, exposing the seductive line of her neck. 'Am I to pander to your ego too, Theo?'

He laughed. 'How can you appear submissive and yet taunt me at the same time?'

She lifted her head and turned to stare at him. Whatever she saw in his face made her squirm harder. Provocatively. Her gaze dropped to his mouth and Theo could no more resist the temptation than he could breathe.

Fingers sliding beneath her knotted hair to hold her still, he caught her mouth in a fierce kiss. Every emotion he'd experienced since waking that morning was delivered in that kiss—passion, arousal, confusion, anxiety and anger. He pinned her against the car so she couldn't move, couldn't put those seductive hands on his body.

Although he missed her touch, a part of him was thankful because, had she had access, he would've lost even more of his mind than he suspected he was losing.

He registered the brief flashes behind his closed eyelids but didn't break the kiss. He suspected Inez had no idea what had just happened. And even if she had, she wouldn't have suspected the true reason behind the paparazzi shots because she was used to being the darling of the press.

Well, she was in for a rude awakening…

She started to open her mouth wider, to return his demanding kiss.

He slowly lifted his head. When she made a tiny sound of protest and tried to recapture his mouth, he forced himself to step away. He'd achieved one part of what he'd set out to do. The second part was a short drive away.

Curving his arm around her waist, he peeled her away from the door, opened it and deposited her inside, all the time trying not to stare down at her legs and imagine how they would feel wrapped around his waist.

He swallowed hard as he rounded the hood and slid behind the wheel.

'Time to head to the club before I give in to the urge to deliver more punishment.'

Her eyes dropped to his mouth and he barely suppressed a groan as she licked her lips.

'For your mercy, I will teach you how to samba like a true Brazilian,' she replied huskily.

Inez lay among the white sheets the next morning, trying hard not to relive the events of the night before but it was as futile as trying to stop a tidal wave.

They'd eventually emerged from the nightclub at two in the morning. She'd been flushed and sweaty from being plastered to Theo's superb body for three straight hours. But the wild racing of her heart had nothing to do with her exertions on the dance floor and everything to do with the man who'd focused on her as if she was the only woman in the whole club.

And *Deus*, had he danced like a dream? Far from tutoring him on the correct steps of her native dance, she'd found herself following his lead as he'd moved expertly on the dance floor.

When he'd caught her to him, her back to his front and replayed the scene in the car park, but this time to music, she'd seriously feared her heart would beat itself to expiration.

In that moment, she'd forgotten that there was a sinister purpose to Theo's plan; that he'd all but admitted she was being used as a pawn in some deadly game he was playing with her father. When he'd laid his stubbled jaw against her cheek and hummed the sultry samba music in her ear, she'd closed her eyes and imagined what it would be like to belong—truly belong—to a man like Theo.

Turning over in bed, she groaned in disbelief at how

susceptible she'd been to his hard body and magnetic charisma. *Santa Maria*, she'd been all but putty in his hands.

Luckily, the fresh air and the long drive back had hammered some sense into her. The moment they'd returned, she'd bidden him a curt *boa noite*, left him standing in the hallway and retreated as fast as her sore feet would carry her.

And she intended to carry on like that. She might not know what his end game was, but she refused to be a willing participant in his campaign.

The last thing she wanted to do was to fall for another manipulator like Constantine.

She was here only because she had no choice but she didn't intend to idle away her time in this house. Theo expected her to stay here for three months, which meant whatever he had planned was not to be executed immediately. Perhaps she could convince him to change his mind in that time.

Yeah, and fairy tales really did come true...

Or she could find out exactly what his intentions were.

She'd seen the look in his eyes when he spoke about her father. Whatever vendetta he'd planned, he intended to see it through.

Helplessly, she rolled over in bed and her eyes lit on the bedside clock. She jerked upright and threw the sheet aside. She might not have anywhere to be on this Saturday morning but lazing about in bed past ten o'clock wasn't her style.

She jumped into the shower, shampooed her hair and washed her body with quick, regimented movement ingrained in her from her time at the Swiss boarding school her father had sent her to just to impress his friends.

Leaving her damp hair to dry naturally, she pulled on an aqua-coloured sundress and slipped her feet into low-heeled thongs. Smoothing her favourite sunscreen moisturiser over her face and arms, she left her room and headed downstairs.

Teresa was crossing the hallway carrying a *cafetière* of freshly made coffee and indicated for Inez to follow her.

She led her out to the terrace that overlooked the immense square infinity pool. Light danced off the water but her attention was caught and held by the man seated at the cast iron oval breakfast table.

His white short-sleeved polo shirt did amazing things to his eyes and olive-toned skin. And loose green shorts exposed solid thighs and lightly hair-sprinkled legs that made her mouth dry before flooding with moisture that threatened to choke her.

'*Bom dia, anjo.* Are you going to stand there all morning?' he mocked.

She forced her legs to move and took the chair he indicated to his right.

'Coffee?' he asked, his voice deep and low.

'Yes, please.' Her voice had grown husky and emerged barely above a whisper.

He nodded to Teresa who smiled, filled her cup then made herself scarce.

Inez sipped the hot brew just as a delaying tactic so she didn't have to look at him.

So far she'd seen Theo in formal evening wear and smart casual and each look had threatened to knock her sideways. But seeing him now, with so much of his vibrant olive skin on show, threatened to topple her completely. She took another hasty sip and choked as the liquid scalded her mouth.

Grabbing the napkin to stop herself from dribbling like an idiot, she looked up and caught his mocking smile. 'You'd rather blister yourself than converse with me?'

She swallowed and fought to present a passable smile. 'Of course not. I was just enjoying the…view.' She indicated beyond his shoulder, where the garden extended beyond the pool and sloped down to the sandy white beach and sparkling ocean.

With a disbelieving smile, he picked up the paper next to his plate and shook it out. 'If you say so—'

Her horrified gasp made him lower the newspaper. 'Something wrong?'

'Is that a picture of *us*?' she demanded through a severely constricted throat. The question was redundant because the picture taking up the whole of the front page was printed in vivid Technicolor.

He'd already seen it, of course, so he didn't bother to glance where her appalled gaze was riveted. 'Yes. Fresh off the morning press.'

'Meu deus!' She reached out and snatched the broadsheet out of his grasp. It was even worse up close. 'It looks as if…as if—' Disbelief caught in her throat, eating the rest of her words.

'As if I'm taking you from behind?' he supplied helpfully.

Humiliating heat stained her cheeks. '*Sim*,' she muttered fiercely. 'With your jacket covering me that way it looks as if I'm wearing nothing from the waist down! It's…it's disgusting!'

He plucked the paper from her hand and studied the picture. 'Hmm, it certainly is…*something*.'

'How can you sit there and be so unconcerned about it?' The picture had been taken with a high-resolution camera but, with the low lighting in the car park, the suggestiveness in the picture could be misinterpreted a thousand ways. None of them complimentary.

'Relax. We weren't exactly having sex, were we?'

'That's not the point.' She grabbed the paper back and quickly perused the article accompanying the gratuitous picture, fearing the worst. Sure enough, her father's political campaign had been called into question, along with an even more unsavoury speculation on her private life.

If this is what they do in public we can only imagine what they do in private…

Her hands shook as she threw the offending paper down. 'I thought this was a reputable paper.'

'It is.'

'Then why would they print something so…offensive?'

'Perhaps because it's true. We were kissing in the car park. And you were pushing your delectable backside into my groin as if you couldn't wait till we got home to do me.'

She surged to her feet, knocking her chair aside. Her whole body was shaking with fury and she could barely grasp the chair to straighten it.

'We both know I was not!'

'Do we? I told you those shorts were a bad idea. Do you blame me for getting carried away?'

'Oh, you're *despicable!*'

'And you're delicious when you're angry,' he replied lazily, picked up the paper and carried on reading.

The urge to drive her fist through the paper into his face made her take another hasty step back.

She abhorred violence. Or at least she had before she'd met Theo Pantelides. Now she wasn't so sure what she was capable of…

'Aren't you going to eat, *anjo*?' he asked without taking his eyes off the page.

'No. I've lost my appetite,' she snapped.

She fled the terrace to the sound of his mocking laughter and raced up to her room, her face flaming and angry humiliation smashing through her chest.

He found her on the beach an hour later. She heard the crunch of his feet in the warm sand and studiously avoided looking up. She carried on sketching the stationary boat anchored about a mile away and ignored him when he settled himself on the flat rock next to her.

He didn't speak for a few minutes before he let out an irritated breath. 'The silent treatment doesn't work for me, Inez.'

She snapped her pad shut and turned to face him. His

lips were pinched with displeasure but his eyes were focused, gauging her reaction…almost as if her reaction mattered.

'Having my sex life sleazily speculated about in the weekend newspaper doesn't work for me either.' She blinked to dilute the intense focus and continued. 'I agree that perhaps those shorts were not the best idea. But I saw the other diners in that restaurant. There were people far more famous than I am. But still the paparazzo followed us into the car park and took our picture.'

Inez thought he tensed but perhaps it was the movement of his body as he reached behind him and produced a plate laden with food. 'It's done. Let's move on.'

She yearned to remain on her high horse, but with her exertions last night, coupled with having eaten less than a whole meal in the last twenty-four hours, it wasn't surprising when her stomach growled loudly in anticipation.

He shook out a napkin and settled the plate in her lap. 'Eat up,' he instructed and picked up her sketchpad. 'You have an hour before the stylist arrives to address the issue of your wardrobe.'

She froze in the act of reaching for the food. 'I don't need a stylist. I can easily go back home and pack up some more clothes.'

'You'll not be returning to your father's house for the next three months. Besides, if your clothes are all in the style of heavy evening gowns or tiny shorts, then you'll agree the time has come to go a different route?'

She mentally scanned her wardrobe and swiftly concluded that he was probably right. 'There really is no need,' she tried anyway.

'It's too late to change the plan, Inez.'

And, just like that, the subject was closed. He tapped the plate and, as if on cue, her stomach growled again.

Giving up the argument, she devoured the thick sliced beef sandwich and polished off the apple in greedy bites.

She was gulping down the bottled water when she saw him pause at her sketch of a boat.

'This is very good.'

'Thank you.'

He tilted the page. 'You like boats?'

'Very much. My mother used to take me sailing. It was my favourite thing to do with her.'

He closed the pad. 'Were you two close?'

'She was my best friend,' she responded in a voice that cracked with pain. 'Not a day goes by that I don't miss her.'

His fingers seemed to tighten on the rock before they relaxed again. 'Mothers have a way of affecting you that way. It makes their absence all the harder to bear.'

'Is yours…when did you lose yours?' she asked.

He turned and stared at her. A bleak look entered his eyes but dissolved in the next blink. 'My mother is very much alive.'

She gasped. 'But I thought you said…'

'Absence doesn't mean death. There are several ways for a parent to be absent from a child's life without the ultimate separation.'

'Are you talking about abandonment?'

Again he glanced at her, and this time she caught a clearer glimpse of his emotions. Pain. Devastating pain.

'Abandonment. Indifference. Selfishness. Self-absorption. There are many forms of delivering the same blow,' he elaborated in a rough voice.

'I know. But I was lucky. My mother was the best mother in the world.'

'Is that why you're trying to be the best daughter in the world for your father, despite what you know of him?'

His accusation was like sandpaper against her skin. 'I beg your pardon?'

He shook his head. 'Don't bother denying it. You know exactly what sort of person he is. And yet you've stood by him all these years. Why—because you want a pat on the head and to be told you're a good daughter?'

The truth of his words hit her square in the chest. Up until yesterday, everything she'd done, every plan of her father's she'd gone along with had been to win his approval, and in some way make up for the fact that she hadn't been born the right gender. She didn't want to curl up and hide from the truth. But the callous way he condemned her made her want to justify her actions.

'I'm not blind to my father's shortcomings.' She ignored his caustic snort. 'But neither am I going to make excuses for my actions. My loyalty to my family isn't something I'm ashamed of.'

'Even when that loyalty meant turning a blind eye to other people's suffering?' he demanded icily.

She frowned. 'Whose suffering?'

'The people he left behind in the *favelas* for a start. Do you know that less than two per cent of the funds raised at those so-called charity events you so painstakingly put together actually make it to the people who need it most?'

She felt her face redden. His condemning gaze raked over her features. 'Of course you do,' he murmured acidly.

'It happened in the past, I admit it, but I only agreed to organise the last event if everything over and above the cost of doing it went to the *favelas*.' At his disbelieving look, she added, 'I do a lot of work with charities. I know what I'm talking about.'

'And did you ensure that it was done?'

'Yes. The charity confirmed they'd received the funds yesterday.'

One eyebrow quirked in surprise before he jerked to his feet. Thrusting his hands into his pockets, he turned to face her. 'That's progress at least.'

'Thank you. I don't live in a fairy tale. Trust me, I'm trying to do my part to help the *favelas*.'

'How?'

She debated a few seconds before she answered. 'I work at an inner city charity a few times a week.'

His gaze probed hers. 'That morning outside the coffee shop, that was where you were going?'

'Yes.'

'What does your father think?'

She bit her lip. 'He doesn't know.'

His mouth twisted. 'Because it will draw attention to his lies about his upbringing? Everyone knows he was born and raised in the *favelas*.'

'It's part of the reason why I didn't tell him, yes. But he denies his *favela* upbringing because he's…ashamed.'

'And yet he doesn't mind anyone knowing about his mother?'

'He thinks it gives him a little leverage with the common man to be indirectly associated with the *favelas*.'

'So he likes to rewrite his history as he goes along?'

'Perhaps. I don't delude myself for one second that my father doesn't bend the rules and the truth at times.'

His harsh laugh made her start. 'Right. Are you talking about, oh, let's see…doing ninety on a sixty miles per hour road, or are we talking about something with a little more…teeth?'

That note she'd heard before. The one that sent a foreboding chill along her spine, that warned her that something else was going on here. Something she should be running far and fast from. 'I…I'm not sure what you're implying.'

'Then let me spell it out for you. Are we talking about harmless anecdotes or are we talking about actual deeds? You know—broken kneecaps? Ruptured spleens. *Kidnap for ransom*?'

Her hand flew to her mouth. 'What the hell are you talking about?'

'Come on, you know what your father is capable of. Do

I need to remind you of what he did to you when you displeased him?'

She followed his gaze to the marks on her arm and slowly shook her head. 'I don't excuse this but I refuse to believe he's the monster you describe.'

His mouth twisted. 'I'll let you enjoy your rosy outlook for now, *querida*. I, too, felt like that once about my own father.'

'Is that what you're going to do to my father? Make him accountable for the things he's done?'

For several heartbeats she was sure he wouldn't answer her, or would change the subject the way he'd done in the past. But finally he nodded.

'Yes. I intend to make him pay for what he took from me twelve years ago.'

Her breath froze in her lungs. 'What did he take from you?'

He turned abruptly and faced the water, his stance rigid and forbidding. But Inez found herself moving towards him anyway, a visceral need driving her. She reached out and touched his shoulder. He tensed harder and she was reminded of his reaction to her touch on his boat. 'Theo?'

'I don't like being touched when my back's turned, *anjo*.'

She frowned. 'Why not?'

'Part of my demons.'

Her gut clenched hard at the rough note in his voice. 'Did…did my father do that to you?'

'Not personally. After all, he's an upright citizen now, isn't he? A man the people should trust.' He whipped about to face her.

'But he had something to do with your claustrophobia. And this?'

'Yes.'

'Theo—'

'Enough with the questions! You're forgetting why you're here. Do you need a reminder?'

She swallowed at the arctic look in his eyes. All signs of the raw, vulnerable pain she'd glimpsed minutes ago were wiped clean. Theo Pantelides was once again a man in control, bent on revenge. Slowly, she shook her head. 'No. No, I don't.'

CHAPTER EIGHT

THEIR CONVERSATION AT the beach set a frigid benchmark for the beginning of her stay at Theo's glass mansion.

The next two weeks passed in an icy blur of hectic days and even more hectic evenings. They'd quickly fallen into a routine where Theo left after a quick cup of coffee and a brief outline of when and where they would be dining that evening.

On the second morning when she'd told him she was heading for the charity, he'd raised an eyebrow. 'What sort of work do you do there?'

'Whatever I'm needed to do.' She'd been reluctant to tell him any specifics in case he disparaged her efforts as a rich girl's means of passing the time till the next party.

He'd returned to his coffee. 'Your time is your own when I'm not around. As long you're back here when I return, I see no problem.'

That had been the end of the subject.

After repeating his warning not to mention anything to her father he'd walked away. The man who'd shown her his pain and devastation had completely retreated.

His demeanour during their time indoors was icily courteous. However, when they went out, which they did most evenings, he was the attentive host, touching her, threading his fingers through her hair and gazing adoringly at her.

It was after the fifth night out that she realised he was

pandering to the paparazzi. Without fail, a picture of them in a compromising position appeared in the newspapers the very next morning.

But while she cringed with every exposing photo, he shrugged it off. It wasn't until her third weekend with him, when the newspapers posted the first poll results of the mayoral race, that she finally had her suspicions confirmed.

He was swimming in the pool, his lean and stunning body cutting through the water like the sleekest shark. The byline explaining the reasons behind the voters' reaction had her surging to her feet and storming to the edge of the pool.

'Is this why you've been taking me out every night since I moved in? So I'd be labelled the slut daughter of a man not fit to be mayor?' She raised her voice loud enough to be heard above his powerful strokes.

He stopped mid-stroke, straightened and slicked back his wet hair. With smooth breaststrokes he swam to where she stood barefoot. Looking down at his wet, sun-kissed face, she momentarily lost her train of thought.

He soon set her straight. 'Your father isn't worthy to lead a chain gang, never mind a city,' he replied in succinct, condemning tones. 'And before I'm done with him, the whole world will know it.'

Despite seeing the evidence for herself two weeks ago at the beach, despite knowing that whatever her father had done to him had been devastating, she staggered back a step at that solid, implacable oath.

He planted his hands on the tiles and heaved himself out of the water. It took every ounce of her self-control not to devour him with hungry eyes. But not looking didn't mean not feeling. Her insides clenched with the ever-growing hunger she'd been unable to stem since the first night he'd walked into her life. And, with each passing day, she was finding it harder and harder to remain unaffected.

It seemed not even knowing why she was here, or the full extent of how Theo intended to use her to hurt her father, could cause her intense emotional reaction to his proximity to abate.

Which made her ten kinds of a fool, who needed to pull her thoughts together or risk getting hurt all over again.

'So you don't deny that you used me as bait to derail my father's campaign?'

Hazel eyes, devoid of emotion, narrowed on her face. 'That was one course of action. But you haven't been labelled a slut. I'll sue any newspaper that dares to call you that,' he rasped.

Her laughter scraped her throat. 'There are several ways to describe someone without using the actual derogatory word, Theo.'

He paused in drying his hair and looked at her. Slowly, he held out his hand. 'Show me.'

She handed the paper over. He read it tight-jawed. 'I'll have them print a retraction.'

Dismay roiled through her stomach, along with a heavy dose of rebellious anger.

'That's not the point, though, is it? The harm's already done. You know this means I'll have to stop volunteering, don't you? I can't bring this sort of attention to the charity.'

He frowned and she caught a look of unease on his face. 'I'll take care of this.'

'Forget it; it's too late. And congratulations; you've achieved your aim. But I won't be paraded about and pawed in public any more, so if you're planning on another night on the town you'll have to do it without me.'

His gaze slowly rose to hers and he resumed rubbing the towel through his hair. 'Fine. We'll do something else.' He threw the paper on the table.

She regarded him suspiciously. 'Something like what?'

'I promised you a trip on the yacht. We'll sail this evening and spend tomorrow aboard. Would you like that?'

At times like these, when he was being a courteous host,

she found it hard to believe he was the same man who was hell-bent on seeking revenge on her father for past wrongs.

She'd given in to her gnawing curiosity after his revelations on the beach and searched the Internet for a clue as to what had happened to him. All she'd come up with were scant snippets of his late father's dirty dealings before Alexandrou Pantelides had died in prison. As far as she knew, there was no connection between Theo's family and hers. The Pantelides brothers, one of whom was married and recently a parent, and the other engaged to be married, were a huge success in the oil, shipping and luxury hotel world. Theo's job as a troubleshooter extraordinaire for the billion-dollar conglomerate meant he never settled in one place for very long. An ideal job for a man whose personal relationships were fleeting at best.

And a man tormented by a horde of demons.

She looked closer at him, tried to see the man behind the wall, the man who'd bared his soul for a brief moment when he'd spoken of his mother's abandonment.

But that man was closed off.

'What does it matter what I want? Frankly, I'm surprised my father hasn't been in touch about this.'

'He has. I refused to take his calls.'

'I didn't mean you. Since I was also the subject in these photos, I'm surprised he hasn't called me to vent his anger.'

His eyelids swept down and shielded his gaze from her. Apprehension struck a jagged path through her. 'He has, hasn't he?'

'He tried. I suggested that perhaps he refrain from contacting you and concentrate on kissing babies and convincing little old ladies to cast their ballot in his favour.'

Shock rooted her to the ground. 'How dare you take control of my life like this?'

'Would you rather I gave him access so he airs his disappointment?'

'What do you care? It's a little late to protect me, don't you think?'

His jaw tightened. 'For as long as you remain under my roof, you're under my protection.'

'*Meu deus*, please don't pretend you care!'

She realised how close she was to tears and swallowed hard. Fearing she would break down in front of him, she whirled round, intent on heading for her room. She made it two steps before he stopped her.

Flinging away the towel, he cupped her cheeks with both hands. 'Stop getting yourself distressed about this.'

'Is that another command?'

His eyes narrowed. 'You're angry.'

'Damn right I am. I wish I'd never set eyes on you. In fact I wish—'

His mouth slanted over hers, hot, hungry and all consuming. Her groan of protest was less than heartfelt and devoured within a millisecond.

A part of her was furious that he'd resorted to kissing her to shut her up. But it was only a minuscule part. The rest of her body was too busy revelling in the feel of his warm bare back and the fine definition of muscles that rippled beneath her caress.

His hands speared into her hair, imprisoning her for the invasion of his tongue as he took the kiss to another level.

His first kiss over two weeks ago had been a pure threat and the two that followed a show of mastery. This kiss was different. There was hunger and passion behind it, but also a gentleness that calmed her roiling emotions and slowly replaced them with a different sensation. Need clamoured inside her; a need to be closer still to his magnificent body; a need to dig her hands into his back and feel him shudder in reaction.

His groan was smothered between their melded lips as she dug her fingers even deeper. Power surged through her when he jerked again.

One hand dropped to her bottom and yanked her lower body into his groin. His erection was unmistakable. Bold, thick and hot, it pressed against her belly with insistent power that made her heartbeat skitter out of control.

She wanted him. Above and beyond all sense, she wanted this man. Her willpower, when it came to the chemistry between them, was laughably negligible.

But she couldn't give in. *Couldn't…*

The gentleness she'd sensed in him was false, she reminded herself fiercely. The bottom line was that in a few short weeks he would walk away. Leave her and her family devastated.

'I'm losing you. Come back, *anjo*,' he murmured seductively against her mouth. He ran his tongue over her lower lip and her knees weakened.

When he cupped her bottom and squeezed, she desperately summoned all her resolve and pushed against his chest. 'No.'

He raised his head and she saw behind the wall. He was as caught in this insane chemistry as she was. A little part of her felt better.

'I can change your mind, Inez. Regardless of what I intend for your father, what is between us is undeniable.'

'Do you hear yourself? You think I should forget everything else and sleep with you just because you made me feel a certain way?'

'That's generally the reason why men and women have sex.'

'But we're not just any man and any woman, Theo, are we?'

He stiffened, and a hard look entered his eyes. 'Are you saying that you've been in love with every man you've slept with?' he queried.

She froze and prayed her humiliation wouldn't show on her face as she tried to stem the memory of Constantine's treatment of her.

His cruel rejection was still an ache beneath her breastbone.

'Inez?' Theo interjected harshly.

'My past relationships are none of your business.'

His slightly reddened mouth twisted. 'Far be it for me to request to be lumped in with your other lovers, but isn't it a touch hypocritical to apply one criteria to me that you haven't done with one of your lovers, in particular?'

'If you're referring to Constantine, let me assure you that you have no idea what you're talking about.'

His hand tightened around her waist. 'Then enlighten me. Why did he dump you?'

Inez broke free. 'We weren't compatible.'

'Or he found out the true reason you were with him and wanted nothing to do with you?'

'No. That wasn't why…' She screeched to a stop as the words stuck in her throat.

'So what was it? Did you really love him or did you convince yourself you did in order to achieve your aims?'

She bit her lip as he shone a light on the stark question. Had she blown her feelings out of proportion? Constantine had been charismatic, yes, but he'd never created the decadent chaos that Theo created in her.

When she'd imagined love, she'd always imagined passion, hunger and a keen pleasure even the slightest thought of that special someone brought. She'd believed herself in love with Constantine and yet she'd never experienced those emotions.

Well, she most definitely wasn't feeling them now.

'I believed my emotions were genuine at the time. But he didn't. He believed I was using him to further my father's campaign.'

'What did he do?' he asked. She looked into his eyes and fooled herself into thinking she saw a thawing of the hardness there.

'He made painful digs at me whenever he gave interviews. He made the tabloids call my character into question…much the same way you're doing now.'

He dropped his hand. 'It's not the same—'

'Yes, it is. Look Theo, I just want to be left alone to do my time.'

He paled. 'You're not in prison, Inez.'

She put much needed distance between them. 'Am I not? How else would you describe my presence here?'

Theo watched her walk away and curled his fists at his sides. The urge to call her back was so strong he forced himself to exhale slowly to expel the need. Her reference to her presence under his roof as a prison sentence had stung badly.

But hell, the truth was irrefutable. He'd forced her to make a choice, and no amount of dinner dates or designer shopping sprees would gloss over the fact that he'd set the tabloids on her as a way to dismantle her father's campaign.

Witnessing her clear distress just now had made his chest ache in a way that confused and irritated him.

Perhaps he needed to step up his agenda, end this dangerous game once and for all and move on with his life.

His brothers would certainly agree. He'd been avoiding their calls for the best part of a fortnight, replying only by email and with curt one-liners that he knew would only go so far before something gave.

He gritted his teeth against the prompt to deliver a swift killing blow to Benedicto da Costa.

His own ordeal hadn't been swift. It'd been long and tortuous. The punishment should fit the crime. Any hesitation on his part now merely stemmed from the afterglow of the chemistry between him and Inez. He freely admitted that theirs was a strong and potent brand, more intense than anything he'd ever experienced before.

It was messing with his mind, the same way the thought of her ex-lover had made him see red for several long seconds. But there was no way he was letting it impede his goal.

Which meant he had to come at this problem from another angle.

He swallowed the acrid taste in his mouth at the thought that Inez had put him into the same class as Constantine Blanco.

Slowly walking back indoors, he turned over the dilemma in his mind. By the time he reached his suite and changed out of his swimming trunks, a smile was curving his lips.

An hour later, he watched her descend the stairs, her duffel bag slung over her shoulder and an overnight case in her hand.

'Did Teresa tell you to pack your swimming gear?'

She regarded him warily. 'Yes. But I thought we were just taking the boat out?'

He shrugged. 'I thought you would welcome the opportunity to sunbathe away from the prying lenses of the paparazzi? There are several decks on the yacht that you can sunbathe on. Or we can swim in the sea, dine alone under the stars. Would you like that?' he asked, then felt a jolt at how much he wanted her to answer in the affirmative. In the past, he'd never taken the time to seek out what pleased his girlfriends beyond the usual gifts and fine dining. It was why he operated his relationships on a strict short-term basis with as little maintenance as possible.

Inez was far from low maintenance. And yet he found himself even more drawn to her.

She glanced pointedly over his shoulder. 'I'll think about it and let you know.'

His unsettled feelings escalated. He reminded himself that they were heading for his boat. She liked his boat. Perhaps she would relent enough to forget that she was angry with him. Forget about Blanco and forget that she was being blackmailed.

Theo was still debating why her feelings meant so much to him when he pulled up at the marina.

* * *

'You've been smiling ever since we set sail.'

Her voice was full of heavy suspicion. Theo's smile widened as he tilted his face up into the sunshine. 'Have I? It must be the weather.'

'The weather has been the same for the last month,' she replied sourly.

He slowly lowered his head and captured her gaze with his. 'Then it must be the company.'

A delicate wave of heat surged up her neck into her cheeks, making him wonder, as he had more than once these past two weeks, how she could have been involved with someone like Blanco and still blush like a schoolgirl.

Theo had looked into Constantine Blanco and had not been surprised to find that he was cut from the same cloth as Benedicto. It was perhaps why Da Costa had chosen to ally himself with the younger man politically. He'd sent his daughter to spy on Blanco and had been double-crossed in the bargain.

Theo's smile slipped as he recalled her hurt when he'd thrown her relationship with Blanco at her. He reached for the glass of wine that had accompanied their late afternoon meal and took a large gulp.

The guilt tightening in his chest since her accusation at the pool squeezed harder.

What the hell was going on with him?

'Have you decided whether you're selling the boat or not?' she asked.

In the sunlight, her black hair gleamed like polished jet, making him burn to feel its silkiness beneath his fingers.

He stared into his drink. 'Maybe. I'll have to weigh up practical usage versus the desire to hang on to something beautiful.'

'But you're a billionaire. Isn't collecting toys part and parcel of your status?'

'I wasn't always a man of means. In fact my brothers and

I worked our backsides off to achieve the level of success we enjoy now.' His smile felt tight and strained.

'Your brothers…Sakis and Arion…'

He looked up in surprise. 'You've been playing around on the Internet, I see.'

She raised her chin. 'I thought it wise to learn a little bit more about my enemy.'

The label grated. Badly. 'What else did you try to discover while you were rooting around my family tree?'

'Your brother Sakis had some trouble with a saboteur on one of his oil tankers.'

He nodded. 'We dealt with that quite satisfactorily.'

'And now your brother Ari is engaged to the widow of the man who tried to throw your company into chaos?' She frowned.

A reluctant grin tugged at his mouth. 'What can I say; we thrive on interesting challenges.'

'You also seem to make enemies with the people you do business with. So far you've led me to believe it was my father who wronged you. How do I know it's not the other way round? That you're not here because you deserved everything you got?'

The stem of the wine glass snapped with a sickening crack. Even then it took the cold wine seeping into his shirt to realise what he'd done.

The top part of the glass landed on the table, rolled off and smashed onto the deck.

Inez gasped. 'Theo, you're bleeding!' She surged to her feet and sprang towards him.

'Stop!'

'But your finger…'

'Is nothing compared to what will happen to your foot if you take another step.'

She glanced down at the broken glass an inch from her bare foot and glanced back at his bleeding forefinger. Anguish creased her pale features.

'Sit down, Inez,' he instructed tersely.

'Please, let me help,' she implored.

Gritting his teeth, he grabbed a napkin and formed a small tourniquet around the gaping wound. 'It's not deep but will need to be cleaned properly. There's a first aid kit behind the bar.'

She nodded, slipped on her sandals and dashed for the bar. Theo stood and moved from the dining table to the wraparound sofa to give the crew member who'd arrived on deck room to sweep up the broken glass. He glanced up as Inez rushed back and set the kit on the coffee table.

Her eyes were turbulent with worry as she glanced from his face to the blood-soaked napkin.

'Are you going to stand there staring at me all evening? I'm bleeding to death here.'

With a hoarse croak, she jerked into action. She carefully cleaned the wound with antiseptic and applied gauze before securing it with a plaster. All through the procedure, she darted quick, apologetic glances at him.

As he stared at her, he felt a different sort of jolt run through him. One he hadn't been aware he was missing until he felt it.

Care. Concern. Fear for him.

When was the last time anyone besides Ari and Sakis had felt like that about him? When was the last time his own mother lavished such attention on him? Inez slid him another worried glance and his breath shuddered out.

'Calm yourself, *anjo*. I'll live. I'm sure of it.'

She exhaled noisily and her agitated pulse pounded at her throat. '*Sinto muito*,' she said in a rush.

'Don't apologise. It wasn't your fault.'

'But…if I hadn't accused you of…'

'You're operating in the dark and want to find out the truth. I respect that. But I can't tell you what my business with your father is until I'm ready. You have to respect that.'

'But…this…' She glanced down at his finger and shook

her head. 'Your reaction…the claustrophobia and the touching thing…I can't help but fear the worst, Theo,' she whispered.

Against his will, his chest constricted at the anguish in her voice. He wanted to comfort her. Wanted to take that look of anticipated pain from her face. He wanted to kiss her until they both forgot why she was his prisoner and why he was beginning to dread the day he had to set her free.

He swallowed hard.

'Let's make a deal. For the next twenty-four hours, no talk of your father or the reason why I'm in Rio. Agreed?'

Her mouth wobbled and her teeth worried her bottom lip as she glanced back at his finger. Her eyes were no less turbulent when they rose to his but he saw determination flare in their depths. 'Agreed.'

Theo stood at the railing on the third floor deck and watched her swim in the pool on the second deck the next morning. She moved like a water nymph, her long black hair streaming down her back as she scissored her arms and legs underwater.

He gripped the rail until his knuckles turned white but still he couldn't take his eyes off her.

'I'm waiting for an answer, Theo,' came the weary voice at the end of the line.

Theo sighed. 'Sorry, remind me again what the question was.'

Ari grunted with annoyance. 'I asked you why I couldn't have one peaceful breakfast without opening the papers to find you wrapped around some poor girl. Seriously, my digestive system has sent me a stern memo. Either I treat it better and not subject it to such images or it goes on permanent vacation.'

Theo heard Perla, his soon-to-be sister-in-law, laughing in the background.

'The answer is simple. Don't read the papers.'

Ari sighed. 'How long is this going to go on for?'

'Everything should be signed, sealed and delivered in a week or two,' he responded, rolling his shoulders to ease the tension tightening his muscles. Another sleepless night, plagued with nightmares. He'd given up on sleep somewhere around three a.m.

'You sound very sure.'

His grip tightened around the phone. As he'd lain awake he'd briefly toyed with the idea of ending this vendetta sooner. And he'd been stunned when the idea had taken firm hold. 'I am.'

'And nothing you're doing down there will affect the wedding? Don't forget it's in two weeks. If you can prise yourself away from that piece of skirt for long enough—'

'She's not a piece of skirt,' he snarled before he could catch his response. Ari's silence made him hurry to speak. 'I'll be at your wedding.'

'Good, since you've missed most of the rehearsals, I'll send you the video of what you need to do. Make sure you get it right; we'll do a quick rehearsal when you get here. I'm not having you mess things up for Perla.'

'Sure. Fine,' he murmured.

He followed the curvy, sexy shape underneath the water and held his breath as Inez broke the surface and rose out of the pool. Dripping curves and sun-kissed skin made his body clench unbearably. He wanted to trace every single inch of her with his hands, his mouth, his tongue. 'Oh, and tell Perla I'm bringing a guest.'

His brother muttered a curse and relayed the message. Theo heard Perla's whoop of delight. 'The love of my life grudgingly agrees but suggests that perhaps, next time, you could be courteous enough to give us a heads-up sooner?'

'Next time? You mean you'll be getting married for a third time?'

He hung up to more pithy curses ringing in his ears and found himself smiling. Without taking his eyes off the figure below, he descended the spiral staircase and walked towards the bikini-clad goddess reaching for the towel on the shelf next to the pool.

Her back was turned and he slowed to a stop as the sight of her tiny waist and curvy hips made blood rush through his veins. Lust twisted through his gut, hard and demanding.

Hell, this was getting unbearable.

He threw his cell phone on the breakfast table and watched her jerk around to face him. The towel she was holding to her hair stilled.

'Hi.'

'Good morning. Enjoy your swim?'

'It was very refreshing,' she replied huskily, her eyes following him warily as he strode towards her. 'So, what's the plan for today?' she asked.

I want to haul you off to my bed and keep you underneath me until we both pass out from the pleasure overload.

He wrenched his gaze from her full breasts, lovingly cupped by damp white triangles, and concentrated on breathing. 'We're headed for Copacabana. We'll stop for something to eat then head back tonight. Or if you want we can stay on the boat and leave in the morning?'

She thought about it for a second and nodded. 'I'd love to draw the boat in the moonlight.'

'Then that's what you shall do.'

Her gaze turned puzzling, weighing.

'What's on your mind?' he asked.

She shook her head slightly and slowly folded the towel. 'Sometimes I feel as if I'm dealing with two people.'

Something hard tugged in his chest. 'Which one do you prefer?'

'Are you joking? The person you are now, of course.'

He froze as the tug tightened its hold on him. His breath came in short pants as he closed the distance between them. 'I thought we weren't going to delve into our issues today.'

'You asked me what was on my mind.'

He nodded. 'I guess I did.' He stared into the pure, make-up-free perfection of her face and something very close to regret rose in his gut.

'Now it's my turn to ask you what's on your mind, Theo,' she murmured thoughtfully.

'It's completely pointless, of course, but I'm wishing we'd met under different circumstances.'

Her mouth dropped open. 'You are?'

The urge to touch grew, and he finally gave in. He traced his thumb over her lips and felt them pucker slightly under his touch. 'As I said, it's pointless.'

'Because you would've been done with me within a week?' she ventured.

'No. I would've kept you for much longer, *anjo*. Perhaps even for ever.'

He forced himself to step away. Once again she'd slid so effortlessly under his skin, opened him up to wishes and possibilities he'd forced himself never to entertain after what their respective fathers and his mother had done to him. She was making him believe in impossible dreams, feelings he had no business experiencing.

He strode quickly towards the pool. A cold dip would wash away the fiery need and alien emotions tearing his insides to shreds. He hoped.

He emerged twenty minutes later to find her polishing off the last of her scrambled eggs and coffee. Over the past fortnight he'd noticed that she ate with a gusto that triggered his own appetite. Or *appetites*.

As he poured his coffee and helped himself to fruit, she reached for the ever-present duffel bag and pulled out her sketchpad.

'Have you thought of doing something with your talent?' he asked.

A shadow passed over her face before she tried to smile through it, but he guessed the reason behind it. Her father.

'I will once I resume my education. I put pursuing my degree on hiatus for a while.'

He didn't need to ask why. 'Until when?'

She shrugged and searched for a fresh page in her pad. 'I haven't decided yet.'

Theo tried not to let his anger show. They'd called a truce for twenty-four hours.

'What will you study when you return?'

'I love buildings and boats. I may go into architecture or boat design.'

He glanced from her face to the pad. 'Boat design, huh?'

She nodded.

He picked up his coffee and regarded her over the rim. 'Why don't you design me one?'

'You want me to design a boat for you?'

'Yes. I'm sure your research showed you what sort of designs we specialise in. It has to be up to the Pantelides standard. But use your own template. Make it state-of-the-art, of course.'

'Of course,' she murmured but he could see the gleam of interest in her eyes as she stared down at her pad.

Her pencil flew across the paper as he devoured his breakfast. She didn't look up as he rose and rounded the table to where she sat. He didn't glance down at her drawing; he was too absorbed with the sheer joy on her face as she became immersed in her task.

Even when his finger drifted down her cheek to the corner of her mouth she barely glanced up at him. But her breath hitched and she jerked a tiny bit towards his touch before he withdrew his hand.

As he walked away, Theo marvelled at how light-hearted he felt.

CHAPTER NINE

THEY DROPPED ANCHOR about a mile away from Copacabana Beach and took a launch ashore.

Inez looked to where Theo stood, legs braced, at the wheel of the launch. The wind rushed through his dark hair, whipping it across his forehead. Stupid that she should be jealous of the wind but she clenched her fingers in her lap as they tingled with the need to touch him.

I would've kept you for much longer, anjo. *Perhaps even for ever.*

Try as she had for the last few hours, she couldn't get his words out of her head. They struck her straight to the heart in unguarded moments, made her breath catch in ways that made her dizzy. Every time she pushed the feeling away. But, inevitably, it returned.

She was in serious trouble here…

A shout from nearby sunbathers drew her attention to the fact that they were not alone any more.

She watched the surge of people and the noise of tourists enjoying a Sunday stroll along the beach roads and suddenly felt as if she was losing the tenuous connection she'd made with Theo last night and this morning. Which was silly. There was no connection. Just a precarious truce.

And an exciting task designing a Pantelides boat, which had made joy bubble beneath her skin all day.

He brought the launch to a smooth stop at the pier and

turned off the engine. Jumping out with lithe grace, he held out his hand to her, the smile on his face making her breath stutter in her chest as she slipped her hand into his.

'I'm in the mood for some traditional food and I know just the place for it. You happy to trust me?'

Safely on solid ground, she glanced up and found herself nodding. 'Yes.'

His eyes darkened. 'It's a bit of a walk.' He glanced at her high-heeled wedges with a cocked eyebrow.

'Don't worry about me. I was born in heels.'

'Then I pity your poor *mãe*.'

She laughed and saw his answering smile.

Gradually they fell silent and his gaze drifted over her face, resting on her mouth for a few seconds before he tugged on her hand. 'Come on, *anjo*.'

He led her along the pier and towards the streets. Ten minutes later, she stared in surprise when they stopped outside a door with a faded sign and a single light bulb above it.

'I hear they serve the best *feijoadas* in Rio,' he said, his gaze probing her every expression.

Inez forced the lump in her throat down as she stared at the sign that had been very much part of a long ago, happier childhood. 'It's true. I…how do you know about this place?'

The hand he'd captured since they alighted from the boat meshed with hers, causing her heart to flutter wildly as he brought it to his lips and kissed the back of it. 'I made it my business to find out.'

Again tears choked her and she couldn't speak for several moments. 'Thank you.'

He nodded. 'My pleasure.'

They stopped in the doorway to allow their eyes to adjust to the candlelit interior.

'*Pequena estrela!*' A matronly woman in her late forties approached, her face lit up with a smile.

After exchanging hugs, Inez turned to introduce Theo.

'Camila and my mother were best friends. I used to have supper here many times after school when I was a kid.'

Theo responded to the introduction in smooth, charming Portuguese that had the older woman blushing before she led them to a table in the middle of the room.

'You want the usual?' Camila asked after she'd brought over a basket of bread and taken their wine order.

Inez glanced at Theo. 'Will you let me choose?'

He sat back in his chair, his gaze brushing her face. 'It's your show, *anjo*.'

She rattled off the order and added a few more dishes that had Camila nodding in approval before she bustled off.

Alone with Theo, she tried to calm her giddy senses. Not read too much into why he'd brought her here of all places. But her emotions refused to be calmed.

He was making her feel things she had no business feeling, considering their circumstances. Her heart was very much in danger of being devastated. And this time the danger signs were not disguised as they'd been with Constantine. She was walking into this with her heart and eyes wide open...

'You're frowning too hard, *querida*.'

Plucking a piece of bread from the basket, she fought to focus on not ruining their truce. 'I think I may have ordered too much food.'

'You have a healthy appetite. Nothing wrong with that.'

'It's that healthy appetite that keeps me on the wrong side of chubby.'

'You're not chubby. You're perfect.'

Her hand stilled on the way to her mouth. In the ambient light, she witnessed the potent, knee-weakening look of appreciation on his face. The look slowly grew until hunger became deeply etched into his every feature.

Desire pounded through her, sending radial pulses of heat through her body to concentrate on that needy place between her legs. '*Obrigado*,' she murmured hoarsely.

He nodded slowly, leant forward and took the piece of bread from her hand. Tearing off a piece, he held it against her mouth. When she opened it, he placed it on her tongue and watched her chew.

Then he sat back and ate the remaining piece.

She eventually managed to swallow and cast around for a safe topic of conversation that didn't involve her father or the dangerous emotions arcing between them.

Whether he noticed her floundering or not, she smiled gratefully when he asked, 'Did your mother grow up around here?'

'No, both she and Camila grew up near the Serra Geral, although she spent part of her childhood in Arizona where my grandmother was from. Their fathers were ranch-owning *gauchos* and neighbours but after they both married they moved to Rio and stayed in touch. Camila is like a second mother to me...'

'Da Costa Holdings isn't a cattle business, though,' he replied, then stiffened slightly.

She smiled quickly, wanting to hold onto the animosity-free atmosphere they'd found. 'No, after my grandfather died, my mother sold the ranch and let my father expand the company instead.' She breathed in relief when Camila returned with their wine and first course.

The older woman's warm smile and effusive manner further lightened the mood. By the time she took her first sip of the bold red wine the slightly chilly interlude had passed.

Theo complimented her on the food choice and tucked into the grilled fish starter. The conversation returned to safer topics and eventually turned to his previous career as a championship-winning rower.

'Why did you stop competing?'

He shrugged. 'I tried a few partners after Ari and Sakis retired. The chemistry was lacking. In a sport like that chemistry is key.' He topped up her wine and took a sip of his own.

'You've been lucky to have had the opportunity to do something you loved,' she replied wistfully.

His smile looked a little taut around the edges. 'Luck is a luxury that normally comes along as a result of hard work.'

She glanced down into her wine. 'But sometimes, no matter how hard you try, fate has other ideas for you.'

His eyes narrowed into sharp laser-like beams. 'Yes. But the answer is to turn it to your advantage.'

'Or you can walk away. Find a different option?'

One corner of his mouth lifted. 'Walking away has never been my style.'

She slowly nodded. 'You wouldn't have won championships if you were a man who walked away.'

His expression morphed into something that resembled gratitude. She couldn't claim she understood all his motives but she was beginning to grasp what made Theo tick. As long as he could see a problem in any area of his life, he would not walk away until it was resolved. It was why he was the troubleshooter for Pantelides Inc.

She'd watched footage of him rowing. His grit and determination had held her enthralled throughout the feature and she would be lying now if she didn't admit it was a huge turn-on.

'But there's also strength in walking away. You walked away from rowing rather than risk partnering up with the wrong person.'

He stiffened. 'Inez…'

She fought the urge to back down. 'I don't want to mess up our truce but I want you to just think about it. There's no shame in forgiving. No shame in letting the past *stay* in the past.'

His eyes grew dark and haunted. 'What about my demons?'

'Do you have a cast-iron guarantee that they will be vanquished by the path you've chosen?'

He frowned for several seconds before his eyes narrowed. 'You're right. Let's not mess up the truce, shall we?'

'Theo...'

'*Anjo*. Enough. Have some more wine.' He smiled.

And, just like that, her pulse surged faster. Hell, everything he did made her pulse race. She took a sip and licked her lips as the languorous effect of the wine and the captivating man sitting opposite her took hold.

She really needed to stop drinking so much. She pulled her gaze from the rugged perfection of his face as Camila returned to offer them coffee.

Inez declined and looked over to see his eyes riveted on her.

'I think we need to get you back to the boat.'

Laughter that seemed to be coming easier around him escaped her throat. 'You make me sound as if I've been naughty,' she said after Camila collected their empty plates and left.

'Trust me, I would tell you if you'd been.'

'Well, the night is still young and I'm not ruling anything out.' She laughed again.

His mouth curved in one of those devastating smiles as he reached for his wallet and extracted several crisp notes.

'I say it's definitely time to get you back and into bed.'

Her breath caught. He didn't mean what she thought he meant. Of course he didn't. But images suddenly bombarded her brain that had her blushing.

As she said goodbye to Camila and headed outside, she prayed he wouldn't see her reaction to his words.

'Hey, slow down, you'll break your ankle rushing in those heels.' He caught up with her outside and slid a hand around her waist.

The warmth of his body was suddenly too much to bear. 'It's okay, I'm fine.' Her voice emerged a touch too forceful and he glanced sharply at her.

'What's wrong?'

She raked an exasperated hand through her hair and tried to stem the words forming at the back of her mind. They came out anyway. 'You're supposed to be my enemy. And yet you brought me to one of my favourite places in the world. You're being so kind and attentive and I can't help… I…I want you.'

The transformation that occurred sent her senses reeling. From the charming, desirous dinner companion, Theo turned into a hungry predatory beast in the space of a heartbeat.

He pulled her into a dark alley between two high-rises. Her heart hammered as he held her against the wall and leaned in close.

'You don't want to say things like that to me right now, Inez,' he grated harshly.

His mouth was so tantalising close, she shut her eyes to avoid closing the gap between them and experiencing another potent kiss. 'I don't want to be saying them either. I can't seem to stop myself because it's the truth.'

'That's just the wine talking,' he replied.

She nodded then groaned when he leaned in closer. Heat from his body burned hers and his breath washed over her face. When his stubbled jaw brushed her cheek, she bit hard on her lower lip to stop another groan from escaping.

'Open your eyes, Inez.'

She shook her head. '*Nao...por favor…*'

'What are you begging me for?' he whispered in her ear.

A deep shudder coursed down her spine. 'I don't know…' She stopped and sucked in a desperate breath. 'Kiss me,' she pleaded.

With a dark moan, he touched his mouth to the corner of hers. Fleeting. Feather-light. Barely enough.

Her hands gripped his waist and held on tight. '*Please*,' she whispered.

'*Anjo*, if I start I won't be able to stop. And neither of us wants to spend the night in jail for lewd behaviour.'

She finally opened her eyes. He stood, tall, dark, devastatingly good-looking and tense, with a hunger she'd never seen in a man's eyes. That it was directed at her made her pulse race that much harder.

'Theo.' Her fingers crept up to his face, dying to touch his warm olive skin. 'Let it go. Whatever my father did, revenge would only bring you fleeting satisfaction.'

His jaw tightened but he didn't look as forbidding as he'd looked before. 'It's the only thing I've dreamed about for the last twelve years.'

Her hand crept up to settle over his heart. 'Have you stopped to think that obsessing about it may just be feeding the demons?'

One large hand settled over hers and he stared fiercely down at her. 'Are you offering me another way to quiet them, *anjo*?'

'Maybe.'

He captured her hand and planted a kiss in her palm. When he glanced down at her, a feverish light burned in his molten eyes. 'He doesn't deserve to have you as a daughter.'

'I can say the same about your parents but we play the hand that is dealt us the best way we can. And when it gets really bad I try to remember a happier time. Surely you must have some happy memories with your mother? And was your father really all bad?'

His mouth tightened. Then, slowly, he shook his head. 'No. It wasn't always bad.'

'Tell me.'

He frowned slightly. 'They thought Sakis would be their last child. I came as a surprise, or so my mother tells me. She used to call me her special boy. My father…he took me everywhere with him. He had a sports car—an Aston Martin—that I loved riding in. We'd take long drives along the coast…' He stopped and his eyes glazed over.

She kept silent, letting him relive the memories, hoping that he would find a way to soften the hard ache inside him. But when his eyes refocused, she saw the raw pain reflected in them.

'I'm not a father, and I probably never will be. But even I know those things are easy to do when life's a smooth sail. The true test comes when things get rough. I find it hard to believe that my brothers and I were ever in any way special to our parents when they turned their backs on us when we needed them most. He could've saved me, Inez—' He stopped abruptly and her heart clenched with pain for him.

'How?'

'One simple phone call to warn me and I wouldn't be here...I wouldn't be afraid of going to sleep each night because of hellish nightmares...' A deep shudder raked his tall frame.

'Oh, Theo,' she murmured. He leaned into the hand she placed on his cheek for several seconds then he pulled away and tilted her chin up.

The vulnerable man was gone. 'This changes nothing. I am what I am. Do you still want me?'

She swallowed. 'Yes.'

Something resembling relief swept through his eyes. 'You have half an hour and a lot of head-clearing air before we're back on the boat. I suggest you use that time to think carefully about whether you want this to go any further. Because, once we cross the line, there won't be any going back.'

CHAPTER TEN

THEO THREW THE reins of the launch to the waiting crew member and turned to help her out. Her bare feet hit the landing pad and she swayed a little when the boat rocked.

Contrary to her thinking he would rush her back to the boat after his pronouncement, Theo had taken his time walking her back down the streets to the promenade and onto the beach that led to the pier.

Hell, he'd even taken the time to help her out of her shoes so they could walk along the shore.

But the plaguing doubt that perhaps he didn't want her as much as her screaming senses craved him evaporated the moment she looked into his eyes.

Burnt a dark gold by volcanic desire, he stared down at her for several seconds before he demanded in a hoarse voice, 'Well?'

She licked her lips and watched his agitated exhalation. 'I still want you.'

'Are you sure? There will be no room for regret in the morning, Inez. I won't allow it.'

'I'm not drunk, Theo. Besides, I wanted you this morning and I wasn't drunk then. Or last week, or the first night we met.'

His nostrils flared as he dragged her close on the deserted lower deck. 'That first night, you felt what I felt?'

An impossible attraction that had no rhyme or reason? 'Yes,' she answered simply.

He swung her up in his arms and strode into the galley and down the steps into his large, opulent suite. Somewhere along the line, her shoes fell from her useless hands. She knew they had because her fingers were buried in his hair, and her mouth was on his by the time he kicked the door shut behind them.

Their tongues slid erotically against each other as they explored one another, his forceful, hers growing bolder by the second. Because she knew he liked it, she nipped his bottom lip with her teeth.

His deep growl echoed inside her before he pulled away. Eyes on hers, he slowly lowered her body down his sleek length. Hard muscles and firm thighs registered against her heated skin and even after her feet hit the plush carpet she held onto him, fearful she'd dissolve into a pool of need the moment she let go.

'I need to undress you,' he said raggedly.

Unable to look away from him, she nodded. The dark purple knee-length dress was form-fitting and secured by a side zip. After a couple of minutes of frustrated searching, she laughed and pointed to the hidden zip beneath her arm.

With a dark curse, he lowered it and tugged the dress over her head.

He dropped the dress. He swallowed. Then he stared so hard she stopped breathing.

'*Thee mou*, you're so beautiful,' he groaned.

The feeling suffusing her was different from her reaction to the incandescent hunger in his eyes. It was pleasure that he liked what he saw, that he might well pardon her for her inexperience.

Eager to experience more of the feeling, she reached for her bra clasp.

'No,' he commanded. He grabbed her hands and placed them on his chest. 'That's my job. *You* don't move.'

He drifted his fingers up her sides, eliciting a deep shiver that brought a satisfied smile to his lips. Her bra came undone a second later and he glanced down at her heavy breasts.

'Do you know how long I've waited to taste these?' He cupped one globe in his hand, lowered his head and flicked his wet tongue repeatedly over her nipple.

Fire scorched through her veins and her head fell back as pleasure surged high.

'Theo,' she gasped as he delivered the same treatment to her other nipple. Caught in the maelstrom of sensation, she wasn't aware her nails were digging into his pecs until he hissed against her skin.

'Take my shirt off, *querida*. I want to feel those nails on my bare skin.'

Fingers trembling, she complied with his demand, pulling the shirt off his broad shoulders and down his arms before giving in to the need to caress his bronzed skin. Heated and satin-smooth, his muscles bunched beneath her touch as she explored him.

But, much too soon, he was pulling her hands away, catching her around the waist and striding to the bed.

Depositing her in the middle of the king-sized bed, he stood staring down at her, one hand on his belt. The power and girth of him knocked the breath out of her lungs and a momentary unease sliced across her pleasure.

So far, Theo hadn't commented on her inexperience but the evidence would become glaringly apparent in a few minutes. She opened her mouth to tell him but he was crawling over the bed towards her, his intense focus paralysing her to everything but the pleasure his eyes promised.

He kissed her again, deeper, more forceful than all the times before. She gave in to her need and buried her hands in his hair, scraped her nails along his scalp and won herself a deep groan of pleasure from him. His lips moved along her jaw to nip her earlobe before going lower to explore her neck and lower.

Once again, he suckled her breasts and once again she lost the ability to think straight.

'You love that, don't you?' he observed huskily when he raised his head.

'*Sim*,' she groaned.

'There are many more pleasures, *anjo*. So many more.'

His lips trailed down her midriff...he kissed his way to the top of her panties before he gripped the flimsy material in his hands. Expecting them to be ripped off—a notion that made her wildly breathless—she was surprised when he slowly and gently lowered them down her legs and drew them off.

Equally slowly, taking his time to savour her, he kissed her from ankle to inner thigh. When his mouth skated over her secret place, her hips arched off the bed in delirious anticipation.

She'd never imagined she'd want a man to go down on her but now she couldn't imagine *not* feeling Theo's mouth on her heated core.

At the touch of his mouth, she cried out, her body twisting as pleasure scythed through her. He tasted her so very thoroughly, his tongue, teeth and lips working in perfect harmony to drive her straight out her mind.

She slid ever closer to breaking point, both fearing and yearning for what lay ahead.

Theo slipped his hands beneath her bottom and pulled her even closer to his seeking mouth. With quick expert flicks of his tongue, he sent her careening over the edge.

Her scream was an alien sound, hoarse and pleasure-ravaged, her grip on the sheets tight as she was buffeted by blissful sensation.

He continued to kiss her until she calmed, then kissed his way up her body to seal her mouth with his.

The earthy taste of her surrender seemed to trigger an even more primitive reaction in him. By the time he lifted his head, his eyes were almost black with hunger.

'Did Blanco make you feel like this?' he grated.

She shook her head. 'No.'

Satisfaction gleamed in his eyes. 'By the time I finish making you mine, you will not remember anyone else who came before me.'

Knowing he would discover her inexperience in a matter of minutes, she took a sustaining breath and blurted, 'I never slept with Constantine. Theo, I'm a virgin.'

He froze in the act of reaching for a condom. Several expressions raced over his face before he spoke. 'So I'm to be your first lover?'

She gave a jerky nod. 'Yes.'

Theo absorbed the news and tried to weigh which was the greater emotion swirling through him—shock or elation. The shock was understandable. But the elation, the fact that he was *pleased* he was to be her first? It'd never crossed his mind that she would be a virgin. But suddenly a few things fell into place. Her blushes, her furtive innocent looks, her surprise at his demanding kisses.

Another feeling rose to curl itself around his chest. Possessiveness.

The fact that he was to be her first made him want to beat his chest like a wild jungle animal. He ripped the condom packet open and stared down at her.

The look of apprehension forced him to slow down. He was moving too fast, possibly scaring her. Time to turn it down a notch.

'I'll go as slow as you want, *querida*, but I won't stop,' he warned. He couldn't. He'd come too far. He wanted her too much.

I would've kept you... Perhaps even for ever.

His own words echoed in his head and yet another emotion swept over him. If they'd met in another time, would she be the one? The idea of Inez as his wife, the mother of his children if he'd been normal, washed over him. His heart raced as he stared down at her, so beautiful, so giving.

Thee mou, what the hell was he doing wishing for the impossible? He wasn't normal…

'I don't want you to stop,' she replied. Then she performed one of those actions that illuminated her inexperience. Her gaze flicked down to his groin and she bit her lip. She had no idea how hot that little gesture made him.

A groan ripped from his chest and effectively wiped away the useless yearning.

Planting his hands on either side of her, he parted her thighs with his and settled himself at her entrance.

'Hold onto me, and feel free to dig your nails into my back if it all gets too much.' He attempted a smile and felt a touch of relief when she returned it.

The seductive bow of her mouth called to him and, leaning down, he drove his tongue between her lips. Gratifyingly, she opened up to him immediately. He deepened the kiss and swallowed her groan.

Carefully, he nudged her entrance, fed himself slowly into her wet heat.

He froze as she tensed. 'Easy, *anjo*. Relax,' he murmured soothingly against her mouth.

With a rough little sound she complied. Except now the tension was channelled into him. The feel of her closing around him threatened to tear him apart. Lying in the cradle of her hips, a sense of wonderment stole over him he'd never felt before. And he wasn't afraid to admit it scared the hell out of him.

'Theo.' She said his name with a touch of imploration and frustration that ramped up his tension. Never had he wanted to make it more right for a sexual partner.

He pushed deeper and felt the resistance of her innocence. Those nails dug in. Pleasure roared through him as he pulled back and looked into her beguiling face.

A face that held a touch of apprehension and breathless anticipation.

'Please, Theo. I want you.'

Her husky entreaty was the final straw. With a hoarsely muttered apology, he breached the flimsy barrier and buried himself deep inside her.

She made a sound of pain that pierced his heart then her head was rolling back on a long moan that echoed around the room. He waited until she had adjusted to him. Then he pulled out and rocked back in.

'*Meu deus*,' she voiced her wonder.

'Inez…' he waited until her glazed eyes focused on him, then he repeated the move '…tell me how you feel.'

'*Fantastico*,' she groaned, and Theo was sure she didn't realise she spoke her native tongue.

Her fingers spiked into his hair and when he thrust into her, she met him with a bold thrust of her own. His breath hissed out.

'You're a fast learner, *querida*.' He increased the tempo and gritted his teeth for control when she immediately matched his pace.

All too soon her back arched off the bed, her chest rising and falling in agitation as she neared her climax. Hot internal muscles rippled along his length and he shut his eyes for one split second to rein in his failing grip on reality. Leaning lower, he took one tight nipple and rolled it in his mouth. Her cry of pleasure was music to his ears. He treated its twin to the same attention then lowered himself on her. Sliding his arms under her shoulders he brought her flush against him and thrust in fast, deep movements.

She screamed once before her teeth closed over the skin on his shoulder. Deep shudders rocked through her as her bliss pulled her completely under.

She bit him harder, her nails scouring his back as she rode the unending wave.

When her head fell back towards the pillow, he raised his

head and looked at her face. The expression of wonder and ecstasy sheening her eyes finally sent him over the edge.

With a roar torn from deep inside him, he gave into the shattering release.

He clamped his mouth shut as new, confusing words threatened to burst free. Praise? Gratitude? Hell, *adoration*? When had he ever felt those emotions in connection to a woman he'd just bedded?

He buried his face in her neck and let the ripples of pleasure wash him away in silence. Until he could fathom just what the hell was going on beyond the chemical level with Inez, he intended to keep his mouth shut.

Inez slowly caressed her hands down his back, not minding at all that she was pinned to the bed by his heavy, muscled weight. Right at that moment, she couldn't think of a better way to suffocate to death. The thought made her giggle.

Theo turned his head and nuzzled her cheek. 'Not the reaction I expect after a mind-blowing orgasm but at least it's a happy sound.'

Immediately her mind turned to the dozens of women he'd pleasured before her. Hot green jealousy burned through her euphoric haze and her hands stilled.

'Hey, what did I say?' His voice rumbled through her. When she didn't immediately answer, he raised his head and stared down at her. 'Inez?'

'It's nothing important,' she replied. And it wasn't.

Earlier this evening, she'd tried to make him see a different way. But he'd refused. This thing between them would last until his vendetta with her father was satisfied. She had no business thinking about what women had come before her or who would replace her once he was done with her family and with Rio.

She endured his intent gaze until he nodded and rose. The feeling of him pulling out of her created a further emptiness inside that made her heart lurch wildly.

Deus, she needed to get a grip. Her hormones were a little askew because she had experienced her first sexual act.

No need to descend into full melt-down mode.

She watched him leave the bed, his body in part shadow in the lamp-lit room. He entered the bathroom and returned a minute later with a damp towel. When she realised his intention, she surged up and tried to reach for the towel.

'No,' he murmured softly. 'Lie back.'

Her face heating up, she slowly subsided against the pillows and allowed him to wash her.

Incredibly, the hunger returned as he gently saw to her needs and when he finally glanced back at her his nostrils were flared, a sign she'd come to recognise as a control-gathering technique.

Her nipples puckered and her body began to react to the look on his face.

'You need time to recover.'

Her body refuted that but her head knew she needed to take time to regroup. When she nodded, he looked almost disappointed. He returned the towel to the bathroom but left the light on as he came back to bed. Getting into bed, he pulled the covers over their bodies and pulled her into his arms.

She settled her hand over his chest and felt his steady heartbeat beneath her fingers. They lay there in silence until another giggle broke free from her jumbled thoughts.

'I'm beginning to get a complex, *anjo*.' He brushed his lips over her forehead.

'I believe this is the part where we make small talk after sex but I can't come up with a single subject.'

She felt his smile against her temple. 'Wrong. Normally this would be the part when I either leave or do what I just did to you all over again.'

Her heart caught. 'And?'

'I'm trying to rein in my primal instincts and not flatten you on your back again.'

Feeling bolder than was wise, Inez opened her mouth to tell him that he needn't hold it back for much longer. Instead a wide yawn took her unawares.

It was his turn to laugh. 'I think the decision on small talk has been shelved in favour of sleep.' He turned her face up to his and pressed his mouth to hers. Within seconds the kiss threatened to combust into something else. He pulled back with a groan and tucked her against him. 'Sleep, Inez. Now,' he commanded gruffly.

With a secretly pleased smile, she slid her arm around his waist, already feeling the drowsy lure of sleep encroaching.

She woke to moonlight streaming through the windows. The bedside lamp glowed and she judged that she'd been asleep for a few hours.

Beside her, Theo lay on his side, tufts of sleep-ruffled hair thrown over his forehead. In the soft lighting he looked younger and peaceful but still so damn sexy her breath caught just looking at him.

She suddenly needed to commit his likeness to paper. Her pad was next door in her suite. Slowly extracting herself from the arm he'd thrown over her, she pulled on his shirt and went to retrieve it.

Returning just as quietly, she settled herself cross-legged at the foot of the bed and began to draw. Every now and then she paused and took a breath, unable to fathom the circumstances she found herself in.

She was in bed with a man who was bent on destroying her family. And yet the overwhelming guilt she expected to feel was missing. Instead she yearned to save him from the demons that she'd glimpsed in his eyes when he spoke of his nightmares.

She swallowed as a well of sadness built inside her. Despite his outward show of invincibility she'd seen his battle. A battle he believed only revenge would win for him…

She froze as Theo made a sound. It was somewhere between a moan of pain and the bark of anger. His hand jerked out and then closed into a tight fist.

His whole body tensed for a breathless second before his chest started to rise and fall in agitated pants.

She dropped the sketchpad. 'Theo?'

'*No. No! No! Thee mou, no!*' The words were hoarse pleas, soaked with naked fear.

Both hands shot out in a bracing position and his head twisted from side to side.

'Theo!' She rose to her knees, unsure of what to do.

'No. Stop! *Arghh!*' With a forceful lunge, he jolted upright with a blood-curdling cry. Sweat poured down his face and he sucked in huge gulping breaths.

'*Deus*, are you okay?' The question was hopelessly inadequate but it was all she could manage at that moment. Because her heart was turning over with pain for what she'd just witnessed him go through.

She reached out and he jerked back away from her. 'Don't touch me!'

'Theo, it's me. Inez.' Tentatively, she reached out and touched his arm.

He shuddered violently and lurched away from her, staring blankly at her for several seconds before his face grew taut and haunted.

'Inez,' he said with a dark snarl. 'I fell asleep?" There was self-loathing in the question, as if he hated himself for having lowered his guard enough to let the demons in.

Her stomach flipped and her fingers curled into her palm. 'Yes. You…you had a nightmare.'

His mouth twisted with a cruel grimace. 'No kidding. What the hell are you doing here?' he snapped, looking around the room with unfocused eyes.

She frowned. 'We…um, we fell asleep together after…' She stopped as heat rushed up her face.

He turned back to her and his gaze slowly travelled over her. He brushed the hair out of his eyes and gradually the dull green lightened into golden hazel. 'We had sex. I remember now.'

She flinched and watched him with wary eyes.

With sure, predatory moves, he lifted the tangled sheet off his body and prowled to where she was poised on her knees. He stopped a hairsbreadth from her.

'Can I…can I touch you?' she asked, unwilling to have him pull away from her, but a part of her longed to soothe the turbulent blackness in his eyes.

His mouth pinched and he took several steadying breaths before he spoke. 'You want to comfort me?'

'If you'll let me.'

Another deep shudder and he closed his eyes. His head lowered until his forehead rested between her breasts. His arms closed around her and tightened so hard she couldn't move. They stayed like that until his breathing steadied.

'Theo?'

'Hmm?'

'Tell me about your dream.'

He tensed immediately and she bit her lip. He raised his head and stared at her.

'Take my shirt off,' he commanded, his voice hardly above a tortured whisper.

Concern spiked through, despite the heat his words generated. 'Theo, you just had a nightmare—'

'One I want to forget.' His hands were on the back of her thighs, hard and demanding as they caressed up to her bottom. He cupped the globes with more roughness than before but there was no pain in the caress. 'Inez, if you want to help me, do it.'

She drew the shirt over her head and dropped it. His eyes devoured her breasts and his tongue darted out to rest against his bottom lip.

Between her legs, liquid heat dampened her folds and he groaned in dark appreciation as his seeking fingers found her core.

'So ready. So tight,' he rasped. With almost effortless ease, he picked her up, pivoted off the bed and sat on the side. Grabbing a condom, he slipped it on and positioned her legs on either side of him.

'You will *make* me forget.' The words were almost a plea but with a promise of things to come. 'Yes?'

Before she could do so much as nod, he pressed her down on top of him. She cried out as he filled her with his hot, heavy length. His hard grip on her hips controlled the rhythm, which grew more frantic with each thrust.

'Theo,' she gasped as pleasure scalded her insides and rushed her towards ecstasy.

'Shh, no talking,' he instructed.

Biting her lip, she stared into his face.

Torment, anger, pleasure and more than a dose of anxiety mingled into an oddly fascinating tableau. He was still caught up in the hell of his nightmare and her heart broke over his anguish.

She tried to catch his gaze, to transmit a different sort of comfort from the carnal that he clearly sought but he avoided her eyes. Instead he buried his face between her breasts and mercilessly teased her nipples until she whimpered at the torture.

He increased his thrusts, bouncing her on top of him with almost superhuman strength that had her reeling.

Her orgasm crashed into her, flattening her under its fierce onslaught before proceeding to completely drown her.

Through the thunderous rush in her ears, she heard his guttural roar as he achieved his own ruthless release.

Sweat slicked their skin and their breaths rushed in and out in frantic pants. This time, though, there were no pleasurable caresses and giggling was the last thing she felt like doing.

With lithe grace, he twisted around and deposited her on the bed. Without speaking, he strode into the bathroom.

Inez lay on the bed, grappling with what had just happened. In the last twenty-four hours she'd glimpsed the man tortured by his nightmares, had seen a side to Theo she was certain very few people saw. Instead of guarding her own heart, she wanted to open herself up even more to him, find a way of taking away his pain and torment.

Had she not learnt her lesson with Constantine?

No, Theo was nothing like that man who'd taken delight in humiliating her. The retraction Theo had promised had appeared in the online evening edition of the newspaper and she was sure she'd seen a look of contrition in his eyes when he'd watched her read it.

Darkness and light.

She was deeply, almost irreversibly attracted to both. Again her heart twisted and she looked towards the bathroom.

A crash came a second later, followed by a pithy curse. She was off the bed and running into the bathroom before she could think twice.

'I'm fine!' he ground out.

She hesitated in the doorway and watched him. His fingers were curled around the marble sink and his head was bent forward. 'What's wrong, Theo?'

'Dammit, woman, I'm not made of glass. And I've been grappling with my nightmares long before you came along, so leave me alone!'

Hurt shredded her inside. 'Don't push me away.'

He locked eyes with her in the mirror and sighed. 'You're too stubborn for your own good, you know that?'

'Maybe, but before you throw me out I need the bathroom,' she lied.

'Fine; it's all yours.'

He started to turn. That was when she saw his scars. '*Meu deus*, what happened to you?' she whispered raggedly.

His glance ripped from her face to where she pointed to his left hip. The marks were puckered and too evenly spaced and shaped to be an accident. But still her mind couldn't grasp the idea that someone had deliberately inflicted pain on him.

'You mean you haven't guessed already, *querida*? *Your father* happened.'

CHAPTER ELEVEN

INEZ STAGGERED BACKWARDS until her legs hit the vanity unit and she collapsed onto it. 'I don't...you're saying my *father* did this to you?' She shook her head in fierce disbelief.

Theo's mouth twisted. 'Not personally, no. He hired thugs to do it.'

She felt the blood drain from her head. Had she not been seated, she would've swayed under the unbelievable accusation.

'But...why?'

He grabbed a towel and secured it around his waist. 'You did your research on my family. You know what happened to my father.'

She nodded. 'He was indicted for fraud, bribery and embezzlement.'

'Among other things. He was also involved with some extremely shady people.'

He turned and strode from the bathroom.

She followed him, the fear she'd harboured for a long time blooming in her chest. 'And my father was one of these shady people?'

Theo turned and watched her. Shocked knowledge flared in her eyes. For a brief moment, he sympathised with what she was going through. Having the truth blown up in front of you wasn't easy.

In his deepest, darkest moments he still couldn't believe how painfully raw he felt at his father's abandonment.

'My father owed him a lot of money on some crooked scheme they were working on when he was arrested and all our assets were frozen. Your father took exception to being out of pocket. When he realised he wouldn't be paid, he decided to pursue a different route.'

Her haunted eyes dropped to the scars covered by the towel and quickly looked away.

'So I'm here to pay for my father's sins,' she whispered raggedly.

That had initially been his plan. Somewhere along the line that particular plan had become questionable. But he'd be damned before he'd admit that.

'Your father made me pay for my father's. Money and power were his bottom line, and he wanted payback. Nothing else mattered to him, not even the tortured screams of a frightened boy…'

He compressed his lips as her mouth dropped open and anguish creased her face. 'How old were you?'

He raked a hand through his hair. Even as a voice shrieked in his head to stop baring his raw wounds, he was opening his mouth.

'I was seventeen. I was returning from a night out with friends when his goons grabbed me. He had me smuggled from Athens to Spain and threw me into a hole on some abandoned farm in Madrid. Ari found me there two weeks after I was taken. After he damned near bled every single cent he could find from every relative and casual acquaintance in order to stump up the two million dollars ransom that your father demanded.'

Her hands flew to her head, her fingers spiking through the long tresses to grip them in a convulsive stranglehold. 'Please tell me when you say a *hole*…you don't mean that *literally*?' The words were a desperate plea, as if she didn't want to believe how real the monster that was her father.

His smile cracked his lips. 'Oh, yes, *anjo*. A twelve-foot-deep *literal* hole in the ground with vertical sides and no hand or footholds. No light. No heat. One meal a day with a bucket for my necessaries.'

'No...'

'*Yes!* And you know what his men did for *fun* when they were bored?'

She shook her head wildly, her eyes wide and horror-struck as he loosened the towel from around his waist and exposed his puckered skin. 'Cigar tattoos, they called them.'

Tears welled in her eyes and fell down her cheeks. Still shaking her head, she walked to the bed and sank down on it. She buried her face in her hands and a gut-wrenching sob ripped from her throat. After the first one, they came thick and fast.

His chest tightened with emotions he was very loath to name. Each sob caught him on the raw, until he couldn't bear to hear another one.

'Inez! Stop crying,' he instructed hoarsely after five minutes.

She shook her head and sniffled some more.

'Stop it or I'll throw you overboard and you can swim to shore.'

That got her attention. She brushed her hands across her cheeks and speared him with wide, imploring eyes.

'If the only people you saw were his men, how did you know it was my father?'

He couldn't fault her for trying to find a different reality to the one he'd smashed her world with. Hell, he'd done that for a long time after his father had been indicted. 'I followed the money.'

She frowned. 'What?'

'I traced the ransom my brother paid through dummy corporations and offshore accounts. It took a few years but I finally found where it ended up.'

'In my father's account?'

'Yes. And since then I've made it my business to find out how every single cent was spent.'

Her shoulders slumped and tears welled again. He could tell the ground had well and truly shifted beneath her feet.

After several seconds, she raised her head.

'Okay. I'll do whatever you want. For however long you want.'

It was his turn to feel the ground shift under his feet. Shock slammed through him as he realised just how much he wanted to take her. To hang onto her.

But not for the sake of revenge. For an altogether different reason; because he wanted her. Not for her father but *for her.*

He shook his head. 'Inez…'

'I can never buy back those two weeks that were taken from you or the horror you've had to live with. But I can try and find a way to make up for what was done to you.'

'How? By giving me your body whenever and wherever I ask for it?'

She paled a little. But the brave, spirited woman he'd come to see underneath all that false gloss raised her chin. 'If that's what you want.'

His mouth twisted. 'I don't want a damned sacrificial lamb. And I sure as hell don't want you throwing yourself on your sword for that bastard's sake!'

'Then what do you want? You have his company. His campaign is falling apart. He will be left with nothing by the time you're done with him. How much more suffering do you need before you let go of this anger? When will you feel pacified?'

Theo started to answer, then realised he had no answer. The satisfaction he'd thought he'd feel was hollowly absent, as was the deep-seated sense of triumph he'd always thought he would feel when this moment came.

Looking into her face, he saw the pain and confusion reflected there and his puzzlement increased. The ground was still tilting beneath his feet but he'd been on this path for too long to let go.

Hadn't he?

He forced his gaze to meet hers.

'I will let you know when I'm adequately appeased.'

Over the next week, she watched as he slowly dismantled her father's campaign piece by piece. Allegations of impropriety surfaced, triggering an investigation. Although nothing was found to indict Benedicto, his credibility suffered a death blow and any meaningful points he'd managed to retain in the polls dropped to nothing.

On the Monday morning after returning from their sailing trip, the calls to her cell phone started. Both her father and Pietro bombarded her with messages and texts, demanding to know what was going on.

She hadn't needed Theo to warn her not to take their calls. After his revelation, each time she saw her father's name pop up on her screen, her stomach churned with pain and disgust.

Although she'd long suspected that her father's business dealings weren't as pure as the driven snow, she'd never in her wildest dreams entertained the idea that he would condone the brutality that Theo had described. Each time she saw his scars—and she'd seen them every night since their return, when he'd moved her into his suite—a merciless vice had squeezed her heart.

And that vice had tightened every time he'd cried out in the middle of the night after another nightmare.

She'd been surprised that first night after their return when he'd pulled her close after a fiery lovemaking and instructed her to go to sleep.

When he kept her with him the following night, she'd boldly asked him why.

'I don't want to be alone,' he'd stated baldly. And each time he'd come awake he'd reached for her, wrapping his trembling body around her and holding on tight until his nightmare receded and his breathing returned to normal.

More and more, her foolish heart had begun to believe that her presence was making the nightmares, if not any less horrific, then at least tolerable.

Or she could just be living in a fantasy land where her mind and heart had no idea what language the other was speaking. Because she was beginning to believe that her heart was more involved in Theo's welfare than was wise. And yet she couldn't control it enough to make it stop wrenching in pain when he suffered another nightmare, or soar with joy when he took her to the heights of ecstasy. Even the knowledge that some time in the very near future, after his goal to destroy her father was achieved, Theo would pack up his bags and leave Rio for good, made her heart ache in a way that was almost a physical pain.

Santa Maria, she was losing her mind—

'There you are. Teresa told me you're still here. I thought you'd be at the centre by now.' She'd shared more details of her volunteer work with him during the times when he'd been *Normal Theo*, not *Revenge Theo*. And she'd been ridiculously thrilled when he hadn't been judgemental or condescending.

She looked up as he entered the living room and crossed to where she sat, applying finishing touches to the sketch she'd been working on since breakfast an hour ago. She'd thought he'd left for the day but obviously she'd been mistaken.

Glancing up at his lean, solid frame and gorgeous face, her heart performed that painfully giddy flip again and she glanced away. 'I took a day off. I'm…I'm still thinking of resigning.'

He stilled then dropped to his haunches in front of her. 'Why?'

She struggled to breathe as his scent surrounded her, making her yearn to lean in closer. 'This whole thing with my father has brought unwanted attention to people who are already struggling with life's difficulties. I don't think it's fair on the children.'

A look resembling regret passed through his eyes before he blinked it away. After a full minute, he murmured, 'No, it's not. But you won't resign.'

Her heart caught. 'Why not?'

'Because I won't allow you to give up something you love doing. The publicity about your father will go away. I'll make sure of it.'

She met mesmerising hazel eyes. 'Why are you doing this?'

He shrugged. 'Perhaps I'm beginning to realise that I was mistaken about how much collateral damage I was prepared to accept.'

Collateral damage. She was grappling with that when he spoke again.

'I have something for you.'

She glanced warily at him. 'Beware of Greeks bearing gifts. I'm sure I've read that warning somewhere.'

His smile held a certain chill but was heart-stopping nonetheless. 'For the most part, I'd urge you to heed that warning. But this one is completely harmless.' He pulled something from his back pocket and presented it to her. The look in his eyes made her stomach flip as she glanced from his face to the box.

'What is it?' she asked.

'Open it and see.'

She opened the velvet case and gaped at the platinum-linked, three-tiered diamond choker nestling between the two catches.

'Are you trying to make some sort of *macho* statement?'

He shook his head in confusion. 'Sorry, *anjo,* you've lost me.'

'This is a *choker.* You want everyone to see that you own me?'

He frowned. 'What the hell are you talking about?'

'Why a choker? Why not a simple diamond pendant?'

'I asked my jeweller to send a few pieces. I liked the look of that one. So I chose it. No big deal, no mind games. I thought you'd like it,' he finished tersely.

She bit her lip and wondered if she was reading too much into it. Much like she was reading far too much into her feelings for Theo and what would happen when things ended.

'It's a beautiful piece of jewellery. But frankly it's a bit ostentatious for my taste.' She snapped the box shut and held it out to him. 'Besides, since my role as paparazzi bait is over, I don't see where I would wear something like that.'

His jaw tightened and he pushed the box back at her. 'I was just coming to that. Ari is getting married next weekend. You're coming with me as my plus one.'

She couldn't stop her mouth from gaping open any more than she could stop breathing. 'You want me to drop everything and fly to Greece with you?'

'I'm sure you can work something out with the charity. I'm happy to make a donation to cover your absence if you like.'

'I...'

'And we're not going to Greece. Ari and Perla are getting married at their resort in Bermuda.'

'Different continent, same response.'

His eyes narrowed. 'Do I need to remind you that we're only three weeks into our agreement?'

Her fingers trembled and she threw the box down on the sofa. 'No, you don't need to remind me. Call me foolish, but I thought we were getting beyond that.'

'I'm trying to, Inez.'

'Then ask me nicely. For all you know, I may be busy next weekend and would need to rearrange my plans for you.'

He raised an eyebrow. 'Busy doing what?'

'Splitting the atom. Shaving my legs. Rehearsing to join a

circus troupe. What does it matter? You didn't bother to ask. You only brought me trinkets and ordered me to be ready to fly off to Bermuda.' Her mouth trembled and she firmed it.

'You're angry.'

'You're very observant.'

'Tell me why.'

She laughed. Even to her ears it sounded as if it could've easily cut glass. His eyes narrowed as she shook her head. 'What would be the point?'

'The point would be that I would listen.'

She placed her feet on the carpet and tried to stand. He caught her hips and kept her seated in front of him.

This close she could see the hypnotic gold flecks in his eyes. She wanted to drown in them. Wanted to drown in him. She tried to calm her racing pulse.

His gaze dropped to her mouth, then down to her chest and a different sort of fever took hold of her.

'That necklace—'

'Is just a necklace. I thought I'd give it to you now so you could get an outfit to match for the wedding.'

'And the trip?'

'I need a plus one. I need *you*. And you can hate me if you want but I'm not prepared to leave you here so Benedicto can hound you.'

'I can take care of myself.'

His eyes narrowed. 'I don't doubt that. But can you tell me that he won't view your refusal to take his calls this last week as a betrayal?'

Her heart skittered. 'And you think he'll harm me in some way?'

He glanced meaningfully at her arm, then back to her face. 'Sorry, *anjo*, I'm not prepared to take that chance.'

Darkness and light. Tenderness and ruthlessness. It was what kept her emotions on a knife-edge where this man was concerned.

'Will you come to Bermuda with me? Please?'

She glanced at the velvet box. 'I will. But I'm not wearing that necklace.'

'Fine. We'll find you something else.'

'I don't need anything—' Her argument died on her lips when he picked up her sketchpad. She grabbed at it but he held it out of her reach. 'Theo, hand it over.' She breathed a secret sigh of relief when her panic didn't bleed through her voice.

'You're supposed to be designing me a boat.'

'I'm still working on it. I'll show it to you when it's done.'

His gaze brushed her face and settled on her mouth. The intensity of it made her insides contract. After a minute he handed the pad over and rose. 'I look forward to it. We're dining in tonight. I'm in the mood for an early night.'

He left the room just as silently as he'd entered. She realised her fingers were clamped white around her sketchpad and slowly relaxed them.

She flipped through the pages until she came to the one she'd been drawing. It was one of many featuring Theo asleep. She stared at it, seeing the vulnerability and gentleness in his face that he covered up so efficiently when he was awake. When he was asleep he was all light, no darkness. There was a boyishness about him that she only caught rare glimpses of during the day.

Darkness and light. Unfortunately, her heart refused to be picky about which it preferred because, awake or asleep, Theo had captured her emotions so efficiently she was beginning to fear she was falling in love with him.

The nightmare started the way it always did. A glow of light signalled the men's arrival. Followed by the rope ladder and the heavy descent of thick boots, tree trunk thighs and towering thugs.

Each time he'd fought back. A few times he'd landed blows of his own. But each time they'd eventually overpowered him. The tallest, toughest one, the one who favoured those smelly cigars, always laughed. It was the laughter not the pain that triggered his screams. It was a never-ending grating sound that churned through his gut and tripped his heart rate into overdrive.

He felt the scream build in his throat and readied himself for the roar.

Gentle but firm hands shook him awake.

'Theo…*querido!*'

He kept his eyes shut and reached for her, holding on tight as the images receded. The irony of it wasn't lost on him, the thought of how much he now needed the daughter of the man who was responsible for reducing him to a helpless wreck night after night for the last twelve years.

As he held on to her the thought that had plagued him for several days now took hold. He no longer wanted to pursue this vendetta. Yesterday, he'd found himself requesting that the board vote a different way to what he'd originally planned. They'd been stunned. He'd been twice as stunned.

He'd mentally shrugged and told himself there was no reason to turn his back on a healthy profit but he'd known he'd changed his mind for a different reason.

Benedicto was all but finished.

But ending it now would mean Inez would be free to walk away from him. And the very thought of that made him break out in a cold sweat.

He'd managed to buy himself a little more time by persuading her to come with him to Ari's wedding.

After that…

His insides churned as he lay in the darkness and felt her soft hands soothe him.

He pushed away thoughts he wasn't brave enough yet to truly examine.

'*Querido*, are you awake?' she breathed softly.

His heart flipped and his arms tightened convulsively around her soft, warm body. 'I'm awake, *anjo*.'

'I'm not an angel, Theo.'

'You are.'

'If I were an angel, I'd have the power to banish your nightmares,' she replied in a voice fraught with pain.

It took several seconds to realise she ached for him.

Pulling back, he stared into her face.

'You didn't do this to me, Inez.'

Her eyes clouded. 'I know. But that doesn't mean I don't wish you healed.'

His smile felt skewed. 'There's no cure for me, sweetheart,' he said, although he was beginning to doubt that. Just as he was beginning to think that the answer lay right there in his arms. If only there was a way…

'Are you sure? There's therapy—'

'Tried it. Didn't work,' he replied. When he heard the curtness in his voice he soothed an apologetic hand down her back.

She relaxed against him and he buried his face in her hair and breathed her in.

'What happened?'

'What, with the therapy?'

She nodded.

He slowly opened his eyes and stared into the middle distance. 'They spoke about triggers, breathing techniques and anxiety-detectors. There was mention of electro-shock therapy or good old-fashioned pills. I never went back for a second session.'

Her head snapped up. 'You mean all that was at your first session?'

He smiled and kissed her gaping mouth. 'I believed what was wrong with me couldn't be fixed by therapy.'

'Believed?'

He realised what he'd said and his breath caught. Was he grasping at straws where there were none?

'I'm beginning to think things aren't as hopeless for me, *anjo*.'

She paled a little but continued to hold his gaze. Slowly,

she nodded. Her luxuriant hair spilled over her shoulder onto his chest as she stared into his eyes. 'I really hope you find closure one day, Theo.'

Simple, frank words, said from the heart. But they froze his insides as surely and as swiftly as an arctic wind froze water.

Because he was seriously doubting that he would ever find peace without this woman in his arms.

CHAPTER TWELVE

THEY BOARDED THEO's private jet late the next Friday. The moment they stepped on board, Inez sensed something was wrong.

Theo paced up and down, his agitation growing the closer they got to take-off.

When the pilot came through, Theo sent a piercing glance at him and the man hurried into the cockpit.

'Theo, sit down. You're making your pilot nervous.'

He barked out a short laugh and threw himself into the long sofa opposite her chair. His fingers drummed repeatedly on the armrest. 'Don't worry; he's used to it.'

'Used to what?'

'My aversion to enclosed spaces,' he answered tersely.

'Your claustrophobia.' Her heart squeezed as she watched his fingers grip the armrest and the skin around his mouth pale.

Unbuckling her seat belt, she crossed to the sofa and sat down next to him. A sheen of sweat coated his forehead and when his eyes sought hers she read the anxiety in them. Reaching around him, she secured his seat belt then took care of her own as the plane taxied onto the runway.

Taking the arm closest to hers, she pulled it over her shoulder and settled herself against him. He tugged her close immediately, his breathing harsh and uneven.

She hugged him harder, and when he tilted her face up to his she went willingly.

He kissed her with a desperation that tore through her soul. For long, anxiety-filled minutes, he took what she offered, until the need for air drove them apart.

'You get that we cannot kiss all the way to Bermuda, don't you?' she said, laughing.

'Is that a challenge? Because I bet I can,' he threw back with a heart-stopping smile.

Inez noticed that his breathing was no longer agitated and breathed a sigh of relief.

'No, it's not a challenge.' She rested her head on his shoulder and caressed his hard jaw. 'How do you normally get through flying?'

His jaw tightened for a second before he relaxed. 'Mild sleeping pills before take-off normally does the trick.'

'Why not today?'

'You're here,' he said simply. After a minute, he asked, 'Why are you helping me?'

'I cannot forget that my father did this to you. And no, I'm not offering myself as a sacrificial lamb. But I don't want to see you suffer either. I want to help any way I can.'

The reminder that her father loomed large between them grated more than he wanted to admit. 'For how long?' Theo demanded more harshly than he'd intended.

She stiffened. 'Sorry?'

'Are you counting the days until I set you free?' he pressed.

Her eyelids swooped down, concealing her expression. 'I...we have an agreement—'

'Damn the agreement. If you had a choice now, today, would you stay or would you leave?'

'Theo—'

'Answer the question, Inez.'

'I'd choose to stay...'

The bubble of joy that started to grow inside him burst when he registered her flat tone. 'But?'

'But… this could never go anywhere.'

A sense of helplessness blanketed him. 'Why not? Because I blackmailed you?'

She shook her head. 'No. Because a relationship between us would be impossible.

Theo's vision blurred at her words. He'd pushed her too far. Hung onto his vendetta for too long. His mouth soured with ashen hopelessness. 'I guess we both know where we stand.'

When she moved away, he fought not to pull her back. She stayed close—out of pity? His mouth curled. He told himself he didn't care but the voice in his head mocked him.

He cared, much more than he'd bargained for when he'd forced her to make that stupid choice. The idea of her walking away from him made his insides knot with a pain far greater than he'd ever known.

The plane hit a pocket of turbulence, throwing her against him. When she stayed close, he let her. Forcefully, he reminded himself of one thing.

He'd never meant to keep her for ever.

The Pantelides Bermuda resort was a breathtaking jewel set amid swaying palm trees and sugar-white sand. The sun beat down on them as Theo drove the open-top Jeep towards their villa.

Stunning buildings connected by dark wooden bridges under which the most spectacular water features had been constructed made for a visual masterpiece. All round them bold colour burst free in a heady mix of blues, greens and yellows that begged to be touched.

Their sprawling whitewashed villa featured high ceilings, cool tiled floors and a four-poster bed that dominated the master bedroom.

A tense Theo who hadn't said more than a dozen words

to her since they landed, instructed the porter to place their cases in the master bedroom and tipped the man before walking outside onto the large wooden deck.

'There's a barbecue later this afternoon. Perla thought we might want to rest before then. You can go ahead and rest if you want to. I'll go and catch up with Sakis and Ari.'

He walked away from her and headed out of the door.

The clear indication that she wasn't welcome stung, although why she was surprised was beyond her.

He'd held ajar the possibility of continuing this thing between them and she'd slammed the door shut.

A small part of her was proud she hadn't grasped the suggestion with both hands, while the larger part, the part that had fallen head over heels in love with Theo in spite of all the chaos surrounding them, reeled with heart-wrenching pain at what the future held.

But, as she'd told herself over and over again on the plane as he'd shut his eyes and surprisingly dozed off, she was taking the right steps now to prevent even more heartache later.

Because there was no way Theo would ever reconcile himself to having her as a constant reminder. Certainly not enough to love her.

The reality was that they'd fallen into bed as a result of some crazy chemistry. Chemistry fizzled out. Eventually, the constant reminder that a part of her was responsible for his inner demons and outer scars would grate and rip at whatever remained after the chemistry was gone.

He was better off without her.

Her heart protested loudly at that decision. Ignoring it, she went into the bedroom and lifted her case onto the bed. The cream sheath she'd bought for the wedding needed to be hung out before it creased beyond repair.

Unzipping her case, she opened it and froze. A red velvet box, similar to the black one Theo had presented her with a few days ago lay on top of her clothes.

With shaky hands she picked it up and opened it. The stunning necklace sparkling in the sunlight made her gasp.

The platinum chain had a small loop at one end, with a large teardrop diamond at the other that slipped easily through the hoop. The design was simple and elegant. And so utterly gorgeous she couldn't stop herself from caressing the flawless stone.

Swallowing a lump in her throat at the thoughtfulness behind the necklace, she jumped when a knock came at the door. Thinking it was Theo who'd forgotten to take a key, she opened the door with a smile.

Only to stop when confronted by two stunningly beautiful women, one of whom was heavily pregnant, while the other carried a small baby in her arms.

'Sorry to descend on you like this, only Theo was a bit vague about whether you were actually resting or if you were up for a visit.' The women exchanged glances. 'I've never seen him so scatty, have you?' the pregnant redhead asked the blue-eyed blonde.

'Nope, normally he's quick off the mark with those hopeless one-liners. Today, not so much. Anyway, we thought we'd come on the off-chance that you were *not* resting and say hello…oh, my God, that necklace is gorgeous!' The redhead reached out and traced a manicured forefinger over the diamond.

Then she looked up, noticed Inez's open-mouthed gaze and laughed. 'Sorry, I'm Perla soon-to-be Pantelides. This is Brianna Pantelides, Sakis's wife. And this little heartbreaker is Dimitri.'

'I'm Inez da Costa. I'm a…' she paused, for the first time holding up her relationship with Theo to the harsh light of day and coming up short on explanations '…business associate of Theo's.'

The two women exchanged another glance and she rushed to cover the awkward silence. 'Please, come in.'

Brianna paused. 'Are you sure?'

'*Sim*...yes, I'm sure. I was just unpacking...' she started and noticed Perla's frown.

'Why are you doing that yourself? We have two butlers and three villa staff attached to each residence.'

'I think Theo sent them away,' she said, then bit her lip as Perla's eyebrows shot upward.

'Did he? Ari did that once too, when we first arrived here four months ago. Then we proceeded to have an almighty row.' She smiled at the memory and placed her hand lovingly over her swollen belly.

Brianna laughed and walked to the sofa. Settling herself down, she opened her shirt and adjusted her son for a feed.

Perla sat on the sofa too and they both stared back at her. Their open curiosity made her nape tingle.

'We won't keep you long. I just wanted to run the itinerary by you because, frankly, I don't trust the men with the information. We have a casual dinner tonight, followed by a quick rehearsal. Most of the guests arrive in the morning and the wedding is at three o'clock, okay?'

'Okay.' She ventured a smile and Brianna's eyes widened.

'Gosh, you're stunning! How did you meet Theo again?'

'Brianna!' Perla admonished with a laugh.

'What?'

Inez fiddled with the clasp of the velvet box and pushed down the well of sadness that surged from nowhere. These two women were not only almost family, they were friends too. Whereas her family was in utter chaos and she had no friends to speak of.

She forced another smile. 'He had some business in Rio. I was...am helping him out with it.'

'Right. Okay.' Perla struggled upright and nudged Brianna. 'We'll leave you alone. I think the guys are rowing in about an hour. It's an experience you don't want to miss if you've never seen it before.'

Brianna gently dislodged her drowsy baby from her

breast and laid him on her shoulder, gently patting his back as she stood.

The door opened as they neared it and Theo's large frame filled the doorway.

His gaze zeroed in on her, then dropped to the box still clutched in her hand before coming back up. Her throat dried at the sight of him and the ever present tingle that struck her deep within flared heat outward.

'Um, Theo?' Perla ventured.

'What?' he snapped without taking his eyes from Inez.

'You need to move from the doorway so we can leave.'

He snorted under his breath and entered the villa. He turned with his hand on the door, causing Brianna to roll her eyes. 'We've given Inez the schedule so you have no excuse to be late.'

'I'm never late.'

'Yeah, right. You were almost two hours late for Perla's engagement party and an hour late for Dimitri's christening.'

'Which therefore means I'll only be half an hour late for this wedding. Now, please go and pester your other halves and leave me alone.'

The women grumbled as they left. He turned from the door with a smile on his face but it slowly dimmed as his gaze connected with hers.

'Did they harass you?' he asked, a touch of wary concern in his eyes.

She shook her head. 'No. They were lovely.'

'I don't know about lovely but I tolerate them.' Contrary to his words, his voice held a fondness that made her chest tighten.

Theo understood family. Enough that he'd been devastated when his had been broken. And yet he'd wanted to rip hers apart.

Despite understanding the reason behind his motives, the thought still hurt deeply.

'Inez?'

She turned sharply and headed back to the bedroom. He followed and grabbed her wrist as she reached out to set the box down.

'What's wrong?'

Her throat clogged. 'What *isn't* wrong?'

His eyes narrowed. 'If Brianna or Perla said something to upset you—'

'No, I told you they were wonderful! They were kind and funny and...and incredible.' Tears threatened and she swallowed hard.

'You only met them for twenty minutes.'

'It was enough.'

'Enough for what?'

'Enough to know that I want what they have. And that I'll probably never have it. So far my record has been beyond appalling.'

He frowned. 'You don't have a record.'

'Constantine used me to get dirt on my father and—'

'I don't want you to say his name in my presence,' he interrupted harshly.

'And what about you? You make me hope for things I have no right to hope for, Theo. What sort of fool does that make me?'

'No, you're not a fool. You're one of the bravest, most loyal people I know.' He said the words gravely. 'It is I who is the fool.'

Theo's words echoed through her mind as she watched the brothers row in perfect harmony across the almost still resort water a short while later.

He took the middle position with Sakis in front and Ari at the back. She watched, spellbound, as his shoulders rippled with smooth grace and utmost efficiency.

'Aren't they something to watch?' Perla sighed wistfully.

'*Sim*,' she agreed huskily.

'I think they do that just to get us girls all hot and bothered,' Brianna complained but Inez noticed that she didn't take her eyes off her husband for one second.

When the men eventually returned to shore, the two women joined them and were immediately enfolded into the group.

Theo glanced her way, a touch of irritation in his eyes. Seconds later, he broke away from the group and came towards her.

'I didn't expect you to be down here. You should be resting.'

'I was invited. I hope I'm not intruding.'

'If you were invited then you're not intruding. Come and join us.' He grabbed her hand and led her to where Ari and Sakis were turning over the boat to dry the underside.

The two brothers gave her cursory glances but barely spoke to her. When Ari abruptly asked Theo to accompany him to the boat shed, her stomach fell.

Perla organised a Jeep to take her back to their villa and when Theo returned half an hour later, his jaw was tight and his movements jerky as he swept her off her feet and strode into the bedroom.

He made love to her with a fierce, silent passion that robbed her of speech and breath before he clamped her to his side and slid into sleep.

Her eyes filled with tears and she hurriedly brushed them away. It was no use daydreaming that things would ever magically turn rosy between her and Theo.

As much as she wanted to wish otherwise, they were on a countdown to being over for good.

The wedding was beautiful and quietly elegant in a way only an events organiser extraordinaire like Perla could achieve despite being seven months pregnant. Inez watched the bride and groom dance across the polished floor of the casino, transformed into a spectacular masterpiece that stood directly on the water, and fought the feelings rampaging through her.

Theo would never be hers. She would never have a wedding like this or have him gazing at her the way Ari was gazing at his new wife.

She would never feel the weight of his baby in her belly or have it suckle at her breast.

Despair slowly built inside her, despite knowing deep down that Theo had done her a favour by bringing her here. He didn't need her to save him from whatever nightmares plagued him. He had a family that clearly adored him, who would be there for him when he chose to let them in.

She needed to stop moping and get on with her life.

Her time in Theo's house and his bed was over. In retrospect, she was thankful she'd let him talk her into keeping her volunteer position. It was a lifeline she was grateful for in a world skidding out of control. The things she couldn't control she would learn to live without.

A tall figure danced into her view and her eyes connected with the man who occupied an astonishingly large percentage of her mind. In his arms was an elegantly dressed woman with greying brown hair and a sad expression. She said something to him and he glanced down at her. His smile was gentle but wary and Inez saw her sadness deepen.

Inez heard the soft gurgle of a baby over the music and turned to see Brianna next to her. 'That's their mother.' She nodded to Theo's dance partner. 'Their relationship has been fraught but I think they're all finding their way back to each other.' She glanced at Inez with a smile. 'I hope that you two find your way too.'

Inez shook her head. 'I'm afraid that's impossible.'

Brianna laughed. 'Believe me, I've seen the impossible happen in this family. I've learned not to rule anything out.' She smiled down at her child and danced away with him towards her husband.

Tears stung her eyes as she watched Sakis enfold his wife and son in his arms.

'What's wrong now?' Theo's deep voice sounded in her ear.

She blinked rapidly and pasted a smile on her face. 'Nothing. Weddings…they make me emotional. That's all.'

His eyes narrowed speculatively on her face before he took hold of her elbow. 'Dance with me.'

He led her to the dance floor and pulled her close.

'You have a big family,' she said, more for something to fill the silence.

'They can be a pain in the rear sometimes.'

'Regardless, you all seem to watch out for each other.'

He shrugged. 'Force of habit.'

'No, it's not. Does Ari know who I am?'

His mouth tightened. 'He suspects. I didn't enlighten or deny because it's none of his business. He's welcome to draw his own conclusions. Why do you ask?'

'Because he's been watching me like a hawk since we got here and he hasn't spoken more than two words to me. That's what I mean. What you have with your brothers isn't habit. It's love.'

His mouth twisted in a way that evidenced his dark pain. '*Love* hasn't conquered the nightmares that have plagued me for all these years, Inez.' The raw pain in his voice made her throat clog. She forced a swallow.

'Because you haven't allowed it to. You resisted any attempt at help because you thought you had to face this demon alone, do things your way.'

The honest barb struck home. He was silent for the rest of the song. Then abruptly he spoke. 'I didn't want to appear weak. I hated myself every time I couldn't walk into a dark room or down an unlit street. I haven't been able to cope with the smell of cigars without breaking out in a cold sweat. Do you know what that feels like?' he asked in a harsh undertone.

She shook her head. 'No, but I know it will never go away if you keep it buried.'

Her warmth, her strength hit him hard and he wanted to reach for her with all he had. Suddenly, everything he'd ever craved, ever wished for seemed coalesced in the woman before him.

'It's no longer buried. A month ago I was still the messed-up boy Ari dug up from that hole twelve years ago. But you did something about that.'

'No, I'm not responsible for that.'

His hand cupped her nape and he whispered fiercely in her ear. 'You are. You've seen me, Inez. I can't sleep with the lights off. I used to panic whenever someone shut a door behind me. That's why I surrounded myself with glass. With you by my side I flew here with no need for sleeping pills.'

'Even though you refused to speak to me for hours.'

He exhaled. 'Things are upside down and inside out right now. Let's just…we'll get through this wedding and head back to Rio. And we will damn well fix this thing between us. Because I'm not prepared to let you go yet.'

CHAPTER THIRTEEN

'I TOLD YOU, you're so much better than a damn sleeping pill.'

Inez laughed as Theo tugged her dress down and lifted her out of it. Leaving it on the floor of the master cabin bedroom, he waited for her to kick her shoes off before he crossed over to the bed. The diamond pendant he'd looked incredibly pleased that she'd worn lay nestled between her breasts.

'Keep that on,' he instructed, just as the plane jerked through turbulence and they fell onto the bed together, a tangle of hard and soft limbs and hot, needy kisses.

'I'm glad I have my uses,' she said, laughing, when he let her up for air.

His face grew serious as he stared down at her. 'You've attained the ultimate purpose in my life, *querida*. Now more than ever you're my saviour: *my* angel.' He cradled her head as he kissed her.

Inez closed her eyes and imagined that she could feel his soul through his reverent kiss. She studiously ignored the voice that mocked that she was deluding herself.

When he finished undressing her with gentle hands, she tried to stem her tears as he made love to her with a greedy passion that touched her very soul.

Afterwards she held him in her arms as he fell asleep. Unable to sleep, her mind drifted back to the wedding.

Theo had introduced her to his mother and again she'd witnessed the sadness in her eyes. When he'd hugged her at the end of the evening and murmured gently into her ear, his mother had burst into tears. Inez had watched as the brothers closed around her and soothed her tears.

She was still watching them when Ari had glanced her way. His measured smile and thoughtful nod in her direction had made her swallow. It hadn't been acceptance but it hadn't been the chilly reception he'd given her either.

As they'd packed to leave, Inez had asked Theo about what had happened with his mother.

'She fell apart completely after my father was arrested. She left Athens and locked herself away at our house in Santorini,' he'd replied in an offhand manner, but Inez had seen his anguish.

Recalling his words about abandonment, she'd gasped, 'She wasn't there when you were kidnapped, was she?'

Heart-shredding pain washed over his face, but a moment later it was replaced by a look even more soul-shaking. Forgiveness. 'No. She wasn't. But I had Ari and Sakis. They were strong for me. And they were that way because of her. I told her that tonight because I think we both needed to hear it.'

His words had resonated deep inside her. But most of all it had been his statement on the dance floor that continued to flash across her mind. *I'm not prepared to let you go yet.*

Her heart lurched. He meant to keep her in his bed for a while yet. Like a trophy he wasn't prepared to relinquish. And her foolish heart performed a giddy little samba at the thought of having a few more moments with him.

She woke to kisses on her forehead and her cheek and opened her eyes to bright sunshine.

'Good, you're awake. We just landed.'

She yawned widely. 'Already? I feel as if I just fell asleep.'

He laughed. 'It's three o'clock in the afternoon. And we have much to do before tonight.'

She stared at his wide grin and her heart lifted with happiness. 'You seem in very good spirits, *querido*,' she commented.

He gathered her close in his arms and gazed down at her. 'There is a reason for that.'

'Tell me,' she murmured softly.

His face turned serious, his eyes fierce as he watched her. 'For the first time in twelve years, I slept through the night without a nightmare,' he muttered hoarsely.

Theo watched her face light up with shocked pleasure before she reached up to clasp his face. Her kiss was gentle and sweet. 'Oh, Theo. I'm so happy for you.'

'I'm happy for *us*,' he replied. With another kiss, he got up and started dressing. 'Get a move on, sweetheart, unless you wish to give the customs guy an eyeful when he boards.'

With a yelp she got up and pulled her clothes on.

Theo's phone started ringing the moment they stepped off the plane. And it wasn't until they were back home that she remembered what he'd said on the plane.

'What did you mean—"we have much to do before tonight"? We're not going out, are we?' She groaned.

He took the phone from his pocket and checked it as another text message came through. She waited impatiently for him to finish.

'No, we're not going out. But we have a guest coming.'

'A guest? Who?'

'I've invited your father to dinner.'

Inez staggered as if a bucket of ice had been poured over her.

'My father is coming here?'

'Yes.'

'And you didn't think to inform me of this? What makes you think I want to see him?'

'We have to. It's time to get this thing over and done with, once and for all.'

'And you don't care how I feel about it?'

'I thought we agreed to fix things when we return to Rio?' he asked with a frown.

'Yes, but when you said *we*, I thought you meant us, you and me. More fool me. Because there is not me without my father, is there?'

'What are you talking about? Of course there is.'

'Then why would you go behind my back to arrange this?'

A tic started in his temple. 'Because it's my fault you're in the middle of all this.' He sighed and clawed a hand through his hair. 'I got a chance to fix things with my mother in Bermuda. We may never get back what we had but I'll take that over nothing. Whatever relationship you choose to have with your own father from here on in is up to you. But this is a hardship I caused in your life and one I have a duty to fix.'

The fight fizzed out of her but the fear that something had gone seriously wrong between the airport and home wouldn't go away.

At seven on the dot, the doorbell rang. She passed her hand over her black jumpsuit and tucked a lock of hair nervously behind her ear as she stood by Theo's side.

The butler entered the living room, followed by her father.

Benedicto da Costa drew to a halt. His narrowed gaze slid from Theo to her, his face a mask of dark anger and cold malice she'd forced herself to overlook in the past.

Now she saw him for who he really was. Images of Theo's scars flashed through her mind and her hands fisted at her side.

'I won't shake your hand because this isn't a social visit,' he rasped icily to Theo. 'And I won't be dining with you, either.'

'Perfectly fine by me. Frankly, the quicker we get this over with the better. But let me remind you that you're here only because of Inez. She may be your daughter but she's under my protection now. I suggest you don't lose sight of that fact. What business you and I have will be finished by week's end.'

Her father's gaze swung back to her. 'Are you just going to stand there and let him speak to your father that way? You disappoint me.'

'That's no surprise. I've been a disappointment from the moment I was born a girl, *Pai*.'

'Your mother will be rolling in her grave at your behaviour.'

She raised her chin. 'No, actually. *Mãe* told me every day she was proud of me. She also encouraged me to follow my dreams. She wanted to be a sculptor. Did you know that?'

'What's your point?'

'She was talented, *Pai*. But she gave it up for you. It was her, not you, who taught me what loyalty and family meant. You were only focused on exploiting that loyalty for your own selfish needs.'

His face tightened and his eyes flickered to Theo, who'd been standing by her with his arms folded, a half smile on his face.

'Is this what I came here for? To be lectured by an ungrateful child?'

Theo shrugged. 'I'm finding it quite entertaining.'

Benedicto growled and shot to his feet. 'If there is a point, *son*, I suggest you get to it.'

Theo grew marble-still, his smile disappearing in the blink of an eye. Pure rage vibrated off his body and Inez watched his nostrils flare as he sucked in a control-sustaining breath.

'*I am not your son*. And you are not worthy to be a father. It's a shame you didn't learn how to be a better parent from the mother who gave birth to you in that *favela* you deny you grew up in. And don't bother denying it again. I know everything there is to know about you, da Costa.'

For the first time since he'd walked in, Benedicto grew

wary. He strolled to the drinks cabinet and took his time examining all the expensive spirits and liqueurs displayed.

Without asking, he poured a measure of single malt whisky and took a bold sip. 'So I bent the truth a little. So what? You've already discredited my campaign. What do you want? My company? Is that your end game? You want to pick up the shares for Da Costa Holdings for peanuts? Well, over my dead body.'

Theo's laugh was menacing enough to cause her skin to tingle in alarm. 'Trust me, a few weeks ago it would've been my pleasure to grant you your wish. But you're wrong on that score. Your company is of no interest to me.'

His wariness increased. 'What's changed?'

Theo's eyes flicked to her and her heart thudded. 'Your daughter.'

'Really?'

Inez shook her head in astonishment. 'Do you really not know who he is, *Pai*?' she asked.

Theo's mouth curved in a mirthless smile. 'Oh, he knows who I am. He's just hoping that *I* don't know what he did twelve years ago.'

Benedicto swallowed, his gaunt face growing pale until he looked ashen. 'I have no idea what you're talking—'

She rushed towards him, anger, pain and disappointment coiling like poisonous snakes inside her. 'Don't you dare deny it. *Don't you dare!*' Her voice cracked and a sob broke through her chest. 'You had a boy kidnapped and tortured! For money. How could you?'

Eyes she'd once thought were like her own turned black with sinister rage. 'How could I? I did it for you. The fancy clothes you strut about in and that fancy car you drive? Where do you think the money came from? I needed it to save the company. Anyway, it was my money. Why did I have to go back to farming just because Pantelides couldn't keep it in his pants or stop his bit on the side from blowing the whistle on him?'

Inez's hand flew to her mouth, her insides icing over. '*Santa Maria*, you truly are a monster.'

Her father's jaw tightened and he addressed Theo. 'Is this the point where you hand whatever file you've gathered on me over to the authorities?'

Theo's mouth twisted. 'So you can bribe your way out of jail? No.'

Benedicto frowned. 'Then what the hell do you want?'

Theo glanced over at her and a look of almost relief washed over his face, as if a weight had been lifted off his shoulders. 'That's up to Inez. And only her. I'm done with you.'

Inez raised her suddenly heavy head and looked from one man to the other.

One stood tall, proud and breathtaking. A man she'd been so determined not to let in. But whose tortured vulnerability had drawn her to him, made her see beneath his skin to the frightened child who was desperately seeking answers.

Choking tears filling her eyes, she turned to the monster who was her father. 'I have nothing else to say to you. I don't want to see you ever again. Goodbye.'

Turning sharply from both men, she rushed out of the room and fled up the stairs.

Theo wasted no time in throwing Benedicto out once Inez left the room. He'd meant what he said—he was done with seeking retribution…had been done almost from the moment he'd met Inez.

Perhaps unwisely, he'd thought the meeting with Benedicto would be swift and cathartic. Instead, he'd brought Inez even more anguish.

He slashed his fingers through his hair as he vaulted up the stairs that led to his third floor suite. Perhaps she'd been right. He'd ambushed her in his rush to get this situation sorted between them.

But he would make it right for her. They would get

through this. They had to. The feelings he'd tried hard to smother had blown up in his face when he'd woken on the plane this afternoon. With the absence of anxiety and fear, the purest reason why he wanted to wake up each morning with Inez had shone through.

The feelings had been so intense he'd almost blurted it out. But he'd decided to wait until she'd confronted her father.

Now he wished he hadn't. He was wishing he'd provided her with that additional support of knowing how much she meant to him before he'd let her father loose on her.

Pursing his mouth in determination, he pushed the bedroom door open. 'Inez, I'm sorry for—'

The sight that confronted him silenced his words and turned his feet to clay. She stared at him, eyes red-rimmed with freshly shed tears.

Because of him. But even that pulse of deep regret couldn't erase the sight before him.

'What are you doing?' he asked, although the part of his brain that hadn't frozen along with his feet could work it out.

Two suitcases were open on the bed, one filled with her clothes. *She was packing...*

The silk top in her hand trembled before she turned and threw it in her case. Then her fingers curled around the edge of the lid.

When she looked at him again, more tears filled her eyes.

'Thank you for opening my eyes to what he truly is,' she murmured huskily.

'Shelve the thanks and tell me what you're doing,' he replied tersely.

One hand swiped at her cheek. 'I'm leaving, Theo.'

'You're what?' His voice rang with disbelief. 'You're going back to your father's house?'

She shuddered from head to toe. 'No. I could never live there again.'

He frowned. 'Then where are you going?'

She gave a tiny shrug. 'I'll stay with Camila.'

He finally got his feet to work and paced to where she stood. When she grabbed her shorts, he ripped them from her hand and threw them on the bed. 'I seem to be missing a link somewhere, sweetheart. Why don't you take a beat and fill me in?'

'I can't stay here.'

A merciless vice squeezed his chest. 'Why not?'

Her face creased in fresh anguish. 'Because he is right. The food he put on our table; the clothes on my back; our fancy education. They *all* came from your suffering.'

'For God's sake—'

She carried on raggedly. 'I never stopped to think about it but I remember the day he came home twelve years ago and told my mother our troubles were over. We weren't exactly poor before then, but after he pressured my mother into selling the ranch he made some bad investments and the company suffered for it. They argued a lot and I used to go to bed every night praying for a miracle just so they'd stop arguing. Can you imagine how I felt when my prayers were answered? And now, all these years later, I find out that what I'd prayed for came at the cost of your—' She choked to a stop, then frantically threw more clothes into the case.

Theo couldn't find an answer as desperately as he tried. He was watching her torture herself and he could do nothing to stop it. '*Anjo*—'

'No. I'm *not* an angel, Theo. I'm a child of the monster, a heartless devil who tortures children and doesn't feel an ounce of regret for it. How can you even bear to look at me?'

'Because you're *not* him!' he interjected fiercely. He took her hands and forced her to face him. 'You're not responsible for his actions. Stay, Inez. We said we would talk about us once we were done with him.'

'But there is no us, is there? We...we just fell into bed because of the circumstances that brought us together. If it hadn't been for my father you'd never have set foot in Brazil.'

'So you're walking away because you think we were never meant to be?' He watched her, forced himself to think how he would feel if she walked away from him. The realisation of what was happening washed over him and ashen despair filled his chest.

'I'm walking away because you need to put everything and everyone associated with your ordeal behind you. Otherwise you will never heal properly.'

He dropped her hand and stared down at her. The ice that had started to build inside him since he'd walked into the room hardened. It crept around his heart and Theo swore he heard it crack. His eyes scoured her beautiful tearstained face, looking for a tiny chink. A tiny ray of hope that would offer deliverance from the quicksand of devastation he could feel himself sinking into.

'So that's it? That's your final decision. You're doing this for my sake but I have no say in the matter?' He couldn't stop the bitterness from lacing his voice.

Her answer was to step back and gather up the last of her clothes. With trembling fingers, she zipped up the cases and lifted them off the bed.

'Inez, answer me!'

She stilled at the door. '*Adeus*, Theo.'

'Go to hell!' he snarled back.

'Table Four need a second helping of *feijoadas*. And a bottle of Rioja.' Camila bustled into the kitchen, checked on the bubbling pot Inez was stirring and nodded in approval. '*Fantastico*. I'll be back in a minute for that order.' She sailed back out on a giddy whirlwind.

Inez wiped her sweating brow and looked over her shoulder. 'Pietro, you grab the bottle; I'll serve up the *feijoadas*.'

Her brother rolled his eyes. 'Who made you queen of the kitchen?'

'I did, when I won the coin toss earlier.'

Her grin came easier today—much easier than it had for far longer than she wanted to dwell on. She still couldn't go for more than ten seconds without thinking of Theo but if she could joke with her brother, that was a good sign that this hollow, half-dead devastation she carried inside her would eventually ease. Right?

'I still think you cheated,' Pietro grumbled.

She lifted one shoulder. 'I'll let you explain to Camila, then, why the Rioja isn't here when she returns, *sim*?'

'Tomorrow, I'm tossing the coin.' He sauntered down the stairs into the basement that served as the restaurant's larder and wine cellar. The smell of the cheese Camila kept in the small space could be overpowering and she smiled again as Pietro made gagging noises.

If there was a bright side to be seen, it was that, amid all the chaos and heartache, somehow she and her brother had grown closer than she'd ever dreamed possible.

They both were yet to decide what they wanted to do with their lives after choosing to walk away from their father and the company, but Camila had encouraged them to take their time. To heal. To reconnect.

When her mother's childhood friend had offered them a job in her restaurant they'd both jumped at it. She'd worked it around her volunteer work and, between the two jobs, it kept her plenty busy.

Keeping herself occupied stopped the tight knot of pain inside her from mushrooming into unbearable agony. In the dark of the night when she lay wide awake and aching was time enough to suffer through the hell of wondering if she was doomed to heartache for ever.

Of wondering if Theo had left Rio in the three weeks since their final bitter encounter. Of wondering if his nightmares were gone for good or if her brief presence in his life had made them worse.

Her hand trembled and she immediately curled it into a fist. Theo was strong. He would survive…

Yes, but he called you his saviour. His angel. And you walked away from him.

'No,' she breathed through the pain ripping through her. She'd done the right thing—

'No what? If you tell me I've got the wrong wine, you'll have to go and get it yourself.'

She shook her head blindly and turned gratefully to the door as Camila walked in. Her quick but assessing glance at her made Inez frown.

'We have a new booking. Table One. And an order of *feijoadas* for one.'

'Wow, you're on fire tonight, sis.'

She ignored Pietro. 'Okay, I'll serve it up and—'

'No, I didn't take a drink order. And I think they want an appetiser first too. Can you go take care of it?'

Inez's eyebrow shot up. 'Me? But I'm not dressed to serve.'

'Pfft. This isn't the Four Seasons, *meu querida*. Besides, it's time you took a break from that hot stove. Tidy your hair a bit and go and take the order.'

Inez looked down at her black skirt and grey T-shirt. It wasn't standard waitress attire but, as Camila had said, this wasn't the Four Seasons. She tucked a strand of hair behind her ear and caught the worried look in the older woman's eyes. It was an expression she'd spied a few times and she reached out and shook her head before the concern could be voiced.

'I'm fine.'

Camila's mouth pursed. 'Good. Then go and attend to Table One.'

With a weary sigh, she washed and dried her hands on her apron. Unfastening it, she hung it on the hook and avoided her image in the small mirror by the door. Her red face from manning the stove for the last three hours would depress her even more.

Plucking a pencil, notebook and menu from the kitchen stand, she nudged the swinging doors with her hip and turned towards Table One.

'You…' she choked out.

Through the drumming in her ears she heard the items in her hand clatter to the floor. A couple of diners glanced her way. Someone picked up the scattered items and placed them in her numb hands. She opened her mouth to thank them but no words emerged.

Every atom in her body was paralysed at the sight of Theo Pantelides.

She heard movement behind her. 'You can't stand here all night, *pequena*. Life will pass you by that way,' Camila said solemnly.

She exhaled shakily and forced herself to move.

Those light hazel eyes never left her as she approached his table. He looked as powerful and as magnificent as ever, even if his cheekbones seemed to stand out a little more than she remembered. His hair had grown a little longer and looked a little dishevelled.

'Sit,' he rasped.

Her heart lurched at the sound of his voice. Licking her dry lips, she shook her head. 'I can't. I'm working.'

'I've received special dispensation from Camila. Sit,' he commanded again.

She sat. He stared at her for a full minute, his eyes raking over her face as if he had been starved of her… Or he was committing her face to memory one last time?

White-hot pain ripped through her. 'Why are you here, Theo?' she blurted.

His eyes rose from her mouth to connect with hers. The breath he took was deep and long. 'I was clearing out the house and I found something you left behind.' He reached down near his feet and laid her sketchpad on the table.

She stared at it, drowning beneath the weight of her despair. 'Oh, thank you.' She paused a second before the words were torn out of her. 'So you're leaving Rio?'

He shrugged. 'There's nothing left for me here.'

Tears burned her eyes as her heart shredded into a million useless pieces. 'I…I wish you well.'

He made a rough sound under his breath. 'Do you?' he asked sarcastically. She glanced up sharply but he wasn't done. 'Problem is, I'd believe those blithe words from the woman sitting across from me. But the woman who drew these…' he flicked over the pages of the sketchpad a few times before he stopped and pointed '…this woman has guts. She was brave enough to draw what was in her heart; what cried out from her soul. Look at her.'

She kept her eyes on his face, her whole body trembling wildly as she gave a jerky shake of her head.

'Look at her, dammit!'

She sucked in a breath. And looked down. The first sketch was the one she'd made of him after they'd made love that first time on the boat. The ones that followed were variations of that first sketch. She'd captured Theo in various poses, each one progressively more lovingly detailed until the final one of him with his brothers, laughing together at the wedding. She'd drawn that from memory on their final night in Bermuda. Staring at the finished picture had cemented her feelings for him.

He turned the page and the image of Brianna and Sakis's baby stared back at her. Dimitri already bore the strong, captivating mark of the Pantelides family. It was that template that she'd used in the following sketches, when capturing her own secret yearning of what her and Theo's baby would look like on paper had been too strong to resist.

'You must think I'm some sort of crazy stalker.'

'There is no stalking involved when the subject is just as crazy about the stalker,' he rasped in a raw undertone.

Her heart flipped into her belly and her whole body trembled. 'You can't be. Theo, I'll ruin your life.'

'I thought my life was ruined before I met you. I was consumed by rage and a thirst for revenge. I let the need for revenge swallow me whole, blinding me to what was important. Family. Love. I thought there was nothing else worth fighting for. But I was wrong. There was you. My life *will* be ruined. But only if you're not in it.'

The tears she'd tried to hold back brimmed and fell down her cheeks. Theo cursed and looked around. 'What's through there?' he asked.

'It's a room, for private parties.'

'Is there a party tonight?'

Before she'd finished shaking her head he was standing and tugging her after him. He kicked the door shut and turned to her.

'Listen to me. You told me I would never see you as anything but the child of a monster. But you forget you're also the child of a loving mother who celebrated every day the special person you are. How do you think she would feel to see you buried here, punishing yourself for what your father did?'

She shut her eyes but the tears squeezed through anyway.

'Open your eyes, Inez.'

She sniffed and complied, staring up at him with blurred vision. 'Now, truly open your eyes and see the wonderful person you are. See the person I see. The brave, talented person who drew those pictures.'

'Oh, Theo,' she cried.

'You have a dream. A dream I want to be a part of.' His hands shook as they traced her face.

'I want that dream to become reality so badly.'

'Then please forgive me for blackmailing you and give us that chance.'

She pulled back. 'Forgive you? There is nothing to forgive. If anything, I should be thanking you for shaking me out of my bleak existence. Even before I truly knew you, you empowered me to fight for what I wanted.'

'So will you fight for us? Will you give me the chance to prove to you that I'm worthy of your love and let me show you how much you mean to me?'

She touched his face and inhaled shakily when he turned to kiss her palm. '*Meu querido,* I fell in love with you so ridiculously soon after meeting you, I swear I'll never confess to you when it happened.'

His stunned laugh brought a wide smile to her face. '*Anjo…*' When her smile dimmed, he shook his head. 'Don't bother to argue with me. I love you with every breath I take. You're my angel and I'll keep repeating it until you believe it.'

'We're not going to have a very smooth-sailing future, are we?'

'No,' he concurred with a laugh then kissed her until her head swam with delirious pleasure. 'But that will be part of our story. And, speaking of smooth sailing…'

'*Sim?*'

'I sent a couple of your sketches to our design guys in Greece. They're interested in talking to you about them. If you're up for it?'

Her mouth dropped open. She waited until he'd kissed it shut before she tried again. '*Really?*'

'Really. And I should bring you good news more often. That happy wriggle does incredible things to my—'

She clamped her hand over his mouth and glanced, alarmed, over his shoulder, just as two text messages beeped in quick succession. He groaned and was about to activate them when a knock sounded on the door.

'*Hell*, I knew I should've found a quieter place for this.'

The door opened and Pietro entered with a bottle of champagne and two glasses.

Theo's expression grew serious as he watched him approach.

Pietro set the bottle and glasses down and stared back at Theo. 'You took care of my sister when I was too much of a *burro* to do so. I'll be for ever in your debt.' He held out his hand.

After several seconds, Theo shook it. 'Don't mention it. Any man who's not afraid to call himself an ass is all right in my book.'

With a self-conscious laugh, Pietro turned to leave.

'Thanks for the drinks,' Theo said. 'But how did you know?'

Inez suppressed a giggle. Pietro rolled his eyes and nodded to the far wall. 'There's a partition to the kitchen. Camila's been spying on you since you came in.'

Theo glanced behind him as the partition widened and Camila beamed at them. Her gaze rested on Inez. 'Your *feijoadas* are good enough, but I always believed your destiny lies elsewhere.' She blew a kiss and shut the partition.

Pietro left and Theo stared down at her. 'Are you ready to start our adventure, *agape mou*?'

'What does that mean?'

'It means *my love*.' His smile dimmed. 'I learnt to speak Portuguese for the wrong reasons. I will teach you Greek for the right ones.'

Her grip tightened on his shirt. 'Were you really planning to leave Rio?'

'Yes. After I persuaded Benedicto to sign over the company into your and Pietro's names, I was done with that soulless vendetta. The thought that I'd lost you in the process nearly killed me.'

'I…what? You got him to sign over the company to us? Theo, we don't want it!'

'It was your grandfather's, then your mother's. It's right that it should be yours and Pietro's. If you don't really want it, I'm sure you'll find a beneficial way to dispose of it.'

She nodded. 'It would go a long way to help the inner city centre and the *favela* kids.'

'Great, we'll make it happen.'

Her heart contracted as she stared into his warm eyes. 'I love you, Theo. Thank you for coming back for me.'

'I couldn't not return, *anjo*, because without you I'm lost.'

She lifted her face to his and he slanted his mouth over hers in a deep, poignant kiss that brought fresh tears to her eyes.

'We need to talk about these tears,' he said drily, then huffed in irritation as his phone beeped again.

'Your brothers?' she guessed.

'And their wives. Ari wants to know if I'm still alive. Sakis wants to know if he can hire you to design his next oil tanker.'

She laughed. 'And their wives?'

He glanced down at the screen and back at her. 'They want to know if they can start planning our wedding.'

She took the phone, flicked the off switch and slipped it into his back pocket. Gripping his waist, she raised herself on tiptoe and leaned close to his ear.

'We will reply to each one of them in the morning. Right now, I want you to take me back to the boat and make love to me, make me yours again. Is that okay?'

'It's more than okay, my angel. It's what I plan to do for the rest of our lives.'

The look of love and adoration in his eyes as he took her hand and walked her out of the room was forever branded on her heart.

* * * * *